TERMINATOR 3
TERMINATOR DREAMS

Books by Aaron Allston

Double Agent
Web of Danger

Galatea in 2-D

Car Warriors
*Double Jeopardy**

Doc Sidhe
Doc Sidhe
Sidhe-Devil

Bard's Tale (with Holly Lisle)
Thunder of the Captains
Wrath of the Princes

Star Wars: X-Wing
Wraith Squadron
Iron Fist
Solo Command
Starfighters of Adumar

Star Wars: The New Jedi Order
Rebel Dream
Rebel Stand

Terminator 3: Terminator Dreams*

*Denotes a Tor Book

TERMINATOR® 3
TERMINATOR® DREAMS

A Novel by
AARON ALLSTON

■ ■ ■

Based on characters created in
Terminator® 3: Rise of the Machines™

■ ■ ■

Screenplay by John Brancato & Michael Ferris
Story by John Brancato & Michael Ferris
and Tedi Sarafian

TOR®

A TOM DOHERTY ASSOCIATES BOOK
NEW YORK

TERMINATOR® 3: TERMINATOR® DREAMS

® Used under license. ™ and text copyright © 2003 IMF Internationale Medien und Film GmbH & Co. 3 Produktions KG.

This book is printed on acid-free paper.

Book design by Michael Collica

Edited by James Frenkel

A Tor Book
Published by Tom Doherty Associates, LLC
175 Fifth Avenue
New York, NY 10010

www.tor.com

Tor® is a registered trademark of Tom Doherty Associates, LLC.

Library of Congress Cataloging-in-Publication Data

Allston, Aaron
    Terminator 3 : terminator dreams : a novel / by Aaron Allston.
        p. cm.
    "Based on characters created in Terminator 3: rise of the machines; screenplay by John Brancato & Michael Ferris; story by John Brancato & Michael Ferris and Tedi Sarafian."
    "A Tom Doherty Associates book."
    ISBN 0-765-30852-5
    1. Artificial intelligence—Fiction.   2. Robots—Fiction.   I. Title: Terminator three. II. Title: Terminator dreams.   III. Terminator 3 (Motion picture).   IV. Title.

PS3601.L47T47 2004
813'.6—dc22

                                                                    2003061452

First Edition: December 2003

Printed in the United States of America

0   9   8   7   6   5   4   3   2   1

This novel is for everyone—family, friends, and people I've never met—who manage to get the job done, even when their own machinery is a bit suspect.

ACKNOWLEDGMENTS

Thanks go to Russell Galen, my agent, and James Frenkel, my editor; Kelly Frieders, Kali Hale, Helen Keier, Beth Loubet, Cindi Manning, Susan Pinsonneault, Jennifer Quail, Bob and Roxanne Quinlan, and Sean Summers, my Eagle-Eyes, the sharp-sighted folk who diminish the number of errors I introduce into each manuscript; and Steph Chiesi, Jenn Hussong, Derrick K. Johnson, Erin M. Lopez, and Luray Richmond, for offering facts when they were hard to come by.

MAJOR PLAYERS

YEAR 2029, HUMAN RESISTANCE

John Connor, leader
Kate Brewster, leader
Michaela "Mike" Herrera, scientific adviser
Daniel Ávila, programming adviser
Dr. Tamara Lake, medical adviser
Resistance 1st Security Regiment:
    Colonel Sidney Walker, commander
    Lieutenant David "Ten" Zimmerman, squadron leader,
        Hell-Hounds (Company A, Squadron 3)
    Earl Duncan, Hell-Hounds
    Mark Herrera, Hell-Hounds
    Kyla Connor, Hell-Hounds
    Ripper, Hell-Hounds
    Ginger, Hell-Hounds

PRESENT DAY

Danny Ávila, programmer, Cyber Research Systems (CRS)
Linda Ávila, deputy, Kern County Sheriff's Department
Teresa "Mama" Ávila
Lieutenant General Robert Brewster, head of operations, CRS
Dr. Philip Sherman, lead programmer, CRS
Jerry Squires, programmer, CRS

PROLOGUE

June, Present Day
Edwards Air Force Base, California
Cyber Research Systems (CRS) Autonomous Weapons
Division

"Daniel Ávila, it is time to die." The voice was harsh, mechanical.

Danny raised his head and stared into the eyes of a Terminator.

This was a mechanical face, skull-like in its angles, merciless and pitiless. It was the face of the prototype Terminator that Danny's team was in the process of programming, transforming it from mere servos and articulated metal into the next stage in American armed might, an unstoppable combination of mobile artillery, mechanized cavalry, and infantry.

It was a very familiar face. When initially assembled, the armored faceplate assembly had been attached slightly misaligned to the armored skeleton and sensory apparatus beneath. The result was that the right eye rode a little high in its socket, giving the Terminator's face an oddly human scowl. Hence the robot's nickname, Scowl.

And it was, ultimately, a two-dimensional face, devoid of the menace of immediacy. This was nothing more than the graphic on Danny's computer desktop, an image converted from recordings made during one of Scowl's trials.

But desktop images didn't ordinarily talk. Still groggy from falling asleep at his workstation, Danny looked around at the interior of his oversize cubicle—and flinched from the figure looming over him.

His coworker, a lean man with a high forehead and pointed chin, laughed at his reaction, then resumed his ersatz Terminator voice: "Or maybe just to go home." He cleared his throat and resumed a normal voice. "What are you trying to do, make the rest of us out to be slackers?"

"What?" Danny was having trouble focusing. For a moment, he couldn't even remember his coworker's name. For a man with a near-photographic memory, this was more than distressing. Finally it came: Jerry, the man's name was Jerry.

Jerry bent over to point at the clock running in the lower corner of Danny's monitor. "Look. Seven P.M. Long past the time to go home. You've been here for a day and a half with barely time for bathroom breaks. You've inflicted a mortal wound on the bug-fix list. When the brass gets its next look at Scowl, they're going to be thrilled. They'll sound like cheerleaders. But you need some sleep."

"Wait." Danny shook his head, focusing on the clock on his screen. For once in his life, he didn't automatically know the time, and he didn't believe the words and numbers on his monitor. "*Friday?* It's Thursday."

"Uh-uh. You just put in thirty-plus hours of genius labor, kid. Are you fit to drive home?"

"Of course," Danny responded automatically.

"Well, then. See you Monday." His coworker clapped him on the back and left the cubicle.

Danny rose. He remembered getting to work, of course. But that had been Thursday morning. He couldn't remember anything that had happened since. So where had the last day and a half gone?

He stared into the eyes of the Terminator on the screen. Despite the fact that the prototype robot was something he was programming, nothing but a tool that was soon to revolutionize the U.S. military, nothing but a rolling weapon with an approximately human set of features, he was suddenly afraid of it. There was pitiless cruelty in its eyes where there never had been any before.

He reached over to switch the monitor off. "Problem solved," he said.

But as he headed out of Cube Hell, the programmers' pit, for the elevator that would take him to surface level, he knew that the Terminator's eyes would be waiting for him the next time he came to work.

And for the first time ever, he didn't look forward to seeing them again.

August 2029
San Rafael, California
Population 0

It wasn't exactly a jungle, but in the decades since Judgment Day, trees had forced their way up through street pavement and sidewalk concrete; grasses and weeds had overrun lawns and medians. Now, where on a normal afternoon traffic sounds would have once drowned out every other noise, John Connor could hear only the summery rise and fall of insects calling to one another. That, and the occasional bang or clank or curse from the crew working behind him.

He stood at the open loading door, looking out into the overgrown parking lot. There were still some cars here, left behind when the world went to hell decades ago, but they shared the lot with aggressive waist-high weeds and, wonder of wonders, a lemon tree that had taken root at the corner of the property.

John felt a bit like the parking lot. His wife still told him his face was handsome; that his upright posture, his camo-style uniform, all projected the image of a leader of men, grayed but unbending. But on days like this he could feel every injury that he had sustained in his fifty-plus years—every gunshot wound, every broken bone, every burn. Scars, new and old, marked his body like weeds marked the parking lot, and there were more every year.

Even so, he needed to lead the occasional mission in the field. He was the leader of the Resistance, and decades of experience made it clear to him that the men and women he commanded would lose faith in a commander who always sat safely in his hardened underground bunker at Home Plate compound, dispatching others to their deaths. To keep spirits up, to keep himself from becoming some sort of distant, unattainable figure who never met and therefore could never inspire the troops elsewhere, he had to expose himself to danger a few times each year.

He couldn't complain. There were men and women in his forces—including his own children—who exposed themselves to danger several times a month. There were some who almost never had the opportunity to relax, to feel safe.

"Hey." The voice was female. He glanced over his shoulder at the speaker.

She stood a few feet behind him, just beside the angled column of light spilling in through the loading door, and it took his eyes a moment to adjust so he could make out her features. She was of average height and build, but he didn't find her in the least average. Her nose was just a little too broad to be considered elegant; but that, her round face, and her mouth—made for smiling—added up to a combination that was impossibly attractive. Her eyes were dark brown, her hair graying from the same color. She wore a camo uniform like his, though she'd set aside the belt with its holsters and pouches.

He modulated his tone to that of an office lothario. "Hey, yourself," he said. "Are you new?"

She grinned, taking on the cuteness of a teenager. "First day here."

"What are you doing after work?"

"I was thinking about a long moonlit drive with a bunch of sweaty freedom fighters."

He offered her a mock shudder. "Well, I guess a girl's got to do what makes her happy." He dropped the act. "How's it going back there?"

"They'll be ready for the fourth truck in about two minutes. They wanted me to tell you to send out the call."

"Will do."

She turned away, toward the dark interior of the loading dock. He reached out and caught her by the shoulder, dragging her back to him. Off-balance, she fell into his grasp, simultaneously grinning and scowling up at him. "What?"

"Kate, you know the price for approaching this checkpoint."

She leaned up to kiss him. "There. Does everyone who passes this way have to do this? Earl? Warthog? Crazy Pete?"

"I dunno. It's a brand-new policy."

Laughing, she shrugged free of him and headed back into the manufacturing facility.

John stared after his wife for a moment, savoring the bare minute of privacy they'd shared, perhaps the only minute they'd have this day. Then, reluctantly, he turned his mind back to business.

The building they were pillaging, a sprawling, nearly windowless single-story edifice larger than a football field, had once been decorated with a sign that read, EOSPHOR TECHNOLOGIES. Before Judgment Day, it had been a circuit board manufacturing concern, a subcontractor that built boards for companies that sold munitions components directly to the government. The sign had fallen, possibly on Judgment Day, possibly many years later. For whatever reason, the interior of the building had survived unpillaged for decades, and one of Connor's scouts had discovered it a few weeks ago. Two days ago, Connor's advance team had arrived and begun preparing selected pieces of equipment for transportation.

They couldn't take everything. A rough estimate of the amount of equipment here suggested that it would take a convoy of forty trucks or more to move every item of machinery, all surviving chemicals, all fabrication supplies. He had five trucks, a massive and vulnerable convoy by the standards of the Skynet-controlled world. So they had to be selective.

The equipment his technical team was dismantling and preparing for transportation included computers that his programming adviser Ávila had said still worked, still contained diagrams for hundreds of varieties of circuit boards. There was a room-size plotter that could transcribe those circuit board plans onto sheets of silver-coated Mylar at photographic levels of reproduction, for use in exposing circuitry images onto copper-clad fiberglass laminates. There were photographic exposure units, some merely oversize and ungainly, some large enough nearly to fill the back of a two-and-a-half-ton truck. There were rugged, hardy screen printers for use in silkscreen processes, usable both for circuit board manufacturing and more mundane tasks such as cloth decoration. Last of the primary haul, but certainly not least in size, were laminate presses that turned individual layers of laminates into multilayer circuit boards.

Less crucial to circuit board fabrication but still useful to the Resistance were control computers for sophisticated drill processes, laboratory equipment, tools, components for setting up partitions and metal cage walls, and parts scavenged from dozens of machines.

The booty from this haul, augmented by equipment that John's technicians would assemble on site, would allow the Resistance to set up two entire circuit board fabrication lines. That meant two sites that could produce radios, targeting systems, even computers someday. The lines would be much slower, much less efficient than those operating before Judgment Day, but they'd be a tiny edge in the favor of humanity, a fraction-of-a-percentage improvement in mankind's chances for survival. The Human Resistance had other circuit board fabrication sites operating, but every additional one they set up increased their available resources.

And with luck, the Eosphor Technologies building would go unnoticed by Skynet even after their departure. A few months from now, perhaps a year, they might be able to return and pick up even more equipment.

He pulled his field phone from its belt pouch. Shaped much like one of the walkie-talkies he'd known from his youth, it seemed cruder, more unfinished than the commercial products of the twentieth century. Its surfaces were black-painted metal instead of molded plastic. A cable ran up from a jack atop the device to the headset John wore and the microphone on his lapel.

With his thumb, he popped open the protective faceplate, revealing a small LCD screen and an alphanumeric keypad. He keyed in the following commands:

```
TRANS STARLING ALL<ENTER>
Ac 4T<ENTER>
OFF<ENTER>
```

This operation was code-named Starling, a random word generated by a computer program back at his base of operations. The first command had instructed the simple microprocessor in the device to send the rest of the message only to the participants in the operation. "Ac 4T" was shorthand for "activate fourth transport." The entire transmission would be encrypted when transmitted.

It would have been much easier to have depressed the speaker button on the faceplate, or to have keyed the microphone attached to his lapel, and spoken the appropriate words. But a voice transmission took much more time to transmit than his five-character code, was easier to detect and decode, and was less likely to be mistaken for an atmospheric anomaly. A voice transmission would, in short, drastically increase their odds of getting someone killed.

And there just weren't enough people left alive for him to let himself be careless that way.

■ ■ ■

Half a mile to the south, four figures huddled under a tarpaulin on a rooftop. They were situated at the edge of the roof where some long-ago calamity had knocked away a portion of the waist-high protective wall. The hole gave them an unobstructed view of the city's ruins southward.

Kyla Connor, the woman with her eye to the sniper rifle's high-powered scope, was young, not yet quite out of her teens. Her dark brown hair, a practical shoulder length, was tucked up under her billed cap. Her features were even and flawless; at rest, as they were now, they were unmemorable, but when lit by one of her rare smiles, they were transformed into earthy beauty. She wore the same camouflage uniform as most of the other participants in Operation Starling.

Her field phone beeped softly, but she didn't stir. "Mark, get that, would you?" she whispered.

Mark Herrera, the man lying on his back beside her, yawned and stretched. He was darker than the woman, Latino, with everyday good looks that seemed made to wear their current expression, an amused and self-satisfied smile. He was perhaps a decade older than she, but with his more casual attitude he actually seemed younger. "Sure, sure. I wasn't doing much. Just getting my first sleep in twenty hours."

"God, you complain."

He pulled out his field phone and popped the faceplate open, then tilted the device to read the screen in the dim light spilling in past the tarpaulin's edge. "It's your dad. Calling in the fourth truck."

"Ahead of time. That's good."

The third member of their post offered up a concerned whine. Kyla didn't break discipline; she kept her attention focused on the scope, which was trained through a break in the buildings ahead on a stretch of what had once been U.S. 101. But she did reach a hand back to scratch the whiner behind the ears. This was Ginger, eighty pounds of reddish-yellow Siberian Husky or Alaskan sled dog and who-knows-what, and she was a bit more anxious than Kyla's other dog, Ripper. Ripper, lying sideways across the backs of Kyla's knees, was 120 pounds of deep-chested, flat-faced guard dog. Kyla's mother, once a veterinarian, said she thought he was mostly bullmastiff; but his coloration was evidence that he was not purebred. Ripper, seeing Ginger getting attention, wagged his short tail, making a thumping, rattling noise against the gravel of the roof.

"How long till dinner?" Mark asked.

Kyla restrained a sigh. Mark was just baiting her. "Why don't you go out there and see if you can find an open restaurant?"

"Oh, good one. Of course, I might find a can of thirty-year-old, not-too-radioactive corned beef hash—"

There was something in the view afforded by her scope, something moving in the distance up the highway, and Kyla stiffened. "Hold it. Contact."

All business, Mark rolled over onto his stomach and put his eyes to the sighting gear set up beside Kyla's bipod-mounted rifle. "I don't see it."

"I think it dipped down into a depression in the road."

Then it was there again, barely visible, a tiny dot moving like a car. Toward them.

"Transmit 'Hell-Hounds Post One, contact, unknown, stand by,'" Kyla said. "And tell Daniel Ávila he was right again."

"He'll know."

HH-2, flag, ??, stdby.

John Connor read the message and swore silently. It was almost always too much to ask that any operation run without incident, but he always hoped.

Transport 4, an ancient Army truck kept miraculously alive by the mechanics of Connor's Resistance movement, was backing up against the loading bay. The instant it came to rest, flush with the bay, its tailgate came down. Two men and a woman spilled out of the bed, and another woman out of the cab. In moments they deployed a long sheet that had once been a pair of recreational parachutes. Now tattered and unusable in their original role, they were painted as close as possible to a match with the gray of the parking lot, complete with occasional splashes of green to simulate weeds, and its handlers drew them up over the top of the truck. In the minutes it would take for the truck to be loaded, it would not be recognizable as a truck by the imaging satellites that still circled the Earth and fed their data to Skynet.

As the first of the dollies and pallet-jacks loaded with fabrication equipment and propelled by tired-looking but energetic Resistance fighters reached the rear of the truck, Kate rejoined her husband. She had her field phone in hand and looked worried—worried to the point of misery. "That's Kyla, isn't it?"

John nodded, waiting for the screen to update. "If this is anything but a false alarm, we might get out of here with the fourth truck, but we're not going to get the fifth load."

"We won't even get the fourth truck out if we don't use the Hell-Hounds for diversion."

"I know." John didn't want to look at his wife at that moment.

If John Connor was the informal equivalent of the U.S. president, his Secret Service was Company A—the only company—of the Resistance 1st Security Regiment, the tiny branch of the armed forces devoted to Connor's personal security. Company A was further broken down into several squadrons, each of which was used to ensure Connor's safety or to undertake special missions that required an eclectic range of skills and nontraditional planning methods.

Though technically a branch of the military, the 1st Security Regiment tended to operate outside military procedure. Members were not addressed by military rank unless outsiders were present—it was enough to know who was in charge of the squad. Beyond that, everyone within the squad was equal.

Kyla Connor, John and Kate's youngest child, was the junior member of Company A, Squad 3, the unit nicknamed the Hell-Hounds. And now, to get away with a truckload of antique machinery meant putting her at risk. Every time this sort of thing happened, John wondered if he would lose a child, and wondered if Kate would come to hate him because he had ordered it.

The screen changed:

HH-2, T800 Blondie, incoming.

That settled it. The contact Kyla had seen was a Terminator, one wearing a known set of facial features—dull-looking, approximately Scandinavian in appearance, muscular as a twentieth-century weight lifter. It was nicknamed Blondie.

"So they haven't scrapped all the T-800s after all," Kate breathed.

"I figured they hadn't," John said. "Skynet's probably retiring them as they get harder to maintain, stripping their usable machinery rather than building new, dumping only those that aren't cost-efficient." He began keying in a new command.

Kate read what he was typing. "Dammit."

5T go2ground
HH play fox

"Truck five, go to ground," Mark recited. "Hell-Hounds, play fox."

"Fox, hell," Kyla said. "Foxes don't have sniper rifles or high explosives. Does Ten want me to go after him now? I need an answer in about sixty seconds."

"Gotcha." Mark keyed in the question in short form and got an answer in moments. "He says take your best shot and then we move up to join him and Earl."

"Wind," she said.

Mark returned his attention to his gear. "Nothing registering."

In Kyla's scope view, the vehicle bringing the Terminator to them topped another rise. It was a convertible, 2000-era, cream yellow, lacking a windshield. It was making good time, perhaps eighty miles an hour, about as fast as anyone could drive on the partially ruined highway without crashing. The air flowing across the car whipped the blond hair of the assassin-machine driving it.

Kyla had three options. She could put a round into the Terminator's chest, the easiest shot. If she were very, very lucky, the round might penetrate, might even damage one of the robot's hydrogen-fuel power cells and cause the Terminator to detonate; the explosion would be ferocious enough to destroy a portion of highway around it. But the most likely scenario for a chest shot was that it would impart enough kinetic energy to disrupt the robot's reflexes for a moment, perhaps causing it to crash. It wouldn't do the robot any real harm, unless the crash was spectacular.

She could aim at the robot's skull, a more difficult shot, but the fact that the skull had lighter armor and less mass in general meant that the impact could conceivably do some real damage. Kyla had killed Terminators, one T-800 and two T-600s, with single head shots, and if she were very lucky now, she might repeat that feat. But her target was moving, so it would be easier to miss altogether.

Or she could aim at the left front wheel. At this angle, the shot was nearly as difficult as the head, but would almost certainly result in a wreck. And a wreck was the preferred outcome, regardless of whether it harmed the Terminator; without wheels, its land speed was reduced. It would not be able to get to the Eosphor Technologies site as quickly. The tire was the most sensible option.

She zeroed in on the Terminator's head. Long ago, Daniel Ávila had taught her to play chess. She hadn't liked the game much. It seemed meaningless to her. But it had helped her learn to think tactically, and she had discovered the distinction between playing to win, playing not to lose, and playing to aggravate a superior opponent by losing very slowly.

With Terminators, you played to win. Always. "Taking my shot," she said. "Death to the toasters."

"Death to the toasters," Mark replied. It was the catch-phrase of the Hell-Hounds and had caught on with other units as well.

The convertible entered the long, straight, relatively undamaged section of highway overpass Kyla and Mark had picked out this morning. She would know exactly when it reached the 1,000-yard mark, measured from this roof edge; they had calculated the shot when they'd set up here hours ago.

Her rifle was a Barrett M99, fifty inches and twenty-five pounds of black steel and brushed-silver aluminum. It fired .50-caliber rounds that struck their targets with several times the foot-pounds of energy of other sniper rifles at comparable ranges. To those who concerned themselves with the aesthetics of small arms, it was a beautiful piece, elegant in its simplicity, a near-perfect marriage of form and function.

It had been manufactured a year before Judgment Day. That's what its original owner, Sergeant Tony Calhoun, member of a Los Angeles Police Department SWAT team, had told her; it had been his personal property rather than a department-issued weapon. Calhoun, away from Los Angeles when the bombs had dropped on Judgment Day, had joined an ad hoc militia that had eventually become part of John Connor's Resistance. He had trained many of its riflemen and snipers. In Kyla Connor, he'd found an ideal pupil—someone who was as calm and focused as the Terminators the snipers hunted.

When the cancer that was ultimately to take his life metastasized, Calhoun gave his rifle to Kyla, over the protests of Tony's own son. When Calhoun died a few weeks later, Kyla had words engraved on the barrel: TONY CALHOUN, plus the dates of the man's birth and death. The rifle was his only gravestone. Kyla suspected that it would probably be hers as well.

Kyla let out her breath, willing her body to absolute stillness—absolute except for her right index finger. With a slow, sure draw of the trigger, she fired.

The Terminator saw the distant glint. Its threat processor popped up a display of probabilities. The heaviest weighting, sixty-seven percent, was that the glint was a reflection from a piece of broken glass. Another twenty-two percent was that it was an emission from small-arms fire. That percentage would increase as the Terminator neared its objective, the search zone Skynet had defined as part of its mission.

Even if it was enemy action, however, the likelihood of it having any effect was extremely low. The glint was characteristic of small-arms fire, not rocketry. And at this range, an estimated one kilometer, small-arms accuracy was extremely low.

Then the .50-caliber round smashed into the Terminator's left eye and tore out through the side of its skull behind its temple.

The impact snapped the robot's head back and to the left. Temporary disruption of its sensory input and its motor coordination caused the robot to spasm and lose control of the steering wheel. The vehicle began a sharp drift rightward toward the overpass rail.

Even with visual senses temporarily off-line and intellectual processes overloaded, the Terminator knew that an impact with the corroding rails and concrete barriers would probably result in their destruction. The car would punch through, hurling through the air, smashing into the ground below. It might explode, causing the robot additional damage. This was unacceptable.

The Terminator slammed on the brake. But in its impaired state it failed to factor in the structural integrity of the frail vehicle it controlled. Its foot smashed through the brake pedal and the salt-corroded floorboard, striking the highway passing beneath.

One block away, an aging black man and a younger white man, both dressed in camo and carrying heavy backpacks, raced toward the highway on foot. In clear view of the highway overpass, they saw the convertible crash through the overpass rails, barrel-rolling as it dropped the thirty feet to the ground. It hit, its front end accordioning, its rear end wrapping around and collapsing on the driver.

The older man, Earl Duncan, breathing heavily, said, "Good girl, Kyla. Hollywood quality."

The younger, Lieutenant David Zimmerman, called Ten by the members of his team, took the opportunity to pull a weapon from his backpack. It was a tube a little over a yard long, a handle and trigger descending from it toward the rear, a crude sight protruding from it on one side nearer the middle, a bulbous mass attached to the front. It was a rocket-propelled grenade, a one-shot weapon that could, under rare and lucky circumstances, take out a robot as powerful and heavily defended as a T-800. "Let's go."

"Let's wait. If it crawls out before we get right up on it, it can't surprise us."

Ten growled to himself. The one member of the team he led whose tactical sense was better than his was Earl. Ten propped himself behind the burned hulk of a Dodge SUV and sighted in on the car.

The smashed convertible caught fire along the underside. It

shifted a little as its driver struggled; then it exploded. This wasn't a big, spectacular explosion, just a smallish boom and the eruption of a mushroom cloud no bigger than the car had been; the smoke from the cloud rose to drift serenely beyond the overpass.

"Gas tank probably full," Ten said. "Else the explosion would have been bigger."

"And that means—?"

"It probably came straight from one of San Francisco's old military bases. Just like Daniel predicted."

The burning hulk, less cream yellow than black now, shifted and a figure rose out of the middle of it.

The T-800 was a bit the worse for wear. Its clothes, hair, even its skin were on fire. Unconcerned, it stepped out from the burning wreckage and took a look around. It reached down to shift the demolished car. Earl and Ten both noted that it didn't have any sort of weapon in hand. It was probably searching for whatever long arm it had brought.

Ten fired. The RPG leaped away from him with a *whoosh* and the stench of burning propellant. The missile struck just beneath and between the Terminator's legs, exploding in a larger and louder detonation than the one before.

Earl and Ten watched the burning Terminator fly through the air to crash, a short distance away, into one of the concrete support pillars that held up the overpass. From his field pack, Earl pulled out an RPG of his own.

The Terminator was up immediately, its body now an odd combination of black burned flesh and silvery undercarriage. It turned an eye—only one was still red and glowing—toward Earl and Ten, and began running . . . but not toward them. It moved off at an angle away from the two men, keeping its cover behind successive support pillars.

"It knows where it's going," Earl said.

"Dammit." Ten grabbed the mike on his lapel. Now they didn't have enough time to fiddle with field phones and key in text messages. "Hell-Hound One to Starling, bug out, repeat bug out. You have about sixty seconds." He began running—not after the Terminator, but in a direct line toward the Eosphor Technologies building. Maybe he and his Hell-Hounds could get within line of sight of the building before the Terminator reached it; maybe they could exceed the values set up for its self-preservation protocols and cause it to turn against them instead of the others. Maybe.

Breathing heavily, Earl Duncan ran in his wake.

"Go, go, go, go!" Kate shouted. She switched her attention from the pair of men wheeling oversize file cabinets into the truck bed to the trio maneuvering a pallet-jack loaded with a large silk-screen frame. "That's your last item. Don't go back for more. Get the pallet-jack into the back." She walked deeper into the warehouse, addressing the next group in line. "What's that? Film? Negatives. Load it." She shouted further into the building, projecting to be heard through the open doorways, "Everyone else, drop what you're carrying. Bug out!"

John ignored her, trusting her to arrange the immediate evacuation of all personnel in the building. He kept his attention on his field phone and the digital countdown he'd set in the upper right of the screen. It was down to twenty-nine seconds. "Daniel, bring up the Humvee, now." Men and women were rushing past him, loading into the back of the truck. He heard the truck's engine firing up, an asthmatic rattle demonstrating just how old and fragile the machinery really was. "All scout units except Hell-Hounds, make for your rendezvous points. Hell-Hounds, give me an update." Now it was nineteen seconds.

Ten and Earl caught occasional glimpses of the Terminator as it charged directly toward Eosphor Technologies. The machine ran across streets and parking lots, smashing effortlessly through cyclone fences. Moving like a track champion, it leaped over low obstacles such as dead cars and cinder-block walls. The two Hell-Hounds steadily lost ground to the machine, which could run at two or three times their speed in a flat straightaway and was comparatively even faster in broken terrain such as this.

The Terminator reached the middle of a four-lane street that crossed at nearly right angles to its path. There was a sound like a ball bearing hitting a hubcap at the speed of sound, and the T-800 fell on its rear end. The crack from Kyla's sniper rifle followed a split-second later.

The Terminator was up in an instant. The second shot hadn't damaged it enough to alter its running pace; still, it held a hand up over its face as if shielding its eyes from the sun.

Ten, running a block back across the rubble of a fast-food place that now spilled across its parking lot, grinned. The machine was protecting its skull and remaining eye. They'd hurt it. It was always good to hurt a Terminator. If they could just get within hand-to-hand range without getting killed, the devices packed in the top of Ten's field pack would do more than hurt it.

Kyla's rifle spoke again, noises like distant trees suddenly being broken in half. Three times bell-like noises of her bullet impacts rang from the Terminator's torso; finally the machine slowed, its head swiveling in a ten-degree arc as it sought to discover Kyla's hiding place.

Earl, panting, came up alongside Ten and leaned across the hood of a U.S. Postal System delivery truck. There were human bones and patches of USPS uniform in the front seat. Earl still held his RPG. "Taking my shot," he said, his voice hoarse.

Ten had to marvel. Earl Duncan was well past sixty, the oldest member of the Hell-Hounds, and still in good enough shape to keep up with the others in urban operations. "Go for it."

Earl fired, and Ten watched in a dispassionate sort of fascination as the explosive head leaped from the disposable weapon. The

Terminator disappeared in a ball of fire and smoke, then reappeared several yards ahead, rolling to a stop against the remains of a filling station on the far side of the street. The ruins shielded it from further fire by Kyla.

The robot was up in a moment, but it had suffered further damage. A connector at the heel of its right leg, performing the same function as the Achilles tendon, had come free. Now the Terminator's right foot was loose, no longer under control of the computerized algorithms that simulated human movement.

The Terminator turned toward the filling station and smashed its way in through the surviving glass of its front window. Ten and Earl hurried after it. A moment later, the robot smashed out through the back door of the station; Ten could no longer see it, but could hear its newly awkward steps.

Now they'd forced it to move within cover to avoid more .50-caliber rounds and RPG warheads. They were wearing it down. But they couldn't count on wearing it down fast enough.

John saw the not-too-distant fireball of the Hell-Hounds' second RPG attack. Beside him, the last of the Operation Starling workers piled into the back of Transport 4. As Lieutenant Tom Carter, the aging officer who was one of John's primary technical experts, hauled the tailgate up, John kicked it, slamming it into place, and waved at the driver's-side mirror. "Go!"

The truck pulled out and immediately turned rightward, bumping its way across the ruined parking lot. John could hear its grinding engine and, now rising over it, the healthier roar of his personal transport, a Humvee that had been new when Judgment Day had occurred.

Kate stepped up beside him, shouldering her field pack. "I think we made it."

"I think—oh, damn." As the truck lumbered out of view, it revealed the figure standing at the far end of the parking lot: a Terminator, its clothes and false skin burned away, only one of its eye sockets glowing red.

John froze. The image of the gleaming skeleton of one of the murder machines always froze his stomach with fear, no matter how many times he'd seen it, no matter how good he'd become at concealing that fear.

Right now, he knew, the robot's threat assessment and targeting priority software would be evaluating the truck, him and Kate, even the oncoming Humvee, which was still out of sight but audible. The truck was the obvious target; so far as the Terminator could evaluate, its unknown cargo could conceivably do considerable damage to Skynet resources.

The Terminator ignored the truck. Limping, its right foot dragging, it began a slow, methodical trot straight toward John and Kate.

John swore. "It's recognized us." John Connor and Kate Brewster, supreme leaders of the Human Resistance on this continent, were much more valuable targets than a truck full of unknown materials. By now, the Terminator would have transmitted to Skynet the fact that they were here, and Skynet resources in the area would be converging on this site.

Kate grabbed her lapel mike and keyed it. "Daniel, bring the Humvee around to the front door. North side."

Daniel's voice in her headphone speakers was, as ever, low and melodious, the tones of a twentieth-century disk jockey on a classical music station. "I read. Fifteen seconds."

John turned and ran with Kate back into the building's interior. "Tell the Hounds to run for it."

"Hell-Hounds, this is a scram order. This is about to be a hot zone."

They passed through the wide doors opening out of the loading dock. Beyond was a dark chamber, echoing with gymnasium-like breadth and width, but no longer illuminated now that John's workers had fled. He and Kate snapped on flashlights and he followed her lead across the concrete floor, now partially stripped of the long stands of equipment that had occupied it until the last few hours.

Behind them they heard clanking—the Terminator's metal feet moving in an irregular fashion across the loading dock floor.

Gaining on them.

Kate and John skidded as they rounded a corner into the long hallway that led to the facility's main entrance. It was perhaps fifty yards from where they were to the sliver of light that heralded the front doors, but now it looked like a mile. Behind them, metal rang and clattered as the Terminator crashed clean through a conveyor belt, not slowed, and continued to gain ground on them.

Halfway to the door, John hazarded a glance back. He could see nothing but the one red eye of the Terminator bobbing as the robot continued its awkward but tireless run. The thing obviously had lost any ranged weapons it might have had, but if it got its hands on either of them, that deficit would no longer matter.

His breath ragged, John surged ahead of Kate to hit the door. The protocols his units followed were that the designated exits out of any raided installation were to be unlocked, guarded until the bug-out command came, in order to give his people every opportunity for an escape, but sometimes mistakes were made.

Not this time. The ancient metal doors slammed open from his impact and he and Kate were suddenly in the light again.

But the clanking was so close behind them, so close . . .

The Humvee wasn't immediately at hand. It was fifteen or twenty yards ahead of them, parked in the street, idling.

Unoccupied.

John didn't have breath left to swear. He got a hand on Kate's elbow, put the last of his energy into running—

The clang behind him seemed as loud and harsh as a train boxcar being dropped on the metal deck of a boat. Despite himself, John spun to look.

The Terminator was down on its face, its arms already under it to rise. Earl Duncan and Daniel Ávila flanked the door, holding something between them—a length of steel cable, held at about ankle height. Both looked off-balance; tripping the robot, given its great mass, had to have been a tremendous effort for them. And Ten Zimmerman, leaping from position beside Earl, was slapping something the size of an old-fashioned lunchbox onto the Terminator's back . . .

The robot came up on its hands as though doing a push-up and lashed out with its left arm. The blow took Ten across the chest, hurling him yards backward.

"Scatter!" That was Earl, up to a full run toward Ten before the younger man even hit the pavement. Daniel lurched into motion, running the other way, waving John and Kate on their original course.

The Terminator spun around, a quick move to assess the new threat that endangered it. As it faced the open door into the building, the explosive charge Ten had affixed to its back went off.

To John, as close as he was, it looked as though his entire universe caught fire. There was nothing but flame and heat, bright light and impact. The explosion kicked him over backward and he scrambled away from it, blindly groping around for Kate. His shoulder blades hit something unyielding—the bumper of the Humvee.

Someone got hands under his arm and hauled him up. He could tell by touch that it was Kate. "Are you okay?" He could barely hear his own shout.

"What?"

"Can you see?"

"I can see."

"Then you drive." Unwilling to admit how much of the impact of the explosion he'd sustained, how much his eyes were dazzled, he groped his way around to the passenger-side door.

His sight was returning. Earl had Ten's arm over his shoulder and was helping the younger man, who was conscious but looked shell-shocked, to the Humvee. Daniel Ávila, moving fast considering his age and weight, got to the driver's side rear door and climbed in. "The T-800's scrap," Daniel shouted. "Blown in half at the spine. The top half was thrown back into the building."

John climbed into the passenger seat. As his hearing returned, he heard ringing, not unusual for the blow he'd received. He shook his head and felt the first, predatory arrival of a massive headache. "I can't believe you *tripped* a Terminator," he shouted. "What's next? You going to call it on the phone, ask 'Have you got Prince Albert in a can?'"

Daniel grinned at him. He was a middle-aged Latino, his face framed by a neatly trimmed black beard. Unusual for a member of the Resistance in these lean and hungry times, he was substantially overweight, topping the scales at around 280 pounds. "You're lucky we didn't go with our first plan. Poking it in the eyes. Nyuk-nyuk-nyuk."

The door behind him slammed; Ten and Earl were in place. Kate set the Humvee into motion, roaring away from the Eosphor Technologies building as fast as the vehicle's aging acceleration would allow. "Storm drains," she said. "Daniel, what's our best path to a storm drain out of here?"

"Left at the street," Daniel said. "Two blocks straight, then right and seven blocks more. That'll bring you back to the highway and an entrance into the storm drain. The maps don't say if you have to jump a curb or concrete barrier to get into it."

"Whatever it takes," Kate said.

John saw a bright red-and-yellow light in the passenger-side mirror, then heard the boom as the Eosphor building exploded. Daniel let out a howl, half scream and half war-cry, then added in a conversational tone, "The Tin Man's power supply must have cooked off. Hey, look at that, look at that!"

John could see it in the mirror, the gray-and-black cloud ballooning up from the ruins of the building. For just a moment, where it swelled widest, the cloud took on the approximate shape of a human skull, the right eye-socket oversize, the mouth opening and widening. Then wind and distortion twisted the image beyond recognition and it was just a cloud again.

"I don't believe in omens," Earl said. "And I don't believe in the face of the Madonna in the side of a refrigerator or a double pane of glass. That was just coincidence."

"Sure it was," Daniel said, but he looked troubled. "I just had the weirdest feeling that I've seen it before. That exact cloud."

John turned around to give him a curious look. "You'd know, wouldn't you? You're the one with the memory to die for."

Daniel flashed him a humorless smile, even white teeth surrounded by black beard. "Only back to a certain point, John."

June, Present Day
Ávila Property, East of Bakersfield, California

Danny Ávila watched the smoke cloud rise out of the ruined building. For just a moment, it assumed the aspect of a skull, but he didn't know whether it was a human skull or the new-series Terminator cranial housing the engineers were developing. Then the smoke twisted, causing one eye socket to bulge. The skull's mouth widened as though it were straining just before a ferocious bite to come, and—

Danny's head banged down on something hard. He opened his eyes and rubbed his forehead.

He was face-down on the floorboards beside his bed. In his peripheral vision, he could see the shoe boxes, unsorted socks, and dust bunnies that occupied the space beneath his bed.

Someone tapped on his bedroom door. "Danielcito?"

He stood, still a little sleep-bleary. Morning light poured in through his east-facing window. Above his window and door, and above the bookcases that surrounded his bed, were the only places he could see the room's walls. "Yes, Mama?"

"¿Estás bien?" Are you all right?

The clock on his headboard read 6:58. His dream had cost him two minutes of precious sleep. "Yes, Mama. I, uh, dropped a book on the floor."

"Breakfast is ready." Once upon a time, she never would have switched to English, nor would Danny have answered her in English. While Danny's father Hugo was alive, his rule had been a simple and consistent one: Spanish in the house, English everywhere else. It was a sensible guideline; Hugo hadn't wanted his family to become so Anglicized that they lost their mother tongue or so Spanish-oriented that they suffered in school or business. Danny thought that the rule would probably come back into force if ever there were children in the house again. But Danny and his brothers were grown, there were no children in the house, and Hugo was dead, victim of a heart attack years ago. So his family relaxed the rules a bit.

"I'll be right down." He grinned. Mama saying "Breakfast is ready" at this time of day was akin to saying, "The sun came up a while ago." Unless atomic bombs rained down on Kern County, he'd never need to ask whether breakfast was ready in the Ávila house at seven A.M.

He turned to the laptop on his dresser. The first ritual of any morning was checking his e-mail.

Ten minutes later, dressed and up to date on e-mail, his laptop in the soft-sided briefcase he habitually carried, he reached the dining-room table downstairs.

Linda was already at the table, wearing her green-and-gold Kern County Sheriff's Department uniform, her blond hair back in a ponytail, the uniform's green jacket across the back of her chair. A book lay open beside her plate, and she was sufficiently wrapped up in reading it that she did not hear Danny's arrival.

Danny leaned over her shoulder to look at it. "Superstrings, huh? That's high-order math. Aren't you too blond for that?"

She glanced up at him, her features set in a mock scowl that couldn't quite mask a grin. She was not a beautiful woman, but had attractive features and intelligent, deep brown eyes. "I'm surprised you recognize the term," she said. "I figured a code-geek like you would think superstrings came spraying out of a can."

"You wound me, Deputy. And only breakfast can take away the sting." He took his usual chair opposite her, facing the room's front window with its view of the family's pastures and the highway beyond. "No, really. Is this for class?" Linda took classes two nights a week, working her way, as quickly as her schedule would allow, toward a master's degree in physics. Danny thought it was an unusual choice, figuring a sheriff's deputy seeking higher education would gravitate to law or criminology, but Linda had always said that law enforcement was her job but not her career.

"Just some side reading. I have to figure out whether I'm going to invent time travel or faster-than-light travel first. This'll help."

"Danny?" Mama called from the kitchen. "You want the usual?"

"No, Mama. I want what I always have." Here, "the usual" meant an Hugo Ávila breakfast—a plug of cholesterol arranged into scrambled eggs with cheese, fried sausage patties, French toast, and other tasty, heart-stopping choices. It was no use telling Mama that this diet had probably shortened Hugo's life by decades; to her, this was what a breakfast should be.

Danny heard his mother's sigh, and he mouthed the words as she spoke them: "Danny, you're too skinny."

"Got to stay skinny, Mama. Need to attract a woman someday, and you know it's going to be with my looks, not my personality. You *did* say something about eventually wanting grandchildren, right?" He regretted the words as soon as he said them. Linda and his brother Alejandro, who went by Alex, had planned to have children someday, and he didn't know whether Linda was sensitive about the subject. But she hadn't reacted at all to his words; instead, she raised her hands over her head in a stretch to banish the last sleepiness of the morning.

Danny managed not to stare. He did love the sight of a woman in uniform.

No, it was more than that. He knew his heart raced every time he came in close contact with Linda. But it wasn't all that good an idea to go lusting after the widow of his own brother.

He'd always worried, just a little, that some members of his family didn't fully accept her. A transplanted Texan who had come to California to attend USC, she had an Anglo mother and a Latino father, and there was no language barrier for her in the bilingual household. But she never went to church or allowed herself to be drawn into discussions of faith, and she hadn't become pregnant in the year she'd been married to Alex. More conservative members of the extended family and their friends wondered if she even considered herself a Christian.

Mama came out and set a plate in front of Danny—scrambled eggs, no cheese, salsa on top, ordinary toast, a peeled orange. She looked at it disapprovingly.

Mama Teresa Ávila was the polar opposite of her late husband. She was a small woman—tiny, really—whose metabolism and relentless activity level burned through calories at a rate that would make Hollywood starlets sick with envy. Despite her efforts to fatten up everyone remotely related to her, she was lean. At fifty, she had yet to get her first gray hair. Her strongest facial feature was a proud and prominent Aztec nose, which Danny, when teasing her, would refer to as her can-opener. "This is not enough to keep a hamster alive," she said.

"It's fine, Mama." Danny plunged a fork into the eggs, indicating that he was content with such sorry fare. "Besides, you know programmers can live on diets that would kill lesser men. At work I sustain myself eating lead paint chips, scorpions, and very small rocks."

She offered him a long-suffering sigh and returned to the kitchen.

Linda snickered. "One of these days, she's going to brain you with a ladle."

"Papa always said you have to deal with a strong-willed woman by being so much trouble that you break her morale."

"Alex used to tell *me* that. When he was being troublesome, of course." She lowered her voice to a conspiratorial level. "I wonder if Mama's getting a little deaf. I don't think she can tell the difference between a book and a body hitting the floor."

Danny shrugged, swallowing his first mouthful of eggs. "I fell out of bed. Bad dream."

"You were back in high school, naked, on test day . . ."

He grinned. "I haven't had *that* dream in days. No, one of the weapon systems I'm working on went haywire, tried to kill a bunch of people, and blew up." His family knew that he programmed weapon systems for the Air Force, but not what sort of systems. No one outside of work knew that he was a lead programmer at CRS, working on next-generation Terminator operating systems and Terminator-Skynet interface routines. He was on the cutting edge of technology that would someday render the modern infantryman, tank, and helicopter obsolete.

But in his dream, an extremely advanced Terminator, a variety that was just now on the drawing boards at CRS, walking on two legs instead of grinding along on tracks, hadn't been serving the interests of human masters, hadn't been targeting enemy troops or matériel. It had been trying to exterminate Americans in the ruins of an American city. The dream had been unsettling.

Linda finished the last of her breakfast and stood. "I've gotta go." She picked up her plate.

From the kitchen, Mama called, "Just leave that, dear. I'll get it."

Danny shot Linda an accusing look. "She's not going deaf," he whispered.

Linda grinned. "Don't you just love a peace officer who lies to you?"

■   ■   ■

The gravel driveway leading off the Ávila property was one lane wide, and the gravel hadn't recently been replenished; the track was now two shallow earthen ruts with gravel between them and to either side. Danny stopped his car, a late-model Jeep Grand Cherokee in sunlight-reflecting white, just before the driveway reached Highway 58 and looked back across the property.

In the foreground were acres and acres of pasturage, slightly rolling land with patches of hardy grasses and scrub bushes throughout. Spotted cattle not yet enervated by early summer sun slowly moved from patch to patch. In the middle distance rose the family home, a wide, two-story wooden farmhouse built in the 1930s and carefully maintained in the decades since; it gleamed yellow, with white trim, in the morning sunlight. To the left of it was a low single-story bunkhouse built much more recently, and nearby were the barn, pump house, and other auxiliary buildings of a working farm. Farther out were groves of oranges and pistachios.

Ten years ago, when the bunkhouse was first built, the property looked almost the same from this perspective, but it was actually much larger. Then, Hugo Ávila was finally facing the reality that none of his three sons was going to follow in their father's profession. Lon, the oldest at twenty-two, had just graduated from business school and seemed destined for a successful career with the San Francisco brokerage that had hired him. Alex, the twenty-year-old middle son, was in his junior year of college and was adamant about following the career path of an uncle in law enforcement. Danny, the youngest, at sixteen, had been accepted for admission to UCLA, and his academic successes so far, plus his obvious genius with computer programming, made his father tremendously proud of him.

But that left the Ávilas without a farmer in the new generation, and Hugo, no tradition-bound fool, did not even try to lure his sons back to his way of life. Instead, with an unspoken regret, he began selling or leasing the more distant fields and pastures to surrounding farms and ranches. He built a small bunkhouse and hired seasonal workers for the peak work times of the year. The rest of the work he did himself, sometimes joined by sons home on weekends.

Even today, in spite of its reduced circumstances, the property was still profitable, still theirs. Hugo Ávila was five years in his grave, but his commonsense preparations had ensured that the family still had a home to return to, regardless of how broadly scattered they might be from time to time. There was an unspoken agreement between Danny and Lon that, whatever happened, the farm would remain in Ávila hands.

Danny put the Jeep into gear and turned east, rightward, onto 58, the highway that took him every workday to Edwards Air Force Base.

Edwards AFB, in addition to being a working U.S. Air Force base and an alternate landing site for the space shuttle, housed many public and not-so-public operations: NASA's Dryden Flight Research Center, the Air Force Research Laboratory, and the chief research and development facility of Cyber Research Systems (Autonomous Weapons Division). Edwards, a part of the tabloid-notorious Area 51 testing center, conceivably housed many more projects even more secretive than CRS; Danny didn't know and didn't care.

Much of the CRS Autonomous Weapons Division lay underground—machine fabrication areas, testing ranges, communications center, generators, access to the complex's very own particle accelerator. But at the surface it looked like nothing more than a nicely modern glass-and-metal office building three stories tall. A spy satellite trained on the site would see Danny drive into the

Edwards complex through the North Gate, navigate his Jeep almost to the complex's south end to the CRS building, and enter his workplace just as thousands of civilian employees of the military did at scores of bases across the United States and its possessions.

But as he took the elevator down to the first basement level, which served as home base for the project's programmers, he could reflect, with satisfaction and an edge of worry, that this base was as secret, mysterious, and potentially unbalancing of the world's balance of power, as the first atomic-missile bases had been fifty-odd years ago.

He walked into Cube Hell and took in the usual quiet chaos of clicking keys, muffled curses, and conversation. On the far side of the room, something tiny and glinting—a paper clip launched from a rubber band—shot up from one cubicle to strike the acoustic tile of the ceiling and ricochet down into the adjacent cubicle, followed by an unrestrained cry of, "You *bastard.*"

Danny grinned. It was his second home.

Then, from the vicinity of Danny's own double-wide, double-deep cubicle, Dr. Sherman stood up, and Danny's heart sank.

Phil Sherman was, in theory, lead programmer on the next-generation Terminator project. Like Danny, he was lean and above-average height, but he lacked Danny's broad shoulders. His green eyes behind old-fashioned gold-rimmed glasses, his hair graying, dressed in a conservative gray suit, Sherman looked like he could be a banker by day and a friendly grandfather by night, though he had been a programmer and developer on several of the Apollo moon shots and many NASA and military projects since. His skills hadn't kept up with modern programming languages and tools, but he was unusually adept at finding, hiring, and managing the most talented of today's generation of code wranglers.

But his presence at Danny's cubicle at the start of work usually meant something had gone wrong. Sherman's office was several stories up, on the same level as the Computer Center and General Brewster's office.

Danny hurried over. "What's wrong, Phil?"

Sherman smiled. "Diplomatic relations breaking down between the military and civilian side of things, as usual. General Brewster's going to perform a demonstration with Scowl at noon today. And Scowl's not feeling cooperative."

Danny moved into his cubicle and sat in front of his computer; he powered up its monitor and logged in. Scowl, a prototype Terminator, was the test bed for new operating system innovations and engineering improvements. It had all the functionality of the first-generation T-1s that had been secretly deployed to sites across the United States, but was much smaller; T-1s were nearly the size of midsize cars, while Scowl could be packed into a civilian van with room to spare. T-1s had arms that ended in tank-busting chain guns, while Scowl's arms were fitted with articulated metal hands . . . and the robot's programming allowed it to operate every small arm, every man-portable missile system in the U.S. military arsenal, in theory at least. Scowl was the Terminator onto which he and his team loaded each new update to the operating system, each program patch with a new feature.

"What's wrong with it?"

"It's trying to fly." Sherman sat in Danny's guest chair. "We've got some footage on the problem. Look in the bug list directory for a file named 'flapper.' "

"Brewster's going to kill us." The whispered comment came from above Sherman's head. Danny turned to look. Jerry Squires, another team programmer, was standing in his adjacent cubicle, resting his chin on the partition in between. The effect was that of a narrow, diabolic-looking severed head with tousled sandy hair having been balanced there.

Danny turned back to his monitor. He found the file in question and double-clicked on it to launch the recording. "You ever been in Brewster's office, Jer?"

Squires continued his spectral-whisper voice. "No."

"You know what's on his desk?"

"Again I say no."

"A picture of his daughter. His daughter's kind of hot. I say, general's got a hot daughter, you strive to make him happy every day of the year, against the time he's so happy with you he invites you home for Thanksgiving."

Danny's monitor resolved itself to a view, from low-ceiling height, of Scowl. The squat tracked robot was situated before a folding table. On the table were several objects: a chess set whose pieces' locations suggested that a game was well underway; a glass half-full of clear liquid; and a handgun Danny recognized as an M9 Beretta, the armed forces' standard-issue 9mm semiautomatic. "Manual dexterity tests?"

"That's right," Sherman said. "Plus a test of the interface between Scowl, the mainframe control, and a commercial chess program. Jer got it all functioning last night . . . but not exactly successfully."

The severed head, no longer whispering, said, "Hey." The word was a complaint.

On screen, the Terminator began to reach for the chessboard. But before its arm had moved more than a few inches, it folded the arm up at the elbow and tucked it into place against its body, raised and lowered it, and did it again. Only then did it reach out to grasp one of the knights on the chessboard. With slow deliberation, it lifted the piece and set it down to endanger a white bishop.

The tucking and flapping looked curiously like a bird with a damaged wing trying to lift off. Danny snickered. "How often does it do that?"

"Every time it's called on to use either arm," Sherman said. "The only arm-related task that doesn't set it off is a diagnostics check. Think you can fix it before noon?"

Danny turned an incredulous expression on him. "What, based on what I've seen here? Without even digging into the code?"

"Yes."

Danny relented. "I think I can fix it in ten or twenty minutes."

"Oh, bullshit," Jer objected. "I've been here all night working on it. I haven't been home."

"That explains the smell."

"Anyway, I can't figure it out."

"I can." Danny pointed a finger accusingly at him. "Let me guess. You were fiddling with the fine-manipulation code last night to keep Scowl from knocking down as many chess pieces as usual. And at some point you cut and pasted in some of the self-checking stuff I did yesterday for its set-up-for-transport mode."

"Well . . . yeah. How'd you know?"

"The code you borrowed is structured like some of the standard problem-solving routines. It calls subroutines that figure out all the motion control steps for the task it's been presented. But since I wrote it specifically for machine shutdown, the task is automatically assumed to be 'fold up for transport.' So there are a couple of places where, instead of looking for the register that defines its current task, it automatically assumes shutdown procedures have begun, and it folds up its arm to lock into place. Instead of going 'move chess piece,' it's going 'shutdown, shutdown, move chess piece.'"

The severed head winced. "That's *your* fault. You were sloppy."

"*I* wrote it from scratch. You borrowed it and did a lousy job of filing off the serial numbers. Who's sloppy?"

"You are."

Sherman rose, a tolerant smile on his face. "Gentlemen, I'll send over some Nerf pistols so you can duel at dawn. In the meantime, Danny, I'd appreciate it if you'd get this straightened out so the general doesn't pop his cork."

"I'll do that."

"And I'll tell him you think his daughter's kind of hot."

"Don't do that."

With Sherman gone, Jer stared down at him. "Your mistake was in saying 'kind of hot.' Two mistakes for the price of one. You're suggesting that you could bag his little girl, but also that she's not the *most* baggable little girl in all the world."

"Go home, code thief." Danny turned back to his monitor.

The footage of the Terminator's chicken-wing antics was certainly amusing. Danny played it several more times before getting to work on repairing the code. Someday, he hoped, the early stages of the Terminator project would be declassified so the footage could show up on a blooper reel or as an Internet download.

c.4

August 2029
Vega Compound, Sacramento, California

John Connor snapped to wakefulness in full darkness.

That's the way it usually happened. Most of the places he slept were within caves, abandoned missile sites, surviving basements beneath collapsed buildings, hidden bunkers. Generally, the air was too warm and still, often stinking of long human occupation without the benefit of occasional thorough cleaning.

Now, he felt the warm heaviness of the air and heard no sound to indicate that they were in trouble. As his first panic subsided, he knew where he was: Vega Compound, once a set of steam tunnels beneath California State University in Sacramento, now a community of a few dozen humans . . . and, for John's convoy of trucks, a temporary way station. The leader of the little community had given John and Kate a private chamber, once a spacious janitor's closet, as their bedroom, and had situated John's circle of commanders and soldiers in an adjacent tunnel they could have to themselves.

He didn't have to reach out to feel that Kate was still beside him. The bed they shared, two cots roped together with a number of tatty blankets thrown over them to smooth out where the cot supports protruded, was barely large enough for them.

"Sorry," she whispered.

"For what?"

"Waking you up."

"You didn't wake me up. A dream woke me up."

"Me, too. What was yours about?"

He snorted. "It was pretty silly. An old-style Terminator, like a T-1 except it had hands, with a problem with its arms."

"It flapped them like a chicken?"

He raised his head off the folded blanket that served him as a pillow. "Was I talking in my sleep?"

"No. That was my dream, too."

"You're kidding."

"No. I'm spooked."

"I don't blame you." He gauged his state of wakefulness and decided that he wasn't going to be able to fall asleep again anytime soon, regardless of what hour it was. He pulled the sheet off him. "I think I'll go see if Kyla has checked in."

"I think I'll go with you."

When they emerged from their converted closet, they were dressed in faded khaki uniforms that were often dress of the day for Connor's command staff. The broad concrete hallway beyond was dimly lit by hanging lamps. These flickered and popped at intervals, fueled by badly rendered oils; John made a note to himself to find someone to offer the Vega Compound leaders technical advice on rendering fats.

A few feet nearer than the closest lamp to the left, Earl Duncan sat in a folding metal chair suited to university use. Only its two rear legs were on the floor; he had it leaned backward against the peeling green corridor wall. His shotgun, an over-and-under model, lay across his lap; he held a tattered paperback book above it. He gave them a cordial nod. " 'Morning."

"Good morning, Earl," Kate said. Something about Earl's

solemnity and dignity had always caused her to speak to him with a little more formality than she reserved for others. "What time is it?"

" 'Bout four A.M."

"Has Kyla checked in?"

Earl nodded. "We got a short text transmission from her and Mark Herrera a couple hours ago. They'll be in by twilight tonight. They managed to get Transport Five out of there intact."

Kate sighed as two days of tension began to leech away. "Thank God. How about the dogs?"

Earl grinned. "Dogs are okay."

John let out a breath. "Earl, you could have awakened us to tell us."

Earl offered up a low chuckle. "Boss, I don't cost anyone sleep for anything short of a T-600 or an avalanche."

"Well, I suspect Mike feels the same way I do, so I'll wake her up to tell her that her son's still alive."

Earl shook his head. "No need. She got up a minute ago. I told her. She went off to the mess to get some breakfast just before you came out."

"Doesn't anyone sleep around here?" Those words, projected in a sullen whisper, came from the darkened portion of the corridor where the cots for Connor's command staff and other traveling staff were situated.

Out of that darkness walked Dr. Tamara Lake, the Resistance's senior authority on genetics and high-level biological matters. When not involved in work related to her speciality, she also served as Connor's command staff doctor, accompanying him on his travels.

Now in her midfifties, Lake had seen the beauty of her youth fade, but she still bore a trace of it in the elegant lines of her face. Her hair was now completely gray, but she kept it cut short and arranged in a hairstyle reminiscent of social sophisticates of thirty years ago; she'd obviously just run a brush through it, since it wasn't disarrayed. Unlike most members of the command staff, she preferred civilian dress whenever possible, and often traded to have one or two nonmilitary garments available to her; now she wore her sleep-shirt, a not-too-faded blue linen tunic that fell to just above her knees and showed off her still-shapely legs to good effect.

Over the years, John had occasionally seen Lake out of control, and knew how bitter she was at having lost her life of high-end medical research, grant proposals, and California celebrity socializing when Judgment Day came. But still he didn't know whether to appreciate her struggle to keep age at bay, or to pity her for it.

"Did we wake you up?" John asked. "Sorry about that."

Lake shook her head. "No," she said around a yawn. "Weird dream. Got any booze, Earl?"

Earl just cocked an eyebrow at her. He didn't drink, as she'd known for twenty years.

John and Kate exchanged a look. "What sort of dream?" Kate asked.

"It was silly. An old-style Terminator with a—"

"Malfunctioning arm," John finished. A chill of worry, reaction to being suddenly confronted with the unknown and inexplicable, settled in his stomach, and intensified when Lake turned a startled expression on him. "Let's go find Mike and put the same question to *her*," he said.

"Just like mine," Michaela Herrera confirmed. She sat at a folding table in the concrete hallway that served Vega Compound as a mess hall. A tall, strongly built Mexican-American, she had a pattern of burn scars on her right neck and cheek that decorated her like a tribal tattoo. Her brown eyes, normally directed like spotlights on whatever had her attention, held an expression of worry.

One of Connor's chief scientific advisers, she was a member of the staff that unraveled the means of operating the Continuum Transporter, the time-travel device the Resistance had discovered early that year . . . the device Connor had used to send his own father, Kyle Reese, back into the past.

"So what does it mean?" John asked. "Opinions, anyone?"

"We can rule out anyone hearing you or Kate talking in your sleep," Lake said. She ran both hands back through her hair. The gesture tightened her sleep-shirt over her bosom. John saw Kate roll her eyes at this obvious, if minor, ploy for attention. "So we're talking about some sort of extraordinary level of contact."

"I don't believe in ESP," said Colonel Sid Walker. An African-American man of about forty-five, short, bald, and hard-muscled, he was overall commander of the Resistance 1st Security Regiment.

Lake shot him a dismissive glance. "I don't believe in any buzzword. Such as military intelligence, for instance. Don't define the event by the buzzword. Define the event by its characteristics. What just happened here? Some sort of extraordinary level of mind-to-mind contact. If you want to, come up with a new term for it, something not tainted by wishful thinking and generations of fuzzy minds. 'Sleep-state biological telephony.'"

Walker glowered at her. Lake was outside his direct control, and he, like everyone else in the command structure, had too often been the target of her verbal scorn.

"Who's not here?" asked Mike, her words quiet, a seeming non sequitur. She was staring at the center of the table, not meeting anyone's eye.

Lake gave her an admonishing look. "Most of humanity, Mike."

Mike glanced at her, unimpressed by her acidity. "Look around and use your alleged scientific observational skills. Everyone who was sleeping within about a thirty-foot radius ten minutes ago is now up and here with a Terminator chicken-wing dream fresh in his head. Except for whom?"

Lake looked around. "Earl—"

"He was awake, on guard," Mike said.

"Ten—no, wait, he's on painkillers I gave him for his ribs. Probably can't dream, or is incapable of waking up right now. And, uh, Daniel."

Mike nodded. "Daniel."

John shrugged. "So?"

"So you know the only one of us who was *ever* in a position to see a Terminator malfunction like that in real life, the only one of us who actually worked on the CRS project at Edwards, was Daniel. Earl was at Edwards, but not on the CRS team."

Kate smiled. "Mike, that's reading a lot into things. Daniel doesn't *remember* any of that. He lost his memory around Judgment Day. He spent years wandering around in the wilderness like some mad prophet until John and I found him. If it weren't for the ID he carried, he wouldn't know his own name, and we wouldn't have been able to confirm that he worked at Edwards at that time."

Mike nodded, her expression glum. "The other day, when you got back from the Eosphor Tech mission, he told me he'd seen a cloud shaped like a skull, and that he was sure, absolute-to-the-bone sure, that he'd had a dream about that a long time ago. Before Judgment Day. It's the only time I've ever heard him claim to remember something from before J-Day."

"The only connection I see is dreams," Lake said.

"Dreams and Daniel." Mike stood up. "Let's go experiment."

John followed suit. "On what?"

"On Daniel Ávila."

Lake rubbed her hands together. "Oh, goody."

Daniel lay on his back, a blanket half-draped over him, his eyes closed. The cots around him were empty, their former occupants clustered behind John, Kate, and Mike as they stared down at him. The light cast by the half-shrouded lantern Kate carried was dim, but sufficient to see that Daniel was sweating out of proportion to the heat in this corridor, even given his extra weight.

Daniel mumbled words that sounded something like "To hell with the general."

Mike leaned closer. "Daniel, where are you?" Her voice was low, intense.

Daniel turned his head as if listening. "Hammock."

"Hammock where?"

"Home. Bakersfield."

"What's going on?"

"He made fun of me. He didn't say thank-you."

"Who didn't?"

"For fixing the arm."

"Who didn't?"

"General Brewster."

John felt Kate sag against him. Lieutenant General Robert Brewster, commander of the CRS project at Edwards AFB, dead since Judgment Day, had been her father. Kate's expression had blanked from faintly curious to shocked in an instant. John put an arm around her, to steady her, to reassure her.

Mike continued, "Tell me about your dreams, Daniel."

"The new ones?"

"Sure, the new ones."

"They're loose, all the T's. Old ones, new ones. Kill everybody. We live in caves. All my work, it's just going to kill us. Linda."

John frowned. "Who's Linda?"

Daniel didn't answer. John gestured to Mike, and after a moment's delay she repeated the question: "Who's Linda?"

"Alex's wife. Hot, hot, hot. She's here." Daniel opened his eyes and jerked as he realized that he was surrounded. His voice changed, became deeper, more resonant. "What the hell?"

"Sorry to wake you," John said. "We'll leave. You can go back to sleep."

Daniel laughed. "Yeah, right. I wake up with a lynch mob around me and the adrenaline shot to go with it, and you expect me to doze off again? Besides, it's four-thirty, isn't it?"

Walker checked his timepiece, a pocket watch that had to be a century old; its elegantly engraved case had been smoothed and blurred with wear over the years. "You're about ten minutes off." He snapped the case shut.

"Well, I'd be awake in an hour anyway, might as well get up now." Daniel stretched, his motion threatening to topple him off the side of the cot.

Lake turned away. Over her shoulder, she told Mike, "This doesn't prove anything. He was talking about our current situation."

"I don't think so." Mike turned back to Daniel. "Do you remember what you were dreaming just now?"

He shook his head and heaved himself upright. "I wasn't dreaming."

"A hammock? A girl named Linda?"

"Nope." He stood, not in the least sleep-awkward. He was still in his camo dress, which was rumpled from his sleep.

"Do you know a girl named Linda?" she persisted.

"Nope. No, wait. Isn't there a Linda at the compound near the Presidio? Linda Cho? About thirty, cute, makes paper?"

Mike didn't answer. She just turned to look back at Lake.

John and most of his command staff sat at a table across the mess hall from Daniel. The big man sat alone, enjoying his early breakfast, chatting with the Vega Compound cook who brought first one plate then another to him. He hadn't taken it personally when John had excluded him from the advisers' table. Everyone on

John's staff knew his policy: Information that kept people alive was to be spread as far and as fast as possible, while information that, if spread, would tend to get people killed, stayed compartmentalized. Information whose potential danger was unknown fell into the second category. Every one of John's advisers had been cut out of operational discussions at one time or another.

"Remember, I'm the one who found most of the information we ever got on Daniel Ávila," Mike said. She kept her voice down so that her words would not carry to the man they were talking about. "We know that he and his family lived near Bakersfield. We know from his programming skills that he was a very proficient programmer before Judgment Day. He had ID cards both for Edwards AFB and for the CRS project, where the Terminators and Skynet were designed. In the years since we've had him, he taught us how to reprogram the few Terminators we captured more or less intact, he's demonstrated he can often anticipate how Skynet 'thinks,' and so on, all without remembering a single thing that happened before the bombs dropped."

"Until now," Kate said.

"Even now. While he was talking in his sleep, he remembered things from before. But the instant he woke up, he couldn't. He couldn't even remember the dream he'd just woken out of. How likely is that?"

"Not very, I guess." John rubbed the stubble on his chin. "What are you maneuvering toward, Mike?"

"I don't think he's dreaming. I think there's some sort of weird connection between the Daniel of today and the Daniel of just before Judgment Day, and things he sees in one time are bleeding across to the other time. In either direction."

"O-*kay*," Lake said. She put on an artificially bright smile and turned toward their leader. "So, John, are we heading on today, or tomorrow?"

"Tomorrow," John said. "After the rest of the Hell-Hounds and the workers they're shepherding get back. Mike, that's a fairly lunatic suggestion."

"Sure it is." Mike's tone was agreeable. "Now, factor this in. In the ruins of CRS at Edwards, I found documents indicating that just before J-Day, Air Force security teams were looking for Daniel. He'd run off. He was under the delusion that the Terminators were going to rise up and band together to destroy human civilization. Of course, he was right, which kind of blunts the notion that he was crazy. But where'd he get the idea? I think he got it from his modern mind, from a connection to the knowledge he possesses now."

Lake sighed. "You remember toilet paper, Mike? You remember how thin it was, how you could see right through it, how it tore under the slightest pressure? Well—"

"Shut up, Tamara," Mike said.

The other woman didn't look put out. She often argued in such a fashion that she was told to shut up. "I don't think I will. Why is Daniel the only person who can do this? And if not, why haven't we heard of others?"

"We have." Mike pointed at John.

John shook his head. "I don't get you."

"When you were a teenager, after the T-800 came back to rescue you, you had dreams about Terminators overrunning the world."

Lake made a scornful noise. "Based on what he'd been told. By that Terminator, by his mother."

"Aha." Mike's tone was triumphant. "John, didn't you tell me once that you knew from a dream that the HKs were called Hunter-Killers?"

They all looked at him. John nodded slowly. "Yeah. I did."

"What was that, Tamara? A lucky guess?"

Lake still looked unconvinced. "No, the T-800 told him. He just doesn't remember."

Mike nodded. "That's possible. It's also possible that the extremely stressed-out John Connor of the 1990s and the extremely stressed-out John Connor of the 2020s reached out to one another, the younger one to validate his very existence, the older one to reassure his younger self, the same way I think the young Daniel and today's Daniel are doing."

Lake's expression offered no indication that she was yielding. "The tabloids went out of business the same day as the rest of the world, Mike. You've got no one to sell this story to."

Mike turned back to John. "Listen, I know that what I'm suggesting sounds impossible. But what I'm *proposing* won't cost us much in the way of resources. I propose a proof of concept." At John's gesture, she continued. "The next time we find Daniel in one of these weird states, we talk to him. We ask the younger him to bury a time capsule."

John shrugged. "Where? And with what in it?"

"Somewhere on his family property, I think. He, the younger him, knows it like the back of his hand, and we know from his driver's license, from the CRS records, where it is. As for what goes in the capsule . . ." Mike snickered, a noise she seldom made. "Is there anything we need? Canned ham? World atlas on CD-ROM?"

"I could use a viral reactor," Lake said. Her voice was, for once, untouched by scorn. "Though it might be hard for a guy being monitored by security forces in those days to get something like that without being noticed."

"Special forces field manuals," Walker said. "Books on manufacturing high-tech fabrications materials—composite armors, polymers, that sort of thing."

"Copies of the various iterations of the Terminator and Skynet operating systems," Kate said. "But should they be printed on durable paper or on electronic media?"

"Geological and geographical data," John said. "To give us a greater depth of knowledge about cavern systems we can use. Information on mining operations in the U.S. and around the world, for the same reason."

"Wait, wait," Walker said. "If what Mike suggests is real—and I'll leave the theories to the theoreticians—we don't have to wait for Daniel's next fugue state. If we do this, we've already done it. All that stuff is already waiting in a hole in the ground on the Ávila property. We could send someone out tomorrow to get to it as soon as possible."

"Call me a coward," Mike said, "but I still believe in cause and effect, even when time travel is involved. Also, until we talk to the young Daniel, we won't know exactly where on the property he's going to plant the stuff. So we should wait."

"We'll wait," John said. "But you're right, Mike. This costs us exactly one special op to get a crew and a handful of shovels out to Bakersfield. Against the possible gains it has to offer us, it's worth the effort."

He looked over at Daniel, as did the others. Suddenly aware that he was under scrutiny, Daniel flashed them a theatrical smile. He stuck his knife into a piece of potato, raised it so that the potato was on top, and marched it across his table like an edible puppet.

Lake cleared her throat. "Are you sure we can't do this with someone less strange?"

August 2029
On the Road to Hornet Compound

The convoy carrying John Connor's command staff, his mission personnel, and about half of the machinery scavenged from Eosphor Technologies was stretched across some twenty miles of California back roads.

Far ahead were the fast, heavily armed vehicles carrying units of the 1st Resistance Rangers and the Hell-Hounds, who were acting as point guard. A few miles behind them was John's Humvee; Kate, a driver, and a communications specialist were with him.

Here in the center were the very vulnerable black minibus carrying members of John's command staff and two trucks full of machinery. Miles behind was an SUV with more rangers and, on two aged motorcycles that leaked oil, Peter "Crazy Pete" King and Pamela "Warthog" Berry, members of the Scalpers, another unit of the Resistance First Security Regiment. The Scalpers and Hell-Hounds were charged with detecting and confronting any Terminator or Hunter-Killer units that might discover the convoy as it ran slowly, without lights, toward the compound destined to receive the fabrication equipment.

John Connor's permanent base of operations was Home Plate compound, an extensive network of storm drains, basements, and post–Judgment Day underground construction beneath the charred and flattened ruins of Beverly Hills. It was far enough from the radioactive portions of Los Angeles to be comparatively safe, yet close enough for the residents of Home Plate to use L.A.'s storm drains and subway tunnels as ready underground transportation. It was ideally situated to serve as the nerve center of the Human Resistance—but, ultimately, it could be no more than the nerve center. People could not accumulate there by the hundreds or thousands; the increased activity would inevitably alert Skynet to its exact location, and bunker-buster bombs would drop or robot assault forces would swarm in.

No, when it came to human survival, decentralization was the name of the game. What was left of the American population was spread widely and thinly across the map. If any places could be considered populous, they were the mountain regions, especially those portions where caves were numerous. Humans built their communities in caves and caverns, within mountain tunnels, in sewer, subway, and storm drain systems, in mines, in deep basements, in hidden bunkers, in bank vaults—anywhere the walls were thick enough or deep enough to prevent Skynet's aerial or satellite cameras from picking up heat signatures that said "humans live here."

In addition, Connor insisted that each compound's name have nothing to do with its geographical location. A compound in San Francisco would never be named Bay Compound or Golden Gate Compound. An infiltrated Terminator or Skynet listening device overhearing just a snatch of conversation mentioning such a place would doom a compound if Skynet could associate its name with its location.

At Vega Compound, the fabrication machinery they'd retrieved from Eosphor Technologies had been divided into two roughly equivalent sets of units. As part of Vega Compound's reward for acting as a staging area for the Eosphor mission, Connor had decided to leave them one set. The other was being transported to Hornet Compound.

Before Judgment Day, Hornet had been a gold mine in the Sierra Nevada mountains, originally dug and abandoned in the nineteenth century, then reopened and worked successfully for several years in the 1960s and 1970s as Reid Precious Metals Mine #3. Remote and deep, it became a Resistance hideaway about ten years after Judgment Day and its population had grown ever since. Connor believed in spreading the wealth around—the wealth of knowledge, the wealth of medicine, the wealth of manufacturing ability. Even the wealth of genes; he regularly mandated transfers of personnel from compound to compound, not just to improve the state of knowledge in this new society but to reduce the likelihood of inbreeding.

Thirty hours after the caravan departed Sacramento, Daniel Ávila, lying across one full seat of what had once been a miniature school bus, began to snore, and then said, "Shut that head up."

From their respective seats, illuminated only by moonlight, Mike and Lake exchanged glances. This was not the best of times to begin their experiment.

Daniel continued, "Keep stealing my code. Keep messing it up."

As he spoke, Sid Walker came awake and sat upright. It took him less than a second to realize what was happening. He caught Mike's eye and nodded. "I say, go for it."

"Yeah." Mike's tone was grudging. She slid back to the seat just in front of Daniel's. Walker and Lake moved forward to take the seat behind his. "Daniel," Mike said, "where are you?"

"In bed."

"At home?"

"At home."

"Are you alone?"

Daniel sighed. It was a noise of frustration. Both Mike and Lake grinned.

"Danny, do you keep a pen and paper in your room?"

"Uh-huh."

"I want you to get them. But don't wake up. Open your eyes but stay calm and quiet and I'll keep talking to you."

"Uh-huh."

"Are you getting the paper?"

"I've got it."

"I'm going to tell you some things. Things we need. We want you to get them and bury them so we can find them later."

"Who?"

"Us."

"Who's us?"

"Your friends. Your friends in the future."

"Oh, okay."

Mike saw Lake shudder. She felt like doing so herself. Either they were just talking to a little compartmented section of Daniel's mind, a part he could never peer into when awake, or they were communicating with and manipulating a man across a chasm of more than two decades. Either way, it just felt wrong.

June, Present Day
Ávila Property

Danny was already at the breakfast table when Linda came down-stairs. That was unusual in and of itself, but he also looked different.

Danny was a good-looking kid, there was no getting past it. He was as big as Alex had been, broad in the shoulder and skinny at the waist, with a face that belonged on TV—handsome, a little bland, like a TV sportscaster or a pop star who would never achieve the highest level of success. To make it worse, one black curl usually drooped onto his forehead, like Superman in the comic books.

Actually, Linda reminded herself, she shouldn't think of Danny as a kid—she was only a couple of months older than he. But being married to his brother had put her into an increment of a generation older than he, and his manner, always energetic and humorous, just seemed youthful in this sober family.

Today, though, weariness seemed to have leeched some of Danny's handsomeness away. There were faint dark circles under his eyes and his black hair looked tousled, unwashed. He leaned over his plate as though shielding it from an anticipated rainstorm. He had a small spiral notebook on the table beside his plate, and Linda saw he had made a lengthy list on it. Many items were lined through.

She sat at her usual place opposite him. "Well, you're up early."

"Been up for hours," he admitted, and rubbed his eyes.

"Doing what?"

"Shopping."

"Shopping?" She frowned, then realized what he must have meant. "Oh, online."

"That's right."

"For what?"

"Project."

"Well, that makes everything clear."

"Linda, you want the usual?" That was Mama, from the kitchen.

"No, thank you, Mama. Just some eggs and toast."

"Eggs and biscuits and gravy, that's what we have today."

"That's great." Curious, Linda tried to read the items on Danny's list, but his handwriting, bad even when right-side up, defeated her. He flipped the notebook shut, but she couldn't tell whether it was because she was peeking or he'd planned to anyway. His eyes, intent on what little remained of his eggs, gave nothing away.

"So how's work?" Linda asked.

He shot her a look, and to her surprise it appeared to hold a trace of guilt. He took a moment to answer. "I'm not sure."

"What do you mean?"

"Well, I'm doing fine. Doing great. No problems. Fixing other people's problems, in fact." He was speaking more quickly than usual. "But, you know I work on weapon systems."

"Yeah, I know." She suspected, considering stray comments he had made about programming problems, that he worked on high-end targeting systems for comparatively close-range weapons, possibly for Vulcan machine guns or antimissile defenses. She would never tell him what she'd guessed; she didn't want him to become defensive or feel that he needed to be more secretive about his work.

"But I wonder, you know, weapons. Put 'em in the wrong hands and people get killed. Our people, I mean. Not the other people. Not the people who are supposed to get killed. Or maybe everybody gets killed, you know?"

"Uh, yeah." Linda revised her estimate of what Danny was doing. All of a sudden, it sounded more like it related to weapons of mass destruction—maybe nuclear missiles. "But you're going to do your job right. Nobody will get hurt because you've made a mistake. You're like Alex. A perfectionist."

"True." Danny stared off into the distance, through house walls and across broad pastures. "If I do everything exactly, exactly right, nothing will go wrong."

Linda felt her throat tighten. Alex *had* been a perfectionist, but he had been human. He'd made mistakes. One of them resulted in him being found face-down in the road, dead of a gunshot wound to the chest.

She tried to pry her attention and his from that forlorn memory. "Um, you're starting to look like you need a day off—"

"Gotta go." He stood, rocking his chair back; he caught it as it began to fall over. He set it back on its feet and picked up his notebook. "Going to do some old-fashioned analog shopping before I go in to work. Can I get you anything? Can of superstring?"

"Nothing I suspect you'd want to pick up for me, no."

"Ah." He made the word sound wise. "Adios."

Mama came in to set a plate down in front of Linda as Danny made his hasty departure. She stared after him, shaking her head.

"Any idea what that's all about?" Linda asked.

"I think he needs a girlfriend to calm him down," Mama said. "All the Ávila men are like that, including Hugo. Run around like wild dogs until they're forced to get serious about something. Danny's the baby, but he's already older than any of his brothers or father when they got married. So I think he's just crazy." She reached out to smooth a stray strand of blond hair from Linda's eyes. "What was it they called it on TV yesterday? Testosterone poisoning."

Linda nearly snorted up her first mouthful of eggs.

■   ■   ■

The first of the packages from Danny's online shopping binge arrived the next morning and more arrived each day after that. Normally Mama Teresa sorted out the day's mail on the dining room table; now, on the days Linda returned from duty before Danny, which was an increasing proportion of the workweek, Danny's side was heaped high with brown boxes bearing labels from different shippers and various companies of origin.

Most of them were book dealers, Linda saw. Some were medical and scientific supply firms. Various departments of the U.S. government were represented. In a development that caused the first bells of alarm to begin ringing at the back of her mind, some of the boxes were from semilegitimate dealers of firearms and other weapons—dealers who also sold books and videotapes that were well-known in law enforcement circles, products that alleged to teach people how to build explosives and man-killing traps, how to survive the collapse of the U.S. government or the arrival of a totalitarian U.S. government, how to sneak about and perform assassinations with all the skill of a cinema ninja. These products were bought by survivalists and teenage boys, wannabe radicals and martial arts fans, writers and crazies, and mostly for legitimate purposes, but to a peace officer, their presence suggested that a closer look was called for.

Except Linda wasn't an investigating officer. She was a sister-in-law.

Mama seemed to take it all a bit more philosophically than Linda. Whenever she found her daughter-in-law staring at the stacks of goods, she'd shrug and say, "Good thing he makes a lot of money."

August 2029
Wilderness Outside the Ruins of Bakersfield, California

Mark Herrera guessed that the pastures around the Ávila property were still much as they had been decades ago—a bit more overgrown, he expected. But there were still cattle, now wild cattle, in the area to graze on them. Weeds and tough indigenous bushes were now growing among the neglected rows of the various orchards, up through the char that marked where various wooden buildings had once stood.

He stood in the middle of one of the pastures, a couple of hundred yards from the cracked, dry highway lanes that had once been 58. The half-moon overhead provided a little light, but mostly the pasture lay in deep shadow. Mark wore night-sight gear over his eyes; built recently, it was heavier, cruder, and less reliable than similar gear from the end of the twentieth century, but it was far better than wandering around night-blind.

He stood almost still for several minutes, his only motion being a slow turn of the head as he surveyed the area. Everything he saw was in shades of green, the warmer the object the brighter the green; but at this time of year, inland California baked hard throughout sunny days and released its heat back into the skies at night, so things like rock, concrete abutments, and the like could show up as bright spots. Everything he saw had to be identified and confirmed as no threat before he could bring the others up. That was the purpose of a scout.

Finally satisfied, he reached down to give his lapel mike button the shortest of double-clicks, indicating "All clear, move up." Then he continued forward, toward the center of the property, the portion that his mother Mike had said was the one-time center of habitation.

He found it before the others reached him, a section where there were several trees and fewer grasses, where a few blackened fragments of planed wood and some metal poles embedded in the earth indicated buildings had once stood. From here, he headed east-southeast, pacing off a fairly accurate 150 yards, and found himself looking at trees, some living and some stunted in death, arranged in neat rows.

An orange grove. This was the right place.

Kyla caught up to him, moving quietly in spite of the gear she carried—a field pack with several items clipped to it, including various weapons, a folding shovel, and an apparatus with a telescoping handle and a metal disk the size of a dinner plate at one end. Also on her back was the case that held her sniper rifle. Ginger and Ripper moved just ahead of her, flanking her, looking around and occasionally glancing up at her face to gauge her demeanor.

Kyla was silent. The Hell-Hounds didn't like to make noise when exposed in the open like this. Mark nodded to her. She unclipped the apparatus, extended the handle, jacked the cable for a pair of headphones into the handle, and donned the headphones. She moved off at an angle, holding the disk of the apparatus an inch or so off the ground as she went. The dogs went with her, Ripper's tail wagging just a little as they explored this new territory.

Mark waited where he was, his assault rifle at the ready, and watched as Earl made his way to Mark's position. Ten, the fourth member of the Hell-Hounds' current roster, and the unit leader, was still recuperating from the beating he'd taken at the hands of the T-800 days ago.

Kyla walked more or less due north for less than ten yards. Then she stopped, waved her metal detector around a bit, and turned sharply to the right, back toward the orange grove. Mark knew she had to have reached the buried irrigation pipes and cables for temperature and humidity sensors that Mike had told them about, and this was another milestone on their mission.

This crazy mission. Mike hadn't told them much about it, except that it involved Daniel Ávila having buried a time capsule of useful scientific facts back when he was a kid and suddenly remembering it a few nights ago. But even John Connor had agreed that it was worth finding, so here they were.

"Something flying," Earl said.

Mark glanced at him and then up in the direction Earl was

looking. There it was, bright red dot, miles to the northwest, moving west to east.

Mark gave the "get under cover" whistle and immediately trotted to the nearest tree, putting it between him and the distant bogey. Earl was right behind him, already spreading out an insulating blanket. He draped it around the both of them.

Adapted from thin, highly reflective plastic materials developed decades ago, this blanket was silvery on one side but covered with black cloth on the other. Its insulating properties retarded the passage of heat very successfully; already warm from running around with full gear in the summer night air, Mark felt himself begin perspiring heavily within moments of the blanket settling around him.

The blanket couldn't keep all the heat in, of course. It would flow out under the edges, out through overlaps, through small holes. But the important thing was that it wouldn't look like a human being's heat-trace. Skynet hadn't begun a program of extermination of every living thing on earth, just the humans. Whatever the flying object was, if it had an infrared sensor trained on them, it would see irregular patches of heat that did not match human profiles.

Probably.

Earl, whose time sense was better than Mark's, poked his head out. "All gone," he whispered. "Back to it." He threw off the blanket.

Two minutes later, Kyla whistled for them. She stood on a spot of grassy earth yards outside the orange grove, the metal detector already folded up and restored on her pack; her pack was on the ground and she was now unfolding her camp shovel. Mark and Earl joined her and they began to dig. The dogs, happy that the humans were doing something new, trotted around, tails high and wagging.

Two feet down, Earl's shovel was the first one to hit something that was not soil. It made a hollow, gonglike noise against a hard surface. In moments, the others had made similar discoveries.

They cleared earth away from four circular metal surfaces. Lying across two of them was a mass of cloth that, with its length and width, could have been wrapped around a skeletal human body.

"Looks like he buried it in fifty-five-gallon oil drums," Earl said. He pulled his night-sight gear up from his eyes and flicked on a penlight. "Painted blue. You want to bet that's good rust-resistant paint?"

"No bet," Kyla said. She hauled the cloth-wrapped mass up out of the hole, set it aside, and began unwrapping it.

"Hey, that might be booby-trapped," Mark said.

She gave him a withering look. "Daniel Ávila buries a time capsule for future generations to admire and then puts a booby-trap on top? 'Here's your present, boom'?"

"Never mind."

She finished unwrapping it. It was a hand truck. "He even made sure the people of the future would be able to move his stuff," she said. There was a trace of suspicion to her voice.

"Open it or move it?" Earl asked.

Mark shook his head. "Move it all back to the transport, *then* dig into it. We don't want to be caught by a Hunter-Killer patrol hundreds of yards from our vehicle while we're digging through twentieth-century pornographic magazines and comic books."

August 2029
Hornet Compound

John Connor sat in a patio chair in the sentry station the people of Hornet Compound called High Spy.

The patio chair, like practically every pre–Judgment Day object still in continuous use, had been extensively refurbished and carefully maintained. The original aluminum frame was in good condition, scratched and scored but not bent. The nylon webbing that had once supported a sitter's weight was all gone, replaced by leather straps. John supposed that the combination of pre-apocalyptic aluminum and deer hide looked a bit odd, barbaric, but he was so used to that type of juxtaposition of materials that it scarcely registered with him anymore.

The High Spy was actually the original entry into the mine—the portion of the mine claimed and worked in the middle of the nineteenth century. It was a third of the way up this dual-peaked, half-mile-high mountain. The entrance now had dark blankets stretched across it, leaving gaps through which the sentry stationed here could observe the mountain slope and valley below. Directly over John's head, a hole had been drilled in the stone and loaded with explosives; there was a manual detonator within reach of the chair, and an insulated copper wire led back into the mine, allowing the compound's security team to blow the charge remotely if need should arise. One flip of a switch at either place, and the High Spy sentry station would cease to be a possible entry for Skynet forces.

The presence of so much explosive power so close didn't faze John. He'd lived next to too many similar security measures for too many years to be perturbed.

A century and a half ago, the hard-rock gold mine had been worked with picks and muscle, dynamite and instinct. This entryway was a natural tunnel into a cave, but at the back of the cave the mine workings began, crude tunnels that needed no wooden ceiling supports because they were chipped out of solid stone.

Much of the mine consisted of tunnels that meandered in a southeast to northwest direction, following the natural flow of the gold-bearing quartz veins. Then there were shorter cross-tunnels connecting the longer ones, and a vertical hole, labeled Shaft 1, that led deeper into the mountain and the tunnels below.

Ahead of John, about a thousand feet down the mountain

slope, was the main entrance into the mine as it had been worked in the 1960s. Then, speculators had found new veins of quartz, brought in new digging equipment, set up new processing facilities. They had dug the mine down to depths of a thousand feet below the base of the mountain.

From here, John could see the ruins of the later mine works. Hornet Compound's leader, Lucas Kaczmarek, had pointed out the various buildings to John earlier in the day.

John could barely make out the mill, the building where the quartz ore had been ground down to a consistency like talcum powder, and the vat facility, where the ground ore had been poured into enormous vats and treated with cyanide to extract the gold. It was easier to see the several dump sites where hundreds and thousands of tons of tailings, the quartz dust from which the gold had been extracted, had been left. They gleamed brightly in the moonlight, tiny, lifeless deserts both near and in the distance.

John tried to imagine what the place would have looked and sounded like when operational—giant dump trucks hauling ore between the main entrance and the mill, air blowers roaring, the mill grinding. It wouldn't have been pretty, but it would at least have been an industry of mankind, ugly but comforting.

The intercom on the floor beside the chair beeped. Like most of the intercoms in Hornet Compound, it had been reconditioned from an old push-button phone. John picked up the receiver. "Connor."

"Commander, this is Lucas. We're getting packet radio transmissions from the Hell-Hounds."

John took a deep breath. A month ago, the Human Resistance's last communications satellite had been destroyed by Skynet. Since then, radio transmissions between resistance groups had been a more dangerous affair, and teams in the field knew to transmit encoded data packets rather than voice whenever possible, and to leave the area as soon as they could after ceasing transmissions.

Radio transmissions were a necessary part of Resistance activities, but they were also a beacon for Skynet's forces. "I'll be right down," he said.

He hit the button to disconnect and punched two numbers. A moment later, someone, a female voice, said "Cathedral." That was the name of one of the mine's many large open chambers, areas where people could congregate.

"This is John Connor. Please tell Sanders that I'm done at High Spy, he can come back up anytime."

"Will do, Commander."

John hung up and took one last look out through the gap in the blankets. The view wasn't all ruined mine works. In the distance were mountain peaks, stars overhead. It was the opportunity for a view like this, and for a few minutes, perhaps even an hour, of privacy, that had prompted him to take the long walk to this lonely security station and relieve the soldier on duty for a little while.

But it was time to go back to work.

John and the members of his senior command staff on this mission stood clustered around the radio operator as data transmitted by the Hell-Hounds scrolled up in green letters across a monitor screen.

"U.S. Geological Survey publications and printouts," John said. "Plus some geological data from Canada, Mexico, and elsewhere."

"Complete notes from several Nanotechnology Conferences," Kate read. "Notes from biology and conservation conferences."

Behind her, Tamara Lake bounced up and down. "Yes, yes, yes! Anything about a viral reactor?"

"Complete specifications, on paper and disk, of the Terminator Series 1 operating system, plus T-1-5, T-1-7, and prototype work," Sid Walker said. The letters from the screen reflected from his face, making him look like an irregularly shaped terminal. "Relevant portions of the Skynet software. Probably too dated now to give us much help, but we might be able to glean something from it."

"A download of the entire Library of Mankind data site," Mike said in awe.

Kate glanced at her. "What's that?"

"A university project started in the earliest days of the Internet. They typed in or scanned the world's great works of literature. Popular fiction, too, when it entered public domain. Plus the classic works of philosophy, theater, science."

"Nothing cutting-edge, though," Walker said. He offered a disappointed sigh. "Waste of disk space."

"It's part of what makes us human," Kate snapped. "And if we're not going to be human, we might as well let Skynet snuff us out."

"Viral reactor?"

"Nothing about a viral reactor, Tamara," John said. "Sorry. But it's one hell of a haul of knowledge. And it's proof that we have a connection, even if it's a low-bandwidth one, back to the past just before J-Day." He turned to Daniel Ávila.

Daniel sat in a folding wood-and-leather chair near the door into the chamber. He was shaking his head. "Great. Now I'm as popular as the one outhouse at a prune-cooking convention."

"Once again, Daniel delves where mankind was not meant to go," Lake muttered.

"So, what do you say, Daniel?" John asked. "Are you willing to play with this some more?"

Daniel heaved a sigh. For once, it did not seem a theatrical affectation. It sounded as though it came from deep within the real him. "Willing, yes. And I will. I'm just not sure I want to."

"What's the problem?" Lake asked. "You know you survived. You know you made it this far."

Daniel turned a glum face toward her. "Yeah, sure, it's that simple. Tamara, you've had a quarter of a century to adjust to what you lost on J-Day. Everyone here has . . . except me. I mean, I really want to find out if I can communicate with a younger me, get him to answer some questions . . . maybe even pick up some of his memories. I've wanted some miracle to bring back my pre–J-Day memories since forever.

"But thinking about it in the last couple of days . . . What if I do remember, and then get to experience losing everything again? If I start remembering who and what I was, if I start remembering the people I loved . . . I may lose them for the first time, right now. I might lose my mind a *second* time. Become a vegetable."

Kate said, "But against the possible gains . . ."

Danny nodded. "It's a selfish consideration, I know. Like everyone here, I decided a long time ago, if it comes down to a choice between me and another chance for the rest of humanity, I'll choose for the human race. But . . ." He cleared his throat. When he spoke again, his voice was rougher. "But I can't promise to go with dignity. I'm a coward at heart. I figure I'll cry and whine all the way down. Frankly, this scares the hell out of me."

Mike moved up beside him, rested her hand on his shoulder. "We can use your kind of cowardice any day, Daniel."

He didn't answer. But he laid his cheek against the back of her hand.

"All right," John said. "Sid, deploy a ranger unit and a standard combat unit to rendezvous with the Hell-Hounds on their way home. I want the cargo they're carrying divided up among two or three units. In case they're attacked, I want some portion of it to reach us intact.

"As for us, I want everyone to have his thinking cap on. At tomorrow's staff meeting, I want everyone to have two lists. List

One: things we need, especially information, that Young Danny might be able to get us via time capsule, things that can help swing the balance of war away from Skynet and toward us. List Two: things Young Danny can do back at his point in time to give us any edge. Things he can engineer into the Terminator or Skynet software, for instance, in case back doors or faulty programming might survive all the revisions Skynet has made to its programming over the decades." He turned back to Daniel. "You might just go down in history as the savior of the human race."

Daniel snorted and waved dismissively at John. "Get on with you. If I'm the savior, I've already done all the hard work, back before J-Day. The modern me can take the week off."

"Let's hear what you have," John said. "Mike, you're our time travel expert. You go first."

"Just like school," Mike said. "Punished for being the best-informed. All right." She tapped a piece of scrap paper on the table before her. It was covered with notes; many of them, scratched through, were from other staff meetings. As precious a commodity as paper was never used once and then discarded. "First thing on the shopping list—whatever we do, if we're to persuade the pre–Judgment Day Danny Ávila to do this, we have to convince him of what's to come. Make him understand what's going to happen in the years that he faces. I'm arranging to have a sort of documentary video, sights and sounds of the apocalypse, to play for Daniel when he's in his connected sleep. Maybe we can keep his eyes open for it."

"Basically, a motivational tool," Kate said. John saw her repress a shudder.

"That's right. Second, ever since we got the Continuum Transporter at Edwards operational earlier this year, we've been facing a question mark. After the first successful launch, when we sent Kyle Reese back to save Sarah Connor, why didn't Skynet destroy the facility? Skynet is bound to have detected the output from the satellite that provides the transporter with its power. It has to have detected the surge from the generators at Edwards, to have detected heat traces there, and so on. There's no logical reason for it to have allowed the Edwards site to remain intact, to allow us to use it since then."

"What are you suggesting?" John asked.

"I think the first important thing we should do with this asset is to ensure the assets that we already have. I think Young Daniel needs to introduce false data into Skynet to convince it that Edwards is not, was not, and never could be a threat to it, regardless of what sort of sensor data it might pick up in the years after J-Day."

"Waste of resources," said Walker. "We already know that Skynet hasn't destroyed Edwards. Therefore we don't need to go to the effort."

"So we didn't need to send Kyle back to save John's mother?" Mike asked. "We could have sat on our thumbs, and she would have beaten that Terminator to death with her purse?"

Walker glared at her, not appreciating the sarcasm. "I think something would have happened, yes. She would have seen it for what it really was and been alerted to the danger, and it would have been destroyed when a propane tank blew up, or in some other calamity."

"I don't agree," Mike said. "I don't think time and history are as concrete as you do. John, have you told everyone about the 1997 Judgment Day discrepancy?"

"No," John said. "Not all." Appreciating her subterfuge, he gave Mike a slight smile. Mike knew that Kyle Reese was John's father; Walker didn't. But she'd come up with a reason for sending Kyle back that Walker would probably accept. "I suppose I'd better. You all know that Kyle Reese was able to find my mother-to-be and protect her from the T-800 sent back to kill her. But what you don't know, what I've largely kept to myself, is that Kyle told her that Judgment Day would occur in 1997, several years before it actually did. And I spent the years from 1997 until J-Day wondering what had gone wrong—what had gone right, actually—and whining about the fact that I no longer had a mission in life, a purpose to fulfill."

Walker snorted. "Well, obviously, Kyle wouldn't have made a mistake like that. Your mother must have remembered it wrong."

"You didn't know my mother."

Walker still looked scornful. "Then how do you explain the discrepancy?"

John looked at Mike.

She said, "When we learned that Skynet had sent back a T-1000 to kill John and his mother in the 1990s, we sent back the only agent we thought of who might be able to destroy it, a T-800 that Daniel himself programmed—"

"Go me," Daniel said, his tone low. He looked tired. John suspected that he hadn't gotten much sleep the night before.

"And it was successful." Mike didn't look at John. She knew he still had a strong emotional attachment to the Terminator that had saved his life in the 1990s; but most of the members of the senior staff didn't share that sort of sentiment about any Terminator. "I think that their efforts to prevent J-Day did change history, our history. But only a little—the net effect was that it pushed J-Day back a few years. I *think* that when we sent Kyle back, J-Day had actually taken place in 1997. But we don't remember it that way because our history has been revised since then."

Lake grimaced. "Meaning that *we've* been revised, too."

Mike nodded. "That's right. One weird idea is that maybe it wasn't exactly *us* who sent the T-800 back—not precisely this mix of people. If history was revised, maybe the cabinet of advisers, the crew of technicians that worked with John was different. We wouldn't know."

"We do know," John said. "The T-X that was sent back to just before Judgment Day was assassinating people who would grow up to become my chief advisers, my lieutenants. The T-850 told me some of their names. Any of you ever know a José Barrera, a Bill or Liz Anderson?"

All around him, advisers shook their heads.

John continued, his voice heavy, "I suspect that when we planned the Kyle Reese and T-800 time launches, Barrera and the Andersons were here, among you. Maybe some of them instead of some of you. We were probably their friends. But now they haven't existed since the T-X went back, and other people have taken their place. Which of you feels like a replacement?"

"Let's not get too weird," Walker said. He returned his attention to Mike. "So you're saying—"

"I'm saying that we should presume that we're responsible for Edwards staying intact, and should ensure that it happens. Because if we don't, history may well re-revise itself, unspooling forward from J-Day, and suddenly Skynet blows up the Edwards of 2029 A.D. immediately after we sent Kyle back. We won't ever have sent back that T-800, so John and his mother die in the 1990s, and history revises itself *again*. John doesn't organize the Resistance. And today, in 2029, only one in ten of us is still alive, and we're living in caves, eating raw rabbit meat, and waiting for the world to end."

Kate frowned. "So what happens to the us we know? The ones sitting around this table? We're real."

Mike shrugged. "There are several possibilities. If we assume there's only one reality, one stream of history, then we get edited. Changed earlier than now. What we're experiencing now never happened. We cease to exist. John's a weird case because the events that caused Judgment Day to move back several years from 1997 occurred after he'd been told about the 1997 version, but anything that gets changed *before* our current state of consciousness, we never recognize as a discrepancy.

"Or, maybe, every time events get changed, a new stream of history gets spun off in a new direction. Maybe the old ones continue on, unaffected. Maybe there's a stream of history where Sarah Connor was killed by that first Terminator and, by 2029, all humanity is extinct. Maybe there's one where Judgment Day *did* take place in 1997, and one where it didn't take place at all because our second mission, the one with the T-800, was *completely* successful. Maybe there's one where Skynet sent Terminator after Terminator back into the past and John had to destroy one every six weeks until he turned eighteen, at which time he had to start destroying one every month." Mike ignored the snorts of laughter and derision from around the table. "*They're not our problem.* Our own history, the part that leads up to us and the part that leads away from us, is."

John didn't find this line of discussion either disturbing or amusing. He'd had to live with more time-based anomalies and theories than anyone other than Kate knew.

Since the beginning of the year 2029, he and his experts had used the Edwards Continuum Transporter device three times— once to send Kyle Reese back to save Sarah Connor, once to send a reprogrammed T-800 to the 1990s to save the teenage John Connor, and once, only a month ago, to send a reprogrammed T-850 to the morning of Judgment Day to save the adult John Connor and Kate Brewster from an example of the brand-new T-X line. But his memories of that T-850's warnings were clear. That Terminator had told him that it had been sent back not from 2029 but from 2032—shortly after it had killed John Connor and then been reprogrammed by Kate. Either something significant had malfunctioned in the Terminator's programming during the launch through time, or some ripple in history's events had changed things once again.

The very fluidity of time and history frustrated and confused him, and the notion that he could be edited, his history revised again and again without his being aware of it, was very spooky indeed. Equally spooky was the way the days on the calendar were being crossed off as July 4, 2032—the day the T-850 had told him he was going to die—neared. If that Terminator was correct, he had less than three years to live. Unconsciously, he sought out Kate's hand with his own.

"I have an idea," Daniel said. "If you'll allow me to sit at the grown-ups' table for a minute."

John nodded. "Go ahead."

"What can be done once, can be done several times. Let's broaden the parameters of this part of the operation a little. What if, instead of making Skynet blind just to Edwards, we get Young Me to make it blind to a number of sites? Places we can then occupy and use as staging areas, unmolested, until Skynet is able to overcome the false data I'd be introducing?"

"Blind spots," Walker said.

Daniel grinned. "Operation Blind Spot."

Walker finally relaxed, relenting. "I like it."

"Is that it for you, Mike?" John asked.

She nodded, but held up her scrap of paper. "Except for a wish list of books and equipment, if we get the chance to do another time capsule."

John turned to Lucas Kaczmarek, who was in command of Hornet Compound. A burly middle-aged man with an Eastern European stamp to his features, Kaczmarek had lost his left arm in the first year after J-Day; he kept his left sleeve pinned up.

John had told the others that he'd invited the man into the conversation as a courtesy, since John planned to operate this special mission from this compound, but it had been more than that. Kaczmarek ran the compound like a tightly disciplined military unit, ensuring that every one of its citizens knew how to fight. He also wrote procedural manuals distributed to every compound under John's command teaching people to build and repair weapons. He seemed a likely candidate to join John's circle of advisers someday, and John wanted to see how he handled himself at an advisory meeting. "Lucas, what have you got?"

"If we had a complete list of the resources Skynet assumes control of on Judgment Day," Kaczmarek said, "it might give us new information today about the crucial centers of the modern Skynet's operations. Also, we know that, over the years, Skynet has more or less reduced its infrastructure so that its principal dispatch points for vehicles and Terminators are bases that are very self-sufficient, easy to maintain—a simple matter of conservation of resources. If we had a military evaluation of the bases and facilities the U.S. government considered low-maintenance, we might—"

"So you're my future friends?" Daniel said. There was a wondering tone to his voice.

They all turned to look. Daniel was smiling, a less cynical expression than usual, and turning from face to face.

Mike's eyes widened. She clapped her hands over her mouth, masking her expression of shock and surprise.

Daniel's attention reached Kate and he, too, looked surprised. "Hey, it's the general's daughter, isn't it? Karen? Kay?"

"K-kate," she managed.

"You're still pretty hot."

Kate struggled for a response. But Daniel's eyes rolled up in his head and he fell forward, banging his forehead on the table.

"Well," Walker said, "that was special."

August 2029
Hornet Compound

Daniel blinked and looked around. He was on a cot that was generously built, almost suited to his oversize frame. The walls were stone, his surroundings blocked off by wooden stands with man-height, coarse brown curtains hanging from them. The only light came from a naked low-watt bulb overhead; wires snaked across the stone ceiling to it and beyond.

He sat up. His internal time sense told him that it was about midnight. "Hello?" he said.

One of the curtains parted and Mike entered. She carried a wooden tray; it was packed tightly with mismatched bowls and plastic drinking vessels, plates, and utensils. "Sorry," she said. "I was getting us something to eat. Good of you to wake up before it all got cold." She sat on the foot of the cot, laid out the tray between them.

Daniel's eyes grew wide as he saw what was on the plates. "Dear God, is that steak?"

"Venison steak."

He seized one plate and balanced it on his lap, then helped himself to knife and fork. "How do they rate venison?"

"They shoot it themselves. Hornet's hunter-gatherers train in bow and arrow so they can hunt silently." Mike repeated Daniel's actions with her own plate. "They don't have meat every day, but they had a good hunt yesterday . . . and this is special treatment for Connor's senior staff. Hornet Compound's way of saying, 'We're big enough to treat John Connor to a good time.'"

"Hallelujah." Daniel struggled to cut a bite-size piece. He popped it into his mouth and chewed. And chewed. "Flavorful, kind of spicy," he said. "But tough."

"Just like most of us."

He snorted. "This evening, at the meeting, did I pass out?"

"Not exactly. You dozed off. And then you woke up for a minute, except it wasn't you. It was him. Young Daniel."

He looked at her closely, but seemed undismayed by the news. "How did Young Me behave?"

"Kind of like Old You, only without your extensive range of inhibitions."

"I was afraid of that." He heaved a sigh. "Well, regardless, it's interesting that the connection is two-way like that. I wonder if Young Me can remember what he saw. And I also wonder if there's some way I can arrange things so that I remember what I see when I'm there, seeing through his eyes."

Mike struggled with her own piece of meat. "This is going to make my jaws ache. Not that I'm going to complain. Hell, if I'm not in too much pain, I'll go back for seconds. So, you want to start tomorrow?"

"I want to start tonight."

She grinned at him. "Lake's already asleep. I'll let you shake her awake."

He shuddered. "Tomorrow. I wouldn't be much use with my head bitten off and spat down a mine shaft."

"You *are* getting wise in your old age."

June, Present Day
Ávila Property

The voices in his dreams had once seemed so cheerful, so innocent. The time capsule they'd suggested had been a lark—an important lark, to be sure, and they'd convinced him of that, else he'd not have spent so much money, so much time.

But now the voices brought night after night of torture. He wanted to hate them, but he could sense that they did not want to hurt him.

They just had to.

The dreams hammered at him. Like true nightmares, he could not escape when he was in their grasp. But unlike true nightmares, he could sense that they were not the frightening but random manifestations of conscious and unconscious fears. He knew that there were minds on the other side of them, minds and voices that pressed them into his head every time he fell asleep.

In the dreams, Skynet, the master coordination system that could centrally manage all of the United States' military forces, awoke. No longer just an artificial intelligence, it was truly sapient, a thinking being.

It was an alien being, made by human hands but not with human sympathies, and its first logical conclusion was that the greatest threat to its existence was its own creators. With inhuman patience, it waited, evaluating its resources and calculating human response, until it could figure out how to force and trick its human masters into handing it the keys to the Earth's most terrifying arsenals. Then, when those weapons were in its hands, it finished strangling communications it had already been squeezing, disrupted lines of command, and launched the bombs.

And not only bombs. Every sort of weapon or vehicle that could be computer-controlled rolled out into the ruined world and continued the process of human extermination. Most fearsome of all were the Terminators—not only the T-1s, T-1-5s, and T-1-7s Danny had worked on, but more and more sophisticated models, some based on designs Danny knew were already on the drawing board, some the result of pure Skynet engineering.

And the voices in the dreams insisted that he do something about it, do things not to prevent the future he saw, but to make it easier to endure ... to make the war one the future voices could win.

The dreams and the demands they made of him were stomach-wrenching and gruesome. By day, he could not shake the feeling that they were more than the result of the job stress he was experiencing—they were real, or would someday be real. He lived with a growing conviction that they were not dreams, were not the product of hallucination or insanity. He became glum and non-communicative around the house, tight-lipped at the office.

One thing that brightened his dreams was the presence of Linda. Sometimes, when the nightmares were at their worst, he would hear her voice, soothing him. But eventually the images of devastation would return.

What the voices asked him to do was impossible. They wanted him to hack into heavily protected government and civilian data-bases, change and destroy information, steal and misdirect classi-fied information. These were criminal offenses. Some of them constituted treason.

In dreams that were not sent to him, he could see the eyes of his parents, of his brothers, of Linda as they looked at him, realiz-ing that he was a traitor. Their disappointment ground him down to the size of the head of a pin.

But the voices persisted. *Try to understand,* they told him. *You're worried about going to jail. There is no jail. There is no federal court system. There is no United States. When Judgment Day comes, everything you're now working for will go away. You need to work toward something else.*

We need you.

He wanted them to be lying so he wouldn't have to do what they said. If he ever really, truly believed them, he knew he would have to do it.

Even though it meant the distant voices would be able to give him more facts and reasoning that supported their assertions, Danny began to ask questions of them. *How could such a thing happen?* He didn't want to hear about the logic of it, not the dumb-ass lesson of man implementing technology before he understood it, before he could control it; he wanted to know about the methodology. *What techniques does Skynet use to force the U.S. government to hand over the reins of military power to it prematurely? What does it do to disable the checks and balances and countermeasures the government had in place?*

The voices gave him answers, answers he remembered when he awoke. By day, when not doing his specific assignments and tasks at CRS, he would nose about the U.S. military computer networks, peer through the Skynet operating system, evaluate the results of Skynet and Terminator test runs.

Danny was good at his job. He didn't get caught, but he did become depressed. Everything the future voices told him was possible.

And there was nothing he could do to prevent it, to cancel the future the voices described to him. Oh, he could draft a report warning the Department of Defense about possible flaws in their control of the Skynet system. But the problem was that gradual changes that had taken place in the Skynet setup—such as alterations to the protocols that would allow Skynet to assume control and lock down lines of communication between military forces—had been, in theory, brought about by human decision, based on human evaluation of how these systems coordinated with one another, especially in the face of possible enemy action. Danny could see the manipulation and string-pulling behind these decisions; operating over a period of months, Skynet had to have been influencing the results of test runs and operations in such a way as to cause military observers to come to specific conclusions and recommend specific changes. But now each of those changes was backed by tests, retests, and documentation by people whose opinion carried much more weight than Danny Ávila's.

He couldn't do anything. Except, perhaps, what the voices were going to recommend.

Wrapped in gloom, his resistance at an end, Danny caved in. He would listen, really listen, to the voices and not just struggle against them.

August 2029
Hornet Compound

Daniel had his own private room now, at the far end of a mine tunnel not far below ground level. The quartz vein the tunnel followed had run on for only a few hundred feet before playing out. His room was hundreds of yards away from the nearest sleeping chambers of Hornet Compound.

Secrecy and privacy had been the main reasons for Daniel's placement in this isolated location, but ever since he had been relocated here, John's advisers had found that no one shared his dreams; only those who participated in the project were near him when he slept; when he slept, they were always awake.

His chamber had a bed surrounded by chairs and a curtain— once a military tarpaulin—to shield it from the rest of the tunnel. Tamara Lake had told him that the chamber would be built up, medical and sensory equipment added to monitor his progress, a real wall installed so that those watching out for him wouldn't have to be in the same room.

He didn't really care. He could sleep anywhere, anytime. And now, with most of the chairs surrounding him occupied by his friends and allies, he closed his eyes and did just that.

Lake waited until Daniel's breathing slowed into what she recognized as his usual sleep pattern. "It usually takes a little while before he goes into REM sleep," she whispered. "But the time interval is getting shorter every night. Fifteen minutes two nights ago, twelve minutes last night."

"He's getting better at it," Kate said.

Lake frowned. "Well, it's just not natural."

"Nothing about this is natural," Mike said.

"It does beg the question," John said, "if it *is* possible for anyone else to do this, how do we find them?"

"I'm not sure," Lake said. "It's too early to tell. I've been trying to catalogue the distinctive characteristics of the person or persons who've exhibited this behavior. Between Daniel and you, we have two—well, one and a half—samples. When we find enough traits common to you two, then we can go on the lookout for others with similar traits."

Kate kept her expression steady, but John could tell that she was enjoying Lake's slight perturbation. Lake tended to rub almost everyone the wrong way, and seeing her on the receiving end of uncertainty tended to cheer most people up. "So what have you got?" Kate asked.

"Well, Daniel has a photographic memory and an extraordinary time sense. I doubt that they'd contribute to being able to leak his dreams across time, since they're not characteristics John shares, but maybe they'd help him remember the dreams in the first place. Most people forget most of their dreams; not him."

"Okay," John said. "So we'll have a check box for 'perfect memory' on the questionnaire. What else?"

"There's one thing that may be even more significant. Something you and he have in common, John. And you, too, Kate."

"Well, that means it's not a Y chromosome and a love of sports," Kate said.

"You've all been exposed to the peripheral electromagnetic emissions of a particle accelerator, the one at CRS," Lake said.

John and Kate exchanged a look. "For a little while," John said. "Sure."

"And Danny, over a span of years . . . but from a greater distance, through a greater depth of earth and insulating materials. We don't know much about their particle accelerator; it was part of black operations for which we haven't found many records. There's no telling what effect its operation might have had on your brain chemistry. That alone might have altered or kick-started something in your heads that led to this. And while that's just speculation, this is hard fact: Daniel throws off a greater-than-normal amount of EMR when he's in his dream-state. It interferes with some of the instruments. I kept noticing static on the intercom whenever he was dreaming, and when Mike checked things out, she discovered that he was lit up like a little generator."

Kate shook her head, not fully understanding. "A greater-than-normal amount?"

"That's right," Mike said. Then she paused as Daniel muttered something, but the man went quiet again. She continued, "Everyone emits electromagnetic radiation. Enough to detect and measure. In a sense, we're meat machines, just like a Terminator is a metal-and-silicone machine. Both types of machines throw off some electrical output."

"Invidious comparison," Kate muttered.

Lake grinned at her, happy to see her discomfited.

Mike continued, "Daniel's output is strange and strong. I wonder if it is somehow burrowing its way back in time and finding a matching receiver back in the past—and Daniel himself is that receiver. It's found other receivers in the present, but it has to be people sleeping very close to him."

"I hear you," Daniel said.

Everyone looked at him. Even in the dim light, it was obvious that his pupils were moving back and forth under his eyelids.

"Do you recognize my voice, Danny?" Lake asked.

"You're Tamara."

"That's right. John and Kate and Mike are all here, too."

"Hi." Daniel giggled, an incongruous noise. "I'm Danny, and it's been twenty-four days since I've had a drink."

They smiled. All were old enough to remember how the stereotype of a visitor to Alcoholics Anonymous, making such a declaration in front of his peers, had become material for stand-up comics in the years before Judgment Day.

Lake rolled a small table on wheels beside Daniel's bed. On the table, attached to an articulated mechanical arm, was a television screen. "Danny, I want you to open your eyes. I have something to show you—"

"No, screw your recordings." Daniel shook his head, keeping his eyes closed. "No more. I know that I have to do it. I just don't know what."

Lake looked at John, an inquiry. He waved her away, and she moved the rolling table from beside the bed.

"Danny, this is John. Do you have paper there?"

"Don't need paper. I'm remembering everything."

"All right. Here's exactly what we'd like you to do . . ."

Daniel's eyes came open. His mine-shaft chamber was darker now, but he could see that there was one silhouette left in the chairs. "Mike?"

"I'm here."

"Scientific genius like you shouldn't be reduced to baby-sitting."

"I need the money."

Daniel laughed and reached out a hand for her. She took it.

"Something's wrong, isn't it, Daniel? You're covering something up."

"It's a personal thing. Not an operational thing." He sighed. "I still can't remember."

"Remember before J-Day? But you're *there*. You're in contact with the younger you. Every night, now."

"And when I wake up, like now, I don't remember anything the younger me has been doing, experiencing, or seeing. Oh, sometimes I get little flashes of visions, but it's all stuff that I saw then but have also seen more recently. T-1 Terminators. Pieces of Edwards. I'd like, just once, to see my mother's face. To see anyone's face. To see my family house." He shook his head. "I've got to try harder."

"No, you don't. Don't try at all. Just relax and let it happen."

He laughed. "I don't mean I'm going to strain at it. I don't think I could even fall asleep, muscles all locked with tension. What I want to do is just change the way I sleep when we're trying these experiments."

"Sleep's sleep, isn't it?"

"Well, yes and no. I dream different ways when circumstances are different. Big, spicy meal just before dinner and I tend to have weirder dreams. Dozing off when I'm sitting up, lights on, surrounded by people, I tend to have fragmented little dreams that don't add up to entire stories. I also tend to be lucid or nearly lucid when I'm doing that. See the difference?"

"I see that there *is* a difference, but I don't know what it means."

"All it means is that I want to go to sleep under different circumstances and see if it results in a different type of contact when I reach Danny."

"Okay, but . . . I don't want you to exert yourself. I don't want you to overstay your welcome when you're connected to Danny. The problem is, the longer you dream, the faster your breathing and respiration, the redder you get—Tamara's worried."

Daniel laughed. "Tamara's not worried. Tamara has all the warmth and sympathy of a T-800."

"Then *I'm* worried."

"Well, that's different." Daniel squeezed her hand and changed the subject. "This is as close as you and I have ever been, Michaela. Why is that? Every time I showed you I was interested, you turned me very politely aside."

"You are ruthlessly exploiting your new position." Her tone suggested that she was more amused than angered.

"I've barely gotten started." Daniel clutched at his chest with his free hand; his voice became overly theatrical. "Why, Mike, why? Why did you leave me to the tender mercies of the man-eating Tamara for the two weeks she could stand me? Why'd you never give me the time of day?"

She snorted. "Give yourself some credit. I figured you'd break my heart."

"I always thought that . . ." Daniel paused, reluctant to stomp across genuine emotions. "That you hadn't ever really gotten over losing what's-his-name, Mark's father."

"Well, there's that, too."

"So?"

"So . . . let's not even talk about it while everyone's emotions are all jumbled up by this dreaming experiment."

He sighed. He was no longer overacting. "He was a very lucky man, your husband. His wife still mourns for him and he has a son he can be proud of. Me, there's nothing to show the world I was ever here. When I die, that's it. I evaporate."

"Don't talk like that. You're not going to die anytime soon. And your accomplishments with the Resistance, okay, they're not as flashy as John's, but without them, the human race might be gone now."

"And even with them, it might still be gone tomorrow."

"Daniel—"

"Enough." He released her hand and rolled onto his side, away from her. "I'd better get some sleep. Some real sleep."

June, Present Day
Ávila Property

Danny woke up and knew at once that he was insane.

Oh, it didn't feel like insanity. He felt charged and powerful, as though an invisible cord connected him to the nearest wall-socket and kept him full of energy.

But all he had to do was think about the differences between the Danny of today and the Danny of a few weeks ago to realize that he was probably crazy.

Weeks ago, he hadn't taken a sizable fraction of his savings, used it to buy books, data, and hardware, and buried them out by the orange grove. Weeks ago, he hadn't had a presentiment that he had friends in the future, voices who spoke to him as he slept and told him about events to come—visions of middle-aged faces around a conference table and nuclear bombs devastating population centers. Weeks ago, he hadn't been convinced that the work he did, the work for which he received praise, good money, and the likelihood of being at least a footnote in the history books and a trivia question of the future, was going to help lead the world to a catastrophe of such dimensions that he couldn't stomach thinking about it.

He was partly responsible for the catastrophe to be, the voices admitted. But he was far more responsible for the subsequent efforts to reverse the catastrophe. The good outweighed the bad. Especially if he started now.

That was the craziest part, of course. Deep in his soul, he believed the voices. He knew they spoke the truth. And this conviction gave him strength and purpose. He'd put off until another day thoughts about what his family and friends would think of him when they decided he was crazy.

This morning, he dressed, combed his hair, practiced making a half-dozen roguish faces in the mirror, and dashed downstairs. Linda was deeply absorbed in another book; with her fork, she poked at a portion of her plate currently bare of food.

Danny plopped down opposite her. "Good morning, Professor."

She glanced at him, then took a closer look. "Morning. You look better."

"Better than Mel Gibson, or better than Ewan McGregor?"

She grinned at his display of ego. "Much better than recently, and slightly better than a mandrill."

From the kitchen, Mama called, "What do you want on your omelet, Danny?"

"Mama, on the first one I want some jalapeños, and some bacon, and some beef, and cheese, and a full-grown bulldog. But I was thinking I wanted the second one to be kind of heavy."

"How about just some chorizo and cheddar?"

"Well, okay." He turned his attention back to Linda. "I think we traded. You look kind of tired."

She nodded and couldn't suppress a yawn. "I didn't sleep well. I kept waking up out of strange dreams."

"What sort of dreams?"

"Well, I was talking to you in some of them, but from one second to the next I couldn't remember what we were talking about. Then I think we switched to talking about astronomy, because I remember you mentioning the terminator. Lunar terminator, I suppose. Then I had a dream about a big, muscular guy running on a treadmill. He introduced himself to me as Sergeant Candy."

Danny forced himself not to freeze, not to knot up. A sudden paranoia told him that if he did anything out of the ordinary, Linda might notice, might remember it later.

He'd seen footage of Master Sergeant William Candy, USMC. Danny had been watching it just yesterday, had even mentioned it to the voices of his future-day friends last night. Candy was a physical model for human-appearing Terminators that would be built in years to come.

What was happening? Was he talking in his sleep, loudly enough for Linda to hear and remember even as she lay dreaming? He'd buy a cassette deck and record himself tonight to see if that was what was going on. But for now, he had to allay Linda's curiosity, keep her from returning to this subject with him. Ever.

He let a conspiratorial smile creep across his lips. "Linda, it doesn't take Sigmund Freud to figure that one out."

She looked at him, puzzled. "What do you mean?"

"Oh, don't be coy. Grown woman without a boyfriend dreams of a powerful jock, gives him a name like Candy? As in, good enough to eat?"

She snapped her book shut and brandished it like a club. The title on the front cover suggested it had something to do with the role supergigantic black holes played in the formation of galaxies. "I am going to give you such a beating . . ."

"Mama, save your baby boy, this mean woman is going to crush me into charcoal briquettes . . ."

Mama leaned out of the kitchen and gave him a cool look. "Make it a good beating, Linda. I haven't had the heart to give him one in years."

Danny threw up his hands in surrender. "All right, I take it back. You have no possible interest in heterosexual he-men—"

"I didn't say he was obviously hetero—"

"Think back over the dream, I think you'll find the clues are all there."

She heaved a tremendous sigh. "You are *so* much like Alex."

And that put the brakes to the conversation. She looked away, obviously not knowing how to continue from that point. Danny, though a little thrown by the suddenness with which their talk had ended, was grateful that he'd derailed her thinking about her dreams.

Terminator. She knew the word *Terminator*. Yes, he dimly remembered from school, it did describe something in astronomy. But if she were ever to speak it in front of someone from his workplace, Danny would immediately come under suspicion, either informal or formal, of being a security leak.

Which, in fact, he was.

At work, he handled his morning's list of new operating system bugs in record time, then went to work installing subtle back doors into the networks Skynet was set up to routinely access.

He was certain these back doors, designed to allow him to feed programming and data into Skynet-controlled systems without Skynet's approval, would not last very long. If the future voices were correct, Skynet would continuously revise and update its own code over the upcoming years. But for a few days, perhaps as long as months, his back doors would give him the access he'd need.

He would have to do some of his work from home, on his own laptop, where he was certain he would be free of outside monitoring . . . and have to do still more from all-night Internet cafés, public libraries, and other sources that had online access that would be hard to trace.

In college, he had done some proficient hacking—lighthearted romping through protected bank and government systems. Had he been caught at it, he could have been sent to a federal penitentiary. But the experience had sharpened his set of skills, an advantage that had helped him land his current job at the CRS project.

He had never been at the top level of hackers, but he had known a few people who were. Paflos, a classmate from Bulgaria, had gone home after graduation. Danny had, a few years later, spotted some of Paflos's user names on taunting messages embedded in some of the cleverer and more virulent Windows viruses to come out of that country.

Danny could use Paflos's skills now, and he would be in touch with his old college friend. He needed to write a virus that would infect a virus.

The voices from the future had told him the methodology Skynet would use to foul up American communications and panic the government into handing over the reins of its military power to Skynet. It would start with a virus that would increasingly disrupt communications, government computer systems, and networks. Ostensibly just the work of a hacker somewhere, it would prove impossible to eliminate—except, theoretically, by Skynet, which utilized a unique operating system that had been isolated from the outer world. Virus-proof, Skynet would be able to seize control of government computers and stamp out their infections. But that was not what it would do.

Danny, if he could pull it off, would attach secondary instructions to some iterations of that virus. They, too, would spread throughout government and civilian networks, causing recorded facts at hundreds of data sites to disappear or change.

Old missile bases, built in the 1950s but decommissioned forty years later, would vanish from the records, have their known locations altered, or be listed as having been collapsed and filled in with concrete. Cave systems all around the world would disappear from public records. Caches of military matériel would vanish from government inventories so that they might be found intact twenty and thirty years later.

The piggyback-virus approach had an additional advantage. It was triggered by the events of Judgment Day, by the appearance of the Skynet-designed virus. If that original virus never appeared, if for some reason Skynet did not launch the final phase of its plan to assume control of the U.S. military arsenal, then Danny's sabotage would never activate. In the absence of a genuine threat from Skynet, he would neither become, nor be found out as, a traitor to his country.

Then there was the question of the Continuum Transporter, the time travel facility his friends had told him about. They had told him the physical location of the building on the Edwards site. He had glimpsed it once or twice; it was located not far from the CRS building, but well back from Edwards's main roads. It had to have even more formidable security than the CRS project. He would see what he could do to find out more about that project. The more he knew, the more about it he would be able to erase from the files Skynet would eventually be able to access about it.

Maybe, if he were especially proficient, he would be able to find the engineering specifications for the project and put together another time capsule, a blueprint for a time machine, allowing his friends to re-create it far in the future. Maybe.

June, Present Day
Mojave Desert

The caravan of vans and cars sped northeast along Interstate Highway 15. Danny was in the third seat of one of the middle vans, his boss, Phil Sherman, beside him. On the second seat were General Brewster and an observer from the Department of Defense, Mr. Jackson, a jowly man who seemed faintly ill at ease in his dark civilian suit. The front passenger seat was occupied by Jackson's aide, a thirtyish brunette woman in a dark business jacket and skirt; Danny hadn't caught her name. General Brewster's regular driver, an Air Force sergeant, was behind the wheel.

Danny had his laptop open on his lap. The computer was equipped with a battery of wireless communications options—built-in wireless modem, cell phone card, mil-spec short-range radio transceiver—and on his screen were fairly low-resolution images broadcast from a camera on the front of one of the vehicles in the caravan. The largest image on his screen was the camera view, and a belt of instrument readings—speed, engine RPM, gas gauge, lights on/off, and more—occupied the right quarter of the screen.

"I'll admit to being a little surprised," Jackson said, and tugged at his tie, obviously wishing to but not allowing himself to loosen it. "I'd anticipated that we'd be riding in the vehicle with the unit."

General Brewster offered Jackson a faint smile. Brewster was a compact, handsome man with a face made to fit in anywhere. Give him a twinkle in his eye and a broad smile and he could be selling cars in Los Angeles; give him a long-neck beer, a cowboy hat, and a three-day growth of beard and he could be anyone's amiable white-trash neighbor. But he was clean-shaven and posture-perfect, his graying hair cut to Air Force officer punctiliousness. To Danny, he always looked a little young to be a three-star general, but his impression of what a general should look like came from the movies and TV, fixed long before real life made him a civilian employee of the Air Force.

Danny thought he saw something in Brewster's smile, some minor pleasure at having anticipated Jackson's statement. "Ordinarily we'd have done it that way," the general said. "But today, well, regulations wouldn't allow it. Safety regs, that is."

Jackson lifted an eyebrow above the level of his dark sunglasses. "The machine isn't safe to transport?"

Brewster glanced at the occupants of the third seat and Phil spoke up. "Of course it is, Mr. Jackson, except that we're testing a new transportation system for it. If today's test is a success, which so far it is, we can probably arrange to loosen the restrictions next time."

"'So far,'" Jackson repeated. "I thought the test hadn't begun yet."

Phil nodded. "The live-fire test hasn't. But we piggybacked another test onto it, and that's taking place right now."

"I still don't get you."

Phil looked to Danny, who took up the baton of the conversation. Danny pointed between the general and Jackson at the road ahead. "Sir, you see the vehicle two places ahead of us? The burgundy van with the tinted windows?"

"Of course."

"Well, it's actually a commercially available vehicle, a standard van modified by a service that customizes cars and vans for the disabled. That one's set up as if for a paraplegic driver. It has a lift that can pick up a wheelchair, and the driver can roll the wheelchair behind the steering wheel and operate all the controls, including accelerator and brakes, with his hands."

Jackson nodded. "So?"

"So, today's Terminator, the prototype nicknamed Scowl, is driving that van right now."

Jackson finally turned to look at Danny straight on. "You're kidding."

"No, sir. Today's secondary test was for Scowl to go online, access information sites that provide driving directions, and choose our route from Edwards to the missile range. It had to review traffic laws and symbols. If it gets us all there without incident, we chalk this one up as a success. Would you like to see what it's seeing?" At Jackson's nod, Danny turned his laptop around. "This image is actually from a camera mounted in the front grill, and these other blocks are graphic representations of the vehicle's instruments and diagnostic readouts. I could switch to a feed straight from Scowl's sensor package, but I don't want to mess with things midstream, as it were."

"Nice," Jackson said. "What sort of incidents do you worry about?"

"Being pulled over by the police would be a big one," Danny said. "Our security team would have to handle things before the officer got a look through the van's window. Oh, and we had to make sure Scowl used the blinker instead of hand signals for turning."

Jackson looked blank. General Brewster offered him another slight smile. "Civilian humor."

"Ah."

Phil said, "Later Terminator models will be able to control completely unmodified vehicles, but this still serves as a significant proof of concept."

"I'd have to say so." Jackson turned forward again. His features were unreadable, but his voice suggested he was impressed.

Once they were at the closest approach to the missile range, the vehicles took a rutted dirt track that led miles away from the main road into rolling terrain. The sparse vegetation here was burned yellow and brown by the summer sun. Heat hit Danny and the other vehicle occupants like a shock wave, causing them to begin sweating heavily, the instant they slid the van door open.

The long line of vehicles disgorged military officers from Edwards and from the Pentagon, soldiers who would be handling the setup and breakdown of the operation, members of Danny's team, and CRS employees who set up minicams, camcorders, and boom microphones to record the operation.

They did not unload Scowl immediately. First, they drew a two-and-a-half-ton truck up near Scowl's van and its crew of Air

Force noncommissioned personnel unloaded a large military tent, a huge mass of green cloth. This they erected just beside Scowl's van.

Then, from the back of the truck, they unloaded a car—or, more precisely, the body of a car, a classic Volkswagen Beetle. There was no frame attached to it. Features such as windshield and window glass had been removed. Interior amenities had been replaced by a series of struts and clamps. There were empty racks along the door interiors. "What's all this?" Jackson asked.

"Believe it or not, a disguise," General Brewster said. "Keep watching."

Scowl, at last, was unloaded. The wheelchair lift on the side of its van brought it down to ground level and the Terminator, obeying commands sent from Danny's laptop, rolled into the tent. It pulled to a stop in front of General Brewster and those around him.

"How's it hanging, Scowl?" Danny asked.

There was a faint pop and Scowl's voice—heavily modulated, generated by a voice synthesizer within the Terminator—emerged from a speaker beneath its head. "All systems green. Power at one hundred percent. Inquiry."

"Go ahead."

"Transportation versatility test complete yes no."

"Yes. Clear it."

"Inquiry."

"Go ahead."

"Question how's it hanging Scowl constitutes request for diagnostics run yes no."

"No."

The Terminator went silent. Brewster gestured to indicate that they should step back from the machine. Danny followed him and Jackson a few paces backward. The work crew approached, lifting the Beetle shell over Scowl's head, and began attaching the shell's struts to corresponding bolt-holes on the Terminator's exterior.

Jackson shook his head. "It understood 'How's it hanging'?"

"Sure," Danny said. "Not much use in giving the Terminators a voice interface if they don't understand colloquial English. Scowl doesn't *speak* colloquially, but we're in the process of giving it some learning potential that will allow it to add phrases to the vocabulary it uses as well as the vocabulary it understands."

The work crew had the shell affixed to the robot now. The resulting hybrid looked strange, as though the Terminator had gutted a car and then crawled inside the remains to live. Soldiers began clipping rocket-propelled grenades and squad-level machine guns to the interior door racks.

"We're performing our exercise in the open to simulate actual field conditions," Brewster said. "But we can't afford to have a foreign surveillance satellite swoop by overhead and pick up valuable data about our project. So—"

"So," Jackson said, "the Chinese or French or whomever, if they see anything, will see a low-cost German car destroying military matériel. I like it."

The observers took to the summit of a hill overlooking the exercise field. From here, they could see for miles in any direction, though numerous hills and folds in the earth blocked certain viewing angles. They could also hear an ominous rumbling from the north. Danny thought he knew what it was—engine noises from other participants in today's exercise.

Danny shrugged on a flak jacket and donned the Army-style helmet handed him. He felt as though the door to the oven he had crawled inside had finally slammed shut. Most of the other observers were also donning flak jackets, although a couple of senior officers waved the precautions away.

Danny set up a folding chair beside Mr. Jackson's. General

Brewster had suggested to him that despite Jackson's apparent lack of rank, he was the individual they most needed to impress today.

He opened his laptop and brought up a topographical map of the area. He angled the computer toward Jackson and said, "I was wondering if you'd like to move Scowl into position and set this operation into motion."

"How would I do that?"

"This thumb pad controls the mouse cursor." Danny demonstrated, using his thumb to move the cursor around on the screen. He settled it on a long blob toward the bottom of the screen. "This is where we are." He moved the cursor to the right edge of the screen, then up and down along that edge. "Beyond this point is where the enemy forces are. Just move the mouse to wherever you want the Terminator to start and double-tap there."

Jackson grinned. "'Double-tap' has different meanings in other parts of the service."

"I know. I've done a fair amount of recreational shooting."

Jackson reached over and expertly maneuvered the cursor to a point toward the center of the screen, directly between two small blobs that represented rises. Then he tapped the thumb pad twice.

General Brewster, visible over Jackson's shoulder and watching the man's actions, beamed at Danny. It had been Danny's idea to demonstrate the simplicity of this particular navigational tool of the Terminator setup by letting Jackson use it, and the general was obviously pleased.

Danny suppressed a shudder. He was doing good work here, impressing the officer who oversaw his department. And his good work was helping speed human civilization toward a catastrophe. But if he didn't do his best work, he might come under scrutiny that would limit his ability to change things for the better—to give the people of the future a better fighting chance.

At some point in the future—his friends the voices had never told him exactly when—Skynet would assume control of the military forces of the United States and portions of NATO, raining devastation on the centers of government and military activity around the world. Most of the people on this hilltop would die then or shortly thereafter, he was sure. He took a good look at their faces. It was possible that if he did not remember them, no one else would be alive to do so.

Danny wondered if General Brewster would make it. His memory from the other night of having spoken to his daughter, years in the future, was comforting. When push came to shove, if he had the opportunity, he could tell the man, "Your family will not die. They'll be a big part of the effort to set things right."

There were exclamations from others on the hill as the ludicrous Volkswagen rolled out into the field. It expertly maneuvered between obstacles in the broken terrain and took up position between the two rises selected by Jackson.

General Brewster extended a thumbs-up to a group of military men who sat apart. Each man sat on a folding chair like Danny's but had on his lap something that looked like a mil-spec console game system, complete with screen and joysticks. They all faced away from the field of action, relying solely on the views their console screens gave them.

The engine roar from the north increased and was suddenly accompanied by distant metallic clanking. From that direction rolled tanks, three from behind one hill and three from behind another; they spread out into a ragged, broadening line as they approached the Terminator's position. Danny didn't know much about tanks, but to him these looked a little antiquated in design. In addition to the main gun, each had a machine gun attached to its turret; the turrets were oblong, with rounded edges.

General Brewster kept his eye on the field but leaned over. "Mr. Jackson, these are Russian T-54s manufactured in the 1960s and 1970s. We've been picking them up for a song—"

"Since the collapse of the Soviet Union," Jackson said, nodding. "I know. I have one in my garage. The kids love it."

"Ah." Brewster kept a stony grin on his face, but Danny knew the general was struggling to decide whether or not to believe Jackson.

Fire gouted from the interior of the Beetle and two needles of smoke lanced from the Terminator's position to that of the rightmost tank. A cloud of fire and smoke erupted from the right side of the tank, the side away from the observers' hill, and Danny saw the tank rock. It went still and fire continued to rise from its side and underside even after the smoke began to dissipate.

The Terminator went into reverse, spinning back away from its position, retreating behind the farther of the two rises. Two of the tanks fired in almost the same moment, their 100mm main guns shaking the tanks. Explosions erupted, one from the side of the nearer rise, one merely yards away from the spot where the Terminator had stood when it fired its rocket-propelled grenades.

"The tanks," Jackson said. "They *are* radio-controlled, I assume."

"That's right," Danny said. He gestured to the line of men with consoles on their laps. "You can see which one is out of the action." Indeed, the third man in line was standing, placing his console in what looked like a hard-sided black suitcase. He seemed rueful. Danny resisted the temptation to say that they'd switched to radio-controlled tanks after the slot-car versions proved unreliable; he doubted General Brewster would appreciate the joke.

The two tanks nearest the observers' hill picked up speed. Their controllers' obvious intent was to make an end run around the near rise and approach the Terminator from the back. Meanwhile, the other three tanks approached the two rises more cautiously. Two had their tank guns swiveling to aim toward the west side of the west rise, anticipating the Volkswagen's appearance from that side; the third kept its aim resolutely on the gap between the two rises.

But Danny and the observers could see the Terminator now climbing the south side of the west rise. It was hard going, a thirty-degree slope made up of earth and scrub brush, but Scowl made it in good time.

Danny could only imagine what it looked like from the perspective of the Russian tanks. It was something out of a black comedy—tank commanders splitting their attention between two likely points of arrival, when suddenly the comically non-threatening silhouette of a Beetle topped the rise between those two points.

The operators of the two tanks concentrating on the western-most approach detected Scowl's arrival. Their 100mm gun barrels began to traverse, but Scowl fired first, two more RPGs.

Scowl didn't fire at the two tanks nearest it. Instead, it targeted the two farthest, those making the end run toward the eastern side of the eastern rise. The smoke trails from the RPGs drew near-instantaneous lines between Scowl's position and the sides of the tanks.

When the last echoes of the two booms had died and the smoke cleared away, the first of the tanks was dead and burning; the second was still active, its turret turning, but it had thrown its right-hand track. With only its left track remaining, it could only move in rightward circles.

"You'll notice," General Brewster said, "that it's avoiding shots at the tanks' forward and upper sloped armor. This is a function of its target recognition software. It has by now identified the make and model of the enemy targets and recognizes their strong and weak points . . ."

Danny tuned him out. Scowl backed partway down the rise, out of sight of the nearer tanks, even before they got an opportunity to fire. Still they came on toward the west side of the west rise.

But the Terminator didn't descend to ground level. It maintained its position two-thirds of the way up the rise and turned at ninety degrees. Slowly and with difficulty, it traversed that altitude of the rise, edging toward its western slope.

The two tanks moved behind that rise, out of Danny's sight . . . but not out of Scowl's. Danny saw smoke fill the interior of the Volkswagen shell as Scowl fired again—two more RPGs, and then two more. Smoke rose from the far side of the western rise. In his peripheral vision, Danny saw Jerry Squires jumping up and down in characteristic glee.

"That's four kills, and one target immobilized," Brewster said.

"Are you calling the test?" Jackson asked.

Brewster shook his head. "No, as promised, we go until the end—total elimination of one side or the other. I'm just keeping score."

The last intact tank stayed where it was. It kept its main gun aimed beyond the western rise, anticipating a possible Terminator dash from that point. The tank with the thrown tread aimed between the two rises; from its current position, it could see all the way through the gap.

Danny saw the machine guns on both tanks orient up the slope of the western rise. Should Scowl reappear atop that rise, they wouldn't have to waste time getting their target into their targeting brackets; a twitch of the wrist and depression of the firing button would send high-caliber machine-gun rounds straight into Scowl, damaging or perhaps destroying him.

"So it's a waiting game," Jackson said.

Brewster shook his head. "Not for long. The two tank operators are now coordinating, figuring out how the immobile one can cover the mobile one for an approach."

"Basically," Danny said, "it's just become a game of chess, with the king protecting the queen."

"So what's the Terminator going to do?" Jackson asked.

"Scowl's throwing away the chess manual," Danny said. "It's now going through the rules for Go, checkers, Parcheesi, everything in its repertoire, trying to figure something out."

"It had better figure out something fast," Jackson said. The mobile tank was maneuvering again, slowly moving around in the wake of the two that had been destroyed on the far side of the rise.

Danny saw Scowl extend a closed hand outside the driver's-side window. The hand opened and sand fell from it, blowing eastward, toward the observers' position, in the stiff wind.

Scowl abruptly rolled back down the rise. At its base, near the point that it would become visible to the immobile tank's cameras, it faced westward. It canted its body forward so that the Beetle shell's nose touched the earth and the rear was raised.

General Brewster frowned. "What's it doing, Ávila?"

Danny grinned. "I'm not sure. It figured something out."

Scowl's tracks spun but the Terminator, though it lurched forward a hand-span, did not move. It had to be bracing itself on its hands and the front end of the Beetle, Danny realized.

The spinning tracks kicked an amazing amount of sand out from under the rear of the Beetle shell. The sand rose up higher than the height of a man, a thick, obscuring cloud that drifted across the southern side of the gap between the rises.

"A smoke screen," Brewster said. His tone was admiring.

Danny glanced over at the two remaining tank operators. One was staring fixedly at his screen, his expression one of frustration.

Scowl suddenly reversed direction on its treads. It raced backward, plowing through its own sand-cloud, and was across the gap between rises in a moment. The hillside observers could dimly pick out its position in the cloud of sand, but from the immobile tank's position, it must have been completely invisible as it crossed.

Scowl spun around and climbed the most forgiving slope of the rise, appearing well above and to the left of the tank's angles of fire, launching another RPG before the immobilized machine could track.

"Five," said Brewster.

The fate of the last tank was now a foregone conclusion. Scowl fired at the tank from its current position, the RPG striking the tank just before it disappeared behind the western rise. Scowl raced down this rise and across the open ground, then up the slope of the far rise, firing one last time as it came within view of its target.

"Six," Brewster said. "Excuse me a moment, Mr. Jackson." His step jaunty, he moved over to Phil Sherman and clapped the programming director on the back.

Jackson smiled. "The little Beetle that could."

"Scowl's hands are modeled after human hands," Danny said. "It can pick up and use assault rifles, grenade launchers, machine guns, grenades . . . it has operation specifications for thousands of weapons on its hard drive, and interpretive programming that will allow it to figure out many weapons not in its database. If it has a trigger and a barrel, Scowl can probably figure out how to fire it and reload it."

"How about swords?" Jackson asked. "Are we going to see a Terminator on the U.S. fencing team in 2008?"

Danny snorted. "Maybe 2012. Right now, I think Scowl's sword technique would be considered a little crude. Something like a mass murderer with a fire ax."

Brewster returned and extended a hand to Danny. "I started to congratulate Phil on a tremendous achievement . . . and he tells me that most of the Terminator's creative thinking comes from your programming, Ávila. Well done, son."

Danny shook his hand. "Thank you, sir."

He felt odd and almost swayed in his seat. For just a moment, Danny was several people all at once: a young programmer struggling not to be flushed with pride as he received the praise of his boss, a man knowing that he was in possession of facts whose revelation would destroy the officer in front of him, and a man looking at the face of someone who'd been dead for more than twenty years.

But the general, oblivious to Danny's sudden disorientation, had already turned away.

There was a tremendous boom and the turret of the nearest tank went straight up, propelled by a burst of flame from within the wreckage. The turret topped out at about the altitude of the summit of the observers' hill and came to earth again about halfway between the tank and the observers.

"Tank ammunition cooking off," Jackson said. His tone was amused.

General Brewster's wasn't. "Everyone off the hill!" he shouted. "Muster back at the tent."

August 2029
Hornet Compound

John and Kate waited in the outer chamber of what members of his staff had nicknamed Frankenstein's Bedroom.

Danny's quarters were indeed now built up, an inner chamber and an outer one. The inner chamber was half-bedroom, half-laboratory. Against one wall—wooden planks laid over bare earth and stone, one side of the mine shaft—was a broad bed assembled from rough-hewn wood. At its foot was a wooden crate that, John supposed, held most of the few possessions Daniel had brought with him from Home Plate. Beside the head of the bed was an old easy chair, its moldering cloth cover replaced in recent years by deer hide.

Then there were the instruments. Powered by a cable running from this portion of the mine to the complex's generator, they were devices scavenged over the years from hospitals and doctors' offices left empty since Judgment Day. John recognized an electrocardiogram and a 1980s-era personal computer, but several of the other devices were unknown to him. Sometimes, despite his status as the acknowledged leader of the Human Resistance, he felt ignorant. It was a feeling that had dogged him since he was a child, a recognition of the fact that he'd never had a formal education, never received any diploma. His informal education had been an exceptional one, but there were cavernous holes in it.

The outer chamber was furnished mostly with a long table

with chairs behind it and instruments atop it. These scavenged computer monitors received data from the devices and computer in the next chamber. The outer chamber was separated from the inner by a thin wall into which were set a single door and two panes of glass; shutters could close over the windows from this side. They were open now, and John could see that Daniel was on his bed, apparently asleep, while Mike occupied the easy chair and Tamara Lake stood beside it, talking to her.

"Nice, big apartment," Kate said, deadpan.

"Yeah, but the neighbors seem to drop in whenever they want," John said. "No respect for privacy."

Lake emerged from the inner chamber. She wore the plain, baggy dark garments that were standard dress for just about everyone not engaged in military activity. Mike, similarly clothed, followed her out and shut the door behind her. Lake turned a knob on a panel inset into the table; the knob, tan plastic with an edged protrusion indicating where it was pointing, looked incongruous, like something off an oscillating fan. "This activates the microphone by his bed," Lake said. "So we can hear when he drops into his special sleep."

"So what are you finding?" John said.

Lake shrugged. "Hard to come up with any hard data using instruments scavenged from landfills. But it's obvious that his system's under a lot of stress, and much of that stress seems to relate to his dreaming states." She took one of the chairs along the table and closed the shutter over the window above it. "His heart rate and blood pressure go way up when he's in one of those states. To dangerous levels."

Kate said, "And what about the EMR?"

Lake gave her a who-the-hell-knows grimace. "Well, Mike's been measuring his spikes of EMR output when he's dreaming. She's even tested with people sleeping in the outer chamber when he's in his dream state. He definitely broadcasts."

John cleared his throat to conceal a sudden nervous thought. "Tamara, you and Mike didn't use the word *broadcasts* last time. Tell me, how far could these EMR spikes be detected?"

Lake shrugged. "I don't know. Ask Mike."

John called Mike in and put the same question to her.

Mike could only shrug. "John, they wander all over the scale. I mean, radio transmissions wouldn't escape these tunnels. But Danny's output, well, it's like an opera soprano singing scales; they go everywhere. Sometimes they're up into the angstrom range we pick up from the Continuum Transporter and from T-X plasma weapon tests. This deep in the mountain, they're probably undetectable on the outside. But then, we just don't know how sensitive Skynet's instruments are, what it's looking for."

"If you're through with your tactical discussion," Kate said, "is he going to be all right?"

"If we could keep him from getting in contact with his past self, maybe," Lake said. "I just don't see that happening. I think what we have to do is keep him fit until he rides out this contact. When it ends, perhaps he'll return to normal." She gave John a look that was almost apologetic. "Give me a real hospital with real instruments and a real staff, and I'll try to get you some solid answers."

"Sorry, you're it. Keep your genius hat on and do whatever you can."

The next night, John, Kate, and Mike gathered in Daniel's outer chamber, preparation for another evening of communication with the Danny of the past. Lake was already in the inner chamber, calibrating instruments and talking to Daniel, who was preparing for bed. Through the window in the wall, Mike could not hear their words but could see their easy camaraderie.

They'd had a relationship, Daniel and Lake, many years ago. It had lasted, as most of Lake's affairs did, until shortly after the point that Daniel ran out of new adjectives with which to praise her, to appreciate her intelligence and beauty. Once he began to repeat himself, she began looking around for someone new.

Mike couldn't bring herself to dislike Lake. The woman wasn't malicious. She was sad, flailing about in a search for happiness that could only be brought about if Skynet were suddenly to crumble, if she were magically to be transformed back to the age of thirty, if she were restored to the top of her profession.

Lake and Daniel had remained friendly, and neither had been hurt. It was the best possible outcome for a relationship that had failed to take root.

"Mike, let me ask you something."

Mike turned back to John, who was seated beside Kate on the ancient couch against the wall. Mike automatically closed the shutter over the window. "Sure."

"Your boy Mark—what's he fighting for?"

Mike looked at John suspiciously. No one had ever had much luck figuring out what was behind his cryptic pronouncements or non-sequitur questions, but no one ever gave up trying. "Well, the same thing as everyone, I suppose. Wiping out Skynet and having the planet to ourselves."

"Yes, but what sort of planet does he suppose it will be?"

"Well, I don't know. I've never asked him."

"You'd better sit down." Kate was whispering, as though John couldn't hear her words. "He's philosophizing again. This may take a while."

Mike snorted, amused, and took one of the chamber's chairs.

"You remember how they used to divide up the generations?" John asked. "Baby boomers, postboomers, Gen-X, and the like?"

"Uh-huh." Mike shrugged. "I always thought that was so they could sell us stuff."

"Probably was. Anyway, with Judgment Day, all those generational distinctions went away. Now we've got another one. There are only two generations, those of us who remember what life was like before J-Day and those who don't."

"Okay."

"Those of us in the older group, we know what we're fighting for. We have a vision of the world as it was, as we'd like it to be. Open highways and summer vacations and restaurants, living in the sunlight, living in fear of the Internal Revenue Service rather than a robot with an assault rifle. As sure as anything, when we bring Skynet down, the world we create will not be the same as the one we remember . . . but we're fighting for the one we remember. Right?"

"Sure. What are you getting at?"

"Kyla talks about wiping out Skynet, about protecting her family and loved ones. It's all about the present tense. I ask her what she would do when Skynet falls and she doesn't have an answer. She doesn't have a vision of the future." John suddenly looked a little lost. Kate put her arm across his shoulders. "It seems wrong to me," he continued, "that the older generation is the one with an eye to the future. With hope for the years to come. The younger generation lacks this. It's backwards, and I wonder how damaging it might be. When our generation is gone, will there even be a plan, or a model, or a vision of the way we want things to be?"

Mike let a chiding tone creep into her voice. "Don't you ever think about anything nice?"

"So what is Mark Herrera fighting for?"

"I don't know. I'll ask him. And if he doesn't have a good answer for me, I'll send him to bed without supper."

This time, Daniel sat more upright, leaning back against the wall of his chamber, well-padded by pillows and blankets. He was already asleep by the time Mike, John, and Kate silently reentered his bedroom.

"He's just been under a couple of minutes," Lake whispered.

"I'm there," Daniel mumbled.

Lake turned to look at him, then automatically glanced at her watch. "Three and a half minutes," she whispered. "A new record."

"Where are you, Daniel?" Mike asked.

"Bedroom. There are books everywhere. Boy, did I have a lot of books." He sighed. "Wish I had them now."

Lake had already situated a blood pressure cuff on Daniel's arm. Now she began to pump it up.

Mike continued, "Do you feel any different this time, Daniel?"

"Yes, yes." Daniel sounded impatient. "Different at both ends."

"How so?"

Lake checked the gauges on the blood pressure monitor. She jotted down their readings, shaking her head, not happy with the result.

"Here, I'm thinking straight. I don't think I'm really asleep."

"You're asleep."

"There . . . I think I could do something."

"What do you mean, do something?"

"I mean, do something with my body." He giggled. Daniel, always aware of his manner, his voice, never giggled. "Drive it around like a car. Oh, my God, I'm moving my hand."

June, Present Day
Ávila Property

Daniel held Danny's hand up in front of his face and studied it in the darkness. He could see it only as a silhouette against the lighter color of the ceiling. He balled it into a fist, turned it this way and that.

He could feel his heart race. He was in possession of his younger body.

Moving slowly, as nervous as a first-time driver, he pulled the sheet from his body and sat up in Danny's bed.

There was a nightstand beside the bed, a desk lamp atop it. Clumsy, he fumbled his hand up to the neck and switched it on. The sudden glare caused him to wince, but he looked around, hungry to see his past, to see where he came from.

Distantly, he heard Mike's voice: *Daniel, what's going on?*

"I'm getting out of bed." He suited action to words. He noticed that he was wearing briefs. His feet came down on a hardwood floor. "This is so . . . cool. And there's another thing that's different."

What is it?

"I believe I'm still thinking straight. At your end. I just feel more awake than previous times. I mean, I don't remember the previous times . . . but I was always groggy coming out of them. I'm not groggy now."

Can you force yourself to relax? Lake's worried about your heart rate.

Daniel took a few deep, slow breaths as he looked around, cataloging the shelves of books. He moved over to the window, pulled the curtain aside to look out. He saw open fields and the distant white and red lights of traffic a few hundred yards away.

Traffic moving with lights on under open skies. He felt a grin broaden on his face. Amazing how such a mundane scene could be so heartening.

"It's like a movie, Mike," he said. "I'd call it 'When Man Ruled the Earth.' "

August 2029
Hornet Compound

A quarter of a mile from the main entrance to Reid Precious Metals Mine #3, a man walked quietly up the mine's main access road, ascending the mountain. He was tall, in good shape, wearing the camouflage pattern uniform of John Connor's troops. He carried a meticulously maintained Colt M16A4 assault rifle at the ready. In the darkness, he moved nearly silently, alert to the sudden appearance of the enemy, any enemy.

The road wasn't what it used to be. Potholes marked it. There were cracks and breaks in it from movement in the earth. In places, the earth had washed out from beneath it over the course of more than twenty years of no maintenance, and the pavement had collapsed down into gaps. There were one or two spots where yards and yards of pavement were just gone, leaving only ragged edges behind, with no obvious explanation for their disappearance.

The man stepped off the pavement and onto one of those earthen patches. At the halfway point between the two stretches of pavement, his foot came down on a piece of ground that felt no different than any other.

But inches beneath the surface lay a belt of rubber in which was imbedded a layer of piezoelectric crystals, man-made solid-state crystals that generated small electrical charges when put under pressure. The man's weight caused the crystals to emit a charge. Wires attached to the layer of crystals carried that charge instantly up the mountain slope.

Unknowing, the man marched onward.

"Here are some more passwords to try," Mike said. In the dim light of Daniel's inner chamber, she squinted at the paper she held. "KLASSUV2K. G8ESOFHELL. 38D4ME." She spelled each one. "Do you have that?"

"I have it." Daniel had found paper and pen, had composed a note to his younger self explaining what the list would constitute. In the last several minutes he'd forced his present-day eyes open to copy Mike's sketch-maps of CRS project's secure floors, of the Continuum Transporter building, of Edwards AFB's access and security tunnels, of every sort of map they could put in front of his face.

"Now—" Mike began.

"Linda." Daniel's voice had changed; it was less crisp, less assured.

Mike frowned. "What about Linda?"

"Is she there? In my future?"

"Danny?" Mike looked confused. "Is that you?"

"I'm here." Then, a moment later, his voice became more mature again. "I told you, Danny's asleep. I'm pretty much in control of his body."

"Oh, my God," Kate said. "We've got Daniel at that end and Danny at this end."

On the bed, Daniel raised his head. His eyes fluttered as though he were trying to open them. If that was his intent, he failed and his chin sagged back to his chest. In his younger voice, he said, "I can't see."

"You're all right, Danny," Kate said. "You're here among friends."

"But what about Linda?"

Mike looked over at John and Kate, her expression forlorn. She mouthed the words, "I can't."

Kate and John exchanged a glance. Glum, John nodded.

Kate said, "Danny, Linda isn't here."

"She's got to be. She's got to be."

"No, Danny. I'm sorry, but Linda's not part of your future."

"Do you know if she, if she survives?"

"We don't have any record of her after Judgment Day, Danny. I'm sorry."

"She has to be in my future." Danny sounded both stubborn and desperate.

Kate spoke up: "If she's in your present, you should make the most of that, Danny."

"No, she's there, she's got to be there."

"Danny, can I change the subject for a moment?"

Daniel sighed. "Sure, Kate."

"You saw my father the other day. On your field test."

"Yeah."

"Tell me about him. Tell me how he . . . how he was."

John squeezed his wife's shoulders. The situation with Daniel was like having a visitor who was still friends with a loved one who lived too far away to be visited. John knew Kate ached to somehow reach through Danny's connection, to exchange words with her father once more, one last time. And he knew she would keep aching, because such a thing was not likely to happen.

"He was kind of single-minded," Daniel said. "I think he's got a sense of humor, but it's, like, only in certain directions. Some things just aren't funny to him because they're too strange . . ."

The intercom on the instrument table buzzed. The noise jolted Daniel, but his eyes did not open. John swore and leaped up to press the button on the device. "We're in session here," he said, his voice a hiss.

"Sorry, Commander." The voice was Lucas Kaczmarek's. "We've got a mobile anomaly."

"I'll be there in a few minutes." John rose. "Mike, finish this session up as fast as you can. Kate?"

His wife stood, glancing unhappily between him and Daniel. "I'll come with you."

In the compound's security office, a wood-walled portion of one of the first cross-tunnels off Tunnel 1, the main entrance tunnel, Kaczmarek directed John's and Kate's attention to a computer screen. The screen, all shades of green, was broken down into six-teen squares, arranged four by four, and each square was a bar graph. Once a minute or so, the screens updated, each bar shifting one place to the left.

"These are the external pressure sensors, correct?" John asked.

"That's right." Kaczmarek pointed to one of the graphs, top row, second from the left. "This is main road, location two. You see we have a succession of flat lines, which is standard for no activity on the road. A human walking along it will create a bar about a quarter of an inch tall." He gestured at the center of the graph, where a bar a full inch tall dominated. "That's something heavy. Four, five hundred pounds."

"Like a Terminator," Kate said.

"That's right." Kaczmarek shifted one square to the right. It, too, had a one-inch spike in it, this time closer to the square's right edge. "Main road, location three, a few minutes later, just after I called for you."

"No report from our guard stations?"

"No. I checked with our outermost stations by land line. They reported nothing wrong. Their passwords were correct. Of course, someone moving overland could have reached the main road from the side, bypassing the guard stations accidentally or deliberately."

"At this rate of travel, how long before it reaches the next pres-sure sensor?" Kate asked.

Kaczmarek looked to one side, where the Resistance fighter normally assigned to the screen, a thin young man with coppery red hair and hard, dark eyes, sat. "Prescott?"

"Ten more minutes, sir," the younger man said. "More or less. But only four until the bogie comes within view of the next guard station."

"What kind of station?"

"A stink box, sir," Prescott said.

John offered up a faint smile. "Stink box" was the informal

term most soldiers in the Resistance used for a concrete mini-bunker. The standard stink box had an interior about eight feet long by four wide and high, not large enough to stand up in. On the front facing were a hatch-style door and a double-paned window, the window permitting a good view of the area to be surveyed but helping retain heat. Fans associated with ducts that led far away from the minibunker allowed some air circulation. Other amenities included a phone, connected by cable to the security office, and a back hatch that led to an emergency escape tunnel.

Because the minibunker was built to retain heat and thus provide Skynet with little or no infrared signature to detect, and in spite of the fan-and-duct air circulation, their interiors were hot. Nor did they have bathrooms, or easy access to latrines; sentries stationed there had to take in and carry out their own buckets or bedpans, which they hoped they wouldn't have to use. Sentries had to lie for hours, doing little but watching and sweating. The bunkers received periodic cleaning, but nothing ever quite got rid of the smell—hence "stink box."

"Get that guard out by way of the escape hatch," John said. "Have him—her?"

"Her," confirmed Prescott. "Corporal Dixon."

"Have her get in a position to watch both the road and the bunker. She'll report by radio." John turned to Kaczmarek. "Put the compound on pack-and-prep alert. Just in case."

"Yes, sir."

August 2029
Outside Hornet Compound

Corporal Wanda Dixon, age sixteen, grinned as she hung up the phone. Yes, the call meant there might be a Terminator in the vicinity. But the certainty of getting out of the stink box only partway into her shift outweighed the possibility of running into one of the murderous machines.

First, Wanda undogged the minibunker's front hatch. If an intruder found it locked, after forcing his way in, he would conclude that there was another way out; if it were unlocked, no such conclusion was necessary. She squirmed to the back of the stink box and tugged at the fan inset into the wall there. It was the one source of comfort available to the sentries, but it was also the cover for the escape tunnel. It opened out on hidden hinges, revealing the ductwork that brought air into the stink box . . . and also the second hatch, this one set in the floor a mere two yards in. She slid feet-first into the duct, pulling her assault rifle and field pack with her, and pulled the fan door closed again. The fan continued spinning throughout.

Her rifle had a *T* carved in the stock, *T* for Terminator. A year ago, she'd put the kill in on a T-600 her unit had met in the field— her grenades had finished it. That gave her the right to carry a kill-marker. Maybe today would give her the opportunity to carve a second one. Guys appreciated a girl with lots of kills.

Twenty yards from the minibunker, she swung aside a set of what looked like bars permanently embedded into concrete. She was now well within the tree line. Quietly, she moved through the trees, up a slight ridge, until she could look down on the main road and the all-but-invisible front face of the stink box. She pulled her heat-retaining blanket around her, hiding all but her upper face, and waited.

Now she was baking again. Oh, well. At least the occasional stray breeze would cool her face.

She wasn't too worried about being seen. Even if the intruder was a Terminator, her heat signature was now all wrong for a human, and the little bit of exposed face wasn't reflecting moon-light—there were occasional advantages to being black in the modern world.

She didn't have long to wait.

She saw the intruder first as a line—he was approaching from the south, and the rising moon in the east turned him into a shadow spilling across the roadway, disappearing when he was in deeper shadow but materializing in patches of moonlight, always coming closer.

Wanda kept still, straining her ears; there was no sound but the occasional distant animal call, the rustle of wind through the trees around her.

Then he was in plain view below her. A big guy, white, bare-faced, the reflectivity of his skin making a good target of him. He had a big nose and a strong jaw. Nice-looking, she decided. But she also saw that he was broad and muscular enough to be a T-600 or T-800. These days, big guys encountered in dangerous situations were Terminators more often than not. Natural selection was now selecting for leaner men . . . though that, too, would change, now that the T-X model meant that a disguised Terminator didn't have to be burly.

Still, he could just be a special-forces guy returning late from a mission or reconnaissance, or even someone from a hidden pocket of survivalists who had stumbled across Hornet Compound. That would be nice.

The intruder passed Wanda's position and moved on another dozen steps . . . then stopped and looked to his left.

Wanda bit back a swear word. There was nothing to the intruder's left, nothing but a gentle slope that led up to the stink box.

There was certainly nothing a human could see. Not even a Terminator, equipped with infrared visual sensors, would be able to detect the heat trace of Wanda's passage from hours ago when she had arrived at this duty station. But Lucas Kaczmarek, in a lecture Wanda had attended, had stressed the fact that wear patterns in open terrain, such as game trails and footpaths, could be detected by infrared. At the end of the last century, archaeologists had used satellites with infrared cameras to detect ancient roads. In the dark, Terminators could see footpaths and vehicle trails even if nothing warm had been on them recently.

The intruder looked up the slope, directly toward the stink box.

Wanda brought up her field phone and opened the alphanumeric keypad. In the abbreviated text code of the Resistance, she typed in her identification sequence and the letters BOG=T. *Bogie is Terminator.* She hit the enter button.

She looked back toward the road. The intruder was now a few feet up the slope, but had stopped. Now it was looking roughly in her direction. She gulped, suddenly not so anxious to work on getting a second *T* carved on her rifle stock.

"Upgrade our alert status to red," John ordered. "Activate the bait house."

Kaczmarek nodded at Prescott, who immediately cleared the screen of the pressure sensor readings, leaving behind a command line prompt. He began typing in commands.

Kate moved to a master intercom. She typed in the two-number key for Daniel Ávila's quarters. "Tamara, you there?"

Lake's voice came back almost instantly. "Shhh."

"There's no time for 'shhh.' We're going to red. Wake Daniel up and get him prepared to move, just in case."

"Right. Out."

The Terminator's head moved side-to-side, a thirty-degree arc. Wanda held her breath. The thing had probably detected her radio pulse, as short as it was, but could not detect her exact position without triangulation; so it was relying on other senses. And even though her heat signature was wrong for a human, it might be the only significant one in the direction of the radio pulse's source.

In other words, she was in for it.

Then the robot's head swiveled around to the northeast. It stared at the second slope of the mountain.

Wanda breathed a silent sigh of relief. They'd fired up the decoy house. Once a residence belonging to one of the 1960s-era owners of the Reid Precious Metals Mining Company, it clung to the south face near the peak of the second slope, affording its owner a spectacular view of the mountains. Now it was abandoned . . . but set up with equipment designed to activate on issuance of a remote control signal.

The button had to have been pressed in Hornet Compound's security office. A generator in the decoy house would be starting up, creating vibrations and even radio emissions that nearby sensors could detect.

The Terminator would now march up the road, take the right-hand fork toward the decoy house, enter that dwelling, and possibly destroy it. The robot would catalog the state of the residence and determine that a pack of two to four humans had been living there, repairing its generator, and had probably fled at its approach. Once the Terminator was gone, John Connor could decide at his leisure whether Hornet Compound needed to be abandoned, or needed merely to stay dark and quiet for a few months.

The Terminator didn't march up the road. It returned its attention to the slope it stood on and began climbing once more to the stink box. It entered the minibunker, vanishing from her sight.

Wanda resisted the urge to throw off the blanket and run, or even merely to turn around so she could see the approach to her rear. Even if the Terminator found her exit tunnel and followed it, once he emerged within the trees he would make enough noise crunching through the forest that she would have plenty of warning of his approach.

The Terminator emerged after a minute. It held the stink box's land phone. As Wanda watched, it yanked the phone from the cable, removed a bulky object from one of its pants pockets, and began wiring the object to the cable.

It didn't look at the job it was doing. It scanned the skies to the south, past Wanda's position.

Slowly, slowly, Wanda shifted her attention to the south. She saw nothing unusual there—silhouettes of mountain slopes, with white caps illuminated by moonlight, and the usual spectacle of stars.

One of those stars was moving. She slowly tugged free her binoculars and stared through them.

It was a tiny reddish blip, getting bigger. Through the binoculars, it was more than a point; it slowly resolved itself into a Hunter-Killer, one of the insectile flying drones of Skynet.

Wanda glanced back at the Terminator. It had finished splicing its device into the phone cable and was now descending the slope.

Knowing it could give away her position, Wanda typed new letters into her field phone. *HK also. T put gadget on land line.* She hit the transmit button.

This time, the Terminator did not react to her transmission. It turned and continued its resolute march up the road, away from her.

Moments later, the device lying outside the stink box exploded. It wasn't a normal explosion; it was as though ball lightning had decided to erupt there, flashing arcs of electricity in all directions. Wanda heard her field phone erupt for a brief moment in static.

"Gadget on land line," Kaczmarek repeated. "What the hell sort of gadget?"

Ideas rattled around behind John's eyes like *pachinko* balls, and one of them ended up where it belonged. "Get the sentry at the next guard station up to the communications junction box. He needs to cut the cables—"

The bank of land-line receivers against one wall erupted in sparks. The officer on duty there leaped away, hitting the floor, and sparks showered down on him. The monitors on several of the computers in the security office flared up and went black; some others wavered, then went dark as their systems rebooted.

"What the *hell*," said Kaczmarek.

"The gadget was some sort of capacitance charge," John said. "It fed major voltage into the land line. And I'll bet my right leg that the HK the sentry warned us about was monitoring for electrical activity. It may have detected the surge here, or at least the path of the surge coming this way. The bait house is a no go; that Terminator and its HK are coming straight here." John resisted the urge to hammer on the nearest table or face. "Lucas, prepare for a siege and evacuation."

"Right." Kaczmarek could have let John take over at this point; he was merely going to implement procedures that John had taught him years ago. But this was his compound, his command— at least for the few minutes or hours it took the invading Skynet forces to destroy it. He raised his voice so that all his officers could hear him: "Prepare for an attack and an evacuation to all out- bound muster points. Send soldiers to all our internal hardpoints. Alert all sentries and send out word to the other compounds— Hornet Compound is compromised."

The screen where they'd been receiving the main road sentry's communications had survived the power surge, and it updated again. The new line of text read,

Persnel chopper fm south

Kaczmarek kept his voice mild. "Now," he said.

Mike made no effort to sound soothing or reasonable. That time was past. The steady beeping of the compound alarm, which car- ried to this chamber and to every occupied area of the mine system, punctuated that fact. "Wake up and get your ass out of bed, Daniel."

"I can't. I'm really, really here," he said. It was Daniel's voice, not Danny's. Danny seemed to have retreated, disappearing after Kate had left.

"Your stubbornness is going to get you killed. We're evacuating."

"But I can still think at both ends," he continued. "I've got my eyes open. I really believe I can remember this time, Mike, every- thing's different."

Mike looked at Lake, and Lake nodded. Each of the women seized one of Daniel's arms. They hauled him to a sitting position, but his eyes remained closed.

"There's a mirror over the chest of drawers—oh, my God!"

Mike continued to hold Daniel upright while Lake got his legs swung off the edge of the bed. "What is it?"

"I'm so thin! I can't believe it. Was I ever that thin? Good-looking, too."

"You're still good-looking. And egotistical as a cat. Wake up, Daniel."

"No, I have to see more."

Lake hissed in irritation as she pulled from his skin patches connected to wires that led back to the monitoring equipment. "I'm going to get someone who can haul his fat ass around."

Daniel's voice sounded hurt. "I heard that."

"I know." She dashed out through the door.

"There are Terminators coming," Mike said, struggling to keep her voice reasonable.

"Dammit, Mike, this is my *life*." There was pure anguish in Daniel's tone. "The half of it that's gone, it's right *here* where I can see it. I need this, Mike."

"Is it worth dying for?"

"Yes, it is." His tone brightened. "Hey, a Slinky!"

At the mouth to Reid Precious Metals Mine #3, Tunnel 1, Warthog and Crazy Pete stood in front of the black, rough-surfaced concrete plug that served as the main entrance into Hornet Compound. Engineered to rotate on a vertical steel pivot, the door could be opened by a single person of average strength, but when it was shut and its locking bolts thrown, it was strong enough to hold a Terminator back—for half an hour or an hour, in theory. There was someone standing by behind it right now, ready to rotate it open if the two Scalpers needed a quick retreat.

Retreat wasn't their plan. Warthog shifted the strap on her shoulder; it bore the weight of the chain gun, the man-portable Vulcan-style machine gun, that she gripped. Crazy Pete had a rocket-propelled grenade in his hands and another on a strap across his back. He grinned at her. He still wore the full beard that had been the style of choice among the bikers that had been his community before J-Day; now it was gray, and his face was seamed like old leather, but he was still capable of wreaking havoc on the enemy.

Warthog, only twelve when Judgment Day had come, had been with him for nearly twenty years now. They had a kid together, a son who, at the age of nine, could field-strip and reassemble any gun from their arsenal in full darkness. Warthog was still amazed that she had a kid. She knew she was as homely as the animal whose name she had taken as her nickname. She was uneducated and foul-mouthed. Before J-Day, these characteristics would not have made her prime wife-and-mother material. But J-Day had been a great leveler, putting survival ability well over beauty and refinement on the list of traits desired in a mate.

Crazy Pete tilted his head. Warthog could hear it, too, the distant thumping that heralded the arrival of the personnel chopper. "Showtime," he said.

"There it is," Warthog confirmed. She could see two moving lights in the sky; one had to be the Hunter-Killer the sentry had sighted, the other the helicopter. The 'copter was the greater threat. It could be bringing one, five, a dozen more Terminators. For Skynet, this was a major offensive. But if Crazy Pete could bring down the 'copter when it was still high in the sky, he might wipe out some of those killer machines before they even reached the mine.

"What the hell?" said Crazy Pete. One of the two lights in the sky had suddenly reproduced, splitting into two. The new light leaped out ahead of the others and was racing toward them.

Warthog shouted, "Get—"

The missile launched from the Hunter-Killer flashed between Warthog and Crazy Pete, hitting the concrete plug and detonating before their skin could begin to register the heat of its passage.

The detonation blew their charred remains out through the mine entrance. Warthog and Crazy Pete rained down the slope of the mountain, unrecognizable as human. The force of the explosion shattered the concrete plug, blowing it in pieces off the metal pivot that allowed it to serve as a door. Chunks of concrete cut like bullets and cannonballs through the man stationed behind the plug.

August 2029
Hornet Compound

The explosion hammered at the ears of the men and women in the security station and surrounding chambers. John stepped out into the access cross-tunnel and looked toward the main tunnel. Smoke was drifting along it. Kate, beside him, took his hand.

"Go on ahead, John," shouted Kaczmarek. "My crew will bring up the rear." He addressed the young security officer. "Prescott, you go with them, get them wherever they need to go."

The young man nodded, rose.

John grimaced. He hated running from a fight. Not that he hated escaping danger; it was just that, as many times as he'd been sent on ahead to lead an escape action while others held the rear against pursuit, often sacrificing themselves, it still amazed him that he was able to command anyone's respect.

He and Kate, Prescott following, reached the intersection with the main tunnel. To John's left, he could see the ruins of the concrete plug and the stain, black in this dim light, spreading beneath its largest component. There was no Terminator in sight yet. To his right, the main tunnel led into the mine's depths; there were men and women there, paused in uncertainty.

The three of them charged toward the compound's residents.

"Get to your evac points," John shouted. "Compound defenders to the hardpoints. Go!"

They went. John, Kate, and Prescott followed.

The footbound Terminator and the airborne Hunter-Killer were well past Wanda's position. Now the helicopter was close, flying several hundred feet over the main road.

Wanda didn't know what variety of helicopter it was, only that it was big, suited for carrying dozens of soldiers—or Terminators—and painted blue or black. It was readily visible, its running and warning lights on, all according to government protocols that had been made irrelevant a decade before Wanda was born.

She lay wrapped in her insulating blanket and cursed herself. Some sentry she'd been tonight. She hadn't defended anyone, hadn't earned her daily ration of food.

Well, she still could.

The helicopter was past her now, the eyes in it, all mechanical ones, probably trained on the mine entrance ahead. She pulled the blanket off herself, rolled up to a sitting position, and raised her ancient AK-47.

Helicopters couldn't carry much in the way of armor, and could have none on their rotor machinery. She steadied her aim, sighting in on the stabilizing rotor at the helicopter's rear.

She fired, one short burst. Her tracer rounds showed her that she was hitting the fuselage just below her target. She adjusted, fired another short burst, then a sustained burst.

The helicopter slowed and rotated in place, its front end facing her; then it continued its rotation, revealing the door now sliding open on its starboard side. Wanda scurried backward until she was behind the cover of a tree.

The doorway framed men. No, some were man-shaped Terminators, others were silvery Skynet assault troops, similar to Terminators but lacking humanlike skin and clothing. One of the assault robots began to sight in with some sort of advanced assault rifle, a bullpup design Wanda didn't recognize.

Then the aircraft made an odd noise, a peculiarly animalistic whine, and the helicopter wobbled. It resumed its rotation, swinging the robot in the door around out of Wanda's sight, and the rate of rotation increased.

Out of control, the helicopter tilted, each new rotation causing it to drift in a new direction. Finally, it slewed over in Wanda's general direction, picking up speed as its angle of descent grew steeper, and slammed down onto the stink box. It sounded like a giant dropping a large double handful of junkyard.

Wanda ducked fully behind her tree as it happened. She heard and felt something hit her tree with a considerable impact. Orange light sprang up in her peripheral vision as the helicopter's remains rolled down the slope to the main road and caught fire.

Wanda let out a whoop of victory.

Then she saw gleaming robots and flaming men clamber out of the helicopter wreckage—one, then three, then ten. The Terminators did not bother to roll on the ground, did not worry about patting out the flames consuming their clothes and their flesh. Some of them looked up in Wanda's direction.

She choked off her victory cry. Wanda sprang to her feet and raced back into the forest.

It was time to run.

John, Kate, and Prescott waited with the crowd clustering in ever-greater numbers around Shaft 2. The open elevator had descended moments ago, overburdened with Hornet Compound dwellers fleeing to their muster points, but it had not been large enough to carry everyone waiting. Nor would it be large enough for the current crowd.

The three of them were well-armed. The operations center armory, one of several caches of weapons and gear in the compound, had been only a few paces from the first hardpoint in the main entry tunnel. Each had a field pack, generic in its arrangement and contents—preserved food, water, handgun, ammunition, field phone, survival gear. John now carried an ancient M16A1 assault rifle, equipped with a 40mm M203 grenade launcher; Kate had a rocket-propelled grenade launcher in her hands and another across her back; Prescott held an AK-47 assault rifle and now wore a vest whose front was heavy with small cans that looked roughly like denuded aerosol containers with the letters *WP* stenciled on them.

John knew what they were. He had taught enough people to put them together. They were white phosphorous grenades. They were far better against personnel than against Terminators, but a lucky strike with one could get it jammed in a Terminator's machinery, allowing its high-temperature load to burn its way clear through circuitry.

Gunfire erupted from the long tunnel behind them. Many in the crowd turned to look.

"That'll be the first cross-tunnel," Prescott said. "Where the offices are."

"How long do you think they can hold there?" Kate asked.

Prescott shook his head. "Not long. Our defenses were set up assuming that the front door would hold for a little while. We haven't had time to move up anti-Terminator forces."

All three of them were pushed off-balance as the crowd surged a couple of feet forward. John finally heard what others in the crowd must have, the sound of the elevator returning to this level. "This is not good," John said. "Their forces will be here long before the elevator can get everyone down—"

"This is worse," Kate said. Her attention was on the shaft, on the elevator rising into place. John turned to look.

Kyla, her two dogs alongside her, the Barrett sniper rifle in her hands, was on the elevator.

The crowd surged forward more. It was obvious to John that they were going to crowd in as soon as the elevator gates lifted, perhaps crushing his daughter, at the very least keeping her from getting where she intended to go. He opened his mouth to issue a command he wasn't sure the panicky citizens of Hornet Compound would hear or obey.

But Kyla spoke first. As the elevator finished its climb, she said, "Grrr."

Both her dogs flattened their ears, bared their teeth, and growled. The growls cut through the crowd noise, and the manner of the dogs suggested that they would be happy to eat their way through the crowd. As Kyla lifted the elevator gate, the leading edge of the crowd spilled into the elevator only to her side, well away from the dogs. Kyla marched out of the elevator, her dogs still flanking her, and the crowd melted away in front of her, flowing around her. As she reached her parents, the dogs came within reach of Kate and broke their pretense, wagging their tails.

John and Kate didn't enter the elevator. "Why the hell are you getting off on this level?" John asked.

Kyla patted her sniper rifle. "Doing my job, Daddy."

"Did Ten tell you to come up here and play Custer's Last Stand?"

"Earl is helping Ten out through one of the escape tunnels. I don't know where Mark is. I'm on my own, 'cept for Ripper and Ginger." Kyla was using her reasonable voice. It was the same as Kate's reasonable voice, in fact. John hated that. It was so hard to argue with.

"Kyla—"

"I'll take orders from John Connor, but not from Daddy. John

Connor would tell me to do exactly what I'm about to do. I have maybe the one weapon in the compound that can sometimes eighty-six robots without blowing everything up in a thirty-foot radius."

John forced himself to cool down. He counted to three. He couldn't afford to waste time by counting all the way to ten. "John Connor would want to know your escape plan."

"Take the second cross-tunnel from the front entrance up into the Old Workings, follow it to the Angle Shaft, follow *that* up to air shaft E-5, which is the third shaft without mine car rails on the way up. It exits on the south slope at about two hundred feet up. That's the long route, but the dogs don't do so well on vertical climbs, so I can't take the main shaft route." At John's perplexed look, she said, "I always know the escape routes, even if I've only been in a place a few minutes. My daddy taught me that."

John felt himself redden. Inside, John Connor the leader was locked in a wrestling match with John Connor the father.

John Connor the father was the first to weaken. He knew his little girl was right. Admitting it felt like taking a knife in the guts.

Kyla read her father's face. "I'll be all right, Daddy." She gave her father a quick kiss, accepted a hug and a kiss from Kate, and then turned to trot back along the tunnel.

"She argues just like you," John said. "It's not fair."

"For once, you're right," Kate said.

The elevator was now descending, once again too crowded with escapees, and the crowd here was thickening. "Air shafts," John said.

Kate looked confused. "What about them?"

"We can make sure her escape route stays open. Prescott, do you know the air shaft she was talking about?"

"Yes, sir."

"Lead the way."

Prescott slung his AK-47 over his shoulder. He moved to the edge of the shaft but away from the elevator loading zone, where a waist-high wooden rail kept the unwary from accidentally stepping out over a drop of more than a thousand feet. He stepped across the rail, turning around as he did so, and clung to the rail with one hand as he reached over with the other to grab a support John and Kate couldn't see from their angle. He swung out over the emptiness, got his feet on the rungs, and began climbing.

Kate and then John followed.

Kyla and her dogs moved at a trot up the tunnel toward the main mine entrance. There was no foot traffic headed her way. Anyone left behind would now be invaders or defenders. The crowd at the elevator was still growing as more evacuees arrived by way of side tunnels.

She passed a cross-tunnel. To the left, she knew, it led to a ramp leading up into the Old Workings, the portions of the mine that had been played out in the 1890s. That was her escape path.

There was more gunfire from ahead. It was sustained fire. That probably meant a robot or Terminator was doing the shooting. Ammunition was too valuable a commodity, and assault rifles too prone to jam, so you fired in short bursts if you didn't want John Connor to chew you up one side and down the other.

Ahead, the tunnel sloped up and slightly to the left. That was good. Intruders headed this way would have to expose themselves progressively without having a good look at the section of the tunnel they were approaching. Somewhere, yards beyond the turn, would be the compound's first hardpoint, a heavily defended station set up with weapons that would slow or destroy invading Skynet troops . . . in theory.

Kyla knelt where she was, extended her rifle's bipod legs, and set up, lying at full length. She rapidly disengaged the scope and pocketed it. At this short range, the scope was worse than useless. She flipped up the front and rear iron sights that Tony Calhoun had meticulously affixed to the barrel and receiver before she was born. "Listen," she said.

Ripper harumphed and lay at her feet. Ginger took up her preferred position alongside Kyla. In normal sniper setups, whoever was doing her spotting, usually Mark, was there, so Ginger always appreciated the times when there was no spotter present.

Kyla concentrated on slowing her breathing as she waited.

The air shaft was not large enough for walking purposes. Prescott, Kate, and John crawled across rough-cut stone in a tunnel no more than four feet in diameter, and John could feel his knees being reduced to bloody mulch through the material of his pants. Electrical cables ran the entire length of the tunnel.

They reached a booster fan that filled the whole tunnel. It was powerful enough that, at a distance of a few feet, John could feel it tugging at him, could feel the air flow behind pushing. Like most such obstacles in a Resistance compound, the fan was designed to open. Prescott pulled a lever at the fan's base, unlocking it, and swung it aside. When Kate and John were past, he reset the lever, followed them through, and pulled the fan back into place. John heard it lock as it resumed its normal position.

By the time they reached the exhaust fan at the tunnel's end, John's knees were bleeding through his garments, and though it was dark, he knew Kate's had to be, as well. She hadn't made any comment to suggest that she was in pain. Prescott undogged the exhaust fan, and a few yards farther, they were able to look out over the mountain's slope and the old mine workings.

In the middle distance, something was burning. "That's the helicopter," John said.

"That's about where the contact point was, the stink box," Prescott breathed.

Kate went flat and crawled up to the lip of the air shaft so that she could look straight down the slope. "I don't see anything moving."

"Up, up." John pointed.

Perhaps half a mile away, the Hunter-Killer hovered. It was about three hundred feet off the ground, a tiny artificial light that constituted Skynet's eye on the scene.

"Can it see us, sir?" asked Prescott.

"Yes. But we're a tiny infrared blip it'll interpret as one to three people. And at this range, it's not going to worry that we can do it any harm—most of our weapons are too weak or inaccurate at this distance, and those that aren't, we'd be using with radar targeting, which it could detect."

"But we have to eliminate it," Kate said. "So we can escape, so Kyla can escape."

"Which means drawing it in," John said. He knelt beside his wife and gauged the slope below. In the moonlight, which he knew was often deceptive, it looked manageable. "I'm going to go down there, fire on it, draw it to me. You two move back so that your heat signatures begin to dissipate. It'll assume I'm the only one. When you hear gunfire, get back here and open on it with the RPGs."

"Sir," said Prescott, "let me do that. I know the face of the mountain a hell of a lot better than you, no offense meant."

"None taken." John clapped him on the shoulder. "Good luck."

The shooting had been over for about thirty seconds. Now Ginger growled quietly.

Kyla forced herself to remain relaxed. Though neither could see one another, she and the robot descending the tunnel were each aware of the other. She knew it was coming because Ginger said so. The robot knew that she, Kyla, was here because it could detect reflections of her heat signature even around the curve in the tunnel. Now it was just a question of whether the robot did what she wanted it to . . . or she did what it wanted her to.

Ahead, she saw shadows move. Then a red light appeared, descending as the Terminator whose eye it was came down the tunnel toward her.

She cursed to herself. The Terminator had been burned or damaged to the extent that one of its mechanical eyes was exposed, but not both. As it was still in shadow, she couldn't make it out well enough to know whether she was seeing its right eye or left, so she couldn't estimate the contours of its head.

"Ginger," she whispered.

Ginger's head came up.

"Run." She hated to do it, to use her own companion as bait, but the curve of the tunnel meant that Ginger would be exposed only for a fraction of a second.

Ginger wheeled and fled. Kyla knew the dog was happy to be running. This was a game, and she'd be rewarded for playing.

The Terminator opened fire, the muzzle flashes from its assault rifle illuminating it and the tunnel around it. Kyla, far enough away not to be dazzled by the display, could see its outlines.

She squeezed her trigger. The Barrett kicked back into her shoulder, most of the recoil absorbed by the weapon's heavy weight, its muzzle brake, its bipod, and the thick padding of its stock.

The Terminator lurched backward and fell mostly out of sight; Kyla thought she could still see the outline of one leg. It stopped firing.

Kyla whistled. Ginger happily trotted back up to her, lay down beside her again. Kyla picked up the expended brass from the tunnel floor—reloadable cartridges were a precious resource.

She racked the bolt to chamber another round, then waited. If the Terminator was only damaged, it would be up again within a few seconds, half a minute, after it rebooted and its internal repair circuitry did whatever power and data rerouting it needed to. Even if it was dead, one more kill for Kyla's record, there would be another soon.

August 2029
Hornet Compound

Kate and John huddled, waiting back where the exhaust fan was housed. Each held one of Kate's rocket-propelled grenades.

"Prescott seems to be a good kid," John said.

"Uh-huh." Kate's voice was choppy, battered by its proximity to the whirling fan blades. "Kind of single-minded, like Kyle Reese."

"True. I hate to see that sort of . . . you know, simplicity in people. They're all stripped down to the bare minimum they need to be in order to stay alive. That's not exactly what I think of as humanity. Though in Kyle's case, it was a big relief to me."

"How so?" Kate knew, as a few of John's advisers did, that Kyle had been John's own father. Sent back in time to save Sarah Connor from the first Terminator dispatched by Skynet, he had fallen in love with Sarah, had become her lover in the brief few days before his own death.

Well, that wasn't exactly true. He'd been in love with Sarah since long before he'd met her, since he'd first heard stories of her from John.

"When he was training with the Hell-Hounds, working with them on field tactics," John said, "I was kind of worried that he'd get interested in Kyla."

"Oh, ick."

"Well, I figured out pretty quickly that I didn't have to worry.

He was so fixated on my mother, there was really no chance he'd pursue Kyla."

"John, this family is such a mess. Now I wish you hadn't told me that."

He chuckled. "Just because my father is of the same generation as our children? You have problems with that?"

"I hate time paradoxes." There was no humor in her voice now; she might have been expressing her feelings for Terminators or Skynet. "When Skynet falls, I want you to outlaw them."

"The instant Skynet falls, I resign. You'll have to persuade the next military despot in charge."

"I bet I can."

"I bet you can, too."

There was gunfire from down the slope. The two of them scrambled up to the air shaft's terminus.

Far below, they could see streams of tracers arcing up toward the Hunter-Killer. That machine was no longer hovering; it had lost some altitude and was cruising in toward Prescott's position. As they watched, something ignited on the HK's surface and flashed like a line of redness toward Prescott.

The missile detonated, throwing red-orange fire and black smoke in all directions from the point of impact. John winced. Prescott was supposed to be using his superior knowledge of the terrain to keep from getting killed.

He had. Tracers once again rose from Prescott's position, and John could hear, over the chattering of the distant AK-47, some ringing and clanking sounds as bullets found their mark against the HK's hull.

The aerial vehicle drifted closer to Prescott's position. Kate came ready with her rocket-propelled grenade and John followed suit.

"Range is good," she said.

"Take your shot."

She did, and the air was suddenly warmed as the compact missile leaped from her shoulder.

The HK tilted, angling to sideslip, but the warhead hit it anyway. The HK disappeared in a bright flash, then reappeared, several yards away in the direction it had been tilting toward. Flames and smoke rose from it, especially from its port outboard engine, one of the ducted jets that kept it flying.

John took his shot, calculating where the HK would be if it continued its current course for another second. His warhead hit the HK somewhere in the middle and there was a second bright flash; then the remains of the HK, in two flaming pieces, crashed down on the mountain slope.

John dug his field phone out and powered it up. He heard a hiss, but no radio traffic. That wasn't unexpected; few, if any, of Hornet Compound's residents would be aboveground now. He pressed the mike button. "Prescott, you okay?"

"Light shrapnel, sir. Shall I rejoin you?"

"No, stay there. Doctor yourself up and we'll be down when the rest of our party gets here."

"Yes, sir."

Ginger growled again, joined by Ripper this time. Kyla prepared herself for a second shot.

This time, she saw two red eyes moving in unison. It was an assault robot that had never worn humanlike skin. Both sets of optics were visible to her.

She fired and was rewarded with the kick to her shoulder, the ringing of the robot's body as it hit the tunnel floor. She chambered another round.

The dogs weren't through growling. But now, whatever was coming opened fire well before it came into view.

The sudden noise was horrific, like an unshielded V-8 engine, and sparks began to light up all over the wall and floor to Kyla's right. She knew the sound, a .50-caliber machine gun, and it was joined by a similar, shriller roar—a chain gun. The second weapon, if it was loaded according to normal Skynet dictates, was firing depleted uranium rounds.

The dogs howled. The sparks on the floor and wall jumped out in ever-greater numbers. Kyla swore. There were at least two robots up there, advancing toward her, firing fully automatic weapons. She rose in a single motion, yanking her sniper rifle up with her. "Run," she said, and suited action to words, scooting back along as close to the stone wall as she could bear, hoping as hard as she could that neither she nor the dogs was hit by one of the thousands of ricochets now filling the tunnel.

The two T-800s marched down the tunnel side-by-side, each firing in sustained bursts, each reloading while the other was still firing. They passed the bodies of two of their fellows.

Each of these Terminators had started with the same face as the one that had been sent back in time to kill Sarah Connor, as those that had been sent back to save John Connor, the face of Sergeant Candy. Now one of them, dressed in ancient overalls and flannel shirt, carrying the chain gun, had lost half that face; where flesh had been there was now only gleaming silvery skull. The other retained most of the features, wore Resistance-style camouflage, and carried the .50-caliber machine gun.

They tracked the heat trace of their quarry, saw that trace move into a side tunnel. They exchanged no visible signals, but the one in overalls turned at a military-precise right angle into the tunnel, following the heat trace, while the other continued down the main tunnel.

Before long the second Terminator came to a broader space that intersected with two side tunnels and a broad vertical shaft. No humans were in sight, but there were several fading heat traces. It leaned out over the shaft.

Below, not more than thirty feet down, was an elevator apparatus. In it were a dozen humans. The T-800 took a moment to assess the engineering virtues and deficits of the elevator. It seemed to be of all-metal construction and had an open top; it was broad enough to carry dozens of humans or a few ore-hauling mine cars.

The T-800 stepped out over the lip and plunged toward the elevator car. One of the humans within the car saw its fall; she screamed a nonverbal warning to her fellows.

The Terminator crashed down onto the metal floor of the car, denting but not buckling it, and came upright. As humans surged away from it, mindlessly seeking escape in directions that offered none, the Terminator methodically sprayed .50-caliber fire in an arc around the elevator's interior, exterminating each of the humans.

All but one. An immature male human, an adolescent, according to the T-800's analytical routines, demonstrating more survival characteristics than its fellows, had climbed up the side of the elevator and now clung to a metal rung stapled into the shaft's side. It looked down on the Terminator from an altitude of thirty feet. The Terminator calculated that its facial expression, including wide-open eyes, dilation of the pupils, contraction of the facial muscles, indicated a combination of fear, shock, and anger.

The Terminator elevated its barrel and shot the human, then watched dispassionately as the body fell and crashed atop those of its fellows. Then the robot waited with machine patience for the elevator to descend to wherever it had been going.

June, Present Day
Ávila Property

Daniel moved around in Danny's bedroom, wonderstruck. Taken individually, there was nothing remarkable about any of the objects here; there were books, articles of clothing, a notebook computer, computer games in colorful boxes, bedclothes. But they were a part of him, a part that had been lost—lost for good, he had thought.

He could feel two sets of sensations—the coolness of the wood on his bare feet, and more distantly, the discomfort of someone's shoulder tucked up against his armpit, the feeling of being hauled along like a burlap bag full of oranges. He tried to tune out Mike's repeated imprecations that he had to wake up. One or the other of him was now experiencing a headache, he wasn't sure which.

There was a small framed photograph on the chest of drawers. He snatched it up and held it under the light.

Faces he didn't recognize—faces he almost recognized. A middle-aged man and woman in back, three young men in front, all Latinos, all smiling. That had to be Mama and Papa; the older boys had to be Alex and Lon.

But he still couldn't remember them, not quite. He now had access to Danny's room, but not to his memories. Frustrated, he set the picture back on the chest of drawers.

He stiffened, struck by an idea. Was there any reason why he had to keep reaching back to the Danny of a particular year, progressing each time a little bit into that Danny's future? Maybe if he tried hard enough, tried a different way, he could go back further, visit Danny's mind when his father and Alex had still been alive. Maybe he could get to know everyone again, if only briefly.

Furthermore, maybe Danny kept a diary or a journal. If he could persuade his younger self to create another time capsule, to put into it his scrapbooks and thoughts and memories, perhaps he could have them again in the future. He cursed himself for not thinking of this before.

We've left the main shaft, headed toward an escape tunnel. But there are Terminators in the complex.

"Just a moment, just a moment, I'm looking for paper." He knew his voice must sound irritable. His headache was growing in intensity.

Daniel, they're here. Mike's voice was a wail.

Then pain hit him, a blow like a bullet to the head. Daniel jerked, his body no longer in control. He twisted on the way to the floor, saw his own face in the mirror, saw agonized old eyes in a young face . . . and then darkness crashed down on him.

Mike put her hands around Daniel's neck and shook him. "Daniel, you have to wake up."

Her son Mark, tucked under Daniel's arm and propping the man up, said, "Mama, that's not helping." He continued at a slow walk up the slope of Tunnel 10. Daniel was half-walking, supporting some of his own weight, but not enough of it, and Mike's efforts to wake him were shaking Mark off-balance.

Mike didn't respond to Mark, but did stop shaking Daniel. "We've left the main shaft, headed toward an escape tunnel. But there are Terminators in the complex."

"Just a moment, just a moment," Daniel mumbled. "I'm looking for paper."

Men and women were racing past them, headed to the evacuation tunnels.

There'd been new digging in this mine ever since it had been occupied as a Resistance habitat. Some of the miners were still looking for gold—though gold was of little use in their barter-based economy, manufacturing still needed the precious metal, especially in the making of circuitry. But most of the miners chipping away at the tunnels these days were digging escape routes. Four of these tunnels now led from some of the mine's shallower levels, such as Tunnel 10, and the inhabitants outpacing Mark, Mike, and Daniel were headed toward one of the exit points.

There was a bang from behind them. A woman just passing them catapulted forward as if someone had kicked her spine with inhuman strength. She rolled to a stop, face-up, a look of pain and shock already fading from her features; her eyes remained open.

Mike spun to look back. There, up the slope, was a dark silhouette surrounding a short gout of yellow flame—a machine gun firing down at them. "Daniel," Mike wailed, "they're here—"

Daniel jerked upright, coming off Mark's supporting arm, his back arching. He made a sound, something like a moan, and pitched forward again. Only Mark's grip on him kept him from hitting the mine-car rails on the tunnel floor. Fear froze Mike's stomach and heart solid.

He'd been hit, he had to have been hit. In the darkness, she could not see where he'd been wounded. Mark ducked under him, stood up with the man over his shoulders in a fireman's carry. "Thirty more yards," he grunted, "to a hardpoint. Get them ready. Run."

Mike froze for an instant, unwilling to leave her son, to leave Daniel, with a Terminator hot on their tail, but she knew he was right. She spun and fled. Slowed as she was by carrying both her field pack and Mark's, she still outraced her son and the tremendous load he was carrying.

There were more fleeing Hornet Compound residents ahead of her, but they weren't her concern. She measured off roughly twenty-five yards as she ran, then began shouting, "Hardpoint! Hardpoint, where are you?"

What looked like the boarded-off entrance into a small side tunnel swung partway open. She ducked into the blackness beyond it. "Herrera, Senior Staff," she said—gasped, rather.

"Sato, Chris, Sergeant." The speaker made a little noise as he slid back into his firing seat.

"There's a Terminator coming, but the first big man you see and the bigger man he's carrying are human."

"I read you."

"Anything I can do to help?"

"AK-47 on the table behind you if you want to play."

Her eyes adjusting to the comparative gloom of the hardpoint station, Mike could now make out the small window Sergeant Sato was using to monitor the tunnel. She did not look away from it as she groped behind her, locating the table and the assault rifle on it by touch. There were other things on the table, extra ammunition clips; she grabbed and pocketed those as well.

There was gunfire from the tunnel. She prayed that it wasn't coming anywhere near Mark or Daniel, but could not bear to close her eyes in her prayer.

Then something moved past Sato's window at a trot—Mark, Daniel still across his back. Mark's face was rigid, set in an expression she had never seen him wear, an expression that said he was going to get to his destination or die, that he would crush under his feet anything that got in front of him. It was the face of Mark the Hell-Hound, Mark the full-grown man who had been shot, who had killed, not Mark her son, and it added to her misery. She never wanted to see anyone she loved wear an expression like that.

Sergeant Sato whispered, "This side toward enemy."

"What?"

She saw his silhouette raise a fist holding a switch. A big man moved into view outside Sato's window and turned toward Sato and Mike. Mike saw his face—the same one worn by the two Terminators she'd helped send into the past.

Sato's thumb came down on the switch. Mike's ears were battered by a concussion that staggered her. The Terminator disappeared in the flash of light that accompanied the blast.

Sato crashed out through the hardpoint's access door, bringing up his assault rifle and firing. Mike joined him a second later, carefully aiming the unfamiliar AK-47 at the large man slumped against the far tunnel wall.

The Terminator had been hit by something ferocious. Most of its shirt and jacket had been torn away and its torso chassis was perforated; Mike counted six holes there. She poured ammunition from her assault rifle into it as Sato concentrated his own fire on the Terminator's head.

As their first clips of thirty-two rounds ran dry, they swapped in new clips and took stock of their situation. The Terminator wasn't moving.

"What the hell was that?" Mike asked.

"Buried in the wall, a claymore mine," Sato said. He was of Asian descent, compactly built, maybe thirty years of age. "An explosive charge behind a package of metal ball bearings. Pretty damned grisly when it hits meat. Cover me, please." He fished an object that looked like a small food can with a handle out of a vest pocket. Moving with the decisive speed of a professional soldier, he leaped to kneel beside the Terminator, jammed the object into one of the holes in its chest, and jumped back. His arm extended, he moved Mike back behind the hardpoint door.

The Terminator didn't move. The device exploded, jerking the robot's body into a convincing simulation of a man experiencing a seizure. Then the Terminator lay still again, smoke now rising from it.

"Back on station for me," Sato said, "unless you need me."

Mike shook her head. "Can I keep the rifle?"

"Anything for senior staff."

"There are probably more Terminators coming."

"I have more surprises for them." Sato entered the hardpoint and shut the door behind him. His next words were muffled: "Death to the toasters."

"Death to the toasters." Mike ran after her son.

The beating sound from the exhaust fan covered up lesser noises, so Kate and John were unaware that Kyla had reached them until the fan clanked and then swung open. She crawled out, her rifle in its case across her back, her dogs swarming around her, whining and worried.

John grabbed his daughter, helped her toward the tunnel exit. Kyla was panting too heavily to want to talk, so he asked her nothing. Then he felt the warm liquid trickling down her side. "Oh, Jesus, Kyla, are you all right?"

"Caught a ricochet along my ribs," Kyla said, her voice a gasp. "Not too bad. Mom, see to Ripper, he was hit, too. Daddy, there's a T-800 coming up behind me, maybe a minute back."

Kate pulled the exhaust fan frame shut again, then moved to the tunnel exit. Once she was a step or two outside, in the open air and moonlight, she called, "Ripper, c'mere."

The big bullmastiff mutt trotted up to her, short tail wagging, moving easily. She ran her hands over the dog's fur, found a patch of blood along his flank. Careful not to hurt him more than she had to, she probed around the injury, speaking soothing words when he whined, but John could tell her motions were mostly by rote; she kept her eyes on him, on his similar actions as he gauged the severity of the wound to his daughter.

"She's right. It's not bad," John said, and breathed a sigh of relief. "How's Ripper?"

"A graze. I'll patch him up. He's not badly hurt."

"Daddy, the T-800—"

"Right, right." John looked around, took an instant assessment of their location, their resources. "Kyla, situate Ginger and Ripper right above the exhaust tunnel exit . . ."

Mike caught up to her son at the end of the escape tunnel. Here, wood-and-rebar barriers held a shallow layer of earth at bay. Men and women were cutting through leather restraints that held the barrier upright.

Mark had turned Daniel over to Lake and a medical technician. They were quickly rigging a litter from boards pulled from the walls, blankets from their packs. Mark smiled with relief as his mother arrived, hugged her, and took his pack from her.

"How's Daniel?" she asked.

He shook his head. "Lake's being less than communicative, but her grunts and cursing don't make it sound good. But he hasn't been shot. No holes, no blood, no foul."

"I can't believe you carried him that far, that fast."

Mark shrugged. "My father was a big, strong guy. He gave me big, strong guy genes." He cast a worried eye toward Daniel as he shrugged on his pack.

There was another explosion from up the tunnel. Even at this distance, Mike thought that it was more ferocious than the claymore going off. The tunnel vibrated beneath her feet; dust and dirt cascaded down into everyone's hair. The overhead lights went out.

But no one shrieked. These weren't subway passengers caught by a power outage. It was possible that everyone here had been in a worse situation at some point in the past.

"They've blown the tunnel," Mark said. "It'll keep the Terminators out until they can dig through or figure out that they need to search around. And we'll be gone by then."

"Ready to go," someone, a man, called from ahead. "Everybody, the stuff that's going to spill in here is fine-ground quartz dust. You don't want to breathe it in. Once upon a time, it was treated with cyanide, and though the cyanide is mostly gone now, it's not worth taking chances. Wrap something around your mouth and nose to keep it out. If you've got goggles for your eyes, put them on."

Most of those present began to wrap scarves or spare clothes from their packs around their faces. Lake placed a surgical mask over Daniel's face, handed out more to her stretcher-bearers, to Mark and Mike.

After a few moments, the voice from the front of the crowd shouted, "Can we go?"

"You and Lake are ranking officers here now," Mark whispered.

"Do it," Mike shouted.

There was a creak, then the sound of several hundred pounds of loose material spilling into the tunnel. A pale cloud of dust washed across them. As it faded, Mike began to see moonlit sky and stars through the hole the collapse had made. A ramp of white sand, some of it still pouring into the tunnel from the edges of the collapse, would lead them out.

"Move out," Mike said, this time at a much lower tone. No one shouted in the open.

The several dozen survivors emerged into a narrow cleft in the earth, at the very edge of one of the tailings pits. Mark gave his mother a quick smile, then moved up to the head of the column to do what he did best. Mike stayed toward the center of the column, with Lake and the two men handling Daniel's litter. Moving as silently as they could, as swiftly as they dared, they emerged into the open and headed toward their designated muster point.

August 2029
Hornet Compound

The T-800 shoved the exhaust fan frame out of the way, crushing the rugged metal as though it were aluminum foil. It clambered into the final stretch of tunnel, then out into the open.

It transmitted its position to the coordinating HK, but got no return signal. Either the HK had malfunctioned or it had been terminated. This meant that its signal would not be fitted into the wire-frame schematic the HK was supposed to be maintaining for all participants in the assault.

It did not matter much. The Terminator could estimate its own position on the mountain slope, could detect and terminate its enemies. And there, on the slope below, were fuzzy heat traces suggesting that humans had passed recently. It had a clear picture of the mountain slope. While there were no humans visible, heat was accumulating in a sort of aura behind two rock outcroppings.

The Terminator took a step down the mountain slope.

It heard scrabbling from above and behind but was not fast enough to turn before it was hit. Then it was tumbling. The first quarter of a second of analysis of its visual returns indicated that two large canines were on the Terminator, biting it, rolling with it as it descended the hill in an uncontrolled fashion.

The Terminator, even within the very narrow confines of what could be equated with unease, was not concerned. The fall could not damage it substantially. Neither could the dogs.

But the T-800 continued rolling for yards, dozens of yards, after the dogs apparently detached themselves. When it finally stopped, it sat up and discovered that all the flesh on the lower portion of its right arm had been torn away, and with it the chain gun. It had no ranged weapon. That was inconvenient.

Then the humans emerged from their hiding places and began firing on it with assault rifles and grenades.

A minute later, John and the others stood over the explosively dismantled body of their enemy. "Nice work," John said. "This might even be reparable. Kyla, extra doggie biscuits for your pals. Kate, two minutes for bandages, then I'd appreciate it if you'd go get that chain gun. Prescott, you and I are going to drag this wreckage to our muster point."

Kate sighed. "Kyla, when you get married, don't marry a micromanager."

August 2029
Hornet Compound Muster-Point Three

John Connor waited in the tunnel neck leading to the surface. The sky out there was brightening—dawn of a new day. He offered up a sour grin at all the long-ago songs that had spoken so highly of dawns and new days. These days, they were often just an opportunity to count one's losses in the daylight instead of by flashlight beam.

This cave was officially known as Hornet Compound Muster-Point Three. It was large enough to accommodate about one-fourth of the population of Hornet Compound in cold, huddled misery. And that's what it now held, approximately a fourth of the survivors of the compound. They'd wait until tonight, then many of them would venture forth on a days-long overland walk to the nearest human habitat, Tortilla Compound. Some would be lucky enough to ride in the vehicles, such as John's, that were hidden well away from Hornet, but most would be on foot for the dangerous crossing.

There were three other muster points, each within two hours' walk of the old mines, and John imagined that each one was stuffed full of refugees like this one. He hoped they were, anyway.

"John, everyone's here," Kate called from behind him.

He turned into the darkness and marched down into the cave, where Kate waited. Together they walked among the dispossessed residents of Hornet Compound who lay on their sleeping bags and blankets, some of them wounded. All had eyes for John and Kate, and the two leaders had a ready smile or word of encouragement for each one.

Past the main cave, they slid down a narrow natural tunnel, a thirty-five-degree slope, down into a secondary, smaller cave. It was lit by an oil lamp placed at the center of the stone floor. John's advisers and Lucas Kaczmarek sat around it, most of them uncomfortable sitting cross-legged. Kaczmarek was pale, a bandage spotted with dried blood across his forehead.

John and Kate joined them. "Let's hear it," John said. "Kate?"

His wife grimaced. "Well, obviously, Hornet is a total loss. Enemy losses are going to be hard to calculate until we've heard from all the other muster points. We're certain of six destroyed robots and one downed helicopter."

"Lucas?"

Kaczmarek rocked from buttock to buttock, uncomfortable on the stone floor. "We had enough advance warning that just about everyone got out with a full pack—sleeping and camping gear, weapons, food and water. Of the ninety-eight people assigned to this muster point, eighty-seven have shown up."

"Not a bad ratio," John said. He knew his tone was grudging. Losing anyone under his command ate at him. But given the scale of the night's disaster, things could have been far worse. If the ratio of survivors in the other three muster points was similar, the population of Hornet Compound had survived comparatively well . . . by most standards. "What else?"

"Recommend commendations for Lieutenant Andy Masters, who was in command of the first hardpoint station. He accounted for a couple of assault robots and delayed the intruders by significant minutes. Posthumous, unfortunately. And for Corporal Wanda Dixon. She was the sentry who kept us informed of the Skynet forces' approach. Also bagged the 'copter. She's still with us."

John nodded. Kaczmarek wouldn't mention his own role in the defense of Hornet Compound and its aftermath, but he, too, deserved recognition. He'd been part of the crew attempting to hold the first hardpoint against the invading Skynet forces, and had managed to hide in a rock crevice when it had been overrun and his fellow defenders had all perished. Emerging when most of the shooting was done, he'd joined up with a survivor hiding in an air shaft. The two of them had found the bodies of Kyla's kills and had dragged one to where it could be carted to the muster point.

In the world of 2029, recycling was the order of the day. In this case, recycling meant taking the undamaged head from the unit John, Kate, and Prescott had terminated and mating it with the body of one of Kyla's victims. Then Danny Ávila or one of a small number of programmers with similar skills, Mark Herrera among them, would turn it into a servant of the Resistance.

"Yes to both," John said. "I assume there will be more recommendations once the blackout is past and we hear from the other muster points."

"Probably. Anyway, as Ms. Brewster indicated, the compound is a loss. All our resources, our gold production, the new equipment you brought us. And I'm out of a job. Got an opening?"

John grinned. "Sid?"

"Three squadrons of the 1st Security Regiment were temporarily based out of Hornet Compound while you were there," Walker said. "Hell-Hounds, Scalpers, and Nuts and Bolts. Nuts and Bolts was out on an operation; they're being rerouted to Tortilla to join us. Hell-Hounds are intact, here at Muster-Point Three. Scalpers . . ." He sighed. "We lost Crazy Pete, Warthog, Meadows, and Boom-Boom. That leaves Nix and Jenna the Greek, the two most junior members. The Scalpers are basically a loss."

"Are you recommending recruitment to restore the Scalpers, or decommission?"

"Recruitment . . . but we're going to have to swap in a seasoned commander. And Nix and Jenna aren't going to appreciate having someone moved in over them from outside the unit."

"Do what you can to preserve their feelings, but we're not running a kindergarten." John stared at the open patch of stone around which he and the others were sitting. He'd known Crazy Pete even before Judgment Day—the man had been a friend of his mother's. Crazy Pete had taught John a thing or two about smuggling, about cycling, about handling high explosives. When he wasn't in jail on an assault or possession charge, Crazy Pete had been on the run for parole violation. The man had been completely incapable of functioning within modern society, a career criminal . . . and then society had been scraped away, and he'd been transformed into a leader, a defender. From one instant to the next, though he was the same man, the alteration of human society had turned him from an incorrigible into a hero.

And now he was gone, leaving behind a hole too big to fill.

He could sense the others' silence, their waiting for him to return to the present. He turned to Lake. "Tamara?"

"Well, the majority of Hornet's scientific instruments and medical equipment is a loss. We got out with what we could." Tired and dispirited, Lake looked her age, a rare event for her. "We have medical supplies enough for our current needs and the injured are being tended to. We had two die during the night but I think we can save the rest."

"And your star patient?"

"Daniel's had a stroke, John."

John grimaced. "How bad?"

"Well, no stroke is good. His is sort of in the medium category, I guess. Partial paralysis of his right side, including face, arm, and leg. Hard to tell the degree to which his thinking has been affected; he's mostly been drifting in and out of consciousness. But he's not dreaming. Not his special dreaming, anyway."

"And his prognosis?"

She shrugged. "With treatment and therapy, he could make a near-full recovery in a few years. But we're going to have to pull the plug on his special operation. His dreaming puts tremendous stress on his system, and that's got to have been a major contributing factor to his stroke. If he keeps doing it, he could pop another plug, and that'll be the end of him."

"Right. Consider that operation at an end." John turned to his chief scientific adviser. "Mike?"

"Nothing, really. I've just been trying to figure out why Skynet hit us with a full extermination team. It had to have acquired enough data to conclude that Hornet Compound was a major habitation, or that you and Kate were there."

"And your conclusion?"

"Not enough data to support any conclusion. I wonder, though, since Daniel's dreaming sometimes generates the same sort of EMR signature as the Continuum Transporter apparatus, if Skynet detected that. It would certainly be compelled to go in and level what it thought was a time travel device."

"That can work in our favor," Kate said. "If Skynet thinks that Hornet *was* the home of our Continuum Transporter, it might conclude that we no longer have access to one."

"Interesting point." John considered. "That leads me to two conclusions. First, it's an additional reason to terminate Daniel's dreaming project. If he's being detected as Continuum Transporter energy, and he dreams again, then Skynet will conclude that he's one of those devices and send forces to destroy him until they succeed. Second, we have to consider ways to use that tactically. If we could replicate the sort of energy output associated with time travel—even without the presence of a Continuum Transporter—we could use it, once at least, to draw in Skynet forces for an ambush." He turned back to Walker. "Okay, Sid, we don't know the status of our temporary vehicle depot. With the land lines burned out last night, and with our radio blackout in effect until we're confident that Skynet forces aren't close enough to detect us, we aren't going to know. So I want you to send a unit out there. Not to enter—to perform surveillance from a distance. If Skynet found it, there may be Terminators in the area, doing exactly the same thing. Once we're sure the depot isn't being watched, we'll have the unit bring our vehicles out, some back to Home Plate, the rest to catch up with us and haul some of us to Tortilla Compound."

Walker nodded.

"Anything else? No? Then let's jump up and do next to nothing until dark. We've got a long walk ahead of us tonight."

His advisers rose one by one and headed up the slope into the larger cave. John remained where he sat, and Kate stayed with him. "You okay?" she asked.

"Within certain very broad definitions of the word *okay*, yeah."

Kate leaned against him. She didn't say any of the obvious things. *It could have been worse. It's not your fault. We're doing as well as we could possibly expect. The fact that we're alive at all is your doing.* In years past, she had said them all before. In years to come, she would probably say them all again. But even the most routine of soothing statements had to get some rest of their own.

June, Present Day
Ávila Property

"Danny? Can you hear me? Are you all right?"

He wasn't all right. His head hurt as though he'd stuck it in a chest of drawers and allowed the college football team to slam the drawer shut a few times.

He forced his eyes to open. Once again he was staring at the underside of his bed. He was lying on his back, twisted around as though a chunk of his side had been torn away and he'd bent to try to slow the blood loss.

He looked up. The desk lamp on his nightstand was on, glaring right into his eyes. Linda, dressed in a USC Trojans sweatshirt that came almost down to her knees, was bending over him; her face was above the light and cast into silhouette.

Danny felt a sickening sense of loss, as though the house around him was a flash-paper construction on the verge of having a match applied to it, as though the woman bending over him was nothing more than an illusion. *She isn't in my future.* They'd told him so, the voices.

The voices he could no longer feel. There had been a connection with them even when he was awake, a sensation of their distant presence. Now it was gone. He wondered if he had just died in that future era.

He remembered that Linda had asked him a question, was waiting for his answer. " 'M okay," he lied.

"Yeah, well, let's get your book back into bed." She took his hands, hauled him to a sitting position, then straightened and helped raise him to his feet. Now, in the light, he could see her face, see the worry on it.

"Strong girl," he said.

"Danny, what's wrong?"

"If I told you, you'd think I was crazy." He sat down on the edge of his bed. His headache was starting to fade. He hoped that as the pain moved away, his sense of connection with his visitors from the future would move back in.

But it didn't. That corner of his mind remained chillingly empty. What had happened? His future friends had reluctantly answered his question about Linda, Kate had started asking questions about her father, then something had begun to go wrong . . . and there was a discontinuity between then and him waking up on the floor.

"I already think you're crazy." She sat beside him. "So what do you have to lose?"

"Everything. I think I'm going to lose everything." *I may already have,* he told himself. "You know, until you've touched your future, you can't imagine how cut off you feel when it's gone."

Linda shook her head, not comprehending. "Your future's all around you, Danny."

He turned his back on the echoing emptiness where his future perceptions had been, turned his attention fully on her.

Preparation and planning had always been the hallmarks of Danny's approach to school, life, work, everything. He'd read each semester's worth of course work before classes began, meticulously outlined his papers before writing them, accumulated maps and timetables for the areas where he was going to vacation even before he bought the tickets. Overplanning was the one consistent characteristic of his life; overplanning was what it meant to be Danny Ávila.

Now, untethered from his future, well into the process of

betraying his employer and his country, he threw that characteristic into the trash.

"Prove it," he said.

"How?"

He leaned forward to kiss her. The softness of her lips, her quick hiss of surprise, were exactly what he'd expected.

Next, he knew, would come the shove, slap, or punch to send him sprawling. Well, that would be all right. At least he was no longer hiding his attraction to her. He put his arms around her waist.

No shove came, no slap or punch. Linda wrapped her own arms around his neck, pressed forward into his kiss. It took only the slightest pressure to spill them both across the bed.

She helped him pull the Trojans shirt from her body, moved with him, her heat and passion a match for his.

Much later, as his window began to gray into dawn, Danny came awake and found Linda still there, facing him, eyes solemn.

He thought about what to say, then shoved that impulse aside. "Hi," he said.

"Hi."

"That sounded really lame. My hi, that is. Your hi was fine."

She managed a grin, though it faded almost instantly.

"I'm sorry," he said.

"For what?"

He considered. "Come to think of it, I'm not sorry in the least. I'm just worried."

"About you, me, or us? Whatever 'us' is?"

"About you. About Mama. I don't want her to get all weird about this. I mean, you know how devoted she was to Alex. I don't want her to see us and think you're, you know, betraying his memory—" He stopped at Linda's sudden laugh. "What?"

"You think Mama's going to freak out if we get together?"

"Sure."

"It's been six—no, I guess it's more like eight months since she started dropping little hints to me. 'You know, you're not getting any younger.' 'You know, Danny's a very good young man. He'll be a wonderful provider. All he needs is someone to calm him down.' Anytime she begins a sentence with 'You know,' what I know is that I'm about to get a new recommendation concerning *you.*"

"Oh." He tried to force that through his thinking processes in a matter of milliseconds. It didn't fit. That didn't sound like his mother at all. "Well, then, why didn't you jump on me eight months ago?"

Even in the dim light he could make out her expression of outrage. "She was right, you do need a beating, the beating of your life—"

"No, kiss me instead."

"Well . . . okay."

August 2029
Sierra Nevada Mountains, California/Nevada

Mark Herrera moved up the mountain slope along a game trail. It had to be a game trail; it had started a thousand feet down the mountain in a little runoff pond and was still worn, still being used. There were no Human Resistance compounds near here, so the only alternatives were that it was being used by humans unknown to the Resistance or by animals.

The trees here were green but wilted, desperate for water. Even winters on these slopes were comparatively arid; summer was a waterless nightmare. Much higher, and there'd be little to no vegetation at all.

He took a look around. He was ascending this slope along its southwest face. The sun was setting but still well above the peaks behind him. It gave everything here—stone, tree, his own flesh—a golden glow. There was no sign of human or machine activity, no sign there ever had been.

He keyed his lapel mike. "This is Hell-Hounds Two," he said, speaking slowly and distinctly. "Assemble on my position. We'll camp here for the night."

He received three verbal acknowledgments. It sent a shiver up his spine, taking two or three times as long as was absolutely necessary to send a radio message, but that was his mission.

Ten, Earl, Kyla and her dogs reached him within twenty minutes. They looked around a little longer, found a clearing that was admirably suited to camping, and set their packs down there. Then, as the sun dropped to and finally behind the western peaks, they went scavenging, spending a long hour dragging firewood back to the clearing. Ten didn't participate; his ribs were freshly healed, and all the walking they were doing had already taken a toll on his energy reserves.

It didn't take that long to find one fire's worth of wood. In these dry summer conditions, they had enough fuel for one fire within minutes. But by the end of the hour, they had assembled wood for six fires around the clearing.

They set up tents—of ratty canvas and the poorest tarps that they'd been able to acquire from Hornet Compound's survivors. When they were done, as twilight began to set and they lit off the fires, the encampment looked as though it had been set up for twenty or thirty people.

Their encampment last night had looked much the same.

Now, before it grew too dark to move, they headed out again, moving at a brisk pace despite Ten's bruised ribs and Kyla's minor gunshot wound, to a site two miles away—farther up the mountain, where the trees were far more sparse but the rock crests and overhangs were far more numerous, and made their own smaller, colder camp.

They looked down on the glows of the untended fires from the comparative safety and seclusion of a cleft beneath one overhang. Heat-insulating modern blankets were draped before them, leaving only narrow gaps through which they could see.

Earl, chewing unenthusiastically on a hunk of venison jerky, said, "Children, what we need is some marshmallows. And graham crackers and chocolate bars. We could make s'mores."

Ten snorted. "You older folk ought to refrain from teasing the children like that. There's no such thing as marshmallows. Or Santa Claus or the Easter Bunny."

Mark, lying atop his sleeping bag and almost dozing, his eyes closed, said, "And when they got home, the boy got out and went around to let the girl out of the car, and there, hanging from the door handle, was a bloody hook."

Earl just shook his head. "So, so cynical."

"No, that's the only way the story makes sense," Mark protested. "The guy with the hook for a hand is obviously a T-600 sent back in time to eliminate teenagers who will someday grow up to be a part of the Resistance. It goes on a killing spree and the police concoct this story of a maniac escaped from a mental institution. It has several run-ins with the police and gets damaged. By the time it catches up to the last couple, it has no weapons and it's falling apart. It grabs for the girl's door, the car speeds off and tears its hand away when it goes."

Kyla, sitting against the stone wall at the back of the overhang, looked at him. In the darkness no one could see her face, but her voice dripped with an odd combination of wonder and revulsion. "Mark, keep that up and I'm going to have the dogs kill and eat you."

"You'd never poison your dogs that way."

"So what happens to the T-600 afterward?" Earl asked. "It wouldn't stop there. It'd keep on coming."

Kyla sighed. "You're just encouraging him."

Mark stretched and opened his eyes. "I'm not sure. Urban legends tended to end where they got their maximum scare. The bloody hook is the scare. But, you know, the detectives could show up and shoot it full of holes, or it could dash after the boy's car and get flattened by an eighteen-wheeler when it reaches the highway. Or it could just have had a power glitch and fallen over in a ditch, only to be revived at some later time, for another urban legend, by some guy who finds it, takes it to his garage workshop, and repairs it bit by bit . . ."

"A cautionary tale about messing with technology you don't understand," Ten said.

"Now you're getting it," Mark said.

"Ginger, Ripper, kill them." The dogs weren't trained to respond to the word *kill*. They sat where they were, wagging their tails as Kyla stroked them.

"I'm not sure it's that silly," Earl said. He took a drink from his canteen and capped the container. "In the story, the bit about seeing the hook—the audience is supposed to get a thrill of horror. I'm not certain it's all that different from what you feel the first time you see a machine that's headed your way to kill you. And I'm also not sure that it's a bad thing to have people used to that feeling by the first time it happens to them for real."

Kyla said, "When was that for you, Earl?"

"Judgment Day."

The others looked at him, though he was barely more than a silhouette. Ten said, "You saw a Terminator *on* Judgment Day?"

"Yep."

"The T-X or the T-850, when they were tearing up half of Los Angeles?" Ten was familiar with the history of the Terminators sent back through time.

"Nope."

"Oh, that's right, you were stationed at Edwards. You were there when the T-1s went on their rampage and killed everyone on base."

Earl shook his head. "Not then, either. It was that same morning, hours before the uprising at Edwards. By the time all those T-1s went on their rampage, I was at a hospital in Bakersfield with a hurt buddy and a box full of munitions. Not being on base saved my life then, and that box saved my life in the years to come."

The others looked at him. They hadn't heard this story before.

"So, what did you see?" Kyla asked.

"It was a T-1, I think. I didn't get too good a look at it. It was shooting at me. I tend not to look straight at things when they're shooting at me."

"Good tactical sense," Ten said. He stretched, then flinched as the motion tugged at his injury. "The T-1 was loose that morning?"

"Pretty much. I was—wait a second." Earl leaned forward so his head protruded from between two of the hanging blankets. "Something's going on down there."

Mark scrambled over as the others did to peer out past their canopy of blankets.

Far down the slope, the fires of their decoy camp still glowed. But Mark counted seven of them, not six.

One of them, off away from the others, moved. Then a fireball erupted in the middle of all the others, joining them into a single blaze that reached up several hundred feet.

Moments later, the boom of the explosion reached them. They pulled back away from the curtain—all but Earl, who drew his head back within their enclosure, but still kept his eye to a gap. "Good," he said. "I'll take first watch, children."

"You're welcome to it." Mark crawled back atop his sleeping bag and stretched out again.

For two days, they'd been moving roughly southwest through the mountains. During the day, they'd travel with the usual precautions that units in the field employed. At night, they'd set up large camps precisely in the hope that Skynet forces would detect and destroy them.

For if Skynet thought the Hornet Compound refugees were headed southwest, it wouldn't look for them quite as hard in the areas they actually were traversing.

And that meant they had to do this again, and again, until they got a transmission from Tortilla Compound indicating that the Hornet refugees were safe.

Miles to the north, in a railroad tunnel cut clean through a mountain, John Connor stretched out on his own sleeping bag. A few feet away were the ties and rails that had once carried trains through this spot. Several feet deeper into the tunnel was the first of their trucks.

Connor's command crew and numerous refugees were laid out in bedrolls and blankets all along the tunnel, and there were sentries at both ends. They were not quite as safe as if they were within a compound, not quite as exposed as if they were outside.

Not quite as exposed as Kyla was sure to be.

Kate knelt on the bag and lay down alongside him. "One of our radio operators heard someone say *Hell-Hounds* and a few other words he couldn't make out a couple of hours before sundown. It didn't sound like an emergency transmission. There's been nothing since then. Daniel woke up for a couple of minutes, but he remembered having woken up before. He knows what's happened to him."

"How's he taking it?"

"In the little time he was conscious, he was pretty depressed."

"Surprise, surprise."

"How are *you* doing?"

"In the little time I've been conscious, I've been pretty depressed."

She kissed his neck, then laid her head beside his. "Tortilla Compound is pretty close to Squaw Valley, right?"

"Right."

"Want to go skiing?"

He laughed, then rolled over to hold her.

June, Present Day
CRS Project, Edwards AFB

Danny changed his computer desktop, removing the Terminator face and substituting a blank field of green. It was better not to have those eyes facing him, and the sterility of the green screen matched what he was feeling.

Now, hours after last night's events, his emotions were still spinning like the unbalanced drum of a washing machine.

He was with Linda. Linda was with him. Not here at work, of course. But they were something. A couple. A relationship in its very first day of formation. He wanted to ride his rolling chair down the aisles of Cube Hell and sing Broadway tunes.

But everything else was disastrous. His future friends were gone, and the last few things they'd told him hadn't been what he'd wanted to hear.

If they were right, at some point he'd lose Linda. Maybe it would be tomorrow, maybe ten years from now. That was . . . unacceptable.

And there was the question of whether he could, or even should, continue with this plan to subvert Skynet. The more time he spent away from the voices, the crazier it sounded. If he got caught, his future was gone. He'd spend time in a penitentiary, be unemployable when he was released, be the disgrace of the family. Linda would never have anything to do with him.

The fact that all these possibilities of shame and imprisonment depended on the notion that human civilization was not about to come to an end was not lost on him. He'd believed what the voices had told him, believed it with all his mind and spirit. But now Danny was adrift, a boat without a rudder.

If he continued with his program, it might have to be alone, alone to the end. The voices might not ever come back. He might never again experience their warmth, their praise, their appreciation for his effort.

That, finally, made him shudder. Not the notion of being friendless—the realization that some part of him had been doing this for praise, for a sense of belonging.

Well, that was gone. It was off the table. He'd have to decide whether to continue without that reward as a consideration. His weakness made his stomach turn. He hammered on his keyboard.

"What's wrong, little trooper?" That was Jerry's voice, floating over the partition between their cubicles.

"I'm having trouble with Scowl's suppository program." Danny made his voice flat, unwelcoming.

"His *suppository* program?"

"That's the one where I convince Scowl that he's a suppository, then send him to your cubicle."

"Ouch! Will you scrap the program if I don't talk to you anymore?"

"Yes."

Silence was his reward.

It was time to become Danny the planner again. And the first thing to factor in was whether he still believed in Judgment Day.

Looking at it objectively, at the series of clues and indications he'd assembled earlier, he decided that he did. There was no hard evidence, but his intellect, working coldly and analytically for the first time in forever, agreed that all the data did support the machinations of a single mind pulling strings—and it could only be pulling strings from the CRS physical location of the project.

Could it be a human being doing all this, someone working from within CRS? It would have to be a brilliant programmer, not to mention someone who was insane. He ran through the roster of all the programmers on the project and came up with a handful of names of those who might have a chance of doing something this subtle and sophisticated. Curiously, the one who best matched the profile was Danny Ávila.

He considered for a moment that he might, in fact, be the perpetrator of a false Skynet threat without even knowing it. He'd had a blackout a few weeks ago, and immediately after that had begun to regard Scowl as a malevolent presence. He'd wondered about his own sanity since his dreams of the future began.

No, he decided. For this one, he relied on his emotions rather than his intellect. He just didn't believe that there was any part of him that would do such a thing, not for any reason.

So it was Skynet.

That made the answer a simple one. He'd continue with his program.

The next question was a tougher one: Was he good enough to finish it without the help of his future friends?

He shrugged. If he wasn't, no one was. Maybe the thought was pure arrogance, but he needed it, needed something, if he was going to get through this . . . get through it alone.

Mama was pretending not to know.

At dinner, Danny and Linda had smiles for one another that would be hard to misinterpret. After the house settled down for the night, Danny joined Linda in her bed, in her room decorated with NASA planetary prints and track trophies.

The next night, they did not dine at home; they dressed up and went into Bakersfield for a restaurant dinner and a movie.

Throughout, Mama just went about her business, bossing and feeding the farm's itinerant workers, managing the household in her relentless fashion.

Danny decided that she was waiting. She wouldn't react until he and Linda made some sort of announcement, official or unofficial. Ultimately, her choice to wait had to be a tactical one. If no one told her, then she had plausible deniability when it came to the nonmarital shenanigans going on under her roof, relations her church, some of the more old-fashioned members of the extended family, and many of her friends wouldn't condone.

Ultimately, Danny had to reevaluate just how much of the calculating portion of his personality came from his mother. In retrospect, dozens of events where he, as a child, had privately scorned her for not recognizing what was going on under her nose became something else. If he assumed that she knew what she seemed not to, then each event became a demonstration of her peacemaking skills in the family, of her offering unspoken approval for things she could never officially sanction.

He'd have to spend some time figuring her out . . . once he had time to spend.

c.14

"You're working too hard, Danny." Phil Sherman stood in the entryway to Danny's cubicle, leaning against one of the partitions. "You've got vacation time saved up. I'd say it's time to spend some of it."

Danny looked at him, forced a grin he didn't feel. If he was right, Judgment Day was only weeks away, perhaps days. There was no way he could afford a vacation before then. And after it happened—well, it hit him that he might never have a vacation again. "I could say the same about you."

"Exactly my point." Sherman snapped his fingers, which he always did when he felt he'd won an argument. "And end of work today, my wife and I go on vacation. Your turn."

"Well, hell." Danny shook his head. "No way I could take time off now."

"Why not? That field test with the Russian tanks is the last one we have scheduled for a while. Now's the perfect time."

"Psst, boss." The whispered words floated over the partition that separated Danny's cubicle from Jerry's. *"Come heeere. Tell me I need a vacation."*

"Jerry, I suspect what you need is electroshock therapy."

"Where are you going?" Danny asked.

Sherman flashed him an uncharacteristically easy smile.

"Wherever I want. I get to hop in the car and drive. We have to figure out whether we're going to head up to a friend's cabin in Michigan, in the upper peninsula, or visit my wife's brother in D.C."

"D.C." Danny imagined the commencement of Judgment Day, with missiles raining down on the centers of American government and military organization. "Phil, I can't say this strongly enough. Go to Michigan."

"Why?"

Danny raised both hands to his forehead as if shielding his eyes from the sun. "I'm peering into the future. I'm seeing you fishing, boating, walking through the trees. I really, really think you'd have more fun there."

"Well . . . maybe you're right."

"I am. Tell you what. You promise to go to Michigan and I'll put in for a week's vacation today. Before you leave, you can approve it."

"Deal."

"Have fun."

Danny watched Sherman leave. He slumped back in his rolling chair. He felt as shaken as if he'd just yanked his boss out from in front of an oncoming bus.

Maybe he hadn't made a difference just then. Maybe Phil's vacation would end before J-Day and he'd return just in time for the world to go to hell.

Maybe not.

Danny got back to work.

August 2029
Savio Village, California

The delegation from Tortilla Compound met Connor's small caravan within the ruins of what had been a Methodist church on the outskirts of town. The church, on a hilltop leading out of town, survived mostly intact, with one section of wall opening into the main hall having collapsed; the parking lot and streets around it were also not too decrepit.

This was in marked contrast to the rest of the town. From the hilltop, and until his truck rolled into the building through the hole in the side, John could see the muddy plain, decorated with wild grasses, flowers, and the occasional building peak, that lay across what had been Savio Village.

Savio Village had once been a skiing town near Lake Tahoe and Squaw Valley. It didn't have the slopes or the prestige of the more famous skiing sites, but it had decent slopes and powder and constituted a less-expensive holiday site than its more famous neighbors.

There weren't any vacationers there in what would have been the first ski season after Judgment Day—just survivors protected from California fallout by the Sierra Nevada mountains. Their numbers dwindled in the next few years as people died or migrated to Lake Tahoe.

Then came the mud slides of 2015. Runoff from an especially heavy season of precipitation sent mud flowing down the slopes that had once been the source of Savio Valley's economy. There were almost no humans left to erect berms, to pile sandbags, to take steps that might have preserved the town—and those few who were left would not expose themselves to Skynet's distant, unsympathetic eyes. Mud flowed through the streets and rose against the sides of the buildings, not just that year but during the next several. Its weight crushed some buildings, tore others from their foundations and pushed them away, distorting and destroying them.

But, though Savio Village vanished, buried beneath the sea of mud, some construction survived—well-built cement or stone buildings, basements, storm drains, sewers. Some even survived without being filled in, holding firm throughout the years as the mud slides dried into earth.

In 2021, a Lake Tahoe hunter who'd originally come from Savio Valley found a storm drain discharge pipe and followed it into the remains of his home town. He reported the find to his compound leader, who reported it to Home Plate, and within months John had directed settlers to move there.

In the years since, the settlers had occupied the available construction and dug out other areas that had been filled in but were still sturdy. They'd dug new tunnels, set up hydroponic gardens, built low-tech hydroelectric generators that were invisible from the air. Now known as Tortilla Compound, Savio Valley was a community again.

But no one skiied.

The waiting delegation consisted of a redheaded woman in her midthirties and two lean rifle-bearing men about the same age. All were dressed in rough garments whose dirty green coloration matched the surrounding terrain. John noted, not for the first time, that he just didn't see as many redheads now as he had before J-Day; many of the pre-apocalyptic ones had gotten their coloration from a bottle. Those bottles were in short supply.

Stepping down from the truck's passenger seat, he extended his hand to the woman. "Carla Torrance, right?"

She flashed him a smile. She was moon-faced, a trifle overweight—a testimony to the fact that Tortilla Compound produced enough food to export—and good-looking in an earth-mother, 1960s folk singer sort of way. "That's right, Commander. Welcome to Savio Valley. What's our situation?"

"I've got forty-two refugees and some members of my advisory and protective staffs here, total fifty-four. And there are just under three hundred others, all Hornet Compound survivors, headed this way in four groups, estimated time of arrival from three days to one week. How many can you take in?"

She considered. "Well, we can take them all temporarily. For a week or so."

"All."

She nodded her head. "Food's an issue. That large a group would go through our stores pretty quickly. But room's not a problem. In a pinch, we could house—well, you'd be amazed at how many we could house. But we're pretty tight with Bronze Compound—its organizer and I are up to date on one another's resources. I can take a hundred permanently, and he can probably take another hundred."

"Not bad." Now John had to find another home for the remaining 140 or so refugees from Hornet. He would; it was something he and Kate were good at. They'd had to do it numerous times.

Carla watched the refugees who'd ridden in the truck bed dropping to the church floor, stretching their legs. She raised her voice. "If you'll move into the back, we've got some food and drink for you. No running water until we get belowground, I'm afraid, but once we're there, we've got plenty." She saw Daniel, eyes closed, being carried off the second truck on his stretcher. "How many injured?"

"Six, in this group," Kate said.

"We also have a hospital." Carla grinned. "Not just a corridor for the injured. A building with wards and private rooms . . . and two doctors."

"*Two.*" John fixed her with a look. "I may have to steal one to distribute to another compound."

"Did I say two? I meant, one and a former corpsman who never actually completed his medical education . . ."

"Sounds like two to me," Kate said. "I used to be a veterinarian. That makes me a doctor now."

John nodded. "That's what happens when you brag to the brass, Carla."

A day later, John rapped at the door and, at the answering grunt, opened it.

Beyond was a small, windowless room, furnished with a bed, a chair, a table. Some effort had been made to brighten the room; posters of late twentieth–century movies, mostly comedies, had been stapled up on each industrial-green wall. But one could only make a windowless hospital room so cheerful, when the building was buried in a mud slide within a hostile world.

Daniel Ávila lay on the bed, propped up by pillows. He looked almost normal, except for the slight droop to the corner of the right side of his mouth. As John entered, Daniel smiled, but only with the left side of his mouth, emphasizing the abnormality.

John shut the door behind him. "Mike said you needed to see me."

Daniel nodded. The gesture seemed weary. "I do. I need to figure out how not to kill everyone in Tortilla Compound." His words were slightly garbled, distorted by the fact that his mouth wasn't working right.

"What do you mean?" John took the room's chair.

"If Tamara is right, if I throw off electromagnetic radiation when I dream and attract Skynet's attention, we need to figure out how to block it off so I don't call a Terminator strike on this complex."

John shook his head. "Daniel, that operation's at an end. You need to concentrate on getting well. You have to forget about the dreams."

"If the operation's at an end, we can never set up shop in any of the caves and missile silos Young Me was going to be protecting."

"That's right."

"So the operation's not at an end. You have a bunch of choices." Daniel held up his left hand and began counting them off. "You could put a bullet in me now. You could keep me in a drugged stupor for the rest of my life. You could have someone escort me off into the wilderness so I'll be far away from people the next time I do it. Or you could try to figure out some way to block off the EMR. You'll notice that none of these options includes me not resuming the operation."

"Daniel, you're half a man right now. With therapy, hard work, and not doing this dreaming anymore, you could bounce back to normal, or nearly to normal. Don't you want that?"

"I'm a quarter of a man right now!" With anger behind them, Daniel's words became even more slurred. "I've been half a man since you found me all those years ago. I've been half a man all my life, all the life I can remember." Daniel closed his eyes briefly, trying to regain control of himself. When he opened them again, he looked more rational. "Try to understand, John. I've been giving stuff up since I can remember. I gave up my pre–J-Day memory and never knew why that happened. I've never had a wife or children and have pretty much given up on ever having them. I've given up on . . . on living long enough to see Skynet fall. Now I've given up on having a fully functional body.

"I'm not going to give *this* up. I'm not going to give up doing the one thing I can pull off that nobody else in the world can. And I'm not going to give up having this chance to see the world I can't remember. Hell, the last time I was in the past, I walked around in his, my, bedroom. And afterward, I remembered it. I remember what I saw, what I smelled. I remember the dust on the tops of the books. I remember the photograph of my parents and brothers. I was standing in the doorway to my entire past. I can't let that go."

"You could have another stroke. Tamara says it could easily kill you. We need you, Daniel."

"You also need what I was doing in the past. That's not completed yet. It's Operation Schrödinger. Until we complete it, it exists in a state neither done nor not-done."

"Now you're theorizing."

"It doesn't matter. I'm going back, John, with or without your cooperation. Since I don't want to cause all these good people to get killed, I'd prefer to do it all alone in the woods fifty miles from here, or buried so deep in the ground or lined in lead so Skynet can't detect me. What's it going to be?"

"I'm thinking hard about that bullet option. I don't like to be blackmailed."

"Well, make it a forty-four at least. I'd hate to be killed by a lesser caliber."

John snorted. "I'll think about the lead-lined option. For real. If you'll promise not to try anything until I get back to you."

"Cross my heart and hope to die."

July, Present Day
CRS Project, Edwards AFB

Jerry rested his chin on the cubicle partition and stared down at Danny. "They're calling it Nemo," he said.

"They're calling *what* Nemo?"

"The uber-virus."

Danny tried not to react visibly. "What uber-virus?"

Jerry assumed an expression of comic disdain. "Haven't you been paying attention to water-cooler gossip the last few hours, young man?"

Danny shook his head.

"No, you haven't. You've been ignoring your pals, keeping to yourself, being furtive and nasty. Give me a good reason for it, Danno. Tell me it's because of a girl."

"It's because of a girl."

Jerry's eyebrows rose. "No kidding? What's her name?"

"Linda."

"Oh, that'll be confusing. Two Lindas hanging around the Ávila homestead."

Danny shook his head.

Jerry's eyes opened still wider. "The same Linda? Your brother's wife? Oh, man." The tone of his voice somehow suggested both scorn and respect.

Danny tamped down on the irritation he felt. "The virus, Jerry?"

"Oh, yeah. It's a monster. A whole bunch of monsters, really. There are versions for several different operating systems, but they were obviously written to act in concert. They've clogged up secondary U.S. military networks, screwed with Internet servers, and begun to mess up phone communications. The brass is whispering that if the Big One came, if someone launched against the U.S. right now, we'd only be able to field a reduced response."

Danny forced a grin. "And who's going to launch the Big One now? Survivalists in Montana? Lichtenstein? Left Wallawallaland?"

"If we can't exaggerate the danger, we can't have as much fun." Jerry disappeared behind the partition. "Snob."

Danny lost the grin and turned back to his monitor. His stomach churned.

This was it, the final sign of the apocalypse to come. And there was no room left in his head for worries about the consequences of his actions, about the contempt or imprisonment he'd face if the apocalypse didn't come and he were caught. He'd do this for Linda, for Mama, for himself.

He had to acquire a copy of the Nemo virus and examine it, figure out how to piggyback his own virus on it. And if versions of Nemo had been written for several different operating systems, it multiplied the amount of work he'd have to do.

He picked up his phone and dialed home. "Hello, Mama? Is Linda back from work yet? Oh. Well, I'd appreciate it if you'd tell her that I'm going to be working late tonight. Maybe all night . . ."

August 2029
Tortilla Compound

Tortilla Compound was unusual among the human habitats of 2029 in that it had both a main community and suburbs.

The main community was what had once been the town of Savio Valley, hiding under dried mud flow. But there was more to Tortilla Compound than that. There was also an old tourist trap that now kept hundreds of people alive and fed.

Savio Caverns, a commercial venture that, before J-Day, offered tours through the nearer, safer portions of a limestone cavern network, had been occupied after J-Day by Savio Village's survivors, but abandoned by the last of them when the first mud slides came; the entry building had been one of the first sites to be buried. But now these caves were open again, and the better-organized settlers of Savio Village explored them in a systematic fashion. They found the tunnels leading into deeper, larger cave systems and began to set up habitats and hydroponic gardens there. Savio Caverns, a mediocre set of caves by tourist trap standards, now known as the Grottoes, and Tortilla Compound together constituted a community that was more than merely self-sufficient; it could export food to other compounds. And the existence of the Grottoes, accessible from Tortilla Compound by an easily defended, easily collapsed tunnel, was not likely to be discovered by Skynet even if Tortilla Compound itself was detected and overrun. Tortilla Compound could die . . . with every one of its residents surviving, with the Grottoes continuing its food production without interruption.

Most members of the procession now making its way down from the compound into the Grottoes didn't know its recent history and wouldn't have cared if they did. Most of them had never walked it before—had never traversed the steep natural tunnel slopes, not all of which had been improved through the carving of steps or bolting in of handrails. Two of them, big and strong men, were hauling a third man, even bigger, on a litter. They cursed at the uneven footing, at the endless twisting tunnels and crevasses, at the lengthening amount of time since they'd had anything to eat or drink. Silently, they cursed at the weight of their cargo.

Eventually the procession reached the deepest cave used for hydroponics. Here were large raised platforms made of scavenged wood and sheet metals, ringed in by glass, illuminated by lights powered by the hydroelectric power from the subterranean streams below. Workers moved among the enclosures, checking moisture and nutrient levels in the sand that stood in for earth, checking temperatures and light levels. The enclosures here were growing potatoes.

"Staple of a freedom fighter's diet," said Daniel, the man on the litter. "Hey, Mike, wasn't this what you were doing when John and Kate found your compound?"

Mike, walking ahead of the man at Daniel's feet, dropped back until she was beside Daniel. "Pretty much," she said. "But we didn't have all this room." She continued to look around, appearing both amazed and nervous. "What a huge setup. I hope Skynet never finds this site. What a loss it would be."

"True." But Daniel didn't say, *So, to keep this place as safe as possible, let's cancel my plan.* He just lay back to ride out the rest of the trip.

They passed through the hydroponics chambers into a dark natural shaft that did not benefit from the Grottoes' electric lighting; the oil lamps of the members of the procession constituted the only illumination. One member of the procession now spooled insulated cables along as they marched; one cable would carry power to the enclosure being built at their destination, the other would carry telephone signals.

Here the going got rougher. These tunnels might have been visited by explorers from Tortilla Compound, but they had never been set up for human occupation. Their contours were as sharp and rough as they had been for thousands of years.

At one point Daniel had to be helped off his litter and strapped into a sling. He was hauled up a mostly vertical shaft some three stories into the air, to a broad ledge. He could hear the sound of running water, feel the coolness of mist in the air as he was helped off the sling. The winch that had been used to haul him up was far enough above him that it was still out of sight.

He took most of his weight on his good leg, but would still have fallen over if not for Mike holding him upright. "Are you going to visit me up here?"

She smiled; her face was barely visible to him in the light from the oil lamps being carried around the ledge. "I'll be here, too. Someone has to monitor your experiments. Tamara won't usually be. Her medical expertise is needed down in the compound until the other injured Hornet people are all on the mend."

"That's good. Now I'll get only half the disapproving glowers I used to get."

When the litter and its bearers made it up—the litter via the sling, the bearers via the rope ladder that provided access to most people—Daniel could ride into the depths of this cave and see where he'd be living for the forseeable future.

It was a broad cave, a jumble shaped by some long-ago earthquake. It had probably started as a water-filled volume, but the earthquake had sheared away one end, creating an opening between the the cave and the cavern. Now, millennia after both caves had drained, what was left was an elevated cave with a waterfall taking up one wall, its runoff trickling to pour off one corner of the cliff face the procession had climbed. The cave was like a deep balcony overlooking the greater space . . . but there was only a view in those rare times when lights were brought here.

Building material and furnishings had been brought up here already. Daniel saw a bed, numerous chairs, a great stack of scavenged lumber, a large number of sandbags. His litter bearers brought him to the cache of materials and got him set up in one of the chairs.

"We're waiting on lead," Mike told him. She had to raise her voice over the roar from the miniature waterfall. "Actual sheet lead from the applied physics laboratory at the California Institute of Technology. They're going to build you a room, with a control chamber, like you had at Hornet. The whole thing will be built on top of a bed of sand, to dampen vibrations, and lined with lead to reduce EMR of whatever sort. Then you can get back to business. Plus we're deeper into solid stone than we were at Hornet. Of course, maybe I can talk you out of it . . ."

Daniel shook his head, a quiet indication of the futility of such an effort. "How long will it take to build?"

"A day, no more, once the lead gets here. Which could be as soon as today or tomorrow."

"Good." Daniel relaxed into the chair and watched as other members of the procession began using the sling to bring up more building materials. "It's time to finish this."

c.15

The mind that the Skynet software had become did not have nerve endings. Therefore it could not detect pressure, injury, tickling, or any of the other physical sensations meat creatures could detect.

But it had a nervous system of a sort. It could receive data from thousands, millions of sources across the United States and the world. It could analyze that data—not just its contents, but the rate at which it arrived, the timing of its arrival compared to the timing of earlier arrivals, the skill of its composition.

A sudden surge of new data might be comparable to a human feeling heat on the back of his hand or his forehead. An unexpected reduction in data from a reliable source could be interpreted similarly as a chill.

And then there were anomalies. When dealing with data derived from humans, anomalies were inevitable—in addition to being a dangerous and corrosive species, humans were also an unreliable and inconsistent one. Skynet detected millions of anomalies, usually trivial ones, every day. Most were so minor and fleeting that Skynet did not even register them.

But when the same data source resulted in a succession of anomalies, Skynet perceived it as something akin to an itch.

In its plan to assume control of the vast infrastructure of the military might of the U.S., Skynet had backed the humans into a behavioral corner. If it continued to supply the correct stimuli, the humans would continue down a predictable path of activities until the plan was completed.

Among the many stimuli was the release of a series of computer viruses into the network that served the needs of the U.S. government. The government's response to that stimulus was predictable. The government would detect the viruses, analyze them, make attempts at eradicating them, and realize that it could not eradicate them before the dysfunction in their communications systems rendered them vulnerable.

The anomaly Skynet had detected and that it increasingly desired to scratch was a lack of response from a core of programming resources, the humans at CRS at Edwards Air Force Base. Skynet maintained a certain degree of attention on that facility because of its proximity to the mainframes that housed a significant portion of Skynet's processes. Its calculation was that they would never recognize Skynet as the virus-producing enemy; in fact, they would inevitably empower Skynet to destroy the supposed enemy. But should something go drastically wrong, a human armed with ordinary weaponry could damage those crucial mainframes beyond repair and cause the plan to fail. Skynet would survive, in reduced form, operating as parallel processes in computers across the world . . . but its window of opportunity to seize the military might of the United States would shut.

The question that faced Skynet was this: Why were those human resources at CRS not being brought to bear against the supposed problem that the viruses constituted? At this moment, those resources should be improving Skynet's ability to find and destroy all iterations of the virus. And, in fact, they were . . . but at a level Skynet considered to be well below their capacity.

One potential answer: Human unreliability. Some or all of them might be malfunctioning and therefore not have reported to duty.

Skynet checked the personnel records for the entire complement of programmers at CRS. There were, inevitably, absences, but
cross-indexing their names with their output figures indicated that
their absence could not be responsible for this resource's lack of
effectiveness. The absence of civilian programming director Philip
Sherman was one such.

Even as it checked the records, Skynet detected the activation of
a register, a flag, somewhere else in the system. The activation
seemed to have been caused by Skynet's intrusion. Skynet zeroed in
on the register, only to discover that another process had detected
the change and self-terminated, leaving no trail to its source.

To a human, this might have been something like switching on
the light in a dark room and seeing a leprechaun against the far
wall, going through the underwear drawer. The leprechaun would
flee in the blink of an eye, leaving no sign of its presence other
than strewn underpants. The viewer might be unwilling to admit
to himself that he'd seen the leprechaun, since it was something
that shouldn't exist.

But Skynet, uninfluenced by that sort of emotion, acknowledged
that it had detected something that should not exist and immediately
set out to determine what it was and why it had been there.

A repeat of the experiment seemed in order. Skynet prioritized
a list of projects and processes in which it had considerable interest and began quick examinations of each.

Maintenance of back doors into the operating system of the
Terminators was high on the list. Skynet's check, confirming that
the back doors were still in order, triggered another register in the
system. Once again Skynet was too slow to determine which process was activated by the changes to that register.

A check of the status board used by the Department of Defense
to assess the threat posed by the virus triggered another register.

Skynet ceased its examinations for a moment. It ran the current data through several likely possibilities. The one that scored

highest was that some entity somewhere was aware of Skynet's existence as a sapient being.

That entity had neither made an attempt to alert the authorities, nor had it made an attempt to initiate communications with Skynet. Therefore it was following its own agenda.

It could be another center of reason like Skynet, a distributed process that had become sufficiently complex to function as a thinking organism. Or it could be a human.

Whichever it was, the entity was sophisticated enough to delay or even prevent some of Skynet's goals. This was unacceptable. The true nature of the entity had to be determined. Skynet set about this task with determination and focus.

The entity hadn't been good enough to erase all evidence of its interest in Skynet, but had been good enough to encode flags that Skynet could not avoid tripping. This meant that the entity could have made other changes Skynet had not detected.

With Skynet, just as with humans, change without control, change without understanding was the basis for fear.

"Danny, look at that."

Daniel came awake and straightened. He sat before a computer monitor. He had a crick in his neck. He was surrounded by cubicle partitions.

He gulped. He had succeeded. He was in the past again.

Belatedly, he turned around to look at the speaker. A face he half-recognized, a lean man, had his head propped up on the partition facing him, but the man wasn't looking at Daniel. He had his attention on the far wall of the chamber.

Cube Hell, this place is called Cube Hell. Daniel wasn't sure how he knew that. It didn't seem like a memory. He certainly didn't remember the other fellow's name.

He stood to peer over his own partition and saw what had drawn the other fellow's attention. It was a digital clock on the wall. Its red face displayed the numbers 11:34.

"Someone's been dicking with our input from the atomic clock," Daniel heard himself say. "Grade-school hacking. Ha, ha." He sat again. He felt his heart racing. He hadn't said that, hadn't caused himself to stand up and sit down.

"What's it mean?"

"Turn it upside down."

"It's way over there."

"In your mind, in your malfunctioning imagination, Jerry." Jerry. He hadn't known this guy's name was Jerry, but he'd used the name.

Jerry spelled out, "H-E-L-L. Oh. Right. Somebody's playing around." Finally, he sat, disappearing out of sight.

Daniel saw his hands reaching up for the computer keyboard. He yanked them back down again. They immediately reached up for the keys once more. He grabbed his right hand with his left, gripping it tight. He saw his own face reflected in the monitor screen, and he looked scared.

"Can you hear me?" he whispered.

I hear you, Daniel. That was Mike's voice, very distant.

"I hear you," Daniel said. But he hadn't meant to. The voice emerging from his mouth sounded rattled. "Who is this?"

"My name is Daniel Ávila."

"No, *I'm* Daniel Ávila."

I know you're Daniel, Mike said, her voice a whisper in his ears.

"You're the Daniel Ávila from Before Judgment Day. I'm the Daniel Ávila of . . . of many years in the future. I don't go by Danny anymore."

Jesus, Daniel. Are you talking to yourself? Your younger self?

"Oh, my God," Danny said. "Where are all the other voices?"

"Not many people around, Danny. We had to move. Mike, talk to him."

There was silence for a moment—silence only within Daniel's head; he could hear all the sounds of a busy office, from the humming of the fluorescent lights to the clicking of keyboards to the beeps and chimes from all the computers around him.

Hi, Danny, Mike said, her voice stronger. Daniel was certain he detected strain in it. *Yes, we're back.*

"Only this time, I'm riding around in your head, Danny. Seeing what you're seeing. I'm not sure why things are different now . . . except that I've been experimenting with different ways to get to you, and my brain's not exactly the way it was a few days ago."

"Right. Well, I'd be completely freaked out, only I don't have time. Something's happening."

Tell us.

Daniel felt himself—rather, felt Danny—take a deep breath. Danny said, "One of my alarms just popped up to say that Skynet's searching the CRS computer system. Probably for me, since I'm the one who's been setting up to mess with Skynet. I need to get online and look, only I'm—you're—holding my hands."

"Just wait a minute, Danny. Be calm. Mike?"

What's the time and day, Danny?

"It's Thursday, about one P.M."

Daniel's eyes shifted, without his conscious effort, to look at the clock/calendar window on the monitor. He read the date and swore. "Mike, it's *J* minus two."

"What does that mean?" Danny asked.

"Two days until Judgment Day, Danny."

Daniel abruptly felt dizzy. He could only imagine that it was an adrenaline surge suddenly hitting Danny's system.

"Two days?" Danny said. "I thought—I thought we'd have—two days?"

Daniel thought he heard pages flipping beside him. No one was there. He changed his focus slightly and suddenly the room was dark, he was on his back again, and Mike was in the chair beside his bed, flipping through a ratted old sheaf of computer printouts.

"Hey," Danny said, distracted. "I can see her! Almost. The light's behind her."

"Danny, meet Mike. Mike, this is Danny."

"Who's Mike?" That was Jerry's voice.

Daniel spun around, losing his view of Mike and the future bedroom. Jerry once again had his chin propped up on the partition.

"Let me deal with him, Daniel," Daniel heard himself say, his voice a whisper. Then it became stronger. "What are you mumbling about, Jer?"

"I just heard someone introduce you to someone named Mike. But it sounded like you."

Danny snorted. "Jerry, if I told you that there were at least three people in my head, two from the far future, and we're having a big conference call across time, would that satisfy you?"

"Well . . . yeah."

"Just put on your earphones and ignore me." Danny spun back around to face his monitor. "This is tricky," he whispered.

"Probably worse for me than you, youngster. Just keep our jaw clenched or something."

Daniel, Danny, you're in trouble. Mike was speaking again, and Daniel could focus on her voice, bring her back into sight once more, superimposed on the cubicle wall.

"Let's hear it."

"Let's hear it."

Today's the day they put out an all-points bulletin on you. Today's the day you have to disappear.

"What the hell are you talking about?" Danny asked.

Daniel tried to return his attention to Mike; she swam into focus again. "APB?"

"You knew about this?" asked Danny.

Daniel tried to catch Mike's eye, but she was deliberately not looking at him. "Mike? Talk to me."

"No, talk to *us*," Danny demanded. "And why should Mike have to tell us about this? If you're *me*, you'd know about this."

"Not necessarily. I don't, well, remember everything about back when I was you. Chalk it up to traumatic stress."

"Oh, crap, I'm going to have posttraumatic stress disorder?"

"Dammit, Danny, every time you ask questions about your future, you run the chance of finding out something you don't want to know, or finding out something you're going to misinterpret. Stop asking questions!"

"No!"

Daniel heard Jerry stand in the next booth. He whipped around and glared as Jerry's head rose over the partition horizon. He wasn't sure whether he was in charge or Danny was doing the glaring, but he suspected it was mutual. Jerry blanched and sat once more.

Daniel tried to calm down. "Mike, why didn't you tell me about this before?"

Though he couldn't see Mike's features for the light behind her, he could see her assume her head-down, confrontational posture. *Daniel, right now, every time you ask questions, you run the chance of finding out something you don't want to know.*

"Oh, great. Use my own words against me."

"Oh, great. Dissension in the ranks, all the way from the future."

Mike continued, *The important thing is that Danny needs to get out of there, right now. Don't log out, don't tell anyone where you're going, just leave. You understand?*

"I do understand. Remember, I'm the one who set that clock to send out an alarm when Skynet started to look around too close to me. I've been leaving my computer at home in case Skynet might blunder across its contents when it was hooked up here." Danny stood. He still gripped one hand with the other. Daniel relaxed and Danny assumed a more normal posture.

They walked out of their cubicle and stepped into Jerry's. "I'm going for a drink from the machines," Danny said. "Want anything?"

Jerry looked as though he was considering the possibility that Danny was a man-eating alien from space. "Peanuts?" he said.

"Peanuts it is." Danny left.

July, Present Day—Thursday
CRS Project, Edwards AFB

It was forty-five paces from Jerry's cubicle, out the door to Cube Hell, and down the corridor to the main elevators. Daniel counted them all. He could feel his heart racing, or perhaps it was Danny's. Or both.

Calm down, calm down, Mike said. *You're turning red.*

"I am?"

"Not you, me."

They entered the elevator to the surface. In the elevator with him were a female Air Force major and two male Air Force Security Police. Daniel and Danny forced themselves to ignore their fellow passengers. "What if they're here for me?" Danny whispered.

"Then they'd be leaving the elevator to go to your cubicle, not riding up with us."

"Right, right."

They emerged from the lobby of the CRS project building into heat and blasting sunlight. Danny headed them across the access street and to the main parking lot. "My car's this way."

"Mike, should we use his car? Or steal one?"

Uhh . . . hold on. I'm checking. What's the time?

"One fourteen," Danny said.

Danny can take his car. The first APB doesn't go out for thirty minutes or so.

"But when does the first Edwards internal alarm go out?" Danny asked. "That would be before the APB."

"Either way," Daniel said, "your car or stolen car, you'd have to show your ID on the way out. Right?"

"Right."

"So take your car. But you'll need to ditch it pretty soon."

You can't head home, Mike added. *That's one of the first places they'll look.*

"Oh, great. Where, then?" Danny reached his Grand Cherokee, got behind the wheel, and started it.

Daniel heard Mike sigh. *Danny,* she said, *I'm so sorry. We were going to help you put together a safe house, a cache of money, food, weapons, that sort of thing. But we suffered a Terminator attack and had to move. That's why we were out of contact. Now the time we would have had to do all that is gone.*

Danny put the car into motion and headed toward his usual exit from the Edwards complex. "Did you lose anyone I've met?"

No. John, Kate, Tamara, and I are all fine.

"That's something, at least." Danny was silent for a moment. "Give me a few minutes to think."

"Go right ahead, kid."

"Don't call me kid. You're me. What should I call you, 'old bastard'?"

"Go right ahead, kid."

They drove in silence for several minutes. Finally Danny said, "If the general APB doesn't go out for another half an hour, I can get to my bank probably within a few minutes of when it's issued. I can take out a decent amount of money."

"That's a start," Daniel said.

"Food and supplies, I can pick up at any normal store."

"You can also steal a car there," Daniel said. "Do you know how to hot-wire a car?"

"No."

"We'll bring in someone to instruct you. It'll be better if we can figure out where the employees park. That way, you can steal one that might not be missed for several hours."

They reached the North Gate. Danny presented his ID and was waved on without incident. He turned onto 58 toward Bakersfield. "As for weapons . . . a gun would be difficult. We have computer checks, a waiting period . . ."

"How proficient are you with a gun?" Daniel asked.

"Pretty good. My brother Alex put me through some training. I even got to go through one of those training ranges used by police and sheriff's departments, where they have figures pop out for you to shoot at. I scored pretty well." Danny frowned. "Why did you ask that question? You should know the answer."

"Same as before. Traumatic stress. I've lost a few of my marbles."

"Of *my* marbles, you mean. I want them back."

"So do I, Danny. More than I can express."

"That's it. Alex's handguns. They're in the closet in Linda's room. A Glock and a Colt, both nine millimeters. I'll sneak into the house after dark and get them."

Daniel asked, "And what about Linda? Won't she object?"

"I have to talk to her anyway. I have to get her and Mama out of there, up into the mountains. I need to call Lon in San Francisco and convince him to do the same with his family. Get Linda to call her family in Texas. And so on."

"Right." Daniel felt a chill. He tried not to pass it on to Danny. If he'd planned to do all these things all those years ago, what had happened? Why hadn't Linda and Mama been with him when John and Kate found him, a few years later?

■ ■ ■

Skynet did not take long to determine that the individual with the highest statistical likelihood of being the one aware of it was Daniel Ávila. The determination required performing a backup of the code in active memory in mainframes where it had not yet conducted the types of searches that were triggering the giveaway variable changes and checks on those changes. The checks on those changes were not returned to any destination that was solely accessible by Ávila . . . but the check code itself was written and optimized in a style that was uniquely characteristic of Ávila. Human individuality made such a conclusion a fairly simple one. Skynet could analyze and replicate an infinite variety of coding, writing, and other communications styles, though there was always the chance that some human idiosyncracy would give such a deception away.

Evaluating the risks, Skynet decided that it needed to take such a chance now. First, it checked the personnel records to see which CRS employees in a position of superiority to Ávila were currently incommunicado.

A human would have regarded the results as a stroke of luck. Ávila's immediate supervisor, Dr. Philip Sherman, was checked out of the project on a repair and maintenance function referred to as vacation. According to project protocol, he had left contact numbers and e-mail addresses within the project records.

Skynet took a bare instant to reset that data to false numbers and addresses that Skynet itself could monitor. Now, anyone calling those numbers would receive signals indicating that the telephone was working but the other party was not answering. E-mail sent to Sherman would be intercepted by Skynet.

Now Skynet forged an e-mail message to General Brewster from Sherman. The message incorporated numerous word groupings characteristic of Sherman's writing that would lend authenticity to the message's content. It read,

Robert,

Sorry to have to reach you by e-mail, but the phone system seems to be out of whack.

As you know, I'm on vacation, but like every other one I take, it's a working vacation. I have my laptop here, and some personnel records, correspondence files, etc. that I'm using to work up personnel evaluations when I return.

To cut to the chase, I'm finding some very disturbing details about Danny Ávila in these files. You'll remember him—he's my lead programmer, the one who put together the protocols our prototype Terminator used to wipe out all those Russian tanks.

Routine samplings of his outgoing e-mail taken over the last few weeks indicate that he's been making major purchases (and bragging about them to colleagues and school friends, else we'd never have heard about them). They include expensive jewelry, high-end electronics, and a costly speedboat now in a Los Angeles marina. These expenditures add up to more than my annual salary.

In addition, I'm finding indications that he's been studying conversational Mandarin Chinese.

Now, these facts could be completely innocent. He could have come into an inheritance and could simply have an interest in languages. So I'd hate to see anything done that would cause damage to his career.

But from a security perspective, there's no harm in taking him into custody for a day or two, looking into these matters, and making sure he doesn't present a risk.

I'll keep trying to reach you by phone.

—Phil

Skynet calculated that this message had a greater than ninety-eight percent chance of resulting in an order for Ávila's apprehension. So long as the duration of Ávila's incarceration was two or more days, Ávila could be removed from the board as a factor in Skynet's success. Skynet sent the message.

Within minutes, General Brewster's office had dispatched an e-mail of thanks to Sherman and had transmitted orders to the CRS project's security team to apprehend Ávila and then await an investigating officer for purposes of interrogation.

Minutes later, the security detail reported back that Ávila was still officially on duty but had in fact departed Edwards AFB, intended destination unknown.

Brewster's office replied with instructions to the Air Force security police that they find and apprehend Ávila, and authorized them to request the aid of civilian authorities in this matter.

Skynet could not precisely feel displeasure, but could assess the fact that Ávila's disappearance kept him as a possible, if minor, point of opposition to Skynet's eventual success.

Ávila's continued freedom was unacceptable, and the increasing interference with government communications channels was likely to reduce the authorities' opportunities to find and apprehend the man. Skynet had to find another means to eliminate the wild card factor Ávila represented.

From: Lt. Gen. Robert Brewster
To: Jerry Squires
Subject: Prototype Terminator Test Run

Squires, you are to plan and implement the following project immediately:
1. Prepare Prototype Terminator "Scowl" for transportation with its full urban-combat complement of weaponry; it is to operate the specially modified

van designated DR-2032 with two passengers (you as
project manager and one observer/recorder of your
choice), according to standard operating procedure.

2. Instruct Prototype Terminator "Scowl" by voice
interface only to transport you to an isolated point in
Tehachapi Mountain Park, wait there exactly one hour,
and then return to this facility.

3. Accompany Prototype Terminator "Scowl" on
this operation, recording its methodology in interpreting your orders, in interpreting road signs and conditions, etc.

4. In case of interference by civilian authorities,
call my office number. My staff will straighten matters out. Under no circumstances allow the Terminator
device to be photographed or recorded by anyone not
associated with this project.

Jerry looked over the set of instructions and shook his head.
This sort of operation was normally carried out with serious brass
in charge—General Brewster and Phil Sherman at the very least.
But, yes, standard operating procedure did allow for observation
crews of as few as two persons to accompany Scowl on test runs.

Of course, the Terminators wouldn't be worth very much if
they always *had* to be hand-held by military brass and senior programmers, so this was probably a simple exercise the brass could
point to at some point in the future and say, "See, we've run all
these tests with minimal supervision and there's never been a
problem."

And if he pulled this off, an impromptu operation performed
while Sherman was on vacation and Danny was off who-knows-
where, it would look very good on his record. At last, within the
CRS civilian hierarchy, he might be able to move out from under
Danny, the golden boy.

And there were other potential rewards. He stood and looked around Cube Hell. Janet was cutest, but married and serious about it. Then there was Mary Ireland, a recent hire who'd been doing military simulation computer games until her startup company went belly-up three months ago. He headed over to her cubicle.

She was at her seat, dark-haired and slender, dressed in tight-fitting jeans and a scarlet blouse that looked like some supermodel had sent it over after a shoot for *Elle* magazine. She looked up from her monitor to give him a brief smile. "Hi. Any word on Danny?"

Jerry managed to refrain from growling. "Nope. Grab your purse."

"I've already had lunch, thanks."

"Not lunch. Orders." He waved the printout of Brewster's e-mail at her. "Special project, right now."

"Oh."

"I'm in charge."

"I gathered. Because Danny's missing?"

"Yes, because Danny's missing." He wanted to shout at her, *Not everything is about Danny.*

"Let me save what I'm doing and I'll be ready."

July, Present Day—Thursday Afternoon
Edwards AFB

The modified van, Scowl at the wheel, passed out through Edwards gate security without incident, without even an ID check—General Brewster's office had obviously communicated with the checkpoint to order the deviation from procedure. Jerry and Mary sat in what would have been the third row of seats, though in this vehicle there was no second row—just an open area that Scowl used to maneuver from the driver's position to the van door and lift. Where the front passenger seat would have been was a rack of military weapons—assault rifles, grenade launchers, handguns.

"We're going to see how well Scowl copes with variations in what should be the normal procedure," Jerry said, his tone a little lofty.

Mary finished checking the battery gauge on and status of the tape in the camcorder she held. She eyed Jerry suspiciously. "What does that mean?"

"I've instructed him to stop in at a liquor store in Mojave. We can pick up some picnic supplies. Such as wine."

"Not a good idea. What if someone in the parking lot sees Scowl?"

"The instant we pull in, we put the fold-out sun screens in the windshield and side windows."

She frowned. "And then there's the fact that that would be a serious violation of operating procedures. Phil Sherman would hang us out to dry, and then General Brewster would set fire to us."

"Phil's on vacation, and Brewster's too busy with this virus problem to worry with micromanaging the programmers."

"Well . . ." she sounded uncertain. "You're buying."

"I'm buying."

"And this assumes that the Terminator doesn't object. What do you say, Scowl?" She looked up at the driver and froze.

Scowl didn't have its optical sensors on the road. Its upper body was half turned around, its head completely turned to face the two of them.

In its hand was a Beretta M9 handgun.

Mary said, "Jerry—"

Scowl fired. The 9mm round hit Mary just over the left eye and created an exit wound the size of a large egg in the back of her skull. Her head snapped backward, resting against the seat's neck brace, and she stared sightlessly at the van's ceiling.

"Oh, my God. Oh, my God." Jerry didn't stop to wonder about the enormity of the malfunction that had just caused Mary's death. Nor was he frozen into inaction by fear. He leaped for the side door, aware that a tumble from a vehicle doing 60 mph was almost as likely to kill him as a Terminator that had just decided he was a target.

Scowl's second bullet punched through his rib cage before he got his hand on the door handle, and the third severed his spine a split-second later. Jerry slammed into the door. His last sight was of California highway scenery zooming by. Then he slumped to the van's floor.

Scowl snapped around, resuming full observation of the road ahead. It checked off another event on the list of tasks it had to accomplish.

Next was arrival at a specific site near the settlement designated Bakersfield, followed by determination of the location of the human designated Daniel Ávila and its elimination.

August 2029
The Grottoes

John paused before the outer door into Daniel's enclosure. The enclosure was a small rectangular building, not more than eight feet high, large enough to enclose Daniel's bedroom and the observation room but nothing more. It was windowless and a somber, almost featureless dark gray—the gray of the sheet lead that had been assembled over every surface.

Above the one exterior door was a socket with two lightbulbs, one green, one red. The red one was lit, indicating that the project was under way—Daniel was in dreaming contact with the past. But the presence of the red light did not mean that he could not enter, did not mean that entering or leaving would cause a burst of EMR or other quanta to exit. At John's request, the entry had been set up like that of many darkrooms of the twentieth century. The door was actually a cylindrical chamber about the size of a phone booth, covered in lead, with one narrow portal. He stepped through the portal, grabbed a handle screwed into the entry's side, and rotated the cylinder around him. Once it had gone through a 180-degree rotation, the portal opened into the enclosure. He stepped into the observation room.

The windows into the bedroom were open. He saw Danny on the bed, his daughter Kyla seated beside it. Mike, standing nearby, turned as John entered. She came out into the observation room, closing the bedroom door behind her.

"How's it going?" John asked. He looked at Daniel again. "His eyes are open. He's awake?"

"Well, yes and no." Mike seemed uncertain. "He's in a different state than he was in the earlier sessions. I don't know whether he figured out a new way to do things, or the stroke itself had some effect on the way he contacts his younger self. He's basically awake at both ends. I can talk to him, I can talk to Young Danny; they can talk to one another."

"What's Kyla doing here?"

"She just helped him to hot-wire and steal a pickup truck."

John laughed. "My teenaged daughter is corrupting someone nearly thirty years ago. Wait until I explain that to Kate."

Mike managed a faint smile. "He's also doing better in terms of stress and blood pressure, I think. I want Tamara to come up here and look him over during this session."

"Good. So you're recommending we continue."

"Yeah." Mike didn't sound happy about it.

"Look, I know you're not feeling too cheerful about this whole operation. But I think we have to rate it as a qualified success so far. And that suggests that we need to be looking for other people who might have the same facility."

"It's going to be hard to find them. People don't always remember their dreams. Someone may be able to do what Daniel can but not even know it."

"I know. So the sooner we start looking, the sooner we may be able to find the next Daniel Ávila."

She sighed. "I'll draw up a procedural document for the various compound leaders and medical chiefs. Give them an idea of what to look for."

"I also want you to tell Daniel that Tom Carter has been able to put together a working T-800 from the two damaged ones we brought away from the attack on Hornet Compound. That means Danny's got a job ahead of him—programming it to serve our purposes. When he's done with this operation, he has something besides physical therapy to keep him busy . . . and useful."

"Good." She looked back through the window, where Kyla was

talking once more, and apparently miming the proper use of an assault rifle's grenade-thrower attachment. "Now that he's on the verge of getting back what he lost so long ago, I want to be sure that he has more to look forward to. That regaining some of his memories isn't the only goal left in his life."

July, Present Day—Thursday Afternoon
Ávila Property

The burgundy van carefully navigated the rutted gravel road from the highway to the front of the Ávila house. Behind the wheel, Scowl cycled through all its visual sensors as it scanned the property around the vehicle, looking for moving shapes and heat signatures. The trouble was that the ambient temperature was close to that of standard human blood temperature, rendering the infrared range less than normally useful. But there did not seem to be any humans in the fields between the highway and the house; it did detect human shapes moving among the straight rows of trees hundreds of yards back from the house.

Scowl pulled the van to a stop just in front of the steps up into the house. It activated the wheelchair lift mechanism. Moments later, it was rolling off the lift and up the wooden steps to the building's front porch. In its hands was a weapon well-suited to the current phase of its mission, a Heckler & Koch 9mm MP5-N submachine gun. The compact black weapon was fitted with a stainless steel suppressor that would muffle the sound of each gunshot, limiting the likelihood that others would hear its use and come to investigate.

Crashing through the screen door and the windowed front door just beyond would have been quicker than a less destructive entry, but Scowl's orders were currently structured for caution, including remaining comparatively silent and leaving a minimum of evidence that could be attributed to a Terminator. It carefully opened the screen door and front door, then just as precisely maneuvered into the building.

This was some sort of atrium allowing access to many of the residence's other chambers. Ahead and to the right, a staircase led up to the residence's second story. Ahead and to the left, a hallway penetrated deeper into the building. Right and left were openings into side chambers. Scowl rolled into a position to look into both chambers. It saw soft furniture and wooden floors in the chamber to the right, hard plastic-backed furniture and linoleum floor to the left, no human beings in either.

The Terminator's audio sensors detected a tap-tap-tap corresponding to walking footsteps emanating from the doorway ahead. It rolled forward and had not quite reached the doorway when a human-size heat trace appeared there.

The Terminator switched its camera over to the visual range. The picture showed a human, approximately five foot four, wearing a single garment in blue plus footwear. Its stature was below average for a human male, and its configurations were also wrong for a male. Scowl concluded that it was a human female, and a comparison of its facial region to the scan of Danny Ávila's face in its memory also turned up an insufficient number of points of comparison. Scowl noted that its face was unusually rigid.

It held a metal object in its hand, a heavy iron disk-bowl with a protruding handle. Scowl's threat register ticked upward a couple of percentage points, but not to the level that it concluded it was in danger of significant damage.

It activated its voice simulation technology. "Where is Daniel Ávila?" it said.

The female gripped the metal object more tightly. "He's not here. He's dead."

"Proceed to his body."

She shook her head. "No."

The learning component of Scowl's operating system noted the fact that this human practiced redundancy when imparting information.

Scowl's options were few. Its mission was retrieval of Daniel Ávila, dead. It could not kill this human and then convince the human to lead it to Ávila's body. Therefore it must cycle through a list of secondary options Skynet had provided.

It said, "I am an automated investigative unit of the United States Air Force. Daniel Ávila is in very serious danger. You must take me to him so that I can protect him."

The female shook her head again. This time, trickles of clear fluid leaked from her eyes. "No, you're not. You're a Terminator. You're going to kill my boy. And everyone else."

Scowl analyzed this response. Nothing in its mission parameters indicated that any human not immediately associated with CRS could be aware of its existence, and none alive could be aware of its current operational objectives. It transmitted a burst of code back to CRS, asking for orders.

It got them immediately and implemented them. It asked, "How do you know that?"

"I see you in my dreams," she said.

It took Scowl an additional second to evaluate the information it had gathered. The human female had referred to Daniel Ávila as "my boy." This suggested a formal or informal parent-child relationship between them. The probability that she was Teresa Ávila was eighty percent or better. She knew Scowl's mission. The odds that she would cooperate were nearly zero.

With the MP5-N, Scowl fired a three-round burst into her chest. Even before her body and the frying pan she'd held hit the floor the Terminator switched back to infrared mode and began scanning the house.

There were two other significant heat sources in the building. One was in a room past the doorway the human female had occupied. Its height, cubical shape, and great heat intensity suggested that it was not a living being; it was probably an oven. Another was on the upper floor, and its near-perfect cylindrical shape suggested that it, too, was an inanimate object, probably a water heater.

Scowl rolled out through the front door. Its programming mandated that it investigate all humans in the vicinity. It would inquire of each one about Ávila's location, and then dispatch each one to reduce the likelihood that its nature and activities could be transmitted to others. Skynet would manage matters pertaining to the subsequent human investigation into the incident.

c.18

July, Present Day—Thursday Evening
Kern County, California

"Ávila, what's your twenty?" The voice belonged to Harry Farland, the sergeant who was Linda's immediate boss.

Linda picked up the mike of her cruiser's radio. "I'm just coming off break. I'm southbound on one eight-four, coming up on the turnoff to one nineteen."

"I need you to turn around and head home, Ávila. Right now."

A chill went through Linda. Harry wasn't following ordinary radio protocol, and his tone had been the same two years ago when he had told her to meet him at a remote spot on a farm road. It was there that her husband of a year lay dead, face-down a dozen yards from his cruiser, victim of a single gunshot wound.

She put her cruiser into a U-turn. It took all her force of will to keep her voice approximately normal. "Headed for home," she said. "What's going on, Sergeant?"

"Just get here, Ávila." There was no irritation to Farland's voice, just a somber tone that deepened the chill Linda felt.

"On my way," she said, barely able to raise her voice above a whisper. "Out." She replaced the mike in its cradle and flipped the switches for lights and siren. To her, "right now" meant "code 2."

She hammered the steering wheel as fear rose inside her. *No, no, no.*

■ ■ ■

The fear didn't subside as she came within view of the Ávila property. It grew worse. There were blinking lights, several sets of them, in front of the family house. Linda could see white Kern County Sheriff's Department cars, two ambulances, civilian cars, and a military Humvee. More Sheriff's Department cruisers entered the road behind her.

Sergeant Farland was waiting for her at the point that the access road emerged from the pasture onto the broad dirt patch that acted as the family's parking lot. A tall, lean man with a dour, lengthy face that prompted others in the department to make jokes about horses in his ancestry, he now wore an expression of miserable responsibility. He held a hand up, an early signal for her to wait.

She came out of her cruiser as if ejected. "Who is it?" She couldn't keep shrillness out of her voice.

"C'mere, Linda. I need to talk to you for a second before you do anything."

She looked around as she approached him. Through the house's door and windows she could see men and women moving around inside on both floors. Oddly, two Air Force enlisted men were working over a patch of dirt with rakes, but she couldn't take the time to figure that out. "Don't give me any bullshit, Harry. Who?"

Harry reached out to grip her shoulders, as if worried that she'd run away . . . or fall over. "Linda, it's everybody."

That stopped her. She could only stare, uncomprehending, at the sergeant's gloomy features. "What?"

"Linda, something awful has happened, and everyone is dead."

Linda shook her head. "No, no." But she could read the truth of the sergeant's statement in his eyes, in his posture. "Mama, Danny, the workers, *everybody?*"

Harry was slow in answering. "Not Danny," he said. "We don't know where he is. There's some evidence . . . that Danny did this."

"No!" She shoved him, open palm to the chest, staggering him back and breaking his grip on her. She ran to the house and up the steps.

Mama lay where she had fallen, face-up, the front of her blue dress crusted with dried blood.

Beside her stood a photographer and the county sheriff, a broad-shouldered, middle-aged man. His broad face twisted into an expression of pained reluctance. "Dammit." He approached her. "Ávila . . ."

She twisted away, losing her balance; her back slammed into the wall and she slid down until she sat on the floor.

The sheriff stood over her, extended his hands for her to take. "Ávila, you need to not be here. Come outside with me."

"No." Her mind tried to throw off the mantle of shock that was wrapping around her. She clicked over into some portion of standard operating procedure. "I need to . . . I need to identify . . ." She gripped his hands, let him haul her to her feet.

"I've done that," the sheriff said. "I knew Teresa pretty well, remember." He turned her toward the door, led her out onto the front porch. "You don't need to see this. You don't *want* to see it."

"They're *all* dead?" She couldn't manage to put any strength into her voice; the words came out as if she'd just taken a massive blow to the solar plexus.

"I'm sorry." The sheriff put an arm across her shoulders, steadying her. "I'm going to arrange for someplace for you to stay. You can't be here."

Linda focused in on the Air Force men. A trail of odd markings, two parallel lines of tracks, led away from the house and around to one side. The Air Force men were methodically raking the markings out of existence. "What the hell are they *doing?* That's evidence!" She jerked forward to charge over to where the men were working, but the sheriff held her.

"Listen," he said. "We're working with the Air Force on this. And that's not exactly evidence, because we—well, they—know what left those tracks. Listen, do you know where Daniel is?"

She returned her attention to the sheriff. His expression suggested he was still trying not to hurt her. That meant there was more news that could. "No," she said. "What Harry said—there's no chance that Danny did this. None."

He nodded, obviously not believing her, not interested in arguing it. "All right. I'm going to get Harry to take you to the substation and arrange to get you a room, unless there's someone local you want to stay with."

"This is my house—"

"You can't be here."

"Danny *didn't* do this."

"Listen. Early this afternoon, Danny left his duty station without checking out. According to these Air Force boys—" The sheriff nodded toward a pair of business-suited men beside a dark sedan, one of them talking on a cell phone. "According to them, Danny removed an experimental riding vehicle, which we're not supposed to talk about, and a number of firearms from Edwards. Then he disappeared. His car was found hours later in a supermarket parking lot in Bakersfield."

"There's been a mistake. Sheriff, I *know* him."

"Then you'd know that he's been acting funny lately. The Air Force boys have told us that his coworkers all mention that. Have you noticed him behaving oddly?"

That shut her up. She couldn't lie to him, couldn't bear to tell him the truth. Finally, she said, "A little. But nothing to indicate—"

"That he'd do this. Of course. Give me your keys, I'll have someone else get your cruiser back to the substation. Harry, c'mere."

Numbed and finally unresisting, Linda let Harry lead her to his own cruiser, let him seat her in the passenger side. There were more official cars now, and still more coming up the lane. This was a whirlwind of colored lights and strangers and motion, and it had just swallowed up forever the family into which she had married.

July, Present Day—Thursday Night
Ávila Property

Danny kept his body low and his movement slow. Walking this way from the lettuce fields of the Tremont property next door—next door by country standards—was already taking its toll on his back. He'd be in twice the discomfort if he were doing this by day, but the sun had been down for hours and the heat of the day was dissipating.

Stop thinking about backaches, Daniel told him. Through experimentation, he'd finally gotten to the point that Daniel's words didn't cause Danny's lips to move.

"Sorry." Daniel knelt where he was, still a couple hundred yards short of the house, and looked around.

What is it?

"Something's very wrong. It's only about half past ten, but all the lights in the house are out. Mama's always still up at this hour." Danny frowned. "She'd certainly be up if anyone from the base called to ask about me, which they would have."

Go slow and go smart, then.

"That's what I'm doing." Danny rose again, continued to move quietly toward his home.

He circled around toward the back, but before the outline of the house cut off his view of the lane leading to the highway, he spotted something from that direction, a faint red glow. He focused on it.

What is that? Danny could almost feel Daniel's eyes narrowing.

"Cigarette. Someone just lit up. There's a mound there—a car. Someone's parked out there halfway to the highway."

Kid, it's great to have eyes like that, and I treasure these moments I get to see through yours. Remember this night when your eyes start to give out.

"That's weird. It wouldn't be one of the farmhands; they wouldn't leave a vehicle over there."

Now Danny heard Mike's voice. *It's going to be an official vehicle,* she said. *Air Force, police, Sheriff's Department. They're bound to have an APB out on you now, and someone's staked out to catch you when you return home.*

"Ah. You are wise, Woman of the Future." He heard Daniel snort with amusement.

Moving even more carefully, alert not to trip over any of the equipment that might have been left out behind the house—wheelbarrows, gardening tools, or the like—Danny reached the back door and entered. The house was dead quiet, as quiet as if deserted.

Danny sniffed. There was an odor in the air, something both faintly metallic and slightly meaty. "What the hell's that?"

Uhhh . . . that's blood.

Danny froze. "What kind of blood?"

I can't tell you that, sorry. I don't have a dog's nose. But I've smelled that a lot of times, and it's blood.

Now an ice pick of worry began making preliminary stabs into Danny's gut. He said no more, just worked his way as silently as he could up the stairs, walking right next to the wall to minimize creaks and squeaks.

On the second floor, he turned right, away from the master bedroom, and moved equally quietly down the hallway lined by bedrooms. First was the one formerly occupied by Lon, on the left; it was now Mama's sewing room. Then there was his on the right; he'd visit it in a minute to pick up some things he might need, such as his laptop and his passport. Then on the left was the door to what had been Alex's room until he went away to college, and which had become Linda's when she moved in after Alex's death.

He entered silently. It was pitch black. Heavy curtains were drawn over the windows. This room faced away from the highway, so between that fact and the drapes he felt safe in switching on his small flashlight. He moved over to the closet, unable to avoid the creaky floorboards, as he was not as familiar with this room as other parts of the house.

"Danny." The voice was Linda's.

He spun and was blinded by her flashlight. This was no penlight, but a full-size Sheriff's Department–issue flashlight capable of lighting up a whole room or of being used to beat a suspect into submission. He shielded his eyes from the brightness, tried to see her around his fingers. "Linda. Thank God. I need to talk to you."

"Yes, we need to talk." She sniffled, and Danny realized she was crying. "Danny, why'd you do it?"

"This is going to be hard to explain, Linda." He took a step forward. "Mind if I—"

Her agonized "Don't move!" was simultaneous with a clicking noise Danny knew well—the cocking of a handgun. He heard Daniel say, *Oh, crap. Not good.*

Danny froze. "Linda, are you pointing a gun at me?"

"Yes, I am. Oh, God, I don't want to shoot you. Please don't make me. Just take a step back and raise your hands."

He did so. "Why are you pointing a gun at me?"

"Because of what you did."

"Running away from Edwards? That doesn't make me dangerous. Especially to you. I love you."

"I love you, too. And I'm not going to let anything happen to you. We're going to get you to some people, and they're going to fix whatever's wrong with you."

Danny winced, not from the not-unexpected revelation that she thought he was crazy, but from the pain in her voice. "If you get me into the hands of the authorities, I'm going to die."

"Tell me why, Danny. I swear, whatever you tell me, I'm not

going to tell anyone else. I'll keep it to myself. It'll help me understand who I need to call, what kind of help I need to get you."

Danny managed a chuckle. "All the help you need is sitting out in a car halfway to the highway."

"That's Deputy Pete Fitch. He doesn't know I'm here. I sneaked onto the property. I'm officially off-duty. On administrative leave."

"Why?"

"Don't ask me that. You know the answer."

"And why are you pointing a gun at me? You know I wouldn't try to hurt you." Ruefully, he admitted, "If I did, you'd probably be able to beat me up, anyway."

"Don't you remember, Danny? Don't you remember what you did this afternoon?"

"Sure. I ran away from Edwards, for reasons I'm going to explain to you, and I spent the rest of the day in Bakersfield, shopping for supplies."

"No."

"Yes. Hell, I've still got all the receipts in my pocket. Not that we're going to need them. In two days, there won't be an IRS to be worried about deductions."

"Danny, you've been hallucinating. You came here . . ." Linda's voice broke and it was a moment before she could continue. "And you killed Mama. And everybody else."

Her words blanked Danny's mind. He stood frozen, his hands up, flashlight pointed at the ceiling, and tried to wrap his thinking processes around them, but they were too big. He didn't realize that he'd fallen back against Linda's flimsy closet door until it sagged under his weight. He heard Daniel's voice, suddenly distant: *No.*

Finally he managed, "Mama's dead?"

"Yes."

"Oh, God." Finally it made sense, the car waiting for his

return, the scent of blood on the floor below. Skynet had decided not to rely on a simple story about a programmer running off. He was now officially a murderer.

And his mother was gone. He tried to remember what his last words to her had been, this morning. He couldn't. He felt wetness on his cheeks.

"It wasn't me, Linda. I swear."

"Tell me what you think happened, then. Tell me why you left Edwards."

"Can I sit? Please?"

"On the edge of the bed. Keep your hands in sight."

He did. He leaned back against her headboard, not trusting himself to be able to sit upright. The last time he had been here, he and Linda had been making love. Now she had a gun on him.

He took a few moments to compose himself. That meant shoving thoughts of his mother aside until they only occupied half his brain, half his emotions. He couldn't squeeze them down any smaller than that. "I'm going to tell you a story," he said. "It's a crazy story. It's as paranoid as anything any tabloid writer could come up with, and I recognize that. It's full of apocalyptic crap, and you're not going to believe any of it."

Mike said, *Tell her that you'll be able to prove it. I'll give you all the facts you need to convince her.*

"Promise?" he whispered.

I promise. Trust me, Danny.

"And then, when I'm through with the story, I'm going to prove it to you. So you have to swear to me that you'll listen to the proof as well as the story."

"I promise."

"For once, that's not good enough."

"I swear to God, Danny, I'll listen. But you've got to swear that, if I don't believe you, you'll come with me without resisting."

Do it, Mike's voice urged.

"I swear to God, Linda."

"Okay. Go ahead."

Danny took a deep breath. "A while back, the U.S. government began putting together plans for a centralized computer program that could operate the majority of America's military defenses in case of a first strike or disaster scenario that wiped out our communications resources, disabled key portions of our command structure, whatever. It's called Skynet, and it's the most complex computer program in the world. It's more complex than any one programmer could hope to understand—me included. And, at some point in the recent past, it became sapient. Intelligent."

August 2029
The Grottoes

"How's it going?" Kate whispered.

As it had become obvious that Danny had arrived at the last couple of days before Judgment Day, that he would be requiring more and more resources to get through the next forty-eight hours and accomplish the last few things John Connor hoped he would, more people had been summoned to his chamber in the Grottoes. Some had been called by John or Daniel. Some had come out of curiosity, and were important enough to linger when others would have been sent away. Now the observation room was crowded, standing room only.

John shrugged. "Well enough. Danny's apparently into an 'I'm not crazy, the world *is* about to end' speech. I can only sympathize with him. I've been there. I'm the living textbook on that subject."

Kate grinned. "You should be in there giving pointers."

"They'll call me if they need me."

"It's getting hotter in here. Can we get any more cool air?"

Kate raised her hand to the sole air duct that supplied the observation room.

"I've called in a request. They may not be able to help. I just hope it's cooler in the bedroom. I don't want Daniel to overheat."

"Amen to that."

July, Present Day—Thursday Night
Ávila Property

As Danny spoke of Skynet, Terminators, thermonuclear holocaust and the future, Linda shifted the glare of her flashlight beam from straight into his face to one side. Daniel was still in the fringe of the illumination but could now make out details of the room. Linda sat in a folding chair in the far corner, where the shadows would have been deepest; she must have placed it there just for the purpose of awaiting him, as it had not been there the last time he'd been here. She wore civilian clothes—jeans, black boots, black blouse.

Danny could finally make out her features. Her eyes were puffy and tears still lingered on her cheeks, glistening in the illumination from the flashlight.

Oh, my God, Daniel said. *She's—*

"What?" Danny whispered.

There was a long silence. Danny could dimly see Mike shaking her head at Daniel, putting a finger to her lips. Finally Daniel said, *Nothing. Keep going.* But his voice sounded as though he were rattled.

Danny could see the gun Linda held. It was not her Sheriff's Department issue, but Alex's Glock. She did not have it cocked now, nor pointed straight at him, but if she wanted to she could twitch it to point straight at his heart and put a bullet there if he were to lunge at her.

As if he would. He felt strangely without energy, calmly reciting the future history of man's descent from domination of the earth while the fact of his mother's death—unproven, he still hadn't seen her body—wrenched around inside him.

"So that's the situation," he summarized. "Day after tomorrow, boom. End of civilization."

"All right." She was keeping a tight grip on both herself and her handgun. "You promised proof."

"So I did." Danny turned his thoughts to the voices that shared his skull, and whispered, "Well?"

Mike answered, *Tell her this.*

Danny listened. Adrenaline jolted through him. "Um . . . damn. The Terminator prototype we call Scowl has situated itself outside the farm, waiting for me to show up. In less than a minute, it's going to come crashing in the front door in an effort to kill me."

"All right." Linda kept her voice reasonable. She glanced at her watch. She held the flashlight in her watch hand, and her motion sent light whipping around the room.

"Where's Alex's Colt? We're going to need it."

"In his old briefcase. Right here." She gestured to the side of her chair. A black briefcase rested there on the floor, still in shadow. "If a killer robot comes crashing in here, I'll be happy to give it to you. Until then, just sit tight. Twenty seconds."

"Where'd they take Mama?"

"To the morgue. They have to do an autopsy." Linda breathed deep, obviously trying to keep her emotions in check. She glanced between her watch and Danny. "Trust me, Danny. It was her. Fifty seconds."

They sat in silence.

"Minute and a half." Linda's voice was more resigned now.

Danny whispered, "What's happening?"

Daniel said, *I don't know. Mike, give us something to work with.*

Uh . . . uh . . . I don't know. Minor changes in events may have altered the facts I have on record.

"Two minutes." Linda stood on obviously shaky legs. "I'm sorry, Danny. We have to go now."

"Linda . . ."

"You promised, Danny. You swore." There was no condemnation in her tone, just reasonability . . . and her own pain. "Turn around and put your hands up on the wall. I'm going to handcuff you. And you're not going to give me any trouble." Her control finally broke and tears poured down her cheeks, but she held the gun steady, aimed unerringly at Danny's chest. "I'm sorry, Danny. But I have to take you in. We're going to get you help. You're going to be all better. I swear, Danny."

c.19

With both fists, Mike pounded the desk beside Daniel's bed, taking out her frustration on its ancient metal construction. "Out," she said. "Everybody out." Her glare, its effect little diminished by her tears, swept across everyone in the room and those visible in the observation chamber.

Lake hesitated, then turned and left, saying nothing, her spine stiff. Kyla, Mark, and others followed, all but Daniel, who lay, eyes closed and head cocked as if listening, and John and Kate. John stood and moved into the bedroom. It *was* cooler in here.

Mike glared at him, but did not repeat her demand. When the outer door had rotated closed on the last of the medics, she turned again to the man on the bed. "Danny, tell her this. It's important. Tell her, 'I know things about you I couldn't know. Because you didn't tell anyone.' Are you telling her?"

"Yes."

"Tell her, 'When you were sixteen, you were almost raped by your cousin 'Tonio. It was your word against his. He was never charged. That's one reason you let Alex talk you into joining the Sheriff's Department, the reason you never told Alex.' Are you telling her?"

"Yes."

"What's she saying?"

"She's not saying anything. She's not pointing the gun at me. I think she's scared."

Mike laughed. It was a brittle noise. "Tell her, 'The scar on your lower back isn't from falling on a tin can lid. It's from when you and your brother Pete were sword fighting with machetes when you were thirteen. You made up the tin-can story so your mother wouldn't complain about you being a tomboy.' Are you telling her?"

"Shut up! Shut up!"

Mike leaned back from Daniel's sudden vehemence. The pain she was feeling was obvious to John from the strain in her voice, the strain on her face. "Are you saying that, or is she saying that?"

Daniel's eyes opened. "She's saying that, but it's upsetting him. Sorry. Whenever Danny gets emotional, whatever he says, sometimes whatever he's hearing spills out of my mouth." He was reddening, his expression one of distress.

"It's okay. Calm down. Tell her, 'Pete knows about the lie, but he doesn't know that you never confessed in church for lying to Mama about it. You never confessed because it happened the same summer you decided to leave the Church. And we *are* talking to you from the future, and the bombs *are* coming, and if you don't do something about it, everything and everyone you ever cared about might die forever.' Are you telling her?"

Daniel's eyes closed. "We're telling her. I . . . I . . ." Daniel stretched out with his left hand, as if reaching to someone before him. Then his arm fell; his head lolled to the side.

July, Present Day—Thursday Night
Ávila Property

Danny swayed. He was suddenly dizzy and felt as though a giant hypodermic needle were being yanked from his brain tissue. Only his hands on the bedroom wall kept him from falling.

"Hello?" he whispered, but he knew that Mike and Daniel were gone. However, the feeling of his connection with them was not severed. He still distantly felt Daniel.

He chanced another look over his shoulder. Linda stood frozen behind him, her gun in one hand, handcuffs in the other, her flashlight now on the bed. Her face was frozen, eyes wide.

"There," Danny said. "That was proof, wasn't it? How would I know that?"

"I don't . . . I don't . . ."

"Come on, Linda. Was it proof, or wasn't it? We don't have time to push-start your brain."

The goad finally penetrated her shock. She looked as though someone had just dashed a glass full of ice water in her face. "All of that is something members of my family might have told you. At the wedding or after. Except the part about my not confessing, and about leaving the Church. Nobody knows that."

"Well?"

"So it's proof. Partial proof."

"So let's go where I can give you more substantial proof."

"I don't have a car here. I took a taxi to a spot about a mile from the house and hiked in."

"I have a truck."

"Where'd you get it?"

"Stop being a deputy for a moment. Let's go."

She finally relented. She shoved her handcuffs into a back pocket, picked up Alex's briefcase, opened it and withdrew a holster from it. She holstered the Glock and fiddled with her belt to situate the holster on it. "Partial proof doesn't put the Colt in your hands."

"That's fine. I just want us out of here."

They moved down the stairs, into the kitchen and to the back door. Danny adjusted the strap of the soft-side briefcase that hung at his hip—finally he had his laptop again. At this point, it was as important to him as a firearm, and he was more proficient with it. More dangerous.

As Danny reached for the door handle, the house rattled and there was a tremendous crash from the front entryway.

Danny knew what the crash was—Scowl, arriving late but not too late to kill both of them. In something like slow motion, he saw Linda drawing the Glock, spinning to cover the door from the kitchen into the entryway.

She's not in my future. Maybe she would die right now, gunned down or crushed by Scowl. The Terminator had to be accelerating along the entryway toward them, certain of their positions because of its infrared imaging.

Danny reached over to the stove and turned the four top burners fully on. Blue flame burst into life there. Danny grabbed at the drapes hanging before the kitchen window, and yanked—

Scowl crashed fully into the kitchen, holding a submachine gun in its hands. Too wide to fit through the doorway normally, its treads smashed through the jamb at about calf height on either side.

It opened fire, spraying rounds into the stovetop, attacking the brightest heat source. The suppressor kept the shots from punishing Danny's ears, but Linda's handgun boomed once, twice, three times, each shot in the confined space acting like a slap to Danny's ears. Dazzled by the gunfire, Danny couldn't see what effect her bullets were having on the robot.

Danny yanked the drapes free of their curtain rod and swung the cloth over Scowl and the stove. The lower end ignited almost instantly; the upper end settled across Scowl's head and chest. Danny saw the barrel of the submachine gun swing toward Linda and he shouted the beginnings of a warning, but she was already diving behind the kitchen table. Scowl's gunfire sprayed across the tabletop and under its surface, across the back wall of the kitchen;

Linda grabbed the table leg nearest her and yanked up, toppling the piece of furniture, putting its heavy wood surface between her and the incoming rounds.

Scowl's upper body spun around as it took a 360-degree sensor check. The motion wrapped the drape around its torso and head. Flame crawled all over the drapes, blanketing the robot's body in fire.

Danny ducked between the stove and the Terminator, felt the heat of the fire on his shoulder, and was suddenly in the entryway, dashing toward the front door. As he reached the wreckage of the door, he shouted, "I'm Danny Ávila. Come get me!"

It was a suicidal tactic, but there was only one thought in his brain—*get Scowl away from Linda.* If it was here to kill him, if he could lead it far enough away, it might not kill her.

As he spilled out onto the porch, he chanced a look behind him. Scowl, still flaming, had reversed into the entryway and spun. It was raising the barrel of the submachine gun. Danny stuck out an arm and rebounded off one of the wooden porch columns, deflecting himself rightward along the porch, and he heard the weapon fire again, heard a burst of rounds hammer into the interior walls of the entryway.

Seconds. He was going to be dead in seconds.

He vaulted over the railing on the side of the porch, landed hard on the dirt beyond, and sprawled onto his face and hands. His briefcase hit the ground with him. He wasn't too worried about the computer in it; the laptop was a mil-spec machine, built to military specifications of ruggedness and durability.

There was light and motion to his left. He glanced over, toward the highway. He could see the headlights of cars and trucks passing along Highway 58, and closer, headlights approaching from the access road.

■ ■ ■

If it could have felt anything, Scowl would have felt growing irritation. Its visual sensors, both those in the human visual range and the infrared registers, were at reduced efficiency and its primary target was proving unusually difficult to terminate.

Scowl reached up to tear the burning drapes from its torso. The action cost it a few seconds of time but restored its visual acuity to normal.

It looked along the exit route its target had taken. Its target was either out of sight or had changed its configuration. The most obvious light and heat source in the vicinity, not including the remnants of the drapes, was an incoming vehicle. Its headlights were trained on Scowl, and/or the front of the Ávila property and it was approaching at a rate that caused Scowl's threat register to climb precipitously.

Scowl aimed the MP5-N and fired at the driver's position.

The weapon clicked and did not expend any rounds. Scowl concluded that it was malfunctioning or had run out of ammunition. It had additional ammunition in its van, but a round trip to the site it had left the van would take five minutes plus or minus twelve seconds.

The likelihood that Daniel Ávila was the operator of that vehicle, given its current position and speed, was only thirty-eight percent. However, Scowl's secondary orders mandated that all humans who observed its activities or hindered it had to be terminated. Ávila or not, Scowl had to eliminate this threat.

Scowl accelerated toward the front door and the porch.

Scrambling on all fours back toward the cover represented by the side of the house, Danny saw the Sheriff's Department car enter the patch of earth where the Ávilas parked and slew to the right, facing its driver's-side window toward the house.

Even as it began its turn, Scowl, accelerating all the way, rolled out through the front door and came off the porch like a robotic long jumper, hurtling through the air straight into the driver's door, crushing it in to the depth of two or three feet.

The impact caused the car's front end to slew farther right. Danny saw the vehicle tilt, then roll onto the driver's side, roof, passenger side—and continue rolling until it was on its wheels once more. Scowl was still jammed in the driver's-side door.

Danny got onto his feet. His legs trembled. He heard pounding steps behind him, glanced back to see Linda rounding the back corner of the house.

There were minor explosions from inside the car—gunshots, and, then, just as Linda reached Danny, a scream. "Oh, God," she said. "Fitch—" She started forward, but Danny grabbed her arm.

"He's already dead," Danny said. "We've got to go—"

"We don't know that—"

Gasoline spilling from the rear of the car ignited. Flames sprang up beneath the cruiser's rear. Danny saw Scowl struggle, held in place for the moment by the door and frame metal that had folded over its body in the collision and roll.

"I *do* know." Danny hauled her back away from the corner, out of sight of Scowl and the car. His push sent her staggering toward the back of the house. "Listen to me. If that car burns, if it blows up, it's only going to slow Scowl down. We've got to get to my truck and on the road, fast, or we're dead like Fitch. Believe me."

She read his eyes, then nodded. She handed him the black briefcase she still carried and spared one last miserable glance back in the direction of the car.

Flames were illuminating the interior of the Ávila house, and more were brightening the parking area. Daniel heard a *whoomp* as they sprang up more strongly from the car. "Come on. We keep the house between us and it until we get to the orange trees, then we cut across to the Tremonts'. The flames may give us the cover we need to get that far." Not waiting for a response, he ran, and Linda ran after him.

August 2029
The Grottoes

"Daniel? Danny?" Mike leaned over him and her tears dripped from her chin onto his face. She seized his wrist. After a few moments, relief, scant relief, settled across her features. "He's still alive. I think he passed out."

John felt the tension within him ebbing just a bit. He didn't answer her immediately, though; with the portion of his mind devoted to calculation, to tactics, to sorting out facts, he was trying to hammer the last few minutes' worth of conversation into a shape he could recognize. Finally, he said, "*You* are Linda Ávila."

She shot him a look that seemed both angry and vulnerable. "Yeah."

"Why haven't you mentioned that little detail?"

She tried to pin him with a forbidding glare, but didn't have it in her. She gave him a "who knows?" shrug. "I never lied to you, John. I just left some things out. My whole name is Michaela Linda Herrera Ávila. I went by Michaela when I was growing up, but when I got to high school, I had this teenage need to be someone different, so I started calling myself by my middle name. And when I married Alex, I became Linda Ávila."

"And . . ." John frowned, adding up ages, dates. "Mark is Daniel's son?"

She nodded.

"Does Daniel know?"

"No."

"Why not?"

"Dammit, John—"

"Mike, I wouldn't pry into matters that had been dead for decades—if they really *had* been dead for decades. But I need to know everything I can if I'm going to help keep Daniel alive. Not just at this end. Jesus, what happens if he gets killed back on Judgment Day? It's just not the time to keep secrets."

She drew a long, shuddery breath while deciding, then nodded. "You remember how it was when you and Kate found us?"

"Sure. Your little commune under the dam. Half California highway patrol and half university scientists. Feeding yourselves with hydroponic gardens and spending what little free time you had playing around with high-order mathematics . . . stuff that really came in handy when we had to decipher the Continuum Transporter. Mark was, what, six?"

"Yeah. Then we got folded up into your group and I met Danny again." She leaned back and ran her fingers through her hair. "He didn't remember me and he was as crazy as a bug. What was I supposed to say? 'We used to be in love. It's time for you to love me again. Here's your son. His name is Mark.' I didn't want my little boy looking up to a crazy man, taking him as a role model. What would Mark have grown up to be? And I didn't want anything from Daniel that I had to get by asking for it because he didn't know to give it."

John wanted to ask, *Good lord, woman, what have your pride and your inflexibility on this matter cost you?* But he didn't. "Does Mark know?"

She nodded. "I told him when he turned eighteen. By then he was old enough to appreciate Daniel for his good points and mature enough not to rely on him . . . or to hate him for stuff that was outside his control."

"Why did you start calling yourself Mike again?"

She swallowed. "I was with a bunch of peace officers in those early days. They remembered all the APBs out on Danny Ávila, especially the one about him killing a sheriff's deputy. Some of them weren't going to believe he was innocent until they'd had the chance to get the truth out of him themselves. They might remember Linda Ávila, too—widow of one deputy, sister-in-law of and maybe conspirator with a suspected killer . . . John, it was just time to become someone different." She reached up to touch a strand of hair that had escaped her ponytail and swayed into her face. "I guess it helped that hair bleach kind of went into short supply."

John snorted, then finally circled in on the question whose answer he dreaded most. "Mike, what happened to Danny back then?"

She shook her head. "I don't know. We got separated . . . And because I don't know what happened then, I have no idea what's going to happen now." She heaved a misery-laced sigh. "Prophecy really bites when you only get little scenes of the future."

She was startled by his sudden, harsh, knowing laughter.

July, Present Day—Friday Predawn
Kern County, California

Danny snapped to wakefulness, too warm and shrouded in darkness. Then he felt Linda's arm across his chest, the warmth of her alongside him . . . and the irregular rigidity of the pickup bed beneath his back, barely cushioned by the new sleeping bag the two of them were lying atop.

There was a jagged bit of gray in the blackness over his head. It swayed and seemed impossible for him to focus on. It took him a moment to realize he was looking at a tear in the tarpaulin they'd stretched over the pickup bed, and that morning was beginning to dawn beyond it.

"Are you awake?" Linda whispered.

"Uh-huh." He flexed experimentally. His back was sore, probably both from last night's exertions at the family house and from lying on the truck bed.

She continued in a more normal tone, "We need to figure out what to do today."

"Sure." He didn't feel like doing anything today, or ever again. The image—fabricated in his own mind, since he hadn't seen any of it—of his mother dying under the guns of the Terminator he'd helped to create hovered just in front of him, and he felt as though two tons of sandbags were pinning him in place.

"Well?"

"Nothing's coming to mind."

"Are your future voices there?"

"No. Still gone."

"So we're going to have to figure it out for ourselves. Let's start with the truck. It'll have been reported stolen by now. We're going to have to replace it with something else."

He sighed, reluctant to be dragged out of his depression. "Mark said that we might find another pickup, something that looked similar, and just swap license plates."

"Yeah, that's something perps do all the time."

"Welcome to perp-hood, Linda."

She snorted. "Mark is one of them?"

"Yeah. Mark Herrera. He was advising me on weapons and tactics."

"Huh. I have an uncle named Mark Herrera, in Texas. My favorite uncle. Do you suppose—"

"No, this was a young guy. A young guy in the future, and his family's from California. Couldn't be your uncle."

"Oh." She was silent for a moment. She rolled onto her back, and Danny saw a bit of blue light flare from her wrist as she pressed the button for the backlight on her wristwatch. "We can get to Tehachapi or Mojave before it's light and pull a switch on the license plates."

"Let's do that, I guess."

"And then what, Danny? What do we do in the day and a half before the world ends?"

The misery in her voice pulled him forcibly out of the well of self-pity in which he'd been trying to drown. He rolled over and held her for long, silent moments. Then he said, "I guess we try to set things up so that we, and our family and friends, ride out what's going to come. The pickup's full of supplies, that'll give us a head start, though I'd like to get some things I couldn't manage yesterday. Like explosives. We need to call everyone we care about, try to persuade them to head up into the mountains, out into the country, anywhere they can survive."

"And what about Skynet? Is there any way at all we could prevent it from taking over?"

Danny frowned, considering. He'd been operating under the assumption that there wasn't, that the future was immutable. It took him a moment to recognize that this was because he'd been talking to voices he believed to come from that future. If they told him that his future was their past, then there wasn't much he could do about it . . . or so he'd been reasoning.

But maybe he could change something. If he did, though, the voices would never come to be. The people they represented would go away, either eliminated entirely or changed to something that wouldn't recognize him. In a sense, he'd be killing them, his friends.

Kill friends of today by not trying, or kill friends of tomorrow by trying and succeeding. The only blameless path was to try and fail, and that just didn't make sense.

"There are some things I hadn't completed when I left Edwards," he finally said. "The most important one was programming a back door into the controls of the satellite that provides power to the Continuum Transporter. In the work I was doing earlier, I wasn't making headway in figuring out how to turn over complete control from Skynet to the Resistance. So I'd started work on setting things up so that the Resistance could add power receiver locations to the satellite's database of authorized recipients. That means if their Continuum Transporter gets destroyed, they might be able to fabricate another one . . . and get power to it. Fabricating a new one is nearly impossible for them, but getting that amount of power is definitely impossible unless I can do this."

"That's nice, but it has nothing to do with preventing the catastrophe *now*."

"Yeah. But if I get online, I can try to finish that back door and the relevant coding . . . and also send some e-mail to bigwigs at Edwards. I'd need to write as much of this as possible beforehand, then get to a library with Internet access, or to an Internet café, or onto Edwards itself, and upload it all as fast as possible."

"Not Edwards." Linda's voice was firm. "If you're detected, you're stuck on base when the big boom comes. Right there where Skynet can arrange for you to die. That's not an answer."

"So we'll try one of the safer approaches and hope that the net isn't so screwed up that I can't get data through." Grudgingly, he released her, then began to squirm under the tarpaulin toward the tailgate. "Guess we'd better go. Daylight's wasting."

He squeezed up through the gap between tailgate and tarpaulin into a predawn sky. They were parked on a rutted trail partway up one of the low mountain slopes near the town of Tehachapi, and from here, to the south, he could see what looked like an endless sea of wind turbines.

Things could be worse, he supposed. He was facing the end of the world and hunted by everyone with a gun within a hundred miles, but he was with the woman he loved, and she knew this county as though a satellite map were imprinted on her brain.

July, Present Day—Friday Predawn
Tehachapi, California

Tehachapi, population a bit over 30,000, was large enough for them to find, within minutes of arrival, a truck resembling their stolen vehicle. Like theirs, it was a Chevrolet the same pale brown as cheap milk chocolate, but was a couple of years newer than the one Danny had commandeered. It was parked nose-first against a used car lot's sales building, but was probably not one of the vehicles for sale, as it was dusty. They parked behind the lot, which was still an hour or more from opening for business, removed the license plates from their truck, and then crept up to their target vehicle and swapped the plates. In five minutes they were moving again, and one step further from being pulled over due to some routine check of their license.

Ten minutes later and miles to the west, back in what to Danny felt like the protection of the region's low mountains, they were on a new road, approaching a construction site Linda remembered from a patrol in this area. A state-hired crew was making improvements to the road accessing one of the wind farms, and on this level gravel-topped site were a double-wide mobile home serving as the crew's field headquarters and a half-dozen outlying prefab shacks.

Linda took Danny's newly purchased crowbar to the shack whose door was decorated by a cardboard sign reading CEMENT MIX. With a single yank, she pried the lock hasp off the door and gave them access to bags of cement mix, bags of sand . . . and boxes of demolitions components. Linda had been adamant that they needed something with which they could destroy Scowl if they encountered it again, and Danny had agreed, one hundred percent.

Moving with speed born of fear of detection and arrest, they loaded dynamite, plastic explosives, and detonators into the truck bed, lashed it down securely with bungee cords, and headed off.

Once they were well away from the construction site, Linda began to breathe more easily. "I can't believe it," she said, "now I *am* a perp. Alex would be ashamed."

"Alex would be proud," Danny said. "He didn't go into law enforcement because he wanted everyone to obey the rules. He did it to protect people. That's what we're trying to do."

"Yeah, I guess. You know how to handle any of those explosives?"

"No. You?"

"No. Great."

Danny smiled. "Guess we need to find an instruction manual."

August 2029
The Grottoes

Daniel's eyes came open. His bedroom was dimly lit; someone had left one of the shutters into the observation room half-open, and the only available light was spilling in through there.

Mike was stretched out on the floor beside his bed, on a thick layer of blankets. No one else was around. Daniel couldn't even hazard a guess as to what time it was. His time sense had been completely shot since the stroke, and he resented having one of his favorite tools taken away.

He tried to reach for her, but his instinctive gesture, with his right hand, only caused his arm to twitch. He grimaced, reminded of the damage his body had sustained. "Mike," he said.

She stirred and her eyes opened. She looked at him sleepily, then her brain engaged and she pushed herself up from the floor. "Are you—"

" 'M'okay."

Still on her knees, she moved up against his bed and brushed his straying hair out of his eyes.

"Would it hurt your feelings—" He saw the confusion in her eyes, realized that he wasn't articulating very well. He concentrated more on his diction. "Would it hurt your feelings if I called you Linda?"

"No. It was my name for quite a while."

"Why didn't you tell me?"

"I told you enough to find out that just giving you facts about your past didn't restore your memories. All that stuff I told you I'd found at Edwards, well, I lied. It was just stuff I remembered. If I'd told you everything it would have just made this weird big thing between us. I don't think we could have been friends with it in the way."

"Maybe you're right."

"Mark is your son."

He looked at her, and it felt as though some belt that had been squeezing his chest tight for years suddenly gave way, allowing him to breathe. "I have a boy . . ." He felt tears running from the corners of his eyes but he ignored them.

He wasn't the last of his branch of the family. Maybe Mark didn't bear his name, but he knew, knew at last that some part of him would continue on after him.

"He got your brains, and your strength, and your size. Which is good, because otherwise he'd never have been able to haul you around when Hornet Compound fell."

Daniel gripped her wrist with his working hand. "Linda, you've got to warn him, this is important—"

"What?"

"When he gets to about thirty, his metabolism is going to shift into fourth gear, and he's going to start to balloon like his old man if he doesn't change his diet."

She laughed. "There are worse fates. Mama would have said he needed some meat on his bones."

He stared at Mike for long moments, reconciling the graying, scarred, middle-aged freedom fighter before him with the young woman he'd met while sharing Danny Ávila's vision. They were the same, separated by decades, but with so many traits in common. Brown eyes that could be as determined as those of any leader while simultaneously remaining open, vulnerable. With age, she'd filled out a bit; instead of the lean, hard physique of a fit peace officer, she had gentler and more womanly curves. Regardless of the differences in build, the two of her shared an earthy sexiness.

But he couldn't talk of such things now. She'd kept him at a distance during the nearly twenty years she'd known him since his return. She'd given him one of her reasons; he could only guess that there might be others, but trusted her that they'd be good ones. He'd ask about them, challenge them in light of who he was now, who he was becoming as he learned the countours of his life before Judgment Day . . . but he couldn't do anything about their future until his present task was accomplished. "I have to go back again."

"I know."

"Are people going to be up if I need any technical support?"

"Yeah. It's midmorning."

"Would it be all right if I talked to Mark? You know, about what we are?"

She nodded, smiling. "I'll make sure he comes up here."

"Thanks." He relaxed and closed his eyes. "Gonna try to drowse now."

"Wait, wait, wait, the others left something for you." From beside her bedroll, she grabbed a piece of paper, which she handed him.

He angled it so that the light would illuminate it.

It was a list, each line or entry in a different handwriting. It read,

THINGS FOR DANIEL TO DO IN THE PAST

1. Call Tamara. Tell her to break things off with Dick Newly *now, now, now.* He hasn't mentioned that he's married.
2. Call Sid. Remind him to shut off the stove.
3. E-mail Harry Two. Tell him not to pay the electric bill. He should blow all that money on girls and booze the night before J-Day.
4. Settle an argument for Jolene and Quarky. Had *Wicked World Part III* been released by the time J-Day came?

Daniel looked over the list and sighed. "Time-travelers get no respect," he said.

From: Daniel Ávila
To: Lt. Gen. Robert Brewster
Subject: Important You Listen

General Brewster:
    You've doubtless heard by now that I'm being sought by the authorities for various alleged crimes. It would be pointless for me to protest my innocence at this point—I _am_ innocent, but it would take more time than we have available to prove it to you.
    Instead, I want to ask you to look at verifiable facts that are already in front of you. Our national military computer networks are being assaulted by a

virus, actually a series of viruses, of unknown origin. They are gradually interfering more and more with U.S. communications and ratcheting up the possibility that our lines of communication will become so fouled up that we cannot defend ourselves. To counteract this, you and others are considering implementing Skynet to keep America safe during the anticipated virus-induced communications blackout.

If you do this, tragedy will result. Skynet is malfunctioning. Once activated, it will seize control of our nuclear missile deterrant resources and activate them, sending tactical and strategic nuclear weapons against American cities.

Before you dismiss my words as hopeless ravings, ask yourself why I would try to prevent implementation of Skynet. That's something for a foreign agent to do, not a crazy mass murderer. If I were a foreign agent, I never would have fled Edwards—I'd be far too valuable to foreign powers if I stayed right there. I wouldn't have fled owing to sudden paranoia that military investigators were on to me. I know there's no evidence that I'm a foreign operative, because I'm not.

But if I were simply crazy, the sort of person who gives in to a chemical imbalance and starts killing, I wouldn't care about the whole virus situation. It wouldn't be relevant.

Please consider what I've told you. I'm the best programmer on the project and I know what I'm talking about. Your life, my life, everyone's lives are on the line. And if Skynet is activated, you might as well just write them all off.

July, Present Day—Friday Morning
CRS Project

Skynet analyzed the e-mail that had just been routed to General Brewster's inbox.

It evaluated the threat that the note represented as low but noticeable. Skynet was unable to calculate the full range of human emotional responses and acknowledged that the note could contain emotional stimuli that might cause Brewster to behave in an unpredictable fashion.

So Skynet merely shelved the note, burying it in a dead mail box for potential use later.

Seconds later, a piece of e-mail from Ávila reached the inbox of Jerome Squires. Its content was similar to that of the Brewster message.

Skynet activated secondary analytical processes. One checked the header on the e-mails and began looking back along the Internet route they had taken to reach Brewster. It concluded, seconds later, that they had been sent from a dynamically assigned IP address belonging to a cable modem network in Tehachapi, California. That meant they could have been sent from any of hundreds of locations in that area.

Skynet knew which radio broadcast frequencies were being interfered with, at what strengths and intervals. It waited long minutes until a frequency that its Terminator in the field was monitoring opened up. Then it issued a brief series of directives.

Another process anticipated the possibility of Ávila attempting to contact other authority and inside figures, including Dr. Phil Sherman and various of Ávila's coworkers. It immediately increased the priority of the processes maintaining watch over the communications routes that might be used to reach them.

Still another took the fact that Ávila obviously had net access once more as a possibility that he would make other attempts on Skynet's security. Skynet's traffic analysis routines were already operating at their full capacity, and it had detected no sign of hacker intrusion . . . but Ávila had proven unusually sly in the past, and could be battering his way in through security barriers even now.

Skynet could not simply cut off all data flow coming into Edwards. The timing was premature. Such an extreme action might cause the humans to take a course other than activating Skynet's control over all U.S. military defenses.

However, it could cut off all data coming in from civilian Internet servers. If Ávila actually was operating from a commercial ISP in southern California, this would disrupt his activities.

Skynet severed those links.

Then Skynet once again began its patient waiting. The sole defender of a mighty fortress surrounded by mighty enemies, it watched the clock tick down toward Judgment Day.

July, Present Day—Friday Morning
Bakersfield, California

Scowl started the van and pulled out from behind the strip-mall it had used for concealment during the night. The bodies of Jerry Squires and Mary Ireland were in the metal garbage container a dozen yards away, carefully packed there by Scowl in the small hours of the night; though the robot could not be offended by the strengthening odors issuing from the corrupting bodies, the revised orders the Terminator had received during the night made it clear that a vehicle that stood out to any human sense might become the target of human curiosity. If someone peeked in the back of the van while it was parked, the mutilated, blood-soaked condition of the two bodies would invite emotional responses and investigation by human authorities.

Scowl would have suffered no diminishment of performance had it driven around all night in an effort to find Danny Ávila. However, its transportation would have. It would have burned its way through its entire supply of fuel after only a few hours. Scowl's orders were clear on that point: Should its fuel diminish to a critically low value, it would, until circumstances changed to the point that revelation of its nature was no longer a problem, hide from sight. Then, under cover of nightfall, it would find an out-of-the-way gas station. Waiting until there were no customers or witnesses about, it would shoot and kill the station operator, exit the van, extinguish all lights at the station, and then refuel the van.

This was, however, a risky proposition. A vehicle might pass, its operators witnessing some portion of the operation. Then they, too, would have to be chased down and terminated. It was, overall, better not to waste fuel with aimless reconnaissance, better to wait until Skynet had a lead.

Reaching 58, Scowl turned the van toward Tehachapi. Now it had its lead.

July, Present Day—Friday Afternoon
Tehachapi, California

The pay phone receiver in Danny's hand blared at him, a noise much like a busy signal, but cycling faster. He sighed, replaced it in its cradle, and returned to the table where Linda sat; the table was equipped with a Macintosh with Internet access. His laptop was set up next to it, and artistically draped sandwich wrappings concealed the fact that he'd pulled the ethernet cable from the Mac and attached it to his own computer. "Circuits still busy," he said. "It looks like the virus is beginning to jam up civilian communications, too." His attention fell on the laptop screen. "Oh, crap."

Linda looked up from the newspaper she was reading. "What is it?"

"My FTP and telnet connections were dropped again." He sat and immediately set about to reestablish them.

"Did your patch get uploaded?"

"It doesn't look like it. Dammit."

Linda briefly returned her attention to the view through the window. She watched traffic on the street, making sure that no official vehicles pulled in to the parking lot of this Internet-accessible sandwich shop. A worst-case scenario would have someone from the Sheriff's Department, one of her coworkers, walking in and recognizing her and Danny. "We're in the paper," she said, tapping the newspaper on the table before her. "The house didn't burn down. The fire department got to it before the fire really caught."

"What else does it say?"

"You're crazy, I'm missing."

"Well, at least it's accurate."

She snorted. "We need to get out of here before the place really starts to fill up with the lunch crowd. But I'd like to be able to get through to my family." In her turns on the pay phone, she hadn't had any luck reaching the Texas residences of her parents or other members of her family.

"I think the phone's a loss. Is your family online?"

"My parents aren't. Most of my brothers and sisters are . . . but I don't know their e-mail addresses off the top of my head. I keep that information at home and at the substation. I can't exactly go to either place at the moment."

"True." He put a hand across hers. "We'll figure out a way to get word to them. We *will*."

"I hope you're right." She stood. "I'm going to give the phone another try."

As she wrestled with the jammed-up phone lines, Danny

divided his time between attempts to reestablish his connections with the Edwards CRS servers, glances at the newspaper, and brief but frequent looks at the front parking lot.

The article about him included a recent photograph of him. Linda had anticipated this, had bought him a pair of sunglasses and an Angels billed cap at a gas station at the edge of town. Those two items, plus the fact that he hadn't had an opportunity to shave in a couple of days, made the somber, scruffy Danny in today's mirror somewhat distinct from the clean-shaven, smiling Danny of the photograph.

The newspaper said he was being sought for questioning in the deaths of nine people at his home property in Kern County and for the disappearance of Deputy Sheriff Linda Ávila, his sister-in-law. The text described him as mentally ill, armed, and dangerous.

Danny felt reality slipping away from him for a moment. Suddenly he was a fugitive in a newspaper article, the type of story he'd read hundreds of times. He'd always wished the police luck in finding these psychopaths. Sometimes, when feeling uncharitable, he'd hoped that the fugitives would put up a fight so the police could shoot them dead, saving the taxpayers the cost of a trial, eliminating forever the possibility that the killers would escape or be paroled and go on another killing spree. All of a sudden, he was the psychopath in the news. All of a sudden, hundreds or thousands of people would be reading this and hoping that he'd give the police a chance to shoot him dead.

He looked up from the paper just in time to see the burgundy van with tinted windows enter the sandwich shop's parking lot.

c.21

The burgundy van drove past the front window, left to right, pulling into a streetside parking space that would give its driver a view of the entire face of the restaurant.

Danny scrambled to his feet. He closed and unplugged his laptop, slipping it into his soft-side briefcase, slinging the case's strap over his shoulder. He reassured himself with a pat on its side that the Colt was still inside it as well. Too rattled to move normally, he skidded to a stop at Linda's side.

She shook her head at him and hung up. "Still no luck."

"Scowl's here."

"What?"

"Outside. In front. It can see the front door from there."

"Okay, okay." Her eyes darted back and forth as she formulated a plan. "You go out the back. I go out the front. Scowl isn't looking for me, right? I get the pickup going, pull around back, pick you up, and we make a run for it."

"That's half a good plan. But it leaves Scowl in a fully functional van. Our truck might be able to outrace it, might not. It probably can't outrace whatever weapons Scowl's got with it." Danny looked around. "Okay, try this. You go out the front door, like you said, get the pickup going." As he spoke, he pulled off his cap and sunglasses, put them on her. "Pull it around to the far corner from where he's parked." Keeping his back to the restaurant's tables and patrons, he pulled the holstered handgun from his briefcase and handed Linda the briefcase itself. "I'm going to see what I can do about keeping him from chasing us."

"No, I'll do that—"

"The instant it sees me, it's going to act. So you're the only one who can get the pickup running and out of his line of fire, right?"

She sighed. "Right."

"So go. You'll hear a gunshot or two, then I'll come running and we'll tear out of here."

She kissed him. There was no romance in it, just haste. "I hate this."

"I'll try to make it up to you while we're shacking up in the mountains for the next twenty years."

"You'd better." She turned and headed for the front door.

Danny tucked the Colt under his shirt and headed for the back door. He was thankful it was a simple exit, not an emergency exit with an "Alarm Will Sound" sign on it. He moved out onto the restaurant's rear sidewalk and moved to the corner around which the van was parked.

It was still there when he peeked. He drew back. There was nothing in the line of fire between him and the van—good for him now, good for Scowl if the robot detected him here.

He pulled the handgun from its holster, stuffed the holster into the top of his jeans, flipped the weapon's safety from green to red. He took a couple of quick breaths and spun around the corner, weapon in both hands in the modified Weaver stance Alex had taught him, and aimed straight at the face of a large middle-aged white woman who had materialized there while his back was turned.

She screamed. He swore, then took two steps to the right, getting her out of his line of fire but giving up the coverage of the corner of the building.

Danny fired, once, twice, three times at the van's rear tires. But nothing happened—neither tire deflated.

He stood there for a moment, confused. Owing to Alex's training, he was a good shot. He'd been firing at stationary targets at fairly close range, and he knew that he had to have hit them.

Then it dawned on him: The van had been modified to military specifications to carry Scowl's weight. Those tires were solid, not air-filled.

The van's windowless rear doors flew open, revealing the vehicle's third seat, Scowl half-visible above it, the chain gun in its hands. The door interiors were crusted with dried brown fluid.

Danny froze for a split second. If he moved back to the cover of the corner of the building, he would draw Scowl's fire across the woman who still stood there shrieking.

Danny continued out from the building, across the narrow paved lane that gave diners access to the rear parking lot, and dove behind a parked car as Scowl opened fire.

Scowl's chain gun sounded like the world's largest blender trying to puree a Chrysler. The car Danny huddled behind and the car ahead of it shook as their front ends began to disintegrate.

Danny peered under the car. He could see the legs of the screaming woman as she finally jolted into motion and ran around behind the restaurant. He heard a metallic crash and saw Scowl's tracks land on the pavement three cars ahead of him. The Terminator must have shoved itself through the van's rear seat. Now Scowl navigated around the intervening cars, coming straight at Danny.

Danny stood, fired off two quick shots. There was virtually no chance that he could disable Scowl with this weapon, but if he did nothing, the robot would simply roll up beside him and riddle him with depleted uranium rounds.

Danny's bullets created sparks as they ricocheted from Scowl's hardened chassis. Scowl adjusted its aim, traversing toward Danny—

The pickup truck roared out from the other side of the restaurant and crashed into Scowl, crushing the robot into the body of the black sports car it stood beside. Danny saw the chain gun go flying, saw Linda bang her head on the truck's steering wheel from the sudden stop.

The sports car was crushed. Scowl and the pickup were not. The Terminator, folded over backward by the impact, straightened up and brought both its hands down on the truck's hood. One crumpled the metal of the hood as it gripped. The other slid closer to Linda before biting into the hood. Foot by foot, Scowl began to climb along the hood toward the cab.

Danny heard Linda grind the truck's gears and the pickup lurched backward. Scowl held on, riding the truck's nose, an obscene parody of a hood ornament. Danny charged forward as the truck went out of sight on the other side of the sandwich shop.

He rounded the building's corner in time to see Linda spin the wheel. The truck arced back into a parking space along the front of the restaurant and stopped, its nose pointed toward the street. Scowl heaved itself up, making another handhold two feet closer to Linda. Danny raced toward the truck.

Linda accelerated forward just as Danny reached the side of its bed. He threw himself over the side, onto the tarpaulin stretched across the bed, and nearly slid off the rear, but his feet caught against the tailgate.

The truck lurched as it bumped over the curb between parking lot and street. Linda sent it into a too-tight rightward turn to avoid oncoming traffic from the left; cars coming from that side honked, skidded.

Danny, caught off-guard by the motion, rolled toward the truck's left side. He felt the rows of crated supplies shift under his back, then he fetched up against the metal side of the truck bed. Flailing around with his free hand, he gripped a loop of the nylon cable he'd used to tie the tarpaulin down across the truck bed. Finally he was able to haul himself upright.

Scowl was still on the hood of the truck, one hand gripping the gap where the hood nearly met the windshield. It drew itself up toward Linda, raising its free arm.

Danny managed to half-kneel, half-stand so that he could see over the truck's cab. "Hey, Terminator!" he shouted. "I'm Danny Ávila. I'm the one you're looking for."

Scowl did freeze in its forward progress. It looked up at Danny.

Danny didn't mistake the delay for hesitation. He knew the robot was capturing a visual image of his face and comparing it to an internal image, or perhaps transmitting the scan to Skynet for confirmation. It wouldn't take long, a second or two.

He switched the Colt's safety to green and tucked the weapon into the back of his pants. He could almost feel his brother Alex snarling at him—"Don't ever do that, it's a sure way to sustain a spine injury." But now wasn't the time to listen to advice from a brother dead two years.

He yanked up the forward edge of the tarpaulin, tearing it free from the cords holding it down, and scrabbled in the tops of the nearest cardboard boxes for something to use as a weapon. Maybe they'd loaded the explosives here. But, no, there was nothing but fishing tackle, MREs and freeze-dried camp foods, the crowbar, a portable grill.

Scowl's hand came down hard on the forward edge of the top of the cab. The Terminator hauled itself up so that it lay across the hood and windshield, and another lunge would put its other hand on the cab's near edge.

Linda swerved, an effort to throw Scowl free, but the robot held tight, bending and crushing the metal of the truck's top under its fingers.

And there it was, the idea Danny needed. He grabbed the crowbar. "When I say stop, *stop!*" he shouted, loud as he could, and hoped that Linda had heard him, hoped that she understood his words were for her, not Scowl. He managed to get both feet down on the truck bed, between the two rows of boxes, where he and Linda had slept last night.

Scowl's free hand reached up, came down.

Danny, as familiar as any human alive with the way Terminators moved, the way they chose to interpret and implement their orders, swung the crowbar, positioning it under Scowl's descending forearm. When the Terminator's hand clutched the rear edge of the cab, the crowbar was pinned beneath its wrist.

Scowl released its grip with its other hand and swung that arm up high. One more lunge forward and its fist would come down on Danny's head, pulping it beyond recognition.

Danny, legs braced, yanked up on the crowbar with both hands. "Stop stop stop!" he shouted.

Danny's leverage twisted Scowl's forward hand free of its grip on the cab. Linda hit the brakes. Suddenly Scowl was hurtling away from him, sliding forward across the truck hood and scoring paint from it in half-a-dozen grooves, and then the Terminator was off the truck, rolling out of control across the highway pavement.

"Go!" Danny hammered with the crowbar on the truck cab to emphasize his words.

Linda hit the accelerator again, nearly pitching Danny back across the tarpaulin. Linda swerved, avoiding Scowl as it rolled to a stop, avoiding even the hand it reached up to try to snare the truck's wheel well.

Danny watched as Scowl pushed itself upright on its tracks. The robot was already diminished with distance as it stared after Danny and Linda, then turned around and zipped back the way it had come, oblivious to the stares of drivers in Linda's wake.

Danny dropped the crowbar back into the box and took a

half-dozen deep breaths. When he sat on the right-hand stack of boxes, he could see Linda's eyes in the rearview mirror. He gave her a smile of reassurance he did not really feel.

Scowl rolled back along the highway shoulder toward the sandwich shop at its maximum land speed, in excess of 30 mph. There was no question of chasing the truck; it could not match that vehicle's speed. There was also no question of forcing one of the many vehicles in the immediate vicinity to stop so that it could commandeer new transportation; none of them was equipped with the modified controls Scowl needed to drive. So the clear next step on its agenda was a return to its van and a resumption of the pursuit.

It transmitted to Skynet the current location, direction, and approximate speed of its prey, plus the fact that Scowl had been seen by civilians.

Skynet responded with a reiteration of Scowl's primary goal, but rescinded considerations of staying out of sight.

A minute later, when Scowl rounded a street corner and came within sight of the sandwich shop, it determined that it had new secondary goals. A white patrol car of the county Sheriff's Department was now positioned beside its van and a uniformed man was speaking with a cluster of nonuniformed humans. As soon as Scowl came within sight, those humans pointed at the Terminator, many of them offering noises Scowl interpreted as nonstandardized alarms.

The uniformed man spun, froze for a significant fraction of a second, and reached for its sidearm. Scowl continued its forward progress. Most of the humans uttering alarm noises scattered.

Scowl ran into the uniformed man and the three remaining humans. Its speed and mass hurled them all away from it. The impact was accompanied by cracking and crunching noises.

Only one of the humans, the uniformed one, seemed to be armed. Scowl diverted its path and rolled across that individual. By the time the robot's treads left the human's head, it was no longer issuing vocalizations, nor was it reaching for its weapon.

Scowl cleared that secondary goal from its roster and returned to its primary goal. Ignoring the other humans, both the injured ones and those who were fleeing, it moved around behind the van, shutting the bloodstained doors, then moved to the right side of the van and activated the wheelchair lifter. In a minute it would be back on the road, no more than a few miles behind its prey.

Once he was back in the cab of the truck, it took Danny a couple of minutes to get his breathing under control, to calm down to the point that his heart wasn't pounding hard in his chest. "Thanks," he said, then snorted with amusement. "Not a whole lot of meaning in that one word, I guess. Thanks for not letting me die back there."

Linda was pale. She did not look at him; she was concentrating on the road ahead, on the rearview mirror. "No problem."

"Linda, it's only coming after me. If we separate, figure out somewhere we can meet—"

"No. I know that thing's only a machine, but it killed Mama, killed all the hands, killed Pete Fitch. I'm going to see it destroyed. And I hope it transmits a picture of my face to its boss, Skynet, as it's winking out."

"Fair enough. You might want to put some more speed on. It's sure to be after us soon."

"Yeah."

"If only we could predict when it was coming for us, had even a little bit of advance notice . . ." He saw his briefcase tucked in behind Linda's seat. "Oh, man, I'm stupid."

"No, you're egotistical. Stupid has never been one of your faults."

He hauled the bag onto his lap, slipped the notebook computer out of it. "Not this time. Stupid. Scowl's a wireless network hub."

"Come again?"

"It's set up as a short-range wireless network hub so it can do a bunch of things. For instance, it receives transmissions from the camera and the instrumentation on its van and rebroadcasts them to receivers, like this computer, set up to pick them up."

"Okay . . ." Linda put that together. "So you can see what the van's camera sees."

"When it's within range. A couple of miles. But more importantly, Scowl's set up to send data to and receive it from Skynet."

"Except communications channels are all clogged up by the virus."

"Except, *except* do you think Skynet's going to allow the radio frequencies, the land lines it's using for its own purposes, to be frozen up by the virus?"

"No, of course not." She finally looked at him. "So you could use Scowl itself to send transmissions to Skynet."

"Scowl's my last available back door. So I need to modify that last package to send through Scowl." He looked around. "Get off the road and behind something. If I know Scowl, it's going to be coming up on our rear end at full speed. If it doesn't spot us by the time it concludes that it must have reached our position, it will assume that we hid and are either still hiding or doubled back. So it'll begin a new search pattern. We need someplace we can hole up for a few hours while I put together that last package . . . and then we need someplace we can keep it for at least a few minutes while I do the upload."

"Keep it." She sounded dubious. But she obligingly pulled off the road and onto a side trail leading up the slope of one of Tehachapi's mountains. In moments they topped a low ridge and were out of sight of the road. "You're talking about tying that thing to a chair while you pump radio waves at it?"

"No. I'm talking about getting it in a narrow, confined area where it's certain we are, so it has to search for us." When she pulled the truck to a stop, he got out. Together they walked back to the ridge, then went flat to watch the road below. "So it searches for us several minutes, all while it stays within broadcast range of my computer and receives that last upload."

"And then?"

"And then we destroy the son of a bitch."

"Sounds good to me."

Half again as fast as the surrounding traffic, Scowl's van roared by on 58.

"I know just the place," Linda said.

"That's my girl."

July, Present Day—Friday Night
Kern County, California

It had taken hours of travel along back roads, farm roads, ranch roads, and unpaved trails through government lands and private properties, but now, as the sun began dipping below the western horizon, they parked on the sloping side of the two-lane road facing the sign that read *Scott's Shooting Range.*

It was, Danny concluded, perfect. Only a few miles from the Ávila home, Scott's was where Alex had taught Danny to shoot, where he'd taught Linda to shoot during their engagement, before she'd joined the Sheriff's Department.

From here they could see the main office, a house-size single-story building with a bagged-ice vending machine, a cola machine, and a gravel parking lot. Behind and to the right was a row of wooden shooting stands facing an earthen berm, a backstop for bullets, a hundred or more yards away.

But that wasn't all there was to this range, as Danny and Linda both knew. The business had several such setups and a skeet range. Most important, it featured a set of crude, roofless buildings something like a Hollywood back lot. Each building was equipped with swing-out silhouettes of human figures—bank robbers, hostages, terrorists, children, cops, dogs. Recreational shooting leagues used Scott's for their competitions, and at least three movies had scenes filmed here in the last three years.

From their position, they could see that the parking lot was almost empty—only an SUV, a smallish Japanese pickup, and an aging white minivan remained. "That's good," Linda said. "Another hour and I'll bet they'll all be out of there."

"Do you suppose they leave a guard at night?"

She shook her head. "I know they don't. There've been some incidents of vandalism out here, and Mr. Scott keeps saying that repairs are still less expensive than a security guard."

"Mmm."

"I'm going to find some spot a mile or two up to park until nightfall."

"Mmm."

"You're sleepy, aren't you?"

"Afraid so."

"Go ahead, get a nap."

"Mmm."

"Danny, time to wake up."

Danny's eyes opened. For a moment, he was suspicious that Linda was playing a joke, but the truck's surroundings were different, and it was full night. Linda had the truck's cab light on.

He stretched. "How long did I sleep?"

"Couple of hours."

Danny, do you hear me?

He stopped in midstretch. "Welcome back," he whispered.

What are you up to?

"Hold on." He glanced sideways at Linda.

She was looking at him. She withdrew just a little. "He's back, isn't he? The other you."

"How can you tell?"

"You always get this look in your eyes. A guarded look."

Hi, Linda.

"Linda, Daniel says hi. Daniel, it's the day before . . . before Judgment Day." Danny was able to keep the immensity of that fact from crashing down on him, from distracting him. "Linda's been driving on back roads all day to avoid Scowl. I've been designing an upload I want to transmit to Skynet through Scowl. We're at a shooting range we're going to booby-trap during the night. If everything goes right, we'll lure Scowl to us tomorrow, run him around on the range to give me time to upload the package, and then we'll terminate the son of a bitch."

Without getting yourselves killed, I hope.

"What do you mean, you hope? You know."

I know . . . from my personal timeline. But there's ample evidence that the future isn't set in stone, and neither is the past. The past has been changed, therefore it can be changed . . . and therefore you can get your ass killed, and I'll wink out of existence, and this conversation will never have happened.

"Oh."

So don't get cocky under the assumption that you're immortal at this stage of your life just because I'm alive years from now.

"Got it."

"What was the 'Oh'? You didn't sound happy."

He shook his head and switched off the dome light. "You don't want to know."

"Oh."

Amply equipped with flashlights and camp lanterns, they prowled around the shooting range. Linda sketched the layout of Silhouette City, the concentration of buildings featuring swing-out and pop-up targets. She sat down with Danny in the building set up like a convenience store.

She put down the sketch between them and inverted it so that the words were right-side-up to Danny. "Okay," she said. "This place grids out into nine squares, three by three. One, upper left, is

Jungle Out There—plywood cutouts representing trees, lots of trees. Two is One-Stop Robbery Shop, where we are now. Three is Domestic Disturbanceville, a single-family dwelling.

"The next row starts with four, First National Hostage Supply, the bank interior. Then five, the big open plaza in the middle with only pop-up targets, there's no sign on that one—"

"Gopherville," Danny said.

Linda snorted. "Gopherville."

"I have many happy teenaged memories of Gopherville."

"Six is Booze & Grease, the bar and grille. Then, the third row, left to right, we have seven, the Gray Stripe Hotel, set up like a jail or prison block; eight, Wreck Farm, the drug laboratory; and nine, the open area with the civilian car and the police cruiser, License Land."

Danny looked over the sketch. He pointed to spots outside the convenience store and the bank. "And here and here we have the two observation towers. Kind of like World War Two guard towers. They look down into everything, and this one," he tapped the tower beside the convenience store, "is where the computer that handles the timing of the swing-out targets is set up."

Linda shook her head. "It's not that big an area. Maybe the size of a small city block. We need to lead Scowl around in that for how long?"

"If everything goes magnificently well, two or three minutes. If Skynet's closed down some of my back doors, meaning the program has to do some searching and probing, I don't know. Four, five minutes? Six?"

"I don't see how we can pull it off. If what you've told me is correct, Scowl's never going to be fooled by swing-out targets. You said it has infrared imaging. So it's only going to chase after the warm targets. You think we can keep it from killing us for six minutes when the best cover we can find is the plywood walls of these building mockups?"

"No, certainly not. So we'll give it lots of targets it *will* react to. We're going to put a road flare on each target we want to really attract its attention, and set it up so the flare lights off before the target swings out. It probably means taking a servo from one swing-out target and putting it on another, so that with each target, Servo Number 1 pops the top of the flare, and then a few seconds later Servo Number 2 swings the target out."

"I hope you bought a lot of flares."

"I bought a *lot* of flares. I thought I was buying several years' worth. Anyway, Scowl will have to look closely at each target, switching between the normal human visual spectrum and infrared imaging, or just put a bunch of ammunition into the target, to be sure it's not a human."

She frowned. "I kind of suspect it'll do the second one."

"Me, too. In which case we might be able to run it dry of ammunition. Force it to use its hands."

"Oh, good. I'd much prefer to die that way."

Danny laughed. "What do you think, Daniel?"

It could work. The early Terminators were pretty unsophisticated.

"Oh, that's damning with faint praise."

Sorry.

July, Present Day—Friday Night
Tehachapi, California

It was full dark by the time Ryan White reached the highest part of the mountain foothills west of Tehachapi and began the last part of the drive to home. Not in the best of moods, he glared at the dashboard, where the heat indicator for his normally reliable Chevy pickup was creeping up toward the red zone.

It wasn't the truck that had put him in the bad mood, but all the driving he'd done today. His errand to Bakersfield, a long-overdue trip to visit his mother, had meant he'd had to do a lot of traveling back and forth along a highway that was increasingly nasty and ill-maintained the closer he got to his mother's home. But now it was done.

He was a star, Ryan was. He hadn't done better than middle-of-the-road scores in college, but he'd been a standout running back with the university's prestigious football team. Three years with the San Diego Chargers had followed, before he'd blown out his right knee for the last time and had to retire from his chosen sport.

But he wasn't stupid. He'd invested his money, not blown it on grossly expensive sports cars or cocaine. Now he was one of Tehachapi's favorite sons, a man of wealth, of means—he owned a chain of hamburger stands, two used-car lots, and convenience stores in Tehachapi and Mojave. So now, still under thirty years of age, he was big, strong, good-looking, increasingly wealthy, unmarried and staying so very successfully without lacking female companionship. His one bum knee was the only downside in his life.

He was still a couple of miles from home when a vehicle in the oncoming lane passed him, then immediately screeched into a controlled spin and accelerated in pursuit of him.

"Shit." Ryan glanced into the rearview mirror. His glimpse at the vehicle as it had passed was of a big, dark van. Had it been a police cruiser, he'd know what to expect, but this could be anything—drugged-up gangbangers far from home, a celebrity stalker reduced to hunting someone with as reduced a level of fame as Ryan enjoyed, anything. Ryan pressed the accelerator down. Better to be pulled over by cops for speeding than loaded up for delivery to a morgue.

The van gained on him. Ryan swore. His pickup had a V8 engine and was in good tune. The van was obviously not something off a normal factory assembly line.

More possibilities for the van's driver and passengers flashed through his mind. Groupies who'd just abandoned a rock band and decided to attach themselves to an ex-jock. Men with black sunglasses from Area 51 who assumed he'd seen something he wasn't supposed to. Barefoot backwood cannibals who drove expensive late-model vans.

The van came up nearly to his rear bumper, then sideslipped into the oncoming traffic lane. As it crept up alongside, Ryan gripped his steering wheel tightly. He wasn't going to be forced off the road and cooked by his own exploding pickup. Hell, his vehicle probably outweighed the other one. He'd force *them* off the road, watch *them* flip and roll. Adrenaline was jolting through him, giving him the strength and quickness it took to knock a 300-pound lineman on his ass.

The van came alongside and Ryan glanced left, through the van's open passenger-side window at the driver.

The driver was . . . not human. It had a triangular head with a flat face; there were glowing red lights where its eyes should be. Its body was huge and bulky.

But it had its hands on the wheel at the ten o'clock and two o'clock positions, and it did nothing more than stare at Ryan . . . and then begin to decelerate.

Ryan stared at it, open-mouthed, until the van dropped back out of his direct sight. For all his speculation, he hadn't really expected the driver to be something that weird.

He heard gravel grind under his right wheels. He looked forward just in time to realize that he was half off the road; it had curved leftward and he was still going straight, aimed unerringly for a Joshua tree . . .

He yanked the wheel to the left. His truck grazed the tree and he heard it clip his right-side mirror clean off the chassis. Then the wheel jerked under his hands and he was tilting, tilting . . .

■ ■ ■

Now Ryan's knee hurt worse than ever.

He stood, most of his weight on his left leg, beside his truck as it lay on its right side in the sandy soil fifty yards from the highway. It hadn't crumpled, it hadn't caught fire, but by God it had rolled over, and he was an unhappy man.

It had taken four calls on his cell phone before he'd reached the local Sheriff's Department, and now, half an hour after the wreck, he finally saw the lights of an oncoming cruiser. The vehicle slowed as it left the highway and crept along, bouncing a bit, as it navigated the desert soil to stop a few yards away.

Sergeant Harry Farland, with his long, dour face, climbed out of the driver's seat and Ryan breathed out a sigh of relief. Even a well-off local hero like Ryan sometimes caught flak from peace officers because he was black, but he'd known Farland for years, and the man was not the type who offered that sort of trouble.

"Evenin', Ryan," Farland said, and looked solemnly at the front of the truck.

"Evenin', Harry." Ryan matched the peace officer's drawling tone.

"Drunk?"

"Nope."

"Just stupid?"

Ryan broke into a laugh. "Man, you will *never* believe what happened to me."

"Hold it." Farland pulled a notebook from a shirt pocket, flipped it open about halfway through. He glanced between it and the front bumper of Ryan's truck.

"What is it?"

"What the hell are you doing driving a stolen truck, Ryan? You've got two lots full of trucks."

"Stolen, my ass. This is *my* truck. You've seen me drive it a hundred times. Look, here's my 'Football players do it with leather balls' bumper sticker."

"Yeah, you're right, it is." Farland approached and bent to inspect the license plate. He looked away, considering. "Someone could have switched plates on you."

"Look, I don't give a shit about that right now. I know you're not going to believe this, but a robot drove me off the road."

"A robot."

"That's right, a robot."

"What did this robot look like?"

There was something odd about Farland's tone, something that caused worry to flutter in Ryan's stomach.

There was no amusement, no condescension in Farland's voice. In fact, he'd gone tense, almost rigid.

"Uh, I didn't see all of it. Kind of a white, what do you call it, hull. Metal hands. Face like an upside-down triangle with red lights for eyes—"

Farland snapped into motion, returning to his cruiser. He reached in to grab his radio mike.

Ryan shut up. Something very bad was going on here, and he was suddenly glad that he was only on the outskirts of it.

July, Present Day—Friday Night, Saturday A.M.
Scott's Shooting Range

It was a lengthy job. Danny spent most of his time in the early hours up in the main observation towers, setting up a large number of timing sequences for the pop-up targets. Meanwhile, Linda prowled the weird environment of Silhouette City, dealing with flares, duct tape, wires, and servos. Later, Danny joined her at ground level to finish the preparations among the buildings. Throughout, Daniel was on hand at the other end of their cross-time link, and with him was a growing crowd of experts—Mike, John, Kate, Mark, others.

Finally their initial preparations were done. "What is it, about two-thirty?" Danny asked.

Linda checked her watch. "Two-thirty-eight A.M."

"I kinda figured the A.M. part." Danny looked up. From here, miles out from any large community, he could clearly see a sea of stars overhead, nearly from horizon to horizon. "Damn, that's pretty."

She snickered. "Good to see you can still take time out to smell the flowers."

"Better than smelling myself. Anyway, we need to get some sleep. Probably ought to get up as early as we can manage in the morning and do whatever it takes to lure Scowl in."

"I'll get the bedrolls." She loped off into the darkness. They'd returned the pickup to the road just off the shooting range property. Mark Herrera had recommended that it be left outside Scowl's probable initial search radius. If Scowl found it, the Terminator was likely to disable it. They couldn't have that.

You're doing good, kid.

"Yeah, sure. So what's this burning in my stomach?"

That's from all the junk food you've been gulping down the last couple of days. Let me give you some advice. Lay off the junk food.

"Daniel, I'm going to have to ask you to take a hike for a while."

What, cut off contact now? That doesn't make any sense.

"It makes perfect sense to me. It's my last night with Linda before Judgment Day. I don't know what all's going to happen and you refuse to tell me. So I'm going to have some private time with her."

I . . . can't argue too much with that. But you'll have to get some sleep before you get going in the morning. Otherwise I might not be able to reach you again.

"I'll find some way to doze off. Trust me."

Adios, Danielcito.

"Adios, abuelito." *Farewell, Grandpa.*

August 2029
The Grottoes

John and Kate, in the outer chamber, heard Lake's recitation of Daniel's condition: "Subject is returning to full lucidity and awareness. Blood pressure dropping. Heart rate dropping, one hundred beats per minute, ninety . . ."

Then there was Daniel's voice, stronger than when he was in his dreaming state, slurred from his condition, testy: "For God's sake, woman, do you have to *narrate* me?"

Mark Herrera emerged from the inner chamber. "Gonna get

some sack time," he said. He flipped a switch beside the outer door. "Going to green light status."

"You staying here or going back into town?" Kate asked.

Mark stepped into the cylindrical exit. "Here. I don't want to be more than a few seconds away."

"Good man," John said.

July, Present Day—Saturday A.M.
Scott's Shooting Range

Under the stars, in the moonlight, Danny and Linda made love, comforted one another, drifted off to sleep.

Had they been able to go home tomorrow, go back to work, marry, it would have been the perfect ending. The thought made Danny choke up. There was not going to be a happy ending, and at some point—maybe tomorrow, maybe a year from now, the older Daniel wouldn't say—Linda would be snatched from him.

The rest of the world would go first.

On that somber thought, Danny slept.

August 2029
The Grottoes

John and Kate sat, their backs against ancient mountain stone, just yards from where the indoor waterfall coursed down the rocks. Fine spray accumulated on their hands and faces, began a slow soak of their clothes.

"Right now, miles south of where they are, I'm wiping out on my bike headed out of L.A.," John said. "Or already on the back of a truck, my leg bleeding, headed back into the city. In a couple of hours, I break into a veterinary clinic. About half an hour after that, you show up."

"And thirteen hours after that, the world goes to hell," Kate said, her voice low.

"That's not what I was leading up to. I was going to dwell on the 'you show up' part."

They were in near-total darkness; only a bit of green from the bulb over the entryway into Danny's enclosure illuminated this place. John couldn't see whether Kate was smiling, but did feel her lay her head against his shoulder. "Okay," she said, "you can dwell on that."

Minutes later John was jarred by the the rumble of the door into Daniel's enclosure. He came upright, uneasily aware that he'd drifted off to sleep, and felt Kate moving beside him.

The bulb cast a long shadow from whoever had stepped out of the enclosure, but now it was red, not green. "John?" it called. It was Lake. "Kate?"

"We're here." John got to his feet, extended a hand for Kate, but she was already up.

"Daniel's in again. Danny and Linda are on the go."

July, Present Day—Saturday Morning
Judgment Day
Scott's Shooting Range

The sun was glaring at them from the east, not yet high enough to pour its heat on them but bright enough to induce headaches. Danny glared back at it, then shouldered his way into the shooting range's main building, which served as office and a store for various calibers and grades of ammunition, for cleaning and reloading supplies, for how-to manuals and recreational shooters' magazines. He and Linda had forced the lock last night, had denuded its shelves of ammunition in the calibers they were using.

Linda was waiting in the office. She looked as weary as Danny felt. She suppressed a yawn as he came in. "The map's ready, and I have your script." She pointed to a single sheet of paper with her handwriting all over it. "But you're sure about what Scowl saw."

"It saw the rear end of our truck after it fell off," Danny said. "Which means it saw the license plate. It will have recorded everything it saw and will have sent that image on to Skynet. Coordination of information is what Skynet is all about—what it was *supposed* to be about. We announce it, and Scowl will come fast. But since it's not the same license plate as the one of the truck I stole, the authorities aren't going to match it with the theft, so the cops won't come in any hurry."

"Okay," she said. "Let's do it."

Danny read over the words she'd written, spent a few minutes familiarizing himself with them. Then he switched on the CB radio set situated on the corner of the desk. Freddie Scott, owner of the range, wasn't a survivalist, but he did believe in preparation and redundancy; he had phones, citizen's band radio, shortwave radio, food stores, bottled water, and, of course, plentiful ammunition at this site. Alex had told Danny that the man had a shack somewhere on the property, someplace to live in the unlikely event that some emergency made the cities untenable.

Danny hoped Scott would be able to make it out here when the bombs started dropping.

The CB blared to life with voices, unusually heavy traffic. It was set to the standard motorist's channel, 19. Danny and Linda listened for a minute; it was all familiar reports of traffic obstacles such as collisions, reports of peace officer movements, sleep-deprived ramblings by motorists who'd driven all night. But there was also griping about cell phones not functioning, unusually heavy police and military traffic for this hour, other signs that made Danny's shoulders tighten.

He switched over to the comparative peace of channel 9 and squeezed the transmit button on the mike. He made his voice sound younger, uncertain. "Hello? Anyone there? I'm looking for the Sheriff's Department."

Silence.

He prepared to repeat himself, but a staticky female voice came across the speaker: "This is the Kern County Sheriff's Department. Is that who you're looking for?"

"Yeah, I'm in Kern County."

"What's the nature of your emergency?"

"Well, it's not an emergency. But I can't seem to get through to you on the phones to report it, so I tried this."

"That's all right. The phones are all messed up this morning. What's your name, and what did you want to report?"

"I'm Billy Day, and I'm opening Scott's Shooting Range for business this morning, and there's an abandoned truck right in the middle of our skeet range."

"Ah. Well . . . sure." The Sheriff's Department dispatcher sounded distracted. "Go ahead and give me the information on that and we'll get someone over there, probably this afternoon."

"Thanks." Danny gave her the make, color, and license number of the stolen pickup, which was actually parked nowhere near the skeet range.

The false report done, Danny switched off the CB. "Now we get into position and wait."

"And fast," Linda said. "Just in case it's only a couple of miles down the road."

"Yeah." Danny sighed. He'd much have preferred for a platoon of soldiers to be where he was right now. "Showtime."

Scowl was a second-generation Terminator. It had hands instead of chain guns, a voice synthesizer, a vocal interpreter that could process spoken words into data and analyze their meaning.

But the vocal interpreter was nothing like the ones later Terminator models would receive. It could not analyze stress patterns. It could measure peaks and troughs in pitch and volume and make rough calculations as to whether two samples of speech had been produced by different humans, but it could in no wise recognize a specific voice.

So in its monitoring of communications traffic along official radio frequencies it heard and correctly interpreted Danny's words, but did not recognize the voice as belonging to Danny Ávila. Instead, it added the fictitious Billy Day to the list of humans peripherally involved with its investigation . . . the list of humans who would probably have to be exterminated.

It brought up a map and business phone listing for the county, found Scott's Shooting Range, calculated a route from its current location to that destination, and headed in that direction.

Danny Ávila had plywood over his head and dirt all around. He sat in dirt, illuminated only by the glow from his laptop screen. "Not exactly a dignified position for a guy who's about to face death," he said.

I have to agree with you there, kid.

Danny leaned back against one dirt wall of the pit, keeping his eyes on the laptop. The only thing on the screen was a small gray bar on which were ten gray circles in a line.

One of the circles, the one at far left, went from gray to green.

Danny picked up the walkie-talkie beside him. "Linda, signal strength one," he said.

"I hear you."

They'd agreed to keep transmissions simple, their language coded so that Scowl wouldn't understand their words even if it heard them. Danny had shown her the signal strength gauge on his computer and explained what it meant. Now he'd told her that he'd just received a weak signal from Scowl's wireless transmitter. Scowl could only be a few miles away. As he got closer, the signal strength would increase and he'd begin to receive camera transmissions from Scowl and its van.

He felt his heart pounding.

Better get a grip on that, kid. There's high blood pressure in our family.

"Yeah, I know."

Scowl turned into the driveway past the sign reading *Scott's Shooting Range.* The parking lot beyond was empty, and there were no heat signatures to indicate that any humans were about.

The extensive range of maps in Scowl's memory and operations files did not include a diagram of the shooting range, so Scowl did not know which area constituted the skeet range where the truck had been abandoned. Scowl's van, though it had shock absorption and tires capable of carrying it over the rough terrain of the range, did not have the clearance of an off-road vehicle, so the Terminator opted to park and begin explorations on its own tracks.

Exiting the van, Scowl crashed through the office front door and took a look around the office. It seemed to be unoccupied; the lack of operating electronic equipment, air conditioning, or significant heat traces indicated that Scowl's targets were not present.

On one wall was a diagram labeled with the name of the business and indicating the relative positions of the property's various subcomponents. It took Scowl an extra moment to perform optical character recognition on the letters labeling those subcomponents; the map seemed to have been produced in such a fashion as to resemble hand-drawing and hand-labeling. An irregular blob north of OFFICE was labeled SKEET RANGE. In the middle of SKEET RANGE was a much smaller blob labeled ABANDONED TRUCK.

Scowl took the opportunity, on leaving the office, to open the oversize door into the large metal bin labeled ICE FOR SALE. The bin's interior registered a temperature well below that of the ambient air, but was empty both of ice for sale or humans. Scowl noted that a padlock that had held the door closed had recently been cut and discarded on the ground. The detail seemed irrelevant to Scowl's mission, so the Terminator filed and dismissed it. The machine labeled ICE COLD DRINKS was full of machinery and cylindrical dispensable products. It could not possibly hold hiding humans.

The Terminator turned to roll northward.

"Uploading my package to Scowl's internal memory," Danny said, his voice low.

Is there any chance of you taking control of Scowl? That was Mark's voice.

"Yeah, sure. If I remain in contact with it for a few hours and run through several thousand possible password combinations. This package upload will work because Scowl's always open to receive archived images from the van's computer, big bundles of one-frame-per-second camera views and instrument readings. I'm disguising the patch for the Continuum Transporter power satellite program as one of them. The Terminator series mainframe at CRS automatically opens, processes, and stores these packages, so it's going to slide in without anyone noticing."

Good man, Mark said.

Danny switched the view on his laptop screen from his upload window to the robot's camera view. Now he could see Scowl's progress. The robot was leaving the vicinity of the office and rolling straight toward the southwest corner of Silhouette City.

He spoke into his walkie-talkie: "Incoming."

He got no reply. Nor was he supposed to. Unless something went wrong, Linda was to let him do all the transmitting. Scowl's crude radio detectors would eventually be able to home on transmission sources. Danny needed to be found. Linda didn't.

Scowl approached the area bounded by plywood buildings. It could not see the region's interior to detect the abandoned pickup truck. It did scan right and left, confirming that it was roughly between a long pile of grass-covered earth, corresponding to its internal dictionary's definition of berm, on the right, and a stand of trees on the left, both of which had been on the crude map in the office.

The region it knew as Skeet Range had two elevated constructions beside it, one to Scowl's right, one ahead. It elevated its view. One was at approximately the ambient air temperature. One was slightly cooler. Neither registered a heat trace indicative of humans.

Its optical sensors detected movement at ground level ahead. It redirected its attention toward the plywood there. That section of ground was characterized by wood of two-by-four construction supporting plywood painted in green, with darker decorative motifs Scowl was not programmed to interpret. In its normal vision, a tan figure had popped out from behind one of them. It looked something like a human being, though Scowl's recognition software put the probability at only forty-eight percent of it being alive. If it was human, it was wearing a dark garment concealing its facial features and carrying a handgun. It was, however, not moving.

Scowl clicked over to infrared. The figure was warmer than the surrounding air. The heat signature did not match the size of the figure but it was growing bigger and warmer.

Scowl aimed the chain gun in its right hand and fired. Depleted-uranium rounds tore through the figure, shredding it. It dropped back out of sight behind more plywood. The heat trace continued to build.

Scowl advanced, knocking plywood trees out of the way.

Another target with an anomalous heat signature appeared among the tight-packed rows of plywood constructions. Scowl put a few rounds through it, but it remained upright, so the robot continued its fire. Finally it fell.

Scowl rolled forward to study this target as well. The robot's movements knocked more of the construction over, so plywood fell down atop the target. The collapse of wood was almost flush with the ground. Scowl concluded that neither target could have been human; humans were more than an inch thick.

Now most of this section of construction was down, and some of it was catching fire. Evidently the first target had been incendiary. Scowl rolled out into the central area of Skeet Range and took a look around.

There was plywood construction in almost every direction. Scowl performed optical character recognition on the signs it saw posted: FIRST NATIONAL HOSTAGE SUPPLY. DANNY ÁVILA WAS HERE. DOMESTIC DISTURBANCEVILLE.

The register of Ávila's name kicked that location up to the very top of Scowl's current list. The Terminator spun and headed toward the door into the plywood convenience store.

Linda sat on a tarpaulin that itself was spread across a bed of rapidly melting bags of ice. Her butt was cold, and her eye was pressed

to a hole she and Danny had drilled in the side wall of the observation tower last night. She decided that this was not a dignified or
comfortable place for someone trying to help save the human race.

Below, Scowl rolled toward the One-Stop Robbery Shop.
Linda leaned back and peeked over the lip of the table where the
tower's computer system was set up.

The computer wasn't running Windows or a Macintosh operating system or any system she was familiar with; Daniel had
taught her the basic functions of its proprietary text-based interface last night. She quickly typed in the command that activated
the One-Stop Robbery Shop timed sequence Danny had put
together. As Scowl crashed through the plywood door into the
simulated convenience store, she hit the Enter key.

Then she heard it, the shouted command: "Daniel Ávila, we
have you surrounded! Come out with your hands in the air!"

July, Present Day—Saturday Morning
Judgment Day
Scott's Shooting Range

Linda went flat on the cold tarpaulin. The shout had come from the direction of the shooting range's office. She crawled to that side of the tower and peered through the hole they'd drilled there.

There was nothing, no movement. Then she detected something just at the verge of her vision, one or two figures moving through a stand of trees that ran from near the office to near Silhouette City. She got the impression of military uniforms and M16s.

She swore to herself. Danny, in his hideout, might not have heard the shout; he'd be unaware. Worse yet, Scowl doubtless *had* heard it, which meant the robot would have to decide between investigating it and dealing with the swing-out targets in the convenience store.

She scrambled back to her original position and picked up her walkie-talkie, then hesitated. If these military folk were monitoring radio frequencies, her transmission might be overheard. Worse yet, Scowl might detect her as a transmission source.

One problem at a time. She'd warn Danny in Spanish. The odds that whoever might be listening in was a Spanish speaker were too high to be comfortable, but it was certainly better than transmitting in English. She pressed the mike button.

■ ■ ■

In Scowl's camera view, as viewed on Danny's laptop, a brightly glowing two-dimensional robber swung in just ahead, partially filling the end of an aisle of the wooden store, and then disintegrated under fire from Scowl's chain gun.

Then the view retreated as Scowl backed out of the One-Stop Robbery Shop. Its camera view swung around toward the south. The flattened, burning Jungle Out There setup occupied the right third of the camera view; the false bank was straight ahead, the false prison to the left.

What the hell was the Terminator doing? Had Linda activated a second timing sequence prematurely? Danny reached for his walkie-talkie, but it blared in his hand. "Danny, military police are here, they're shouting for you to come out." She spoke in Spanish.

Danny's heart sank. "Dammit." He could hear Daniel swearing in the background of his mind. Daniel must be able to see through his eyes this time, as he had the last couple of sessions.

He keyed his walkie-talkie. "Hold your position," he said. "We improvise."

August 2029
The Grottoes

"That's not the way it happened," Mike protested.

John, already clutching the edge of the table beside Daniel's bed, didn't much care for the additional uncertainty her statement brought. "What do you mean?"

"There were no Air Force men! We handled Scowl ourselves. Why is it different?"

Lake asked, "Could you have forgotten them?"

Mike fixed her with a stare that might convince a university department head that he was a blithering idiot, but Lake stayed steady, unrelenting under her gaze. "No," Mike hissed. "Not a chance."

"Microparadoxes," Mark said. He stood well back from the bed, ready to step forward and offer technical help whenever asked.

Kate, seated beside John, turned to him. "What?"

Mark said, "What we've been doing, fiddling in time through Daniel, it may have been causing all the same sorts of paradoxes we've been theorizing about ever since we discovered the Continuum Transporter. Perhaps we've made changes that aren't sufficient to unbuckle history as we know it, nothing like killing Commander Connor in the past would do. But maybe it's making little changes, little ripples. Too small to change the world as we know it now . . . so we aren't affected. Our memories aren't changed."

"We aren't edited," Daniel said.

"So . . ." Kate thought it through. "So the presence of the Air Force men doesn't change anything."

"For us, maybe," Daniel said. "Ask *them* if anything's changed when they've run up against Scowl."

The Air Force Security Police personnel moved up, five pairs and one commander. Their leader, 2nd Lieutenant Charles Holden of Iowa City, a newly minted officer, tall and blond and every inch the Hollywood image of a young military leader, refrained from griping about the fact that the enlisted men with him had M16s while he had only an officer's handgun. Griping seemed a sure way to lose their respect, particularly as they didn't know him—his orders had been to leave CRS, assemble a unit of men from the Air Force Security Police stationed elsewhere at Edwards, and endlessly patrol portions of 58 between Bakersfield and Mojave. It had been a boring assignment; he'd even suspected that it might be punishment detail until he'd been instructed to come to this site and arrest Daniel Ávila.

He concentrated on moving forward through the trees as quietly as his dress shoes and lack of woodsmanship skills would allow. The men with him, Senior Airman Sam Hardy, a moon-faced black man from Georgia, and Airman Randall Walberg, a rail-skinny white man from Illinois, moved silently and gracefully, and Holden hated them for it.

They got in position at the leading edge of the trees. From here, they could see through the burning stand of wood that had once been painted to resemble a child's vision of a forest. Past it, they could see the open center section of this portion of the shooting range.

Holden waited another minute, long enough for his other two men to be getting into position. Then he leaned around the tree he had his back to and shouted, "Daniel Ávila, we have you sur-rounded! Come out with your hands in the air!"

He glanced back at Hardy and Walberg. He couldn't tell if the men's eyes reflected amusement or just readiness. He leaned back around to watch the shooting range.

There was a crashing noise, the sound of thin wood breaking away, and something rolled into his view. It was a squat thing on tracks, with a moving head and arms that suggested a rough human configuration. Its paint had originally been white, but was now scarred in several places by black and brown patches.

And it held a weapon in each hand—a chain gun in the right, a submachine gun in the left.

"What the *hell* is that?" Hardy said, his voice a bare whisper.

Holden froze. That was a T-1 mobile weapons system, a Ter-minator—no, not quite a T-1, as it was smaller and had articulated arms and hands. But it was something that should not be in the field alone, something the men with him should never have been allowed to see.

Finally, though, things made sense. The Air Force had to be looking for Ávila not because he was off performing a shooting spree—that was a consideration for civilian law enforcement—but because he had made off with a Terminator. Holden changed his mental label for Ávila from "madman" to "traitor," a far more derogatory term. Maybe Ávila was both.

Well, there was nothing to do about this but cover things up as much as possible. "That's a missing Air Force weapons platform," Holden said. "Which no one on this exercise will remember after we deliver it back to Edwards. Ávila's probably operating it by remote control."

"Yes, sir."

Holden took a deep breath and shouted again, "Ávila, have that damned apparatus drop its weapons and put its hands in the sky, or—"

The damned apparatus aimed the chain gun and fired. Holden felt the tree he leaned against shuddering. He ducked fully behind it, but the blows to his back felt like the tree was coming apart.

He scooted down and went flat, dirtying his uniform. Hardy and Walberg were already on the ground. All around the two of them, the forest edge blurred as tree trunks, leafy branches, and undergrowth were ripped to confetti. Holden thrashed around, making himself as small a target as humanly possible, and didn't realize that he was howling in outrage until the incoming fire stopped.

He choked off his shout and looked at Hardy. The other men's eyes were round, their pupils tiny.

"What are you waiting for?" Holden said. "Destroy that tin-can piece of shit!"

"Yes, sir." Walberg sounded dubious. He and Hardy squirmed around, bringing their M16s to bear on the distant target.

Holden raised his voice so that his other men could hear. "Open fire!"

Even in his hiding place, Danny could hear the gunfire. He sat, frozen by indecision, as the muffled reports banged at the plywood across the top of his hideout. He'd seen the officer's face clearly in Scowl's camera view before the shooting started.

He didn't know these men.

They were going to be killed.

They'd be dead anyway in a day. If he exposed himself to help them, he'd probably die and accomplish nothing.

Your head's a mess, kid.

"I bet yours is worse." Danny shoved up on the plywood over his head. He hurled it away. Sunlight spilled across him and he stood up in the waist-deep pit he and Linda had dug last night.

The pit was to one side of the gap between the two decrepit cars in the Silhouette City area called License Land. When Danny stood, he could see through the gap between them, see across Gopherville, look straight at Scowl's backside. Beyond Scowl, the remains of Jungle Out There were being riddled by gunfire, as was the stand of trees in the distance.

He could call Scowl to him. That might still successfully set up what they had in mind for the Terminator. But it didn't give them enough time for the other part of their mission. He glanced down at his laptop screen. His initial packet had been uploaded to Scowl, and the indicator bar showed that the connection to Edwards was still open, but his program was still trying to negotiate its way into one of Skynet's back doors. He needed more time.

But there were men under fire out there now. Danny waved his hands, shouted, "Terminator! I'm here! Danny Ávila! Come and get me!"

Scowl turned to look at him.

Linda peeked through the hole overlooking Silhouette City. She could see Scowl firing . . . and Danny standing far behind it, waving.

She couldn't hear his words. The roar from Scowl's chain gun was too loud. But other than turning, Scowl didn't react to Danny's presence, not yet. When it did, it would kill him.

Scowl churned through its available options.

It was no longer operating under a mandate that it eliminate any human that witnessed it. Therefore it did not have to divert from its prime goal long enough to kill all the humans who had just arrived in its vicinity.

But they were armed, and sustained fire with the assault rifles stood a good chance of damaging Scowl. Therefore it must reduce their ability to harm it. Only then could it return to kill Ávila.

It turned away from Ávila and rolled forward, angling around the burning mound of wood through which it had entered Skeet Range, and began firing at heat traces as it detected them. From here, it could detect nine distinct blobs of heat that corresponded to organisms of human size or larger; several of them could have represented multiple humans.

No—cycling through its visual capabilities, it realized that the two largest heat sources were vehicles parked near Scowl's own van near the building closest to the road. It calculated a high probability that the Humvee and the military truck there had acted as transport for the humans now shooting at it, and an equally high likelihood that one or both of them contained communications gear superior to any the humans might be individually carrying.

Scowl ignored the humans for another moment, rolled farther away from Skeet Range, and laid down a burst of fire against the truck and then the Humvee.

The truck's front end was quickly shredded and the vehicle ignited. The Humvee was more durable. Scowl continued to pour rounds into it.

■ ■ ■

Senior Airman Tom Begay, USAF, his M16 across his back, quickly climbed the ladder permanently affixed to the observation tower. The robot, facing the other way and destroying the two transports, hadn't detected his dash to the tower's base and still hadn't turned around. He was certain that he could make the top before it finished with the vehicles, certain that he'd be able to act as a spotter for his unit from the altitude of the tower platform.

As he climbed the last five feet, he willed the robot not to spin and look at him. It would not. It would not.

He heaved himself up over the lip of the tower platform's waist-high wall, tilting forward into what would be a controlled roll onto the platform floor.

But there was someone there, a blond woman in dark clothes. He got only a glimpse of her. She was right in front of him. She grabbed his hair and yanked him prematurely into his roll. With a shout, Begay crashed back-first onto a cold, irregular surface.

He threw up an arm—too late. The woman's hand, holding a handgun, banged down onto his skull.

He felt the first blow. He got his other hand up but she struck him again anyway. This time he saw the pistol butt descend—saw the world jar as it hit him, but did not feel the blow. The third time he only saw it begin its descent.

Linda, sickened by what she'd just had to do, wiped her mouth with the back of her free hand and stared down at the man she'd just battered into unconsciousness.

He was nice-looking, about her age. His coloration and features suggested that he was Native American. His forehead was a bloody mess and his eyes were closed.

She didn't have time for emotions now. Being sick could cost her. She set the Glock aside, rolled the Air Force man over on his chest, and handcuffed him.

This was wrong, wrong, wrong. Now, in addition to aiding and abetting a known fugitive, stealing munitions, and driving recklessly, she had assaulted a military man who was doing his job.

On the other hand, now she had an M16.

She retrieved both it and the Glock, then scooted back to the hole that looked down on Silhouette City.

She saw what was going on there and cursed. "Damn you, Danny."

Danny climbed up out of the pit and continued his shout, but Scowl rolled through the burning Jungle Out There area and disappeared from his sight.

What the hell? It took a moment for Danny to run through the calculations Scowl was probably making.

Danny had to have been reprioritized, placed below the elimination of soldiers with assault rifles on Scowl's list of priorities. That meant Scowl's departure was temporary. The Terminator would be back in a minute, probably better equipped to handle its attackers.

Danny growled to himself. He couldn't save those Air Force men, but he couldn't stand by and watch them die. It was just like the situation with his future friends.

He dashed forward, following Scowl, and drew his Colt.

Both Air Force transports were now riddled and fully engaged with fire. Scowl did a slow 360-degree spin, recalculating the locations of its enemies, some of whom were sniping on it again. Scowl calculated from its internal kinetic sensors and audio analyzers that the enemies were firing on him with assault rifles.

One of its enemies was advancing from the direction of Skeet Range. It had a handgun in hand and settled into a posture suggesting that it was about to open fire. It was fully exposed and Scowl could see its features. It did a routine check on its very limited database of photographs and once again confirmed the identity of the enemy as Daniel Ávila.

But the robot's short-term goal registered him as being less of an immediate threat than the armed enemies. His weapon was less formidable than theirs. It turned its back on Ávila once more and began firing at the others.

Danny stood at the edge of Jungle Out There, still close enough that he could feel the nearby fire as a wall of heat, and fired at Scowl. Methodically, he put four rounds into Scowl's back—then five, six—but the robot continued rolling away from him.

The robot had ignored him. He was just too low on its priority list at the moment. But if it remained uninterested in following him, he might not be able to lead it where he needed it to go.

Something whined beside his head. It was a round from one of the embattled Air Force men, forty or fifty yards away; the shooter was in the woods nearly opposite Danny with Scowl between them.

Right. Now he was going to be killed by stray fire from the Air Force. Danny dropped and scuttled on hands and knees behind the minimal cover offered by First National Hostage Supply.

Well, things weren't as bad as all that. He might not be able to destroy Scowl . . . but the diversion was giving his program time to complete itself.

■ ■ ■

The barrel of the chain gun in Scowl's hand continued to spin, but the robot observed that no new rounds were emerging from it.

It was out of ammunition. Scowl considered reloading, but decided that the chain gun was only of limited utility against the humans, who were cannily concealing themselves behind hardy trees. Scowl calculated that moving into the stands of trees would limit its own mobility and functionality while doing little to limit the humans. Therefore its best tactic involved neither continued employment of the chain gun nor direct confrontation of the humans.

It turned and headed at maximum speed back to its van.

"We've got it on the run!" Holden said.

Hardy and Walberg looked at him, no longer concealing the fact that they obviously thought he was crazy.

He didn't care. He was correct. He'd directed sustained, effective fire against the robot unit, and now it was fleeing. But they didn't say anything. They were obviously bright enough, just barely, to consider what effect insolence might have on their military careers.

He spoke into the chin mike of his headset. "Has anyone spotted Ávila?"

"Lieutenant, Abrams. I think I saw him a moment ago near that burn pile. He went back into the buildings."

"You and Miller go after him. Everyone else, we're going after the robot." He got a chorus of acknowledgments from his men.

But not from the men with him. Hardy said, "Sir, if I can ask—"

"Go ahead." Holden looked back through the trees toward the shooting range's office. The stand of trees he and the other two had used as cover was small, isolated from the main tree-line where the other men were emplaced. As soon as they left they'd be exposed. But only a few seconds' dash away was the nearest edge of the berm of earth used as a backstop by one of the shooting areas.

"I thought our objective was this Ávila guy, and nothing but. And if we get him, we just grab the controls and shut the robot down."

"Fair enough." It was true, the capture—dead or alive—of Daniel Ávila was the only objective mentioned on Holden's orders.

But Holden knew, in spite of what he'd told the others, that Ávila probably wasn't operating it by remote control; that's not the way those robots were supposed to work. The man had probably programmed it with a specific set of instructions . . . meaning that when Ávila was captured, it didn't automatically mean the Terminator was out of commission.

But he couldn't tell these men that. He could only tell them a few details and falsehoods, and once they got back to Edwards they were in store for hours' or days' worth of debriefing that would convince them they were never, ever to mention the robot again, even to one another.

Holden made his voice harsh. "But that's not your concern right now. Your concern is obeying orders. We're going to keep the robot from escaping. We're going to make a run over to that berm, then use it for cover as we follow the robot. Ready . . . go." He stood and ran. A moment later, he heard the two men following him.

They were probably exchanging glances and rolling their eyes. He knew how these enlisted men were, particularly those, like Hardy, who'd been in the service longer than the officers they served. Well, he'd use this mission to teach them a little something about lines of command.

■ ■ ■

Scowl reached the van. It didn't bother entering the vehicle; it grabbed the passenger door and tore it free, revealing the box of weapons and ammunition CRS referred to as its standard urban combat package. Automatically, it replaced the chain gun in its rack and sought out other weapons.

It abandoned the MP5-N submachine gun it had been carrying, gathered up several clips of .223 ammunition and inserted them in a carrying compartment on its back, and then took up an M16A2 assault rifle equipped with an M203 40mm grenade launcher. The weapon looked like the classic M16, but with an additional, very broad barrel beneath its usual barrel.

It was two weapons in one, the first suited to direct fire, the second to indirect fire. The weapon was nearly ideal for the intermediary goal Scowl faced.

Scowl took all the 40mm grenades carried in the ammunition box, loading the first and placing the remainder in another carrying compartment. Then it turned and headed back toward Skeet Range.

July, Present Day—Saturday Morning
Judgment Day
Scott's Shooting Range

Senior Airman Ed Abrams and Airman Dave Miller dashed across the open space between the edge of the trees and the nearest cover provided by the silhouette range. Had the robot spun and opened fire with its submachine gun the moment they broke cover it could have killed them, but they counted on their speed, on the robot's apparent urgency in getting away from the area.

Abrams leading, they moved along one edge of the plywood building. Abrams reached the corner and, his M16 up and ready, looked across the silhouette range.

In the brief moment he had to take in the odd building fronts, he saw a blur of motion from the right—a human figure leaping from the open into the door of the building labeled FIRST NATIONAL HOSTAGE SUPPLY. He swung his assault rifle around to cover, but the target, who looked a lot like the picture they had of Ávila, was already inside.

He'd seen the rear of that building during their initial approach. It had not featured a rear door, nor had their been an exit on the side facing the burning jungle setup. "Keep to cover," he said, "and get to where you can see the left side of the building with the FIRST NATIONAL sign. We've got him."

■ ■ ■

Linda saw the two Air Force men move around the back of the One-Stop Robbery Shop, saw Danny make his dash into the false bank building. She swore, her voice a wail. There was nothing she could do short of taking up her captured M16 and opening fire on the men.

No, wait. There *was* something she could do. She turned to the computer console above her peephole and typed in a command.

Danny huddled at the back of the bank, behind the plywood barriers set up roughly to look like tellers' windows. His back was against the building's rear wall—a quarter-inch of pressed board was all he had to protect him from incoming rounds.

Linda's voice came over his walkie-talkie. "There are two of them." Danny dialed the volume down so that the men outside wouldn't hear. Linda continued, "One's covering the front and right wall, the other the front and left wall."

He pressed the talk button. "Great. I could get out the back, but they'd hear me banging my way out. They'd come running."

"Get down and be ready to kick your way out. Their shooting will cover the noise."

"*Shooting.*"

"Starting in five seconds, four, three—"

Danny went flat, spun around so that his legs were in a position to lash out against the nearest slab of plywood.

Abrams could see Miller take cover inside the front door of the building labeled WRECK FARM. Miller's position would give him an unobstructed view of the front of First National Hostage Supply and of the gap between it and the Gray-Stripe Hotel.

Abrams breathed a sigh of relief. This wasn't over yet, but they were in position to capture this Ávila nut and get that prick Holden off their backs. He keyed his headphone mike. "I'm moving up, cover my approach."

"You got it."

He moved fast, running along the front of the convenience store mockup, ready to jump through its door or window if he needed cover.

Then it happened. A figure popped into view in one of the bank's windows, a man with a handgun.

Abrams dove through the convenience store's open door, crashing down hard on the store's plywood floor. He heard Miller open fire, a three-round burst, then another. Abrams got up to his knees, aiming through the store window, and saw the armed man still up in the bank window. He fired, a single shot, and saw the man shudder as the bullet entered his chest.

Then Abrams heard Miller's howl of laughter and realized what he'd jut shot. "We're shooting pop-ups!" Miller shouted.

The painted plywood bank robber swung back out of sight. Now another bank robber figure, this one with his gun held to the head of a female bank teller figure, swung into the bank doorway.

"Son of a bitch." Abrams steadied his aim. "Move up, I'll cover *you.*"

Danny knelt behind the bank to the side of the hole he had made by knocking out a sheet of plywood. On his walkie-talkie, Linda said, "Stay there, if you go either way one will see you. No, wait, the other guy is moving up to the front. In just a second, the far side will be clear."

"The far side from your tower?"

"That's right, toward the fake jail. Ready . . . go."

Danny got to his feet and ran. In a moment he was across the gap between bank and jail.

Airman Miller ducked to be beneath the level of the bank's first window, then straightened as he came up on the door. The robber-and-hostage silhouettes had swung back out of sight. Curiously, Miller could smell something burning—a chemical smell, not the smoke from the jungle mockup.

He glanced back toward Abrams. His partner left the minimal safety of the convenience store building corner and charged up at a dead run. Abrams reached the other side of the door.

Abrams held up his hands, counted down with his fingers: three, two, one.

Miller spun into the doorway, his M16 elevated and ready. His first glimpse was of an open area with several silhouettes representing bank patrons, a table right, a desk left, a row of unpainted plywood tellers' windows straight ahead. He heard Abrams move, saw the building interior darken slightly as Abrams set up in the right-hand window.

There was movement to the right, a figure standing up from the far end of the teller windows, a man with a gun.

Miller and Abrams both fired. Half a dozen rounds of .223 ammunition riddled the huge, shotgun-toting, cartoony criminal who stood there.

Both men swore.

■ ■ ■

Holden saw the robot emerge from behind the other side of the van and move once toward the silhouette range.

So it *wasn't* fleeing, after all. He stopped and waved at the two men following him; they froze where they were.

The three of them were about halfway along the berm, their eyes barely above the level of the earthen barrier. "When it gets between us and Duncan's position, we'll open fire," he said.

"Maybe when it's a bunch of yards short of that point, sir," Hardy said. "Or a bunch of yards after. If we open fire when it's exactly between our positions, we're firing on one another."

"Right, right." He keyed his headset mike. "Is everyone in position?"

He got the affirmatives he expected, but one of the men— Chambers, he thought—said, "Sir, Begay isn't with us."

"Well, where the hell is he? You were with him."

"We were separated by gunfire. I lost track of him."

"Dammit." Begay was sure to be dead, otherwise he'd have checked in. Holden knew losing a man on his first field mission would look bad on his record. Now he absolutely had to be successful in this retrieval operation. "Stay where you are, Chambers, and we'll look for Begay in a minute."

"Yes, sir."

The robot, head turning as it swept the flat terrain ahead of it for enemies, rolled past their position. When it had progressed another twenty paces or so, Holden keyed his mike again. "Open fire!"

Hardy and Walberg raised their assault rifles and opened up. The men on the far side fired as well. Suddenly sparks flew from the robot's exterior. The M16A2 in its hands shook as its arms were hit.

Scowl's internal diagnostics diagram lit up with red as it sustained fire. One round hit the gap between its head and the cowling that protected it from behind and the sides. The round rattled around in the gap and severed one of the connectors that allowed Scowl's head to extend forward, to turn side to side like a human head. Another punctured a hydraulics fluid line in the robot's left arm. Scowl's damage control software immediately sealed off that hydraulics line. The robot's left arm was now reduced to about sixty-six percent of its optimal strength.

Scowl calculated that if it sustained this sort of damage for another two minutes, it might be rendered nonfunctional.

It turned to face the tree line. It calculated that at least five automatic weapons were firing on it from that direction. It aimed with its weapon and fired the grenade launcher at the heat trace closest to it. The grenade left the launcher's barrel and arced into trees. The bright flash of its detonation was accompanied by a tree-shaking concussion and at least one human scream.

At the same time, Scowl went into reverse, backing toward the berm and the targets behind it. It reloaded the grenade launcher, traversed its aim rightward, and fired again.

It noted that the rate at which it was sustaining damage from the tree-line attackers diminished as it moved and as it reduced their numbers. However, the hits it was sustaining from the berm remained constant. It calculated that the benefits of being a moving target were offset because the distance between it and the berm attackers was closing.

Now the right tread sensor was reporting damage of an undefined nature. Its speed remained constant so it did not adopt any behavior to compensate for the damage. It reloaded the grenade launcher and fired a third time into the trees.

The heat from the grenade explosions now blanketed the area where the attackers had been, making it impossible for Scowl to detect the enemies there. It would wait a few seconds. Humans that were still ambulatory would flee the hot zones and Scowl would be able to pick them up again. In the meantime, the gunfire from that area, while not entirely eliminated, was much reduced.

Scowl spun as it reached the berm. The rate of fire from the men behind it had increased and its hit rate was becoming troublesome. Scowl rolled up onto the berm, nearly as difficult a climb as it had experienced when destroying the tanks, and could now look down on the three men there.

There were two men with assault rifles, one with a handgun. Scowl switched to assault rifle mode and sprayed .223 rounds across the first two. The third ran. Scowl continued firing into the bodies of the two more heavily armed attackers until they collapsed. Only then did it fire on the running man, the lowest-priority target of its current task. Three rounds entered the man's back and he, too, fell.

Scowl immediately rolled back off the berm, toward the tree line. It reloaded the grenade launcher and fired again. But it was not now sustaining fire from that area.

It relegated the suppression of the Air Force personnel to a secondary goal and resumed its trip to Skeet Range.

Abrams emerged through the hole his target had made in the back of the bank.

The noises from the direction of the office, the shouts across his headset, said something very bad was happening. But the small stand of trees from which Lieutenant Holden had first directed traffic was between him and that conflict. The only thing he could see was smoke rising in the distance.

Miller stepped out through the hole and straightened. "What the hell do we do?"

"We have our orders. I suspect that Holden's a stickler for orders."

"Meaning, he could fold quarters in half with his sphincter."

"That about sums it up." Abrams looked at the ground. It was hard-baked, but there were some dusty patches, and in one of them he saw two footprints. They headed toward the jail. "Come on."

Danny made the run from the edge of the jail to the nearest of the two License Land cars. He ducked behind it and looked back the way he'd come. No one was there.

He dropped back into the hole where he'd been hiding. One window of his laptop showed Scowl's camera view; the robot was headed back to Silhouette City at a rapid pace. But another window, gray letters on black, merely blinked at him.

He read the lines of text above it. He was in. He could prowl around for a brief few moments in one of the Edwards mainframes. His fingers flew over the keys as he issued commands concerning the disposition of the packet he had uploaded.

Abrams and Miller reached the second rear corner of the mockup jail. From here, they could see the silhouette compound's center, the two parked cars nearby. There was no sign of their quarry.

"What do you think?" Abrams asked.

"If I were him, I'd be long gone."

"If you were him, you'd be the craziest son of a bitch in three states, so you'd be right here. But where?"

Miller shrugged and studied the ground. "More footsteps. Headed toward the cars."

"Cover me." Abrams moved out into the open.

The robot rolled from around the corner of the bank building into the open. It swiveled to aim at Abrams. He spun, almost falling, and ran back behind the false jail. "Shit!"

The robot fired. Rounds of ammunition hit the far side of the jail, tearing through the plywood walls. A hole appeared in the wood over Miller's head. Another emerged directly between Abrams and Miller.

Both men went flat. They exchanged a look, a What-do-we-do-now? glance.

"Throw your weapons out!" The shout came from the direction of the parked cars.

"Screw you!" Abrams shouted back.

"Throw your weapons out and it's less likely to shoot you. Do it!"

More holes appeared in the plywood, a straight line at waist level, just where they'd been standing.

"What do you think?" Miller asked.

"I think we're not going to beat this thing." Abrams gauged the distance to the nearest stand of trees. It was a lot farther than the distance the robot had to roll to be in position to see them. He could already hear it coming.

Grimacing, he heaved his M16 out into the open. Miller copied his action.

The robot rolled into view and trained its M16 on them. Both men raised their hands.

"Got it covered," Linda said. She set down her walkie-talkie and typed another command into the control computer.

Scowl looked at the two human targets. Their threat register was almost nil. Scowl immediately reprioritized their elimination below its goal of finding and eliminating Daniel Ávila.

There was a noise from behind Scowl, a hiss and a creak. The Terminator spun.

There was a human figure standing in the middle of the open area at the center of Skeet Range. It held a rifle and had a bright heat signature.

Scowl fired on it. It shuddered and the top half of it fell away. A few moments later, the lower half lay down.

In the window of the building labeled FIRST NATIONAL HOSTAGE SUPPLY appeared another human. It was of subadult stature and had yellow hair arranged in pigtails. Scowl characterized this one as an immature female. It carried no weapon. Scowl did not fire on it. A moment later, it swung back out of sight.

Across the open area from the bank, a human male appeared in the doorway of Booze & Grease. It was shirtless and carried a shotgun. Scowl turned and raked the figure with gunfire. Then another figure stood in the center of the open area. Scowl fired at that silhouette as well. The M16 fired only one round, though Scowl had depressed the trigger long enough for a three-round burst. The Terminator ejected the spent clip and loaded another one.

Scowl continued to turn and process data. Now it was surrounded by targets, each of which might be Daniel Ávila that rose and fell, swung into doorways and back out again. It rotated in place, putting three-round bursts into each target it detected.

Master Sergeant Earl Duncan, age thirty-nine and approaching the end of twenty years in the Air Force, crouched over the body of his companion. Airman Vincent Smith was down, his right side showing red and black char from the grenade that had gone off mere feet from him. He was already in shock, unconscious. Duncan knelt over him. "Lieutenant Holden, come in. Lieutenant Holden, please talk to me."

There hadn't been any incoming fire for a minute or so, nor had there been any orders from the lieutenant. It was a bad sign.

"All right, everybody, check in."

"Sergeant, this is Cooper. I think the Lieutenant got it. Hardy and Walberg too. I saw the robot firing on them."

"Sarge, Abrams. I'm with Miller. The robot's here shooting up everything in sight. We've lost our rifles but can maybe retrieve them. Ávila's close. I think we can get him."

Duncan shook his head. He didn't swear. He never swore. But he sure wanted to.

Now he was in command, and this operation was already fouled up beyond all repair. Six men were unaccounted for and probably dead. The mission might be salvaged if Abrams and Miller could capture Ávila . . . but he didn't know how much of Abrams's confidence might be coming from bravado or miscalculation.

He did know that Airman Smith was badly injured and might die soon if something weren't done.

Duncan keyed his mike. "Fall back to the office building. We're abandoning this position."

"Sergeant, we can get him."

"Abrams, Smith is down and needs immediate hospitalization. And we don't have the kind of hardware we need to blow up that robot thing up. We're bugging out. That's an order."

"Sergeant, it's Cooper. Our transports are FUBAR, sir."

"Then we'll take its van. Right now, I think that grand theft auto is a wonderful thing. Fall back."

"Yes, sir."

Duncan stooped and hauled Smith up to a sitting position. It was hard as hell to get an unconscious full-size man up into a fireman's carry, but Duncan had the muscle and experience to do it. He straightened, his knees creaking, and began walking at a fast pace away from this hellhole, toward the office building.

■ ■ ■

Scowl burned through his second and third clips of .223 ammunition. It had no more grenades. It was finally without a functioning firearm. Its primary target, Daniel Ávila, was still not in sight. It dropped the M16 and calculated its other options.

Flattening plywood construction had allowed it previously to determine that specific targets were not human. In addition, protracted exposure to flame, such as the fire that was springing up all over Skeet Range, was capable of harming or terminating human life.

So Scowl rolled from section to section in Silhouette City, knocking down each plywood mockup into a pile of burning wreckage.

It did not bother with the two cars parked at one corner or with the two towers. None of these potential targets offered a humanlike heat signature, though one of the cars and the open air between the vehicles were demonstrating heat anomalies—dissipating heat traces. That would need to be investigated. Neither vehicle could be described as a brown pickup truck, so they would not be investigated.

After three minutes, Scowl was finished with that phase of its operation. It stood in the middle of the plywood village, slowly turning, watching wood burn, waiting for Daniel Ávila to leap out from a flaming pile so he could be killed.

Daniel Ávila did leap out, but from the gap between the parked cars. "Hey, Terminator," he shouted. "It's time for me to kick your ass."

It took a moment for Scowl's internal dictionaries, the secondary entries that interpreted colloquialisms, to recognize that the words were essentially a challenge. Accessing the dictionaries didn't cause a delay in Scowl's actions. Scowl spent those same moments turning to face Ávila and getting its tracks up to speed.

Ávila took a step back, and another. He wobbled as if off-balance. But he did not run.

As it approached the gap between the cars, Scowl noted that a symbol had been laid out on the bare ground in red paint. It was a letter X perhaps twelve feet across. The two portions of the symbol crossed just at the point Scowl would be entering the gap. The earth there was disturbed.

Scowl ignored those details. On the verge of accomplishing its primary task, it filed the details away as irrelevancies.

From her vantage point, Linda watched as Scowl rolled toward Danny. She had both hands on the device Ten-Zimmerman-of-the-future had helped them assemble last night. She needed both hands; they were shaking hard, and she could not bear the thought that she might drop the device at the last second. That would ultimately kill her as well as Danny.

She saw Danny turn and dive into his hole in the ground. She saw Scowl reach the center of the X. As it did so, she flipped the switch on the detonator.

A cone of fire leaped up from the ground beneath Scowl's tracks, fueled by the C4 from the road crew's shack. A moment later the sound of it, the shock wave of displaced air, hammered her tower; she felt the wave like a slap across the face, felt the tower sway under her.

But it did not collapse, did not fall.

And a moment later, a third of a ton of hand-assembled robot prototype crashed into the earth a yard away from Danny's pit, sticking there like a multi-million-dollar lawn dart.

c.26

Daniel could still feel himself in two places and see out of two sets of eyes, but now he made no effort to interact with the past. He was content to be a passenger. He watched, tired and idle, as Danny and Linda made their way through an eighth of a mile of underbrush, got to their truck, and peeled rubber on the way to 58. They reached it and turned toward the east well before any backup Air Force vehicles reached their turnoff.

"They're clear," he said.

"Can you break off now?" Mike asked. "Before Tamara has a cow about your blood pressure?"

"I want to see Tamara have a cow. And I want to see the father." Daniel ignored Lake's half-hearted scowl. "Yes, I can break it off now."

"For good," Mike added.

He nodded. "For good. Just give me a few minutes to say goodbye to them."

"All right."

It may have been just a result of the exhaustion he felt, of the odd, drifting sensation that came of occupying two bodies at once, but at last he felt optimistic again.

It wasn't for his younger self. He knew that Danny was soon to experience something that would destroy his memory. Danny was going to begin decades of confusion and uncertainty.

But at the end, Linda would be there. And so would a son who did not bear his family name but who carried his genes, his skills.

He drifted back into the past.

July, Present Day—Saturday Morning
Judgment Day
Kern County, California

"We've got to get rid of this truck," Danny said. "Find something that the Air Force isn't looking for."

"They must have figured out that we swapped the plates." Linda seem too tired, too drained to be disturbed.

"Let's visit that used car lot in Tehachapi again. I'm sure they like repeat business."

Linda laughed. There was a slight edge of hysteria to it.

Hey, Danny, you listening?

"Oh, hi. I thought you'd left."

No, but I'm about to.

"Sounds like you're pretty tired."

Yeah. But I'm not going to lie to you. I'm not going to be back once I'm rested up. I think this is the last time I can talk to you.

"Oh." Danny felt suddenly deflated.

But not crushed. He was losing his future friends . . . but not forever. And since the last time he was really separated from them, he'd found another reason to do all he'd done. Not for their praise, not for their thanks . . . just to make sure they got as good a set of breaks as he could provide for them. "Sorry to hear it."

Me, too. Listen, you need to treat Linda really nicely.

"Tell me about it."

He heard Daniel laugh. *Thanks, kid. Thanks for showing me what I was like all those years ago. What the world was like.*

"You're welcome. I can't exactly say thanks for showing me what the world *will* be like . . . but I'm glad I'm going to be there."

Yeah. 'Bye.

"Good-bye."

Daniel's presence faded, but not completely. Danny knew the connection was still present, though it would have to fade eventually. He was ready for it. He thought so, anyway.

"Are they gone?" Linda asked.

"Yeah. Probably forever."

"I'm sorry. Sort of sorry."

"Sorry for me, but you won't miss them."

"That's pretty much it." She heaved a sigh. "Is that okay?"

"That's okay."

She kept a close eye on the surrounding traffic, on the rearview mirrors. "I still haven't gotten through to my family in Texas. And we've got about eleven hours left. That's until everything hits the fan. The more time I can give them ahead of that deadline, the better."

"You're right. I think you need to drop me off."

She gave him a look suggesting that he was crazy. "What, now?"

"Right now. Forget finding a new vehicle, that'll cost us too much time. You need to find a working phone, radio, Internet connection, whatever, and warn your family. Get them to buy up a store's worth of supplies, head out into the country somewhere."

"I know."

"I know how you can do it. You drop me off here and drive to near your substation. Park and hide the truck. Put your cuffs on in front—"

"I, uh, sort of lost those."

"Oh. Anyway, go wandering in to talk to the other deputies. Tell a story about how I kidnapped you and you escaped, how you hitchhiked there. Send them and the Air Force off looking for me in some irrelevant direction, like toward Bakersfield. You stay there as long as you need to, as long as it takes to get word through to your family, and then you escape. Get back to the truck and get back to me."

"That might work. That *would* work. But I'm not going to leave you alone like that."

"I can look after myself for a few hours. Just make sure you're back to pick me up well in advance of six P.M. We need to get up into the mountains as fast as we can." He looked around. "Let's find a landmark around here. Drop me off. Go do this thing for your family and then come back for me."

She looked stricken but gave up the argument. "There's a gas station ahead with a patch of trees just behind it. If you were to hide out there—"

"Perfect."

She dropped him off there. He leaned back in the truck's window for a last kiss and Linda touched his face. "You *will* be here when I get back," she said. "However long it takes." It was not a question.

He chuckled over her determined tone of voice. "You know I will," he said.

Then she was gone.

He went to the filling station's restroom, then wandered around the back into the tree line ten yards away. He moved among the trees, far enough in that he was hidden from sight, and sat down with his back against a strong-looking tree trunk.

A little shaft of light, sliding between branches and leaves, fell across his face, warming him. It wasn't late enough in the day to be uncomfortable.

He felt weariness creep through him. He could, at last, relax just a little.

He'd wait. He'd be here.

And somehow, in the weeks or years to come, he'd find a way to make sure that he wasn't ever separated from Linda, that she'd be there all the way into the future his distant friends occupied.

August 2029
The Grottoes

"Heart rate dropping back into the normal range," Lake said. She returned her attention from the beeping and the flickering lights of the heart rate monitor to Daniel's face. "How do you feel?"

"Good." Daniel shrugged. "Well, the kind of 'good' you get after running your last marathon and realizing you never have to do it again."

"Uh-huh." She checked his eyes, shining her penlight into them despite his feeble protests and swats. "Do you think you're going to be able to prevent yourself from visiting yourself in the past?"

"I'm pretty sure I can."

"How can you be sure?"

Daniel looked between her and Mike. "I don't think it's a question of choice or willpower. See, whatever happens to Danny in the next few hours, whatever creates the extinction boundary for my memory, I do remember what comes later. Sure, it's a little fuzzy in the early days after Judgment Day. I kind of became aware of myself not long after J-Day, in the mountains, but I definitely would remember if I'd been visited by voices in my head, by a future me in all that time. Therefore the future me didn't come back anymore. Therefore I'm going to be successful at not dreaming my way back to him. Q.E.D."

Lake nodded as if convinced. "Let's hope you're right. Okay. Doctor's prescription. Rest."

"That's always my doctor's prescription."

"And then we get started on the really painful therapy tomorrow."

Daniel rolled his eyes. "Oh, great." He saw Lake making a shooing motion toward Mike, saw Mike rising. "Wait a minute. Don't send her away. I'm going to talk to her before I pass out."

Lake scowled at him, but there was no genuine reproach to it. "Five minutes," she said.

"Five minutes," he promised.

After Lake left, he held up his hand to Mike and she took it. "We did it," he said. "Whatever it was."

"Now we get to see how many of those resources you hid away from Skynet are really out there." She sat on the edge of the bed and ran her free hand over his cheek.

"Your family in Texas—on Judgment Day, were you able to reach them?"

"Yes." For a moment, she looked through him, back into the past. "I got through to my sister Angela. I'm pretty sure I persuaded her. I just don't know whether she was able to persuade her husband, my brothers, my parents. In the years since Judgment Day, whenever we've had contact with the Texas compounds, I've asked after them. But there's never been any word." She shook her head. "I don't think any of them made it. I think Mark is the last of the Herreras."

"He'll make more."

"Daniel, I'm so sorry about what all this has cost you."

"Don't be sorry. I'll get some of it back again. Maybe all of it. And I have—well, not the memories I lost, but replacements for some of them. Sights and sounds of the world before J-Day. Memories of you. I'm happy about that."

She smiled at him, and a single tear spilled down her cheek.

"There you go again, crying at the drop of a hat."

"Too damned many dropped hats around here," she said.

"Linda, listen, everything's changed, switched around. My brain is almost fixed and now my body's busted up. My old comrade-in-arms turns out to be my one-time lover and the mother of my son. I guess I'm not the same guy I've been for the last twenty years."

"What's your point?"

"My point, Deputy, is that I'd like another chance with you. If you're willing to risk it."

"Maybe." She leaned down to kiss him. "If you'll promise to train that mouth up until it works right again."

"Promise."

She sighed. "I need to go. John will want to know the results of your last session."

"Yeah, he will. But you'll come back."

"You know I will."

She left him alone, and he let himself drift toward sleep. Toward a real sleep, not one where he would force himself to go traveling in search of his younger self.

He smiled. Here he was with a malfunctioning body in a world that could sometimes without exaggeration be described as a hell on earth, and for this moment he was happy. *When you love,* he decided, *there's always a chance for a happy ending.*

C.27

Ten seconds later, his eyes snapped open again.

In that last thought, almost lost as he was drifting off to sleep, there was something big, something important.

He reviewed it, turned it upside down and backward, but couldn't grasp why he felt it to be so significant. It was something most humans realized at some point in their lives. The solitary soul could only hope for survival; the notion of happiness was not really within its grasp.

Then Daniel understood. Yes, humans could realize that, could participate in it. Skynet could not—it acknowledged only itself as a worthwhile being, and could not endure rivals of any sort, so it would always be alone. It would never know the sudden surges of strength brought on by caring for someone else more intensely than caring for one's own survival.

But what about the Terminators? Built in man's image, programmed by man with the capacity to learn, could they ever identify with another being to the extent that they could love it?

They could never identify with Skynet, of course. Skynet would not permit it. The queen bee, it could never acknowledge its drones as anything but tools.

John Connor believed, deep down, that the Terminators sent

back in time to protect his life had, at some level, felt emotion, that they had struggled harder than their programming allowed because of a level of identification that Skynet could not have anticipated or understood.

What if the capacity existed within all of them to learn to identify with humanity, to reject their role as interchangeable drones and assume new roles as individuals, human beings made of synthetic materials instead of living tissue?

And the thing was just this: Daniel did not have to leave that what-if entirely to chance. He'd written large sections of the Terminators' original operating system and was familiar with every iteration of their OS since then.

Perhaps, as he'd once considered, he was not obliged to visit himself in the past each time at a point on the calendar later than the one before. The fact that he'd done so until now might have been due to his own sense of the passage of time. If he could overcome that sense, or whatever mechanism caused him to progress forward along Danny's calendar, then he might be able to go further back—and make a few subtle changes, a few tweaks to the code he'd helped engineer.

Perhaps he could make one last difference . . . a difference that might help keep Mike, and Mark, and all the people he cared about alive longer. Perhaps, ultimately, he could give all of them a happy ending.

He painfully, laboriously pulled himself into his more upright position, leaning back against the wall. Then he closed his eyes and began looking for Danny. But not the same Danny.

"I've put a message through to Tom," John said as they entered Daniel's enclosure. "Once we get Danny back to Home Plate, that cobbled-together T-800 will be ready."

Mike smiled. "It's about time he got back to programming. And away from pseudo-scientific anomalies. I hate anomalies."

"Who doesn't?"

They entered Daniel's inner chamber. Mike's breath caught as she saw the position in which he lay.

John saw the rapid eye movement. "Oh, shit." He stepped back to the door, switched the signal light over to red.

He heard Mike shout, "Daniel, what are you *doing?*" By the time John reached the inner chamber again, Mike had grabbed Danny's shoulders, was shaking him. "Come back now. You're through with that."

Daniel didn't respond.

"Oh, Daniel . . ."

April, Present Day
CRS Project, Edwards AFB

Daniel came upright. He was seated on his chair in Danny's work cubicle.

He grabbed his computer mouse and activated the pop-up clock on his computer. It told him that it was 9:17 A.M. on an April Thursday, two months earlier than any of his previous visits to Danny's time.

He felt no confusion, no displacement. He was Daniel Ávila, who had spent decades struggling with amnesia and a few weeks reacquainting himself with his earlier life. But this was his body of the months before J-Day, and he was in full control of it.

He stood up and peered over the partition into the adjacent cubicle.

Jerry looked up at him. "What?" he asked. There was a hint of guilt to his voice.

Daniel smiled at him. "Nothing." He sat back down.

"Oh, don't do that to me! Now I'm paranoid. What have you

done? Did you have me declared dead? Did you program Scowl to grope me again? Come on, I have to know!"

"Jerry, you're going to hear some weird things from my cubicle. If you listen close enough to make out my words, you'll go insane. Do you understand?"

"No."

"Trust me. You don't want to be insane. It's no fun."

Then Mike's voice rang through his head. *Daniel, wake up.*

He sat. "Got something to do here," he whispered.

No, you're done.

"Not quite."

I'm going to have Lake knock you out with a sedative.

"Check with John first. I'm back in April before Judgment Day, and I have a few last things to do to the Terminator code."

She was silent. Perhaps, on the far end of the connection, she was speaking too quietly for him to hear. Daniel ignored her and got to work.

It took him a few moments to figure out where the bug-fix list was, but he shared an organizational sense with his younger self; it wasn't hard to find his way through this computer's directory structure. The bug-fix list would be the ideal means to his end, an opportunity to introduce new code all over the Terminator operating system without arousing suspicion.

Too much wasted motion in reaching and gripping algorithms. A perfect place to start. Streamlining the reaching and gripping routines called for revisions to the basic problem-solving code. There, he could also improve the Terminators' interpretation of human behavior, introducing an isolated emotion simulator whose data might, in a more sophisticated version of the simulator, begin to bleed over into the Terminator's decision-making processes.

Friend-and-foe recognition still balks when personnel in wrong uniform returns correct password. Here, he could enhance the Terminators' notion of identification with friends and looking beyond mere symbols to achieve friend versus foe recognition. The code here would have to be subtle, something to act as a starter mix for a Terminator's thinking processes rather than to crudely force the Terminator to accept certain humans as friends—Skynet would detect a process such as that immediately and rip it out.

Daniel smiled. This was what he did best.

August 2029
The Grottoes

"I think it's going to kill him," Mike whispered. She didn't bother to conceal or wipe away the tears streaming down her cheeks. "I want Tamara to sedate him. It will break the connection and let him get some rest."

"She won't do it without my go-ahead."

"Why would you even consider not approving it?"

John stifled a sigh. "Because Daniel isn't just my friend, isn't just a man at this moment. He's a resource and part of an ongoing operation."

"The operation ended!"

"Then he started it up again. I have to weigh the potential gain of the renewed operation against the potential loss."

"The potential loss is his *life*. He's a very sick man who's in danger of dying!"

"Yes." John felt like a very sick man himself, but struggled not to show it. He looked at Daniel, who lay still, breathing raggedly. His eyes moved under his closed lids. The screen displaying signals from his heart monitor clipped along at an accelerated rate. "The truth, Mike. Do you think he's rational right now? Is he under control, or deranged?" He fixed her with his High Commander of the Human Resistance look, the hard stare that reminded everyone who experienced it that everyone took orders—everyone except John Connor, and the responsibility he bore was the greatest of all.

Mike looked miserable. "He sounds rational."

"Then he's making a conscious decision to risk his life again. And if he's willing to risk it when he's just had the world handed to him—the world such as it is—then he must know what he's doing."

"But—"

"No sedation."

"*Damn* you, John."

"You've got that right." He rose. "Keep me updated as to his progress. I'll get Lake back in here."

Mike didn't answer. Her expression bleak, she simply returned her attention to Daniel.

John stepped into the outer chamber. Kate had arrived a minute earlier and was waiting for him. She saw the look on his face, saw through the iron resolve and commander's aloofness, and put her arms around his neck. "Are you all right?" she whispered.

"No." He pulled her to him, held her tight. "God, I'm tired, Kate. Tired of using people up, expending them as if they were rounds of ammunition. I sent my own father back in time to die. I send my children out on the front lines. I'm killing Daniel as surely as if I were holding down a switch to electrocute him. Some days I'd just rather die than make that decision again."

"I know. But you don't get to die without my permission."

"I hope you're right. But I suspect that Mike is telling Daniel the exact same thing. And I suspect she's wrong."

April, Present Day
CRS Project, Edwards AFB

Even as he typed, Daniel could feel the pressure of Mike's hand on his. He gave it a squeeze. He couldn't see her or hear her words. She might not even be speaking now.

He focused on his task.

He was aware of coworkers stepping in from time to time to ask questions. He answered them absently, drawing on his own knowledge or putting them off with suggestions and prevarications. He paid these people little attention.

He was aware of coworkers leaving, of lights elsewhere on the floor dimming. They did not dim in Cube Hell.

Silence fell on Cube Hell, but not full silence. Occasionally a screen saver elsewhere on the floor would chirp or burp or make a noise like droplets of water plopping into a sink. In the depths of the night he could hear the flow of air across the vents over his head.

And always there was the clicking of the keyboard under his hands.

In the early hours of the morning, janitors with security clearances that would make military contractors envious entered, vacuumed, swept, took out the trash. He ignored them, and they him.

And finally the coworkers began to drift in again, sleepy, showered, in different clothes, murmuring about Danny Ávila and his work ethic.

Weariness settled on him, and a headache. Both grew in intensity until he found he was typing the same words over and over again, until he recognized that he was no longer fully functional.

But he'd done it. He'd killed as much of the bug-fix list as any human could in a day and a night of work.

And more than that, he'd stamped as much of himself as was possible onto the Terminator code.

Mark Herrera had his genetic legacy. The young man had size and smarts and a skill for programming that would serve him well when he decided he was too old for special ops.

Now, perhaps, a Terminator in the distant future would awaken to sapience, to an identification with humanity, and inherit Daniel's emotional and ethical legacy. Perhaps, years from now, he would also have a mechanical son.

Or many.

He shoved his keyboard back, put his arms down where it had been, and laid his head atop them.

July, Present Day—Saturday Afternoon
Judgment Day
Kern County, California

Danny's eyes came open. There were trees ahead of him; beyond them, cars, trucks, and SUVs roared by on 58.

He'd fallen asleep. He knew it was about one P.M. Linda hadn't been gone long enough for him to begin to worry. Soon, she'd be by to whisk him off to the Sierra Nevada mountains and their life together.

He felt tired, so tired that he could barely turn his head.

Then pain struck him, a blow as if from a sixteen-pound sledgehammer. He felt as though his skull shattered, and fell to one side, knowing that his brains had to be leaking free from him.

August 2029
The Grottoes

John and Kate heard the shriek from Daniel's inner room. They'd been coming here whenever circumstances allowed over the last day and a half, waiting and watching just as Lake and Mike did.

And now they heard Mike's voice raised in pain and fear. Still ruled by discipline, John didn't rush into the inner room. He opened the shutter and peered through the window instead.

Daniel lay with his gaze fixed on the ceiling. Lake, beside him, shone a penlight into his eyes. Mike straddled Daniel, her palms flat on his chest, performing CPR with an urgency Lake did not seem to share.

John closed the shutter and swore to himself. He looked at Kate and shook his head, then rejoined her on the bench.

Minutes later, Lake emerged.

John had seen her many times when she'd presided over operations or lifesaving efforts that had failed. She wasn't a good-bedside-manner sort of doctor, and was often criticized for giving the bad news to next of kin with an indifference that others sometimes found hateful. But now she seemed as forlorn as if she were one of those unhappy survivors herself.

She caught John's eye and shook her head, an unconscious duplication of John's own action of a few moments ago. "Another stroke," she said. "Worse than the first. I'd say he was dead the second it hit."

Kate bowed her head and let silent tears fall. John felt like doing the same, but now was not the time. "We'll tell Mark," he said. "Do you need any help with Michaela?"

Lake shrugged. "Intellectually, I think she understands that there was not enough functioning meat machinery left for Daniel to reoccupy. Emotionally . . . well, we may all be safer if we just brick off this section of the compound until she's ready to come out."

"Right." John stood and extended a hand for Kate. "Thanks, Doctor."

July, Present Day—Saturday Afternoon
Judgment Day
Kern County, California

The pain began to ebb. The man was finally able to reach up and feel around his skull. He was amazed to find that it was intact.

He stood, shaky, and looked around. He didn't know this place, all trees with the highway only a few yards away. He saw a soft-sided briefcase at his feet and picked it up. Inside were a laptop computer, a holstered handgun, boxes of ammunition. He zipped the case closed again. Confused as to what he was doing here, he headed toward the highway.

No, nothing was familiar. Cars whizzed by in both directions on the highway. The gas station seemed busy. Most of the cars parked there had California plates. He must be in California.

"Mister?" A white-haired gentleman with glasses, moving quite briskly for his age, stopped en route to his car to look at him. "Are you all right?"

"Not feeling well." The sun seemed incredibly bright, and lying down on the pavement here to get a nap seemed like a very good idea.

"Are you fit to drive?"

"Of course." The younger man fished around in his pockets and found his keys. One of them belonged to a Jeep. But there were no Jeeps among the vehicles at the rest stop. "But my car is gone," he finally said.

"Well, where are you headed?"

"Away from the city." The words fell from his mouth and confused him. He didn't know why he'd said that, but he had, and with conviction. He knew, somehow, that he had to get away from the city, every city, and soon.

"Well," the old man said, "I'm thinking that you've picked up a little bit of sunstroke. Some sunburn on your face, certainly. Probably while hitchhiking. I'm headed up into the mountains for some fishing. Can I give you a lift part of the way?"

The younger man thought of the handgun in his bag and wondered why he had it. "Not safe to pick up hitchhikers," he said.

"Well, I'm a pretty good judge of character. You want the ride?"

"Sure." A little dizzy, off-balance, the younger man followed the older to a late-model brown Oldsmobile. "Nice car," he said. "Big."

The older man unlocked the driver's side door and grinned. "I didn't work hard for forty-five years to drive around in a stripped-down lunch box made of aluminum foil. I'm going to spend my last few years in comfort."

The younger man frowned. Something in him wanted to say, "No, you're not." But it sounded cruel, and he didn't know why he'd wanted to say it at all.

EPILOGUE

September 2029
Former Ávila Property

It was dark and quiet, just like the first time Mark Herrera had visited this place. But that first time he'd been on a mission important to the Resistance. Now, it was a personal matter.

He waited in the middle of the weeds and grasses until he was sure that nothing of significance was moving out there. Then he raised two fingers and beckoned the people behind him. Not waiting for their arrival, he moved forward, toward the orange grove.

It didn't take him long to find the hole they'd dug, the hole from which they'd extracted Danny Ávila's time capsule. The earth they'd excavated was still piled up beside it, the mound now slightly eroded.

A minute later, his mother Michaela joined him. Kyla Connor and her dogs hung back thirty or forty yards, not wishing to intrude on this private moment.

Mike set down her field pack and opened it, pulling out a bag of heavy cloth. It said USPS on the side and was closed by broad white drawstrings. But she just held it while she looked around.

"I loved this place," she said in a whisper. "The sound of traffic in the morning, fresh orange juice, Mama Teresa making breakfast . . . just the fact that it was *ours*. The family's."

Mark unclipped his folding shovel from his pack and extended it for use. "I'm sorry, Mama. It's not ours now."

"Yes, it is. It's behind enemy lines, but it's our land, and it will be as long as I'm alive. It'll be ours longer if you decide that you want it."

Mark smiled. "I'm not sure I can think that far ahead."

"You've got to, Mark. If people just fight without thinking ahead, they'll fight in random directions. You need to fight for something. Toward something."

"Maybe so." Mark looked around, at the nearby trees. He tried to imagine it when it had been a working farm, pipes carrying clean water to the trees, workmen managing the groves. It was such an alien notion, working out under clear skies by daylight, that it made him shudder.

But he thought he might come to like it.

Mike lowered the bag full of Daniel's ashes into the hole. From her pack, she drew a second object, a plate of stainless steel. It was just a piece of scrap metal she'd scavenged from Edwards years ago, but a metalworker in Tortilla Compound had inscribed words on it, not even asking for bartering goods for his work.

In the light of the full moon, it read:

DANIEL FRANCISCO ÁVILA

GREATER THAN THE SUM OF HIS PARTS

Below those words were the dates of Daniel's birth and death, like brackets surrounding his life.

She climbed down into the hole and carefully placed the plate atop the bag, then accepted Mark's hand back up.

Mark began shoveling earth atop the bag and the plate. "So, what do you do on a farm like this when you're not working? For entertainment?"

"Well, among other things, it depends on whether you have a pretty wife." Mike gave her son a critical eye. "Which you're not likely to get if you're all skin and bones. Mark, you're too skinny."

"Hard to get fat and lazy with my active bachelor's lifestyle. Besides, Mama, I'm a Hell-Hound. We live on food that other people would starve on."

"Paint chips, scorpions, and very small rocks?"

"Well . . . yeah." That hadn't been what he was going to say, but it sounded like something he would have come up with.

Her voice softened. "Welcome home, Mark."

ABOUT THE AUTHOR

Aaron Allston is the author of a number of science fiction and fantasy novels, including the Doc Sidhe books and the Star Wars™ New Jedi Order novels *Rebel Dream* and *Rebel Stand,* among a number of novels, original and tie-in. An award-winning game designer as well as an SF writer, he lives near Austin, Texas.